COLIN PORT and DR MOIRA HAMLIN come from very different backgrounds but have both lived and worked in Africa, London and the West Country. They worked together for five years and it is their joint interest in fun and excellence which drove them to write this book.

Colin is a career detective who retired in 2013 as a Chief Constable. He has worked for the UN International Tribunals and was ACPO (Association of Chief Police Officers) lead for International Policing. Described by the *The Times* last year as 'one of the country's top detectives', he is no stranger to controversy or newspaper front pages and headlines, nor to challenging the status quo or the Establishment. Colin currently runs his own leadership and management consultancy.

Moira is a Chartered Clinical Psychologist who worked in publishing before training and practising as a clinician in her specialism of addiction. The author of numerous academic publications this is her first joint work of fiction. Moira was a magistrate for 17 years and held a number of Non-Executive Director positions before becoming the Chair of a Police Authority and the Deputy Chair of the national body for Police Authorities. Moira is currently on the Governing Council of University of Bristol and a Company Director.

G000167654

LOOK THE OTHER WAY

COLIN PORT
AND MOIRA HAMLIN

To Lester
with many happy memories
Moira x

in friendship
Col.

SilverWood

Published in 2015 by the authors
using SilverWood Books Empowered Publishing®

SilverWood Books Ltd
30 Queen Charlotte Street, Bristol, BS1 4HJ
www.silverwoodbooks.co.uk

ISBN 978-1-78132-348-9

British Library Cataloguing in Publication Data
A CIP catalogue record for this book is available from
the British Library

Set in Sabon and Univers by SilverWood Books
Printed on responsibly sourced paper

You may choose to look the other way but you can never say again that you did not know

William Wilberforce

Chapter One

The cramps in Joel's stomach started again. It was always the same when he was waiting to give evidence. Nerves; he would have been concerned if he wasn't a little nervous. He was a witness against a feral street gang who were on trial charged with raping and robbing a 16-year-old girl.

As he sat in the Central Criminal Court, better known to the world as the Old Bailey, he was bored and did what he often did: he went into number one court, not just because it had some of the most interesting cases but because this was where the characters were to be found: the barristers, the solicitors, the accused and the villains, who weren't necessarily the same people, and, of course, the judge.

Today the pathologist, Professor William Grieg, was in the witness box. Joel resented the way experts were questioned being accorded respect, dignity and understanding. Whilst in his view the real experts, the police and in particular the detectives, were treated like something the barrister scraped off their shoe. Grieg was droning on about how to break someone's neck. Joel thought this was fairly straightforward; after all, who hasn't fantasised about breaking the neck of someone close to them? He certainly had. He imagined breaking his DCI's neck earlier in the morning when she failed to recommend him for promotion once again. A pleasing few minutes passed while Joel continued the fantasy about his DCI. Perhaps he should pay more attention to the learned Professor?

The defence barrister was cross-examining Professor Grieg when the pathologist made an unforeseen and astounding revelation. He said, 'Anyone could break another's neck in one move given training or the right circumstances. The size of this defendant's forearms just make it much more likely pressure on the neck could result in death.'

The barrister looked close to an asthma attack gasping for air, he'd forgotten the old lawyer's adage: don't ask a question unless you know the answer in advance. The accused, it transpired, cleaned cars for a living and had forearms the size of Joel's thighs. Joel saw the jury turn and look at the man sitting in the dock, who, unfortunately for him, was wearing a short-sleeved T-shirt emphasising the size of his arms.

'Shit,' said Joel under his breath. Why hadn't he thought of this before when Robert told him the story about his daughter? He jumped up and strode out of the court while the barrister tried to gloss over his gaffe. Joel didn't directly look at the judge, but felt his glare at the audacity to walk out of court in the middle of a cross-examination burning his back. Joel had other matters on his mind.

Exiting the court, Joel switched his mobile on and punched in the number of his friend Robert. Frustratingly there was no reply. The answerphone clicked in.

'Robert, it's Joel. I think I've got a possible answer.'

Returning to number three court, Joel found there was no sign of him being called as a witness. He couldn't get out of his mind what he had seen and heard in number one court. His thoughts turned to his home of Budleigh Salterton, a quiet, genteel town in east Devon, famous for its pebble beds from the Triassic age, which came bottom of a survey for towns giving value for money to homebuyers. This never affected Joel: he inherited his house from his grandfather. It was a world away from Somerstown, an inner-city area squashed between Kings Cross and Euston in London, with very high levels of deprivation and home to the street gang he was giving evidence against today.

Many residents of Budleigh Salterton were secretly pleased it was once described as, 'Britain's most overpriced, dreary place'. Take Joel's friend Robert who lived there. A surprising choice for this former BBC journalist, but Robert was old-school, different from those whose map of the world seemed to extend from Primrose Hill to Chelsea and scenic Oxfordshire, and beyond forays to Heathrow it became an indistinct black hole.

Snatches of conversation with Robert flew through his mind. 'I don't believe that guy killed her, Joel. Why would he? He had a good job, his family was looked after, Jess was kind to him, and she thought he could do better for himself. Why would he kill her? Kem was a gentle, gentle man. It doesn't make sense. I dread to think how he has coped with prison, especially a South African prison.' These conversations had taken place many, many times when Joel and Robert were in The Feathers: the same pub in which they first met.

'Joel, come on, were you dozing?' Joel heard a voice say.

'I was just thinking,' he uttered incomprehensibly and looked up to see Billy, one of the DCs from the office, shaking his shoulder.

'Suzy has been trying to get you,' said Billy. 'Someone called Robert who said he is a friend of yours told her you were trying to call him urgently.'

'DS Grant,' the court usher shouted. It was Joel's time in court. His forgotten cramps returned. God, Joel thought as he went into court, this's all I need now. The conversation he intended to have with Robert was lodged firmly at the forefront of his mind.

Joel spent the remainder of the afternoon giving evidence, and being examined and cross-examined. He'd had better days in court. At one point the judge said, 'Officer, are you with us this afternoon?'

Joel replied, 'I'm sorry, My Lord, I've just heard some disturbing news.' For a split second Joel thought of doing what an old DS, who came from Yorkshire, advised him to do if he ever got into trouble in the Crown Court.

'Drop your trousers, lad, get your dick out and run up and down the aisle wobbling your lips.' Joel thought better of this; he was in trouble but not so much. He'd keep it in reserve.

Reprieve came mid-way through his cross-examination as the court finished for the day. Joel was glad he was reminded not to speak to anyone about the case as he used this as an excuse to make a speedy exit.

As he walked into Ludgate Hill to phone Robert, he remembered the first time his friend told him how his beautiful daughter, Jess, had been killed in South Africa. Everything looked fantastic for the future of Jess and Matthew, her fiancé. They were visiting Matthews's parents when she was murdered in the country of Matthew's childhood and of Jessica's dreams – South Africa. Jess's death broke Robert, and Joel remembered how he vividly recounted a conversation with the South African police officer, who told him, by phone, Jess's neck had been 'snapped like a rat in a trap'. Joel contemplated the South African police seemed to have a little to learn about victim care.

He returned Robert's call and told him what he had seen and heard in court. Robert was excited but they agreed to discuss it in more detail when Joel went to Budleigh at the weekend. Joel decided to join Suzy and Billy for a drink, and it transpired they shared the judge's concern about his demeanour in court. Over the next few hours and a couple of bottles of wine, Joel told them about Jess's murder and Robert's concerns. They now understood!

Leaving Suzy and Billy, Joel arrived back at his flat more than a little the worse for wear. As he walked into the kitchen he remembered promising to ring his girlfriend Sarah but had completely forgotten. Sarah lived in Budleigh Salterton and owned a dress shop there. Joel first met Sarah in The Feathers, one evening when he was with Robert. He was interested from the outset in this dark haired beauty who had been an investment banker in the city, but left banking to pursue her childhood dream of running her own business and was making a real success of it.

Joel's worries suddenly came into greater focus when the phone rang. It was Sarah. She was clearly very annoyed with him, but in her restrained, assertive style. He went into listening mode; in his haze he thought it might have something to do with his slight difficulty in talking! Late night conversations with Sarah tended to be a little one-sided; she usually mentioned him transferring to Devon and Cornwall Police and the improvements it would give to their lives together. Joel felt it was to stop him going out on the town with his friends. These conversations never went well. Sarah became exasperated and said they should talk when he was sober; Joel should have rung her back but fell asleep instead.

He woke up with a jolt. Perhaps it was the wine or perhaps too many coffees during the day, but images of the court kept whirling round. He knew Robert would be awake, so when he rang it was no surprise his friend was still up at 1am. Joel asked Robert to describe Kem, which he did by describing him as 'scrawny'. Robert reiterated what he told Joel on many occasions over the years: he never believed Kem was guilty and thought the South African Police had made the facts fit in relation to the first black man they suspected. Not for the first time, Robert asked Joel to go to South Africa and see what he could find out about the case. Again Joel told him he could not. As he switched his light off he noticed a text from Robert:

J it all stinks. Please just go. Can get u on the 19.30 2nite to CT.

In spite of the serious message, Joel smiled to himself. Who would have thought the near octogenarian former BBC journalist would master text speech? Mind you, if the veteran presenter David Dimbleby could get a scorpion tattoo on his shoulder, what next?

After a restless night Joel got ready for work and went to see his DCI, Fiona Henderson, as soon as she arrived at the office in Islington. Joel had known her for a long time: they joined the police together and continually vied for the top student award at training school. Henderson won. He had thought they were attracted to each other, but when he discovered she was in a relationship with a sergeant, Joel's interest waned. They worked together from time to time, but Henderson was always, always more ambitious than Joel.

She was sitting there in her faux designer outfit, rehearsing for her next promotion board, he thought. 'Morning Joel,' she said with a patronising smirk, 'I hear it didn't go so well at the Bailey yesterday?'

Joel felt annoyed with Billy and Suzy, who must have told her. So much for mates, he thought. 'What do you mean?' he asked.

'I bumped into Edward Whitaker, the defence lawyer, last night at dinner.' She added, 'He sounded quite confident of an acquittal following your performance yesterday.'

Joel thought, Bastard, but what he said was, 'We'll see what happens, Guvn'r. The jury will see through all that shite Whitaker pumps out. I am going to be finished at lunchtime and have the weekend free. Can I take four hours off this afternoon to go down to Devon?'

DCI Henderson responded in her usual no nonsense manner, 'No you can't have time off. We've too much on at the moment. I want to see you back here. Start concentrating on work and you won't get caught out in the witness box. Anyway, you might have to work tomorrow on the five-handed robbery job Reuben picked up this morning. That's going to go on all weekend.'

Joel knew he needed a break. He had worked fourteen days without one; what would European Working Time Directive zealots think about it? A lot, he thought! The episode in court made him think; his concentration had drifted, a sure sign he was overtired, and so if he couldn't have the weekend off, he was left with no alternative but to report sick. He didn't like doing it, but he realised it would be for the best.

Joel walked out of Tolpuddle Street police station and went to the Angel Tube. It was a drag getting to the Old Bailey by Tube, but it was far better today than getting a lift with the others and everyone going on about his performance yesterday.

As Joel walked into Upper Street he reflected once again how, as a resident of the South West, he ended up in Tolpuddle Street police station, named after the martyrs. Puddledown, the home of the martyrs who marched to London in the 1830s, was about sixty miles from Budleigh Salterton. Joel didn't feel like a martyr going to court this morning, though; he felt like a sacrificial lamb.

On the Tube he was still arguing in his head with Henderson, and he was losing! But he had to focus on the case; he didn't want to lose it because of his performance. He also thought about Robert constantly. The attraction of having a break in South Africa was becoming more and more appealing, particularly on the hot, sticky Tube.

Back in the witness box, Joel was glad he'd had the opportunity to think about his evidence overnight, despite the alcohol! Whitaker resumed his cross-examination.

'Just to confirm then, Officer, you have not discussed your evidence with anyone overnight?' snarled the pompous arse Whittaker.

'Only my DCI,' said Joel.

'What's that? I told you specifically not to discuss this case with anyone,' interrupted the judge, last night's claret showing in his complexion which almost matched the red of his robes.

'I apologise, My Lord,' said Joel, 'but I was taken aback this morning when I went into my office and DCI Henderson said I hadn't done well yesterday. I was very shocked.'

The judge said, 'What did you say to him, Officer?'

'I just said my evidence was a matter for you and the jury, not for anyone else, My Lord,' answered Joel.

'How did he manage to comment on your evidence? Was he in court or did someone else speak to him?'

'DCI Henderson is a woman, My Lord. Apparently she saw Mr Whitaker at dinner last night and he told her, My Lord.'

At this point Whitaker did turn as red as the judge's robes and leapt to his feet. 'Perhaps I can explain, My Lord.'

The judge turned to the jury and told them there were some issues he needed to discuss with counsel and they should go home for the weekend. He emphasised they were not to discuss the case with anyone, looking at Whitaker as he spoke! He then returned to his chambers, asking counsel to join him.

Joel left it for the barristers to fight out with the judge, but not before he noticed Whitaker glaring at him. He was off. He thought about phoning Fiona Henderson, but not for too long.

Outside the court and breathing the fresh air, he thought again about the hand grenade he had metaphorically thrown into the court. Taking the phone out of his pocket, he dialled Robert's number and said, 'Robert, it's Joel. Book the ticket, I will go tonight.'

'What made you change your mind?' asked Robert.

'It's a long story, we'll talk later. Let's just say I need a change of scenery. Quick,' replied Joel.

Hanging up on Robert, Joel then spoke to Billy in the office. 'Billy, it's Joel. Is the Guvn'r around?'

'She is doing promotion board preparation or having her nails done, not quite sure which,' said Billy.

'Ever the joker. Where is she, Billy?'

'Honestly, Joel, I don't know.'

'Can you report me sick please, Billy?'

'What's up?'

'Let's call it sleep apnoea.' Joel felt this was an accurate description following his lack of sleep over the last two weeks.

Joel went back to his flat and packed. He knew Sarah was out for the afternoon and, taking the easy option, he sent her an email saying he would ring her when he got to South Africa. His finger hovered over the send button for a second, then with a shrug he pressed it. He knew Sarah would try and ring him, but he had no intention of answering his phone to anyone this afternoon.

The break in South Africa would be ideal. He could rest, sleep, but most of all he could help a friend with an issue which had worried Robert for many years. Joel certainly wasn't cheating on his colleagues, he was just exhausted.

Chapter Two

Joel settled into his business class seat, sipped his champagne and amused himself looking around his fellow passengers, making up stories about their lives and wondering how many of them were on the sick like him.

While others tapped their sales charts into their laptops, Joel watched the latest film release. He kept his eye on the micro-person a few rows away, who was winding his lungs up ready to yell the minute the air pressure hit the cabin, "s the k", "spot the kid", being a favourite expression for finding himself next to the inevitably noisy presence on an aircraft.

Contrary to the reviews for the latest Hollywood thriller, Joel found his mind drifting away from the obvious plot, and snatches of his first encounter with Jess started to intrude.

Walking into The Feathers, strains of Mariah Carey's 'I Had A Vision of Love' reaching me from the room next to the bar, I saw one of my neighbours sitting in the corner with a beautiful young woman with long dark hair who was humming along to the tune.

The neighbour smiled at me. 'It's Joel, isn't it?'

'Hi, yes,' I replied.

'I've seen you around. I'm a neighbour of yours,' said the man. 'You live in your grandfather's old house, don't you? Nice to meet you. I'm Robert, this is my daughter Jess.'

She gave a small smile in greeting and I thought how attractive she was, even in jeans and a loose fitting shirt, yet she seemed unaware of the impact she had on others.

'Are you on your own? I nodded. 'Then come and join us,' invited Robert.

Jess told an anecdote about her first year at university, and while I fancied her I could see she was not interested in me. 'Matthew comes from South Africa and is doing law. He wants to be a barrister.' It was clear from the way she talked about him that Matthew was her boyfriend and she was pretty keen on him. Any desires I might have had quickly evaporated.

Trying to impress her, I found myself saying, 'I'm going to join the police in October.'

'Whatever for?' she said with a slight frown.

Rather taken aback I responded sharply, 'I want to do something for others not myself, and it is a good career.'

'Well, you two are getting on well,' said Robert ironically.

This first encounter epitomised the sparring relationship Jess and I developed over the next few years.

Joel was jolted back to the present by pained screams from "s the k" in the row in front, he had just trapped his hand while reclining the seat. Pity it wasn't his head, thought Joel unkindly. The steward was there in a flash, trying to relieve the pain of the little stinker in front and managing to calm him down after a few minutes by wrapping a mock bandage around his hand. Joel thought personally the steward was more interested in "s the k's" mother than the kid.

Finally, the steward turned to Joel and said, 'Another glass of champagne, sir?' looking at Joel in an apologetic way.

'Yes please.' Joel sighed. It was going to be a long night. His thoughts returned to Budleigh, Jessica and now Matthew. He remembered one of his first encounters with Matthew.

'But Matthew, the police here are very different from South Africa,' I remembered saying.

'Not that different from what I have seen. Look at the poll tax riots and the way your lot beat everyone up,' Matthew responded.

'Bollocks,' I said. 'They came looking for a fight and they got one.'

Jess said, 'God, Joel, you've only been in the police a few months and you are already indoctrinated.'

'You should try facing a baying mob with stones and bricks being lobbed at you. My mates were there, you weren't.'

'Actually, I was there. Not in a demonstration, but with my father. You and he would get on well, you share the same views: slightly to the right of Attila the Hun,' Matthew said dryly.

＊

Joel's views mellowed over the years, and he certainly had more in common with Matthew now than back then!

His reminiscing continued, moving now to Jess and Matthew's engagement party.

If Jess and Matthew knew I had just come from setting up a drugs operation round the corner from their flat, I wouldn't be welcome at this party. Too many of the rich, trendy Chelsea-ites liked stuffing powder up their noses. I hoped none of them would be here tonight.

'Joel, this is George, Matthew's father,' Robert said to me.

'You're the policeman I've heard so much about,' said an imposing man, wearing a regimental tie, with characteristically clipped military tones. Clearly he still kept himself very fit and there was a slight trace of a South African accent.

'Yes I am, but don't believe everything you hear from the media,' I replied, glancing at Robert.

'Joel doesn't like the press, he thinks they are unfair to the police,' replied Robert.

'I understand your views here in the United Kingdom, but I don't have any problems with the press at home. Most of the editors are personal friends,' George said dismissively. 'If you will excuse me I need to go and circulate.'

'What an arrogant shit,' I said, turning to Robert.

'Yea, got it in one. He is so different from Matthew. That's what happens when you can buy and sell many people, including members of the government and the media.'

'He's clearly ex-military, so where did he get his money?' I queried. 'Please don't say he's an African mercenary?'

'No, No, nothing as controversial. He's just naturally confident or, as you say, arrogant. He was in the army, intelligence corps, then the Secret Intelligence Service, and afterwards made a fortune in something connected with mining.'

'Interesting life,' I mused.

'Yes,' said Robert, 'but Jessica is marrying Matthew, not his father, although I worry about their plan to go to South Africa. I'm not sure she understands the reality of living there. Visiting while doing research is not the same. It's funny that George also studied in London at The School of Oriental and African Studies, but I expect it was quite different in the 1960s than in Jess's time. Mind you, he was still in the army then, not the rebellious student type.

I didn't know it then, but my last sight of Jess was later in the evening when Matthew had his arm around her waist and she was laughing in that distinctive style of hers which turned my insides to liquid. They looked a perfect match, and although I still fancied Jess, I had grown to like Matthew in spite of myself. He'd better be good to her though.

How things had changed following Jess's death. Matthew returned to the United Kingdom and was now a barrister in the Temple. He had told Joel about how he was a very junior, junior on a case against the government involving members of the Kurdish organisation, the PKK. The government wanted to deport them because of their terrorist links, but this was successfully defended. During this time Matthew reviewed various documents originating from the Intelligence Services, and for the first time gained a real insight into an element of his father's background.

George never talked much with Matthew about his time in SIS, and during the case Matthew mentioned to him how he'd considered SIS were responsible for some of the issues exposed in the trial. He had seen intelligence from them which purported to come from agents, but when examined was found to be summaries from publicly available information. This proved devastating for SIS, who were supporting the government's assertions there was no risk in the repatriation of the people, despite the same people having been agents for them in the past, which was exposed in the media.

The judge formed an opinion the view of SIS could not be considered as reliable. Additionally, the person responsible and head of department was James Davies, a former colleague and personal friend of George Corfield. Matthew's father had spoken to him, and told Matthew he was doing immense damage to the United Kingdom by the approach being taken. Matthew responded by saying it wasn't him; indeed, he was a very small cog; it was the amateurs in SIS who were doing the damage. This hurt Matthew as he had always been very proud of what his father had done.

George did not like this rebuttal and ended up shouting at Matthew, telling him to grow up and get in the real world. Matthew retorted by saying he was in the real world, not his father's private club. Matthew went on and said it was Davies in particular who let everyone down. There was a lot of good material from SIS, but because of the friend's laziness the government case was flawed. Davies was severely criticised by the judge and resigned quietly, only to re-emerge as George's lead representative in the United Kingdom.

Joel thought about Matthew recounting this story and how the relationship between the father and only son appeared to have deteriorated over the years.

"S the k" erupted into life again, literally as some of the remnants of his supper were deposited into the aisle. Once again the steward rushed to the rescue. 'I'm so sorry,' said his mother, 'he's usually so good at travelling, I can't understand it.'

I can, Joel thought, all the orange juice and chocolate he's been stuffing for the last five hours.

The steward cleared up the mess and once again asked Joel if he wanted a drink. 'Why not?' Joel said as the steward leant forward and said with surprising indiscretion, 'I think you deserve it,' nodding towards "s the k". He seemed to have lost interest in the mother too. It suddenly struck Joel he had no idea of the time difference between South Africa and the United Kingdom. Were they ahead? Yes, he supposed they were. Joel looked at the screen and saw South Africa was two hours ahead, which meant they'd be landing at 7.30am local time. He concluded he should get some sleep but the storm he left at the Bailey kept intruding on his efforts. Then Sarah came into his thoughts. She hadn't tried to ring, or at least he hadn't received a call, which was not surprising as he had switched off his phone in the airport lounge. It would be rude to disturb everyone else, he had reasoned with himself. It was going to be a difficult conversation in the morning. He wasn't looking forward to it.

The cabin lights went on about two hours before landing, much to Joel's annoyance as he hadn't managed to get much sleep. Breakfast was better than he remembered; BA had obviously gained a chef.

Going through immigration was a breeze, and the bags came through quicker than they managed in Heathrow these days. Joel came into the arrivals hall and was confronted by a sea of faces and welcome boards with strange sounding names. He started to make his way to the taxi rank when he saw a board from the Victoria and Alfred hotel saying 'Joel Grint'. He wondered if that was supposed to be him and went over to the young man holding the board.

'I am Joel Grant.' The man didn't seem to mind the difference in name; he took Joel's bag, and Joel jumped into the hotel car privately thanking Robert for his foresight. An hour later they were still in the car as they had hit Cape Town rush hour.

'Not far now, boss,' said the young driver.

Ten minutes later, at the hotel reception there were two envelopes waiting for him, one with 2,000 rand and another with a South African cell phone and a note from Robert advising him to use it. Here is someone who knows the country, Joel thought. I could do with him being here, not back in Budleigh.

He was shown to a nice loft bedroom overlooking The Waterfront and Table Mountain. It was time to catch up on the sleep he had lost thanks to "s the k" on the plane, although in fairness it was not just because of "s the k". It was due to his travels back through the past as well.

When his luggage arrived Joel took a hot reviving shower. He seemed to spend hours in there, but in reality it was about ten minutes. When he got out, wrapping himself in the fluffy white towels and then the complimentary dressing gown, he lay on the bed and fell asleep. It was twelve o'clock before he woke up again and he was completely disorientated, despite the fact he was only two hours ahead time-wise. Nevertheless the speed and activities over the last twenty-four hours were having an effect. He looked at his watch again and thought he might as well do it now. The next ten minutes were filled with a very uncomfortable conversation with Sarah, who could, had she chosen, have been a skilled advocate. He tried to explain why he left without speaking to her personally, why he was so tired and why he needed to help Robert at such short notice, but it all fell on deaf ears. She was incandescent.

Sarah said she told Fiona Henderson, who phoned her, he had gone to South Africa. Joel was annoyed Sarah had seen fit to pass on this information, but why shouldn't she? It was no secret. He thought he felt like a coward in respect of both women, but tried to rationalise it by thinking about how he was helping Robert and possibly an innocent man.

Joel felt like a scolded schoolboy. He had been put in his place, but on balance, he did indeed deserve it. Didn't he? He had behaved like a twat. In fact, using a word from one of his favourite novels, he behaved like a cad. But anyway, he'd done the deed, and now what was he to do?

He wandered along The Waterfront during the afternoon, with an occasional visit to a café or bar but he was still tired, eating shortly after 6pm and having an early night. Surprisingly Joel was sound asleep immediately; he feared he would not be able to sleep, worrying about what he'd left behind. He was wrong.

Joel was up at 6.30am and went out for an early morning walk. Feeling the sun on his face, he could have easily fallen into holiday mode. The day before he considered going on an organised tour trip to Robben Island, but didn't think he should; he was here to work, not on holiday. For different reasons he resisted the township tours.

While it was still touristy, he bought a ticket on the Big Red City Tour, a bus tour all around the city, which would certainly aid his orientation. Well this was the way he rationalised it in his mind. The advantage of the first bus of the day, which Joel booked, was after the first few stops it went straight to the cable car at Table Mountain, and by 10am he was at the top of the mountain. The views from all around were magnificent, overlooking the city and the bay; he could actually just see the outline of Robben Island. He caught sight of a dassie darting among the rocks, and found it hard to believe this animal, which looked like a guinea pig, was closely related to the elephant. It was as near as he'd get to an elephant on this trip, he mused, as there was no time for a safari. Joel decided against walking down the mountain by himself; following for once the tourist advice, he came back down around midday and re-boarded a bus to Green Point, where he had a late lunch before walking back to his hotel. After the day around Cape Town, Joel felt relaxed and ready for what lay ahead.

The following morning he was up at 7am, breakfasted at the hotel then caught a taxi to the offices of Independent Newspapers in St Georges Mall.

Chapter Three

Joel read the newspaper cuttings, the coverage of the murder, the arrest and the conviction of Kem at the newspaper office. He had been sentenced to death for a 'gruesome barbaric' crime according to the Cape Times and its sister paper the Cape Argos. His lawyer said he would appeal, although Joel could find no coverage of his appeal in the papers.

He had identified the lawyer, or advocate as they were known in South Africa, who represented Kem in court, as Henri Weltzen, and his attorney as Frederick Weisner. Joel couldn't find any details about Weltzen, but Weisner was still practising and his offices were just around the corner, also in the business district of Cape Town where it seemed most of the larger firms of lawyers were based. Joel called the attorney's office from a café he'd found nearby. He asked to speak to Frederick Weisner and was put through to the attorney's private office. He again asked to talk to Frederick Weisner, and when asked what it was about he simply said, 'the conviction of Kem Siblisi.'

The officious receptionist or secretary, whatever she was, said, 'Are you a relative?'

'No,' said Joel, 'I'm a British police officer.'

There was silence for a moment, then the receptionist said, 'One moment, please. What is your name?'

Joel gave his name and waited. The receptionist came back moments later.

'I'm sorry, Mr Weisner is with a client at the moment but will be free to telephone you later this afternoon.'

Joel said, 'I was rather hoping to see him in person.'

The receptionist sounded shocked. 'You are in South Africa?' she queried.

'I'm in the Crimson Café, not too far away from your offices. This is my mobile number. I'll wait here for the call.'

Joel hung up. He didn't want any prevarication from the secretary about how difficult a personal meeting would be. Secretary: Joel pondered the origins of the word. In medieval English it meant 'keeper of secrets', which of course many of them were – whether personal secretary, Secretary of State or company secretary.

He settled down, drinking tea and watching legal and business Cape Town at work, speculating on the secrets the pedestrians held. He enjoyed people watching. His mind was drifting back to England: to Sarah, to Robert, to the mess he'd left at court, wondering what was happening when his phone rang. It was 'Little Miss Helpful' from Weisner's office.

'Mr Weisner can see you now, Mr Grant.'

It seemed only moments since he'd put the phone down, but when he looked at his watch it was actually nearly two hours. 'OK. I'll be with you in five minutes,' said Joel. 'I know where your office is.'

'Mr Weisner works across the street from our corporate offices at 10 Bree Street. Push the entry phone and I'll let you in.' She was actually starting to sound almost helpful, thought Joel.

He had known lawyers working in different buildings in London. Strange how practices are the same 6,000 miles away. Then he thought, no it's not strange. Part of the South African legal system is Common Law, and partially based on English law. It wasn't long ago, perhaps a hundred years or so, when the senior judges in South Africa were British and were sent out here on three-year stints.

Joel paid his bill, left the café and walked to the office. He pushed the entry phone and was told by the same secretary to come up to the first floor, which he did.

On entering the reception he was met by a beautiful blonde woman in her thirties sitting behind a mahogany pedestal desk. He noticed she didn't seem used to visitors; her suntanned legs, which were wide apart, filled the gap between the pedestals. It was very difficult for Joel to concentrate on her wonderful smile when the main image in his mind was under the desk.

Joel said, 'Hello, I'm Joel Grant. Thank you so much for getting back to me and arranging things, it is very kind.'

'My pleasure,' said the legs.

A door opened onto the reception area, and a white man with white hair neatly trimmed close to his head and a small beard peered out. His spectacles were on the top of his head, which gave him the appearance of being slightly taller than his 5 feet 6inch slimline frame actually was.

'Please come in, Mr Grant. It's always a pleasure to meet members of the British Police Service. I'm Frederick Weisner.' He held out his hand and Joel shook it.

Joel walked through the doorway into the paper-strewn office. There were files of papers everywhere: on shelves, filing cabinets, on desks, even on the floor.

'Please take a seat.' The diminutive lawyer pointed to two fireside chairs. 'These used to be in my old office and belonged to my grandfather. He bought them from a German family who were selling up and going to the United States. They were called Goldman, and I understand they own most of Hollywood now. Well that's the rumour, but my grandfather maintained he'd got them for a real bargain.'

Joel thought, what a nice way to ease into a conversation. Not the usual, 'Please take a seat, how can I help you?' He felt he was going to like Weisner. 'They look in really good condition,' said Joel, who suspected they were early to mid-eighteenth century and probably worth a considerable amount. 'Are they German?' he asked.

'English, I think,' replied Weisner.

They weren't English, thought Joel, but they were valuable. He knew a little about furniture. He loved going to auctions in England; he liked the theatre, the competition, and the challenge. He had bought and re-sold a lot over the years, quite successfully.

'Coffee? Tea? Water?' said the lawyer.

'Perhaps some water, if I may.' The receptionist was there in a flash with two glasses of water, which she placed on the card table separating the chairs. Joel noticed the table as well. It too was antique and *was* English.

The two men weren't sitting opposite each other, but sat as though they were facing an imaginary fireplace. In fact the fireplace had been replaced with a wall, featuring what was clearly a family portrait of Weisner with two children and a partial view of Table Mountain.

'Kem Siblisi – now there's a name from the past. What brings Scotland Yard knocking at my door enquiring about a man convicted of a sexually motivated murder, who for many years sat on death row awaiting execution. I should add, Mr Grant, it is my firm view Kem is innocent. I was convinced at the time and I have remained convinced over the years. It defies my training. It defies logic, but I know that man is innocent.'

Joel had rehearsed how to start the conversation many times while in the café, but the opening address from the defence lawyer was so clear, so confident, he reconsidered his approach.

'Mr Weisner, I should make it clear from the outset I think I agree with you. I should also make it clear that, while I am a police officer, I am not here in that capacity. My close friend Robert Bennet is the father of Jessica Bennet who was killed, allegedly by Kem Siblisi. He too does not believe Mr Siblisi is guilty and has asked me to help him find the truth.'

'Ahhh, the truth. "The search for the truth", I believe you British police call it.'

'Well, in relatively recent times,' Joel interrupted, as he suspected he knew where the lawyer was going.

'Yes, yes, I'm aware of some of the miscarriages which have taken place in your country,' said Weisner. 'Every miscarriage is a crime, not just for those convicted and the original victims, but fundamentally for the rule of law. Believe me, Mr Grant, there have been many, many more miscarriages in this country, and Kem is but one of them in my view. But tell me, though, why does the white father of a white woman sexually assaulted in a foreign country not believe the local servant did it? Some twenty years after the event? Please excuse my rather blunt assessment, but I hope you understand.'

'Of course,' said Joel. 'Robert Bennet is a former journalist who has worked in South Africa and has always had serious doubts about Mr Siblisi's guilt. These doubts, like your own opinion it would seem, were not based on facts or knowledge, but on intuition.'

The next half hour was taken up with Joel explaining his conversations with Robert over the years and his recent revelational experience at court. Then Weisner went through Kem's court case, the appeal, and his efforts to keep Kem alive at a time when South Africa was executing as many people as the United States of America, a country many times its size in terms of population.

'Mr Weisner, would you mind if I asked you questions about the investigation and police procedures?' Joel said. 'I know you've touched upon them, but there are a couple of quite specific areas of interest for me.'

'Of course,' the lawyer replied as the receptionist glided in with two more glasses of water.

'Thank you very much. Mr Weisner, I'm sorry, I forgot to ask how long do I have?' Joel asked.

'As long as it takes.'

'Thank you so much, but I have another request before we start again. It's practical, but when I was in the café I drank rather a lot of tea. Could I please use your bathroom?' The receptionist chuckled at the polite request.

'Of course. Marta, please show Mr Grant where the bathroom is.'

Chapter Four

Joel hurried to the bathroom; the realisation of potential relief caused him to become desperate. Although he was a thousand miles or so away from where the siege had taken place, *The Relief of the Mafeking* came to mind as he stood there. How poignant, he thought.

Joel rejoined the lawyer, who was talking to the receptionist about Kem's family. 'Go now and ask her please, Marta.'

Weisner and Joel sat down again. 'I hope you don't mind,' Weisner said, 'I have asked Marta to go and see if Kem's sister can come here to see you. She works at one of the hotels nearby.'

'Which one?' Joel asked. It would be too much of a coincidence if she worked at Joel's hotel. He was relieved to find out she didn't.

Joel felt a little pressurised. He would have preferred to have been a lot more prepared before meeting Kem's family; he didn't want to build their hopes only to have them let down.

Weisner continued, 'What are your questions?'

'The first, is quite straightforward. I can't find any trace of Henri Weltzen, do you have an address for him?' Joel asked.

'I'm afraid Henri passed away about three years ago,' replied Weisner. 'He was a good man, I miss him. I was in court most days, so I hope I can help.'

'I'm sorry. I'm sure you can, Mr Weisner. I hope my second is not too indelicate: Kem Siblisi admitted to the murder of Jess to the police but denied it in the court. I have read the newspaper accounts of the trial, but what happened, Mr Weisner?'

'Well, let's look back – "review the situation" I think detectives call it. Here we have the murder and sexual assault of a white English woman in South Africa at a time of tension between our two countries. Apartheid was still at its peak, although the Pass Laws had just been abolished. There was no sign of forced entry to the house and no strangers had been seen in the grounds. A black servant was seen by his co-workers running away from the house a short while before the body was found. He still had two hours to work, and everyone else was accounted for by the police.

'The police have their suspect, who they arrest, torture – and I use that word deliberately, Mr Grant – and the suspect admits the murder, saying he was sexually aroused by Jessica Bennet. There are no marks or signs of abuse on Kem when I see him. He admits the murder to me, but when I ask him to detail what took place in order to prepare for the court he cannot give me anything other than the basic facts, then admits he didn't attack Jessica but was forced to confess. We plead "Not guilty", but the court does not believe us. Straightforward. International incident resolved, black man admits offence, denies it in court, found guilty and sentenced to death.'

Joel was amazed at the calm, measured way Weisner related the summary. It was so clear and concise, but at the same time terrifying.

'A couple of supplementary questions, if I may. Why did Kem admit the murder to you and then deny it?'

'Mr Grant, this was a man whose only dealings with white people was as an inferior being, because that's how Apartheid was designed to make people feel. His only dealings with white people would have been with his employers, who were reasonable employers as we found out, which further aggravated the situation in the eyes of the court, and the police who stopped him and imprisoned him under the Pass Laws, which severely restricted the movement of black people. So a white man purporting to be a lawyer comes into his world and tells him he is here to help him when he has just been tortured by whites. Who should he trust?'

'So what did make him trust you?' asked Joel.

'I would like to think it was my approach and attitude, but I suspect it was my reputation with others. I was in a real dilemma: he had admitted the crime to me, but now was denying it. It was his description of his "waterboarding", I believe the CIA call it now, which convinced me he was telling the truth and allowed me to continue to represent him.'

Joel said, 'I thought waterboarding was relatively new?'

'No, no, Mr Grant. Believe me, it's been around a long time. Don't forget you are in the country which invented concentration camps and Apartheid. We have many dark secrets.'

'But why did Kem leave work early, and why was he running?'

'He said Jessica had told him it was okay to go home and tell his family his news.'

'What news?'

'He was going to do a correspondence course as a precursor to an external LLB from London University. Jessica had made enquiries and it was possible. Unfortunately no one else knew, including her husband-to-be. There were no documents, so the prosecution just said it was lies.'

'Very interesting,' said Joel. 'About Jess's body, Mr Weisner. Do you know if the pathologist visited the scene? Who was it? Where would the remaining exhibits be stored? And where did the post mortem examination take place? I'm sorry to bombard you with questions.'

'Not at all,' said Weisner. 'In those days I do not recall a pathologist visiting a scene. It was only those who became forensic pathologists who latterly started visiting scenes. It's still not usual. Photos, videos, and samples are usually taken by the police for them to examine retrospectively.'

'Were there photos of the scene?' Joel asked.

'Yes, I have copies on my file. They're pretty basic. I will get them for you.'

'What about other exhibits, clothing, etcetera?'

'Normally any clothing belonging to the deceased would be kept at the hospital and destroyed,' Weisner explained. 'Kem's clothing may have been taken and possibly retained by the police, if they bothered. In fact, thinking about it, I know they didn't bother to take his clothing from him, because when I first saw him he was still wearing his work uniform. They would have taken it from him prior to court, though.'

'Uniform? What do you mean?'

'Many people gave, and still give, their house staff uniform. It is supposed to be a perk, but I suspect with some, particularly in the old days, it was more about power.'

'What will have happened to that?'

'Probably destroyed by the police, or possibly returned to the family. Let me get the photographs.' The lawyer got up, turned to a pile of paper in the corner of the room and pulled from it three blue files, each about ten centimetres thick. From one of the files he pulled a brown envelope, then placed the other files on the floor and handed the envelope to Joel.

In the envelope Joel found ten black and white photographs, mostly depicting the body of a young woman lying strewn on the floor of what looked like a very expensively furnished room, the walls lined with hundreds of books. The other images were of the wider room. Joel immediately noted the French windows of the room and what looked like the only other door into the room were both closed. The furniture did not appear to have been disturbed and the bookshelves looked as if a librarian kept them in order. Nothing seemed out of place except the torn clothing on Jessica's body.

'Did they take any photos at the post mortem examination?' asked Joel.

'Yes, but they wouldn't be supplied to me as a matter of course. I'd inspect those at the court,' replied the lawyer.

'I don't want to be crude, but I seem to recall reading in the newspapers Jess's knickers had been pulled down. This point was laboured by the prosecution. Did they find that at the post mortem?'

'No, everyone who gave evidence mentioned it. George Corfield, the staff, the police.'

'But how did they know? The photos don't show that, the dress has not risen up.'

'Mr Grant, this was twenty years ago in South Africa. The police will have adjusted her dress, pulled it straight, prior to the photographs being taken, to preserve the young woman's dignity. It's not unusual.'

'But how can these photos purport to represent a murder scene? What use are they to the investigation and court case?' Joel was flabbergasted.

'That's how it was. We had to rely upon oral testimony a lot more than in England.'

Joel was stunned by the experienced South African jurist's comment. Oral testimony is fine, but descriptions are personal and recollections differ. Photographic evidence is still open to interpretation but any interpretation was bound to be flawed if the scene had been tampered with prior to the photos being taken.

At this point the receptionist returned and said, 'Thembi wasn't there today.' For the second time that day Joel felt relief, but this time of a very different kind. His lack of appreciation of South African investigatory practices, particularly twenty years ago, confirmed to him he really wasn't ready for Kem's family.

'Mr Weisner, I am conscious it is getting late for you and your staff,' Joel said, indicating the receptionist. 'I know it's unusual, but would you mind if I took these papers back to the hotel and went through them overnight?'

'I'm sorry, Mr Grant, I can't allow these papers to leave my office. Things go missing from hotels here, and I would never forgive myself if anything happened to these documents. You are very welcome to come back in the morning and continue with your questions and research. We have a spare office. You may have noticed this is not a busy office. Most of the work takes place across the road.' He indicated the main office building, and added mockingly, 'This old, cantankerous partner with his ideals for justice has been placed out of sight of the rich, powerful clients.'

'That's not true and you know it,' said the receptionist in a protective, almost maternal, way. 'It's your name that brings those clients to this firm. You're the one they want to meet. You're the one they want to review the evidence before it gets to court. You are this firm!'

'Hush, child,' Weisner said to the agitated young woman.

'I don't mind staying late tonight. I need to get on with the Landry file anyway. I've got a good three hours' work and I can certainly do it better at night, when you're not here.'

'Well if you don't mind keeping Mr Grant company, Marta, that would be very good, I think. What do you think, Mr Grant?'

'As long as he keeps quiet,' Marta responded, quickly and firmly.

'I promise,' said Joel equally quickly, delighted at the thought of researching the documents tonight rather than having to wait another day.

'All right,' said Weisner. 'All the information you want is in these three files,' indicating the blue folders, 'and don't stay too late, Marta! I will see you in the morning, Mr Grant?' It was a question not a statement, and Joel nodded. Five minutes later Weisner departed with a kiss on the cheek from Marta. Saying good night, he left Joel going through the documents. It was 6pm – I'll be finished by eight, Joel thought.

Again the time flew by, Joel reading and making notes which he would clarify with Weisner in the morning. Marta brought him coffee 'to keep him awake', but it was now 8.45pm and he was hungry.

He closed the files, arranged them in a neat pile on the card table and put his notes in his rucksack. He stood up, stretched his arms and back and walked out into the reception area.

Marta looked up. 'Finished?' she asked.

'For the moment,' Joel said. 'What about you?'

'Yes, quite finished.'

'I'm sorry to have kept you so late. I didn't realise. I'm starving –

my stomach always tells me when I need a break. Are there any good restaurants here?'

'Yes, but there are also some good ones on The Waterfront nearer to your hotel.'

'Are you hungry? Would you like to join me?' Joel thought it was only polite to ask given she had put herself out for him.

Surprisingly, she said, 'OK. The Waterfront is more or less on my way home and I can give you a lift in my car.'

Perfect, thought Joel, who had been wondering how safe the streets of Cape Town would be at night, even for a relatively fit man. He also thought he'd leave his rucksack in the office, just in case.

Marta locked the office and set the alarm. They made their way into the basement where, to Joel's surprise, there was an enormous underground car park.

'It goes across the road to the other office,' Marta said, 'that way Papa can sneak into the corporate boardroom to be presented to the clients without them knowing he isn't allowed in their building normally.'

'Papa?' said Joel.

'Yes. Didn't you realise he's my father? I'm a late child. I didn't come along until he was fifty. My mother left us, and he and our nanny brought up my brother and me. She did try and get custody when it suited her,' Marta continued, which Joel found surprisingly open, 'but she was unsuccessful.'

They got into a silver Audi A5 and drove the ten minutes to the hotel. During the drive, Marta's openness continued, and Joel discovered she had been married to a well-known rugby player when she was twenty-two. Joel was fascinated by the story, but still more fascinated by the legs of his companion moving as she changed gear negotiating the night-time traffic of Cape Town.

Marta parked the car at the hotel, and they walked to the Baia Seafood restaurant a short distance from the hotel. Marta chose an excellent South African Chenin Blanc, although she merely sipped hers. Joel managed to enjoy it fully!

The conversation with Marta over dinner was captivating for Joel, who was developing an interest in his dinner companion. She'd previously had plans to be a lawyer like her father, but the husband had different plans for his trophy wife. She would stay in and breed for him. Marta soon discovered he was a bully, bigot and abuser. The final straw came

31

when he discovered the reason she was not getting pregnant was due to the contraceptive pills she was taking, not because of any particular medical issue. He went berserk, beat her up and her father ensured she pressed charges. To do this to a national hero was tantamount to treason, and many of her new friends cut her adrift. Marta wasn't bothered by this response; in fact, it was another form of release.

Marta left South Africa for a time and lived in New York, working for Africa Rights Watch, developing policy in relation to sub-Saharan Africa. Her job entailed regular visits to the region, which in turn allowed her regular visits back to see her father. When she had a spare moment, she would catch an overnight plane from Nairobi, Kigali, wherever, spend a few days with him, then return to the centre of the continent.

She missed South Africa and her father. She still hungered to be a lawyer, so came back, trained with the firm and qualified. There were those who didn't want it to happen, but her father made sure it did.

'So you're a lawyer as well?' Joel asked, now knowing the answer.

'Yes, and you, like many in the past, thought I was my father's pretty secretary. Well I may be an attorney, but because of my ex-husband's connections I work with my father, which I frankly prefer rather than the self important knob-sticks across the road.'

'I did think you were his secretary, yes, but pretty? Now I never noticed.'

'No, I'm not surprised. You barely took your eyes off my legs when we were in the car. Not to mention when you first came in the office. Don't think I'm just a dizzy blonde, Mr Grant. Did you notice I was blonde, given your other interest?'

God, she could be fierce, thought Joel, who responded, 'Of course I did, and believe me, I certainly don't think you're dizzy. And it's Joel, not Mr Grant, Marta. Are you a natural blonde, by the way?'

Marta almost split her sides laughing. 'You're a cheeky bastard, Mr Grant. Is that grey in your hair natural?'

'Certainly not. I've spent a fortune getting these highlights put in,' Joel said. His hair over the past couple of years had become a grey–blond mix. They both laughed out loud. This was not going the way Joel had planned; he was enjoying Marta's company too much.

They recounted tales of their life experiences, Joel's mostly made up of anecdotes from his policing career, including the recent event at the Old Bailey, and Marta's her experiences in South Africa societies. She was quite specific in using this term; she was adamant it was still very much divided by the 'haves': the white minority, and the 'have nots': the majority of the black majority.

Marta talked about her brother, who was a zoologist and lived near Pretoria. She clearly thought the world of her little brother. She also revealed, while working for African Rights, she had met a British police officer, so she knew a little about the way Joel was approaching his inquiries. In fact she knew a great deal. He wondered how closely she had known the police officer, who was from the provinces, not the Met. Marta, in her forthright style, asked Joel about his personal life. Was there a wife? Children? Girlfriend? Joel found himself being very open – well, relatively open. He disclosed he'd been married; it broke down and his ex-wife had taken his children, who were now twelve and ten, to live in Canada. He tried to stop it, but knew the courts would have ruled against him so he did not pursue his case. He saw his children as often as he could, and intended to spend some time while on the sick visiting them. He'd had relationships since but nothing serious, and for some reason he didn't mention Sarah.

Marta left about 10.30pm. They agreed to meet the next morning in the office. She said, 'Thank you, Joel, I've really enjoyed tonight,' then leaned forward, kissed him on the cheek, turned and left.

'Me too,' murmured Joel thoughtfully as Marta left the hotel car park.

Chapter Five

Joel needed a clear head in the morning so went straight to bed, not tempted by the hotel bar. At first his mind was twirling with thoughts about Marta, Sarah, life, then he subliminally refocused on what he had found today and his research tomorrow. It was strange how his mind did this: always came back to the matter in hand, despite other delicious thoughts.

The next thing he knew was the phone ringing at 7am. 'How's it going, Joel?' It was Robert.

'Robert, I've only been at it one day, give me a chance,' Joel responded, waking up and thinking what time it was in the United Kingdom.

'What have you done? Who have you seen?' Robert pressed.

'For God's sake. It's not easy here, Robert, you should know that. I've read the media coverage of the trial and I've had a preliminary chat with Kem's lawyer, who I'll be seeing again in the next few days.' Joel thought it was better to slow things right down, otherwise he wouldn't be surprised if Robert jumped on a plane to get involved. That was the last thing he needed. He'd also worked out it was 5am in the United Kingdom.

'I know, Joel. I'm sorry, but I was just keen to hear.'

'Robert, now you've called, the lawyer said Jess was organising a correspondence course for Kem, and that's why he'd left early – to tell his family. Do you know anything about it?'

'I remember it being mentioned at the trial, but there was no documentary evidence, no course papers, nothing. But it's the sort of thing Jess would have done. I seem to remember it was for a law degree from London, she was at SOAS so she would have ready access to material. It's just none was found, so everyone assumed he was lying.'

'But wasn't this Jess's first trip to the Corfield's home?'

'No, no, she'd been a number of times. It was the first time since

34

they'd got engaged, and it was a sort of introduction into South African polite society. When she'd been before, she was with Matthew and researching her dissertation.'

'Okay,' said Joel, 'but if Kem was lying, how did he know about the course?'

'That's what his lawyer said, but the prosecution just alleged he'd seen the course in a book or magazine in the library at the Corfields. One of Kem's jobs was to keep it tidy.' Joel remembered the photograph of the well-ordered books in the library.

'I understand. Thanks, Robert, that's really helpful. As soon as I have anything I'll let you know. How are things generally? Much happening in the grand metropolis of Budleigh Salterton?'

'I think you'd better speak to Sarah. She's still very annoyed with you.'

Annoyed. Mmmmmm, thought Joel, just a little. 'I rang her when I got here.'

'Oh, I didn't know,' said Robert. 'I think she blames me, though. It's unlikely you'll get the blame.'

You are probably wrong there, old boy, thought Joel. 'Listen, I'll ring you at the end of the week, but the signal is not good here, so leave it to me to ring you when I'm in the hotel or something.'

'OK, Joel, I can take the hint,' Robert said quietly. 'Speak to you at the end of the week.'

They said their goodbyes and ended the conversation. Joel got up, showered, dressed and then had breakfast, but this time in the Crimson café. He had spotted the food the previous day and thought he'd try it out.

Joel walked to the office and rang the buzzer at 8.25am. A voice from the other side said, 'You're early, come back at 8.30,' coupled with a laugh. It was Marta teasing him. The buzzer opened the door and he walked up the stairs and into the reception area. He noticed Marta was wearing trousers this morning.

'Morning,' she said. 'Sleep OK?'

'Great thanks, what about you?'

'The same. I'm not used to painting the town red anymore, and believe me, going for a meal is like painting the town red for me.' They both laughed. 'I have put your files in that office over there,' she pointed to a small office, which was very ordered compared to Weisner Senior's. 'It's my office for when I need peace and quiet, so don't make a mess. Joel, thanks for last night. I enjoyed it.'

Joel said, 'It was the least I could do. You did me a real favour staying late last night.' Joel went into the office where there was a cup of coffee waiting for him. 'Thanks for the coffee,' he added.

'Don't get used to it! Papa will be here shortly and I made some for him.'

What a woman, thought Joel. One minute soft, the next tough. He settled down at the desk. A couple of minutes later, Weisner Senior arrived, popping his head in to Marta's office.

'Good morning, Mr Grant, how are you this morning?'

'I'm good thanks, Mr Weisner. How are you?'

'I'm fine. I think you will have some questions for me. I have to go to see my colleagues and a client at 10.30.' Joel heard an 'Hmphh' from the direction of Marta. 'Would you like to start now?' Weisner asked.

'Yes please.'

'Bring your coffee.'

Joel followed him into his office, and was about to join him in the fireside chairs when the lawyer said, 'Please close the door. Marta is always complaining she can't work with me talking. It's actually her eavesdropping.' This elicited another 'Hmphh' from Marta, and as Joel closed the door she smiled at him. He winked at her.

'Before we start, Mr Grant,' said Weisner, 'you took Marta out for dinner last night. I presume it was to say thanks for staying behind. It was nice of you, she has had no life recently, but you must understand Cape Town is a village and people talk.'

Good God, thought Joel. He shouldn't have been surprised, Marta had told him. 'Mr Weisner, I was grateful to Marta and neither of us had eaten, I'm sure she told you that.'

'I haven't spoken to Marta about it. I received two phone calls from your fellow diners earlier this morning. It's a village, Mr Grant. I am delighted Marta had a break from her work. I mention those calls merely to illustrate the point: people talk, they love to gossip here. They will want to know who is asking questions about Kem Siblisi, and who is having dinner with old Weisner's daughter. Is it the same person? Take care who you talk to and what you say, Mr Grant.'

'I understand, Mr Weisner. I am grateful.' The only people he had spoken to were admin people at the local paper. Interesting, he thought.

'Now your questions,' said the professor to the student.

They talked for nearly two hours. Joel learnt a lot about the South African investigative process and court procedure, and a great deal about

Kem's trial. At 10.25am the door opened. It was Marta.

'Time's up,' she quipped.

'Please excuse me. I must go, and I will not be back today. How long are you here, Mr Grant?'

'As long as it takes,' Joel replied, repeating what Weisner had told him the previous day.

'You will have more questions, I'm sure. Please feel free to use this office as a base and to leave your papers securely. Marta will know my movements. Please ask any questions when you wish, directly or through Marta.'

'Thank you, you are very kind,' Joel responded.

'Not at all,' said the lawyer, leaving the room with another kiss from Marta, who said, 'Speak to you later.'

Joel asked, 'Where is the coffee, Marta?'

'Why?'

'I was going to make some.'

'You are so clearly not South African, Joel Grant. It's in there.' Joel made the coffee and settled down to reviewing the file again.

Joel asked Marta if she had any blu tack and was it OK to put the pictures on the wall. She said she had seen many dead bodies, having worked in central Africa and being a lawyer in South Africa, where the murder rate was over forty a day. Joel was not surprised by this comment. He put the pictures on the wall to refer to them as he read and reread the documents. He looked at the pathologist's report a number of times. It was short. The part, which was of particular interest, was the explanation death had occurred by the deceased being held by the neck and the head being pushed back sharply, breaking the neck and stopping the blood supply to the brain. The pathologist also described the clothing, how the left side of Jess's dress and bra had been ripped and how her knickers were pulled down from the left hand side, but Joel reminded himself the police must have told the pathologist this.

Shortly after midday Marta brought in another coffee and some lemon drizzle cake for Joel. 'I made this,' she said. 'Unless you need to go out for a meal?'

'No, this is great, thank you,' said Joel.

'Joel, I haven't contacted Thembi Siblisi today,' Marta stated. 'I got the impression you weren't ready to see her.'

'Thanks, that was very astute of you. I'm afraid I think it's just a little too early, and I don't want to raise the family's expectations.

But won't she have got to know you were looking for her? Your father explained how this place is village-like.'

'She would have known. It would have been a subject of gossip, but I didn't go to the hotel. I thought it was a little early too, and I saw your face, so I'll do it when you're ready.' As if to illustrate the point, she said, 'Did Papa mention gossip in the context of who was in the restaurant last night? I saw three of his clients or friends, one of whom is the editor of the Cape News.'

'Yes, he did.' God, thought Joel, she's good. She's bloody good.

Joel confirmed what her father had told him, Marta said she hadn't mentioned it last night because she thought Joel might have become self-conscious. She was correct, he concluded.

The rest of the day passed by with Joel going over the files. There were few phone calls into the office, but one was clearly from Mr Weisner. Joel heard Marta say, 'Yes…mmm… Yes… Seems so… Hmphhh,' third time today, thought Joel, 'I'll ask him, he may be busy… OK, I'll let you know.'

The phone call ended. 'It seems my father likes you and wants you to have dinner with him tonight at home. Is that OK?'

'That's very kind of him. What time? Where is the house?'

'It's at 6pm, so I'll pick you up from your hotel at 5.30. It seems as though he doesn't want you seen out in public!' She laughed.

Joel looked at his watch. It was four o'clock. He told Marta he'd better go and get changed. The walk to the hotel would do him good, and the streets were still busy. She said she would see him later.

Chapter Six

As he made his way to the hotel, his head was full of questions from the information he'd taken in during the day. He needed to find out what had happened to the potential exhibits, and he hoped they hadn't been destroyed: there were many cases in the United Kingdom where they hadn't, and they had been found in the most unlikely places.

Marta's Audi swung into the entrance to the hotel car park. Joel was inside talking to the doorman, and he didn't notice her arrival until he spotted another customer staring at the door, seemingly stunned. Joel turned around and saw why the customer was stunned. It was Marta walking from the car, no longer wearing the trouser suit she had been wearing earlier but a short flouncy silk dress with matching red high heels. Her blonde hair flashed electric in the sunlight; she looked incredible.

Joel walked out towards Marta. She leaned forward and kissed him on the cheek, whispering, 'Put your tongue back in your mouth.' Joel was not only taken aback by her appearance but also by her comments. 'You English, I thought you were more subtle.'

'I don't know what you mean,' Joel managed to blurt out as they both got into the car, 'but I have to say you look beautiful.'

'Thank you,' she said. 'I have tried, I'm glad you noticed.'

'So did half of Cape Town, I think,' said Joel mischievously.

They both laughed and chatted about 'the South African male' on the way to Marta's Father's house. It was a relatively short drive to the house, with its own grounds, situated in the affluent area of Bishopscourt.

As they drove into the property Joel noticed the number of people busying themselves in the grounds, 'I'm surprised your father has so many people working here,' he said, perhaps somewhat naively.

Marta said, 'Most of them are ex-clients who he took pity on. At one time he had ten people living here, but he managed to find some jobs. I think there's only about five now. They've been with him ages, and are so loyal towards him.'

As they pulled up, Weisner came out, hugged Marta and said, 'Joel, how nice to see you. Thanks for coming,' shaking his hand at the same time.

'No, thank *you*, Mr Weisner. This is really very kind.'

'Joel, please call me Frederick. Marta does when she's annoyed with me.' He laughed. 'Come, come in.'

He led the way into the house, and as he did Marta whispered in Joel's ear, 'Told you he liked you!'

'Annette,' Weisner said to a middle-aged black woman who was in the hallway, 'this is Joel. He is a friend of ours. Joel, this is Annette. She has been here longer than I can remember, and she takes care of me.'

'And it's a big job, isn't it, Annette?' Marta interrupted.

'Oh Marta, you look gorgeous,' Annette said.

'She doesn't need flattery, thank you,' Weisner said to Annette.

'Every woman needs flattery. What would you know, Frederick?' she responded. Joel thought the relationship between the Weisners and Annette was very different to what he had imagined of most South African householders.

'What do you want to drink, Marta?' Annette asked.

'Surprise me, and Joel will have the same, won't you, Joel?'

Weisner said, 'You see what sort of house this is, Joel? Dominated by women at every turn.'

Annette served everyone a Sundowner, made from Cape Brandy, lemon juice and Amarula liqueur. 'Good choice, Annette. Can I afford this?' Weisner said.

'No, but it is not every day your daughter brings home a handsome young friend.'

Weisner said, 'He is a friend of both of us.'

'He's still handsome,' said Annette, 'isn't he, Marta?'

'In an English sort of way,' she responded.

Weisner could see Joel was embarrassed by these comments, and said, 'So, what have you found out, Joel?'

Thank goodness, Joel thought. He felt as though he was having an out of body experience. 'Well I'm still researching,' he said. 'I'm really interested in getting to the police and hospital to see if they have any exhibits.'

'If I can give you a little advice, try the hospital first. Who was the pathologist? Tomas Hessen?'

Joel replied, 'That's right.'

'Mmm, he wasn't forensically qualified at the time, I think but you should go to the hospital first. You could use the British police angle, they will be impressed. Don't talk to the pathologist, talk to the admin people. They will help, if they can. I may be able to assist.'

'Police? Are you a policeman?' Annette interrupted.

'Yes, from London,' Marta responded on his behalf.

'Oh how exciting.'

'Yes, Annette, from Scotland Yard. You love those crime thrillers, don't you?' said Weisner teasingly.

'Oh yes, I love them all. *Ashes to Ashes*, *Midsomer Murders*, *Silent Witness*, *Taggart*. But he's not like any of them, Marta.'

'See what I meant, Joel? We may as well not be here the way they talk about us. It's definitely a woman's world.' Everyone burst out laughing at the irony of the statement.

'Why should I go to the hospital first?' asked Joel. His natural inclination would have taken him to the police first.

'Because you may meet resistance at the barracks,' Marta answered.

'That is quite true,' Weisner added. 'They have come a long way, but they don't like people poking around in the past very much, believe me. Regardless of that, I do feel your best chance is the hospital. Has Kem's sister contacted you yet, Marta?'

'Not yet,' Marta replied. She felt she wasn't lying.

'Pity, she may be able to arrange a visit to the prison for Joel.'

Joel said, 'Is that really possible?'

'Depends,' Weisner replied, 'where they are in the visiting cycle and how much time they have added up.' Weisner explained Kem was in Pollsmoor prison, where his family could add up their visitors' passes to have long visits or multiple visitors. 'Let's eat. That's why you're here – well partly.'

They enjoyed a wonderful evening, with Weisner holding court and telling tales – some sad, some mad and some downright bad – of the days gone by in South Africa, which showed how things had changed. They ate an avocado salad starter followed by a minced beef dish called bobotie, and a milk tart for pudding. Annette said she had picked a traditional South African menu for the new arrival. Joel liked it.

The evening ended with Annette saying, 'Is it not time you went to bed, Frederick? You were up early this morning and you don't want to bore Marta and Joel anymore.'

Weisner looked at Joel, shrugged almost as if he was saying 'What can I do?' and nodded in agreement. Joel and Marta left after saying goodnight to everyone, thanking them for a wonderful meal. They got into the car, and Joel said, 'Annette and your father have an interesting relationship. She's very maternal.'

'Maternal may be how it's portrayed, but that's for outside consumption. They are lovers and have been for years.'

Joel didn't say anything immediately. He simply considered what he'd just been told. It broke all the rules, all his preconceptions of relationships in South Africa. Yes, he knew there were inter-racial relationships, but he had presumed they were restricted to the young, not people of Annette and Frederick's generation. He had watched *Django* on the plane and assumed all relationships between the white elite male and black women would be based upon the power and control of the male, or a variation of the slavery portrayed in *Django*.

'I would never have guessed,' Joel said eventually. 'It must be rare.'

'What? Men and women falling in love?' Marta snapped.

'You know what I mean, Marta. Powerful white lawyer and black servant.'

She interrupted before he could continue. 'She's not a fucking servant, she's as much part of our family as I am. She was our nanny and has been incredible for my father since my mother left. They have a great relationship which, because of people with your views, has to be hidden.'

This time Joel snapped in response. 'What do you mean, my views? You know fuck all about my views. I have no experience of this country and was basing my comments on my understanding of the culture. Don't associate me with prejudice. There's enough in the United Kingdom that I don't understand, let alone in this place. I wouldn't pretend to understand it. I'm sorry.'

Marta was not expecting such a response, assertive but reasoned, and most of all conciliatory. Why wasn't she expecting the response? She liked Joel; it was what she should have expected. She liked him a lot.

'I'm sorry,' Marta said. 'It's just I'm tired and I was labelling you with the prejudices I've seen from others. Fancy a drink at my flat? Peace?'

'Peace,' Joel surrendered. 'I'll get a cab back to the hotel, then you can have a drink too.'

She said, 'Joel, you English! I'm asking you to stay the night.'

Joel was shocked again: the second time in five minutes. This country, these people. What next? he thought, but then he remembered an experience when he was a young detective. He'd been handed a business card by a woman in a pub. The card read, 'Roses are red, violets are blue.' He then turned it over, and it continued, 'I fancy a fuck, how about you?' Joel, as the good old *News of the World* would have said, made his excuses and left! Which certainly was not going to happen tonight.

'Well?' said Marta. 'Do you want to stay?'

'Let me just analyse the proposal,' Joel said, and immediately followed with, 'Yes.'

'That was the correct analysis, Joel Grant. Any other answer and you would have been walking back to the hotel, and that's not a good thing for a stranger to be doing at this time of night.'

'That's why I said yes,' Joel quipped, but then quickly added, 'only joking, honest.'

'Mmmmmmmm,' said Marta, 'your British sense of humour.'

They arrived at the flat in Greenpoint, which Joel recognised as not far from The Waterfront, and Marta drove into the garage area after the barrier had been opened by the security guard, who waved a greeting to her. She parked the car and was about to get out when Joel reached across, put his arm around her and kissed her. She responded by kissing him back and holding his head between her hands. The kiss seemed to continue for minutes, then Marta murmured, 'Come on, let's get inside.'

They left the car and walked arm in arm to the lift, which took them to the fourth and top floor of the flats. On the short lift ride they were like two lovers who couldn't keep their hands off each other, kissing and touching. They couldn't help themselves.

Marta opened the flat door and guided Joel through to her bedroom, where they continued to kiss while undressing each other. They were on the bed in seconds and were quickly exploring each other's bodies in the intimate way only lovers do.

They made love throughout the night, interspersed with sharing thoughts and secrets with each other about their lives, their views and lovers. Joel was again circumspect about Sarah. He said he had a girlfriend who he lived with, but didn't go into detail. This seemed to satisfy Marta's natural curiosity and Joel's conscience. Marta was not in a current relationship. She said she found relationships difficult after her marriage. Joel was thankful for this piece of information; at one point during the night he'd had visions of a large South African bursting through the door and tearing him apart. How would he explain that to Sarah or, more importantly, Fiona Henderson?

As if out of nowhere, Marta asked, 'Joel, do you really think Kem is innocent?'

'I don't know. I need to gather a lot more information. Your father seems to think so.'

'Yes, but sometimes Papa lets his heart rule his head. He's been wrong before, otherwise he wouldn't have married my mother.'

'But then you wouldn't be here.'

'That's nice, thank you,' said Marta.

'Anyway, all of us make mistakes. We are all wrong sometimes, even great South African freedom fighters make mistakes.'

'No they don't. He's a great man and I won't hear a word against him.'

'What, your father?' Joel said.

'You know who we're talking about, Joel. Madiba. Another example of your British humour?'

He kissed her gently, softly, on her face, her body and hair. This woman had something special. He didn't know what it was, but it was there.

At 6am the alarm rang out. It was an old alarm clock with bells on top. Marta explained it was a present from her father a long time ago to make sure she never missed breakfast.

'Breakfast? queried Marta.

'Just a coffee, thanks, I have to get back to the hotel and get changed.'

'I'll drop you off on the way to work. Now, as I was saying, breakfast?'

Marta gave Joel coffee, orange juice, muesli and croissants. He looked around the flat, which was tastefully furnished. In a modern complex, with its polished wooden floors and French doors opening out on to a balcony, again with beautiful views of Table Mountain. The flat was decorated with many Art Deco features; a favourite of Joel's at auction rooms.

Marta dressed ready for work while preparing breakfast. God, she looks good, Joel thought. He could have done with going back to bed with her. They left at 7am, and Marta dropped Joel off ten minutes later. As he was about to get out of the car, he leaned across and kissed her.

'Thanks for breakfast,' he said, 'best hotel in town.' He saw Marta look sternly at him. 'Only joking. British humour and all that.'

Marta smiled. Joel added, 'I really enjoyed last night, Marta, it was great.'

'So did I,' she said. 'Now get a shower and into the office. You've got work to do.'

Joel alighted, the car drove off and he walked into the hotel. When he left there about twelve hours earlier he'd had no idea what would happen during the course of the night. What would the next twelve hours bring? he pondered.

Chapter Seven

Joel showered, changed and walked to Weisner's office. It's just like work, he thought, although a little later in the morning than in London. He rang the bell and the door was opened immediately. He walked in, closed it behind him and walked up the stairs. Marta was just coming out of the office he was using.

'Your coffee is on the table, sir.'

'Sir? Goodness you're formal this morning,' Joel said.

'Just being business-like.' She laughed. 'Papa will be ringing shortly. You said you had some questions. Do you want to speak to him, Joel?'

'Yes thanks,' said Joel, remembering their discussion in bed earlier.

'Joel, please don't tell him about last night. He is, despite what he may display, quite old fashioned.'

'Marta, I wouldn't dream of mentioning it to anyone. It was between us, and is no-one else's business.' He kissed her gently and held her for a moment.

'Thank you,' she said almost coyly.

Five minutes later the phone rang. It was clearly Weisner. Joel heard Marta say she thought he wanted to speak to him, and seconds later the phone rang on his desk. He picked it up and heard a voice say, 'Good morning, Mr Grant. I see my daughter got you home safely last night.'

Joel grasped Weisner wanted to keep the business relationship formal. He responded, 'Yes, thank you, Mr Weisner, I am very grateful to her and to you too for your kindness and hospitality.'

'Not at all,' said Weisner. 'Now you have some questions, I think.'

'Please. They may sound basic, maybe naïve, but the answers would be helpful.'

'Those are the best type of questions, Mr Grant. Now what are they?'

'Firstly, do you know if Kem is right or left handed?'

'Oh dear, let me think now.' There was silence for a moment, then, 'Left-handed. I recall him signing a document with his left hand. Yes, yes left, definitely left, but what's the significance?'

'Oh I just wanted to know. It may help me understand the scene a little better.' Joel didn't mention to Weisner it was actually a little to Kem's detriment, given the condition of the clothing described in the evidence. 'Now the pathologist, is he still around in Cape Town?'

'Yes he still works at the Groote Schuur Hospital, but I would not suggest you go to him. Well, not just yet. He is even more cantankerous than me and will get very defensive about his work when you tell him who you are and what you are doing, if he doesn't already know!'

'Ah, the village.'

'Precisely,' said Weisner. 'What are you after?'

'I want to see if I can find the exhibits in the hospital. I know it's a long shot, but it's what has happened in the UK: exhibits have been found in the strangest of places.'

'Ah, that's definitely administration, as I said last night. Doctors wouldn't know or be interested in that sort of thing. I thought about the British police angle, but I don't think you should use it yet. If you go to the Administration Department, ask for Dr Joseph Boucher. I will ring him, he will be expecting you.'

'I thought you said doctors wouldn't be interested?' queried Joel.

'He's a Doctor of Philosophy, very bright. Ask for him,' replied Weisner.

'OK, thanks. And my last question, for the moment, do you have any contacts in the police?'

'Many, many contacts,' said Weisner, 'but it's who would be the best for you to speak to. Leave that one with me, I will think about it. It could be career limiting for them if the wrong people found out, so we may have to think very carefully about your approach.'

'Thank you.'

'No more questions?'

'Do you have a photo of Kem?' asked Joel.

'No, I'm afraid not. Why?'

'I'm interested in his physique.'

'OK, that's easy. Very thin, long legs, long, thin arms, not much fat or, for that matter, muscle.'

'Mmm, that's how Robert described him. Thanks,' said Joel.

'Can I speak to Marta again please?' Frederick asked. Joel had not mastered the phones and went to the office to get Marta, who had clearly been listening to his side of the conversation. She spoke briefly to her father and returned to Joel.

'Papa was right about the police, Joel, you will have to be careful. Some are very good people, some are very bad.'

'Same the world over,' commented Joel, 'only the percentages differ. How far is Groote Schuur Hospital from here, Marta?'

'Only five minutes by car. Give Papa a little time to talk to Joseph Boucher. That's who he was hinting at last night. I would suggest you aim to get there about twelve o'clock when it will be quieter, lunchtime. I will give you a lift.'

'No, I'll take a taxi. You've got work to do, and anyway people might see me with you.'

'Are you ashamed of me, Joel Grant?'

'Don't be silly,' he said.

'OK, I understand, I think.' She thought she knew what he was alluding to.

Joel spent the rest of the morning reading, thinking and jotting down little notes for himself. Again he lost all sense of time until he became aware of Marta at the door.

'It's almost 11.45am, Joel, time to go. I have a taxi waiting for you.'

My goodness, she's good, he thought yet again. 'Thanks, Marta.' He gathered his papers, and as he was about to leave the room he turned and kissed her on the lips, whispering, 'See you later.'

'I hope so,' she responded as Joel went out of the door and got into the Toyota.

The driver said, 'Groote Schuur Hospital, sir?' He arrived at the hospital twenty-five minutes later; the traffic was horrendous. As he paid the driver, he asked if he could pick him up. 'No problem,' replied the driver, handing him his card and adding, 'Anything for a friend of Mr Weisner, he's a great man.'

'Thank you so much. See you later.' Joel walked into the brick and colonnade dominated structure. Access to the Admin Department was from inside the main building, he walked to the enquiry counter and asked for Dr Boucher.

'Is he expecting you? It's lunchtime,' said the receptionist. Looking around he saw Marta was right, it was quiet.

'Yes, my name is Joel Grant.'

'One moment please.' The receptionist made a brief call, and said in a surprised manner, 'He's coming down to see you.'

A little while later, a six foot tall white man in his forties, wearing what looked like a tired well-worn suit, walked into the reception area. He went over to Joel and said warmly, 'Dr Grant, how nice to see you. So good of you to come over. I am Joseph Boucher, Head of Administration. It's not often we get visitors from the United States.'

Joel was puzzled and was about to respond when Dr Boucher whispered in his ear, 'Just go with it.'

Joel thought he understood, and said, 'Nice to meet you too.'

Dr Boucher took Joel to his office, where he said, 'I'm sorry about that, but you never know who's listening. Frederick explained what you are doing and, like him, I think using the British police approach would be unwise. Your investigations will not be popular with some in this hospital who know the Corfield family. In fact, they are one of our largest donors and benefactors. People in this country don't like being reminded of the past. We've had that with the Truth and Reconciliation Commission, and they now want to look forward.'

'I don't want to get you into trouble,' said Joel.

'Not a problem. Now Frederick only gave me the briefest of details. How can I help?'

Joel explained he was trying to find out if there were any exhibits left from Jess's post mortem.

'Well, that should be fairly straightforward. We South Africans are great bureaucrats and hoarders, believe me. Let's have a look.' Dr Boucher went to his computer and started searching. After five or so minutes, he said, 'I think you may be in luck, Dr Grant.'

'I'm not a doctor,' Joel said.

'It doesn't make any difference. I learnt a long time ago being called "Doctor" opens doors, and if you don't mind I will call you Doctor in case anyone is listening. I hope you don't think I'm paranoid, I'm just being careful. Now come with me.'

Dr Boucher led Joel out of the office, through what seemed hundreds of double doors and down as many stairs until they reached what was the bowels of the building and an area signposted 'Archive'. They were greeted by a stern looking man in a brown coat.

'Ah Hector, this is Dr Grant,' said Boucher. 'We're looking for arc/23451bd, do you want me to get it?'

'Not at all, Doctor. Please go into the research room, I will bring the material to you.'

'Thank you so much, Hector, very kind.' Hector wandered off, and Dr Boucher showed Joel into a bare room with a waist-high table in the middle and a desk with two chairs at one end. There was, given the depths they had plummeted to, no natural light in this room.

The door to the room opened. 'Sorry, Doctor, I'm having trouble finding the material. I just need to try the annexe. This is very unsatisfactory, I'm sorry.' Hector continued, 'that reference came from the old Salt River Mortuary, that's why it's in the annexe.'

'Not at all, Hector, I'm grateful. I know if it's here you will be able to find it. It probably hasn't been touched for many years.'

Hector left them to resume his search. 'Doesn't look good then?' said Joel.

'No, no,' said Dr Boucher, 'if it is still in the hospital, Hector will find it. The records show it has not been removed, unless someone has stolen it!'

Ten minutes later, during which time Joel discovered Dr Boucher had done most of his PhD, which was actually in engineering, at Salford University and they swapped stories about the pubs and clubs of Salford and its neighbour Manchester, the door was burst open by a cardboard box, measuring about a metre long by half a metre wide and deep, followed by Hector who was negotiating the doorway.

'Let me help you,' said Dr Boucher.

Hector said, 'No need. It's big but light.' Joel's heart sank. Hector placed the box on the examination table, added, 'I'll leave it with you doctors,' and left the room.

Out of his pocket Dr Boucher produced two pairs of latex gloves. 'I've seen the films,' he smiled at Joel.

The box was well sealed, and Dr Boucher opened it with a pocket-knife he had with him. Inside were a number of brown paper envelopes, each marked with the name 'Jessica Bennet' and a description of its contents. Joel counted eleven envelopes, marked 'brassiere', 'pants', 'left shoe', 'right shoe', 'ring from left hand', 'nail scraping from left hand', nail scraping from right hand', 'necklace', 'underskirt', 'earrings' and 'dress.' Eureka! thought Joel. He felt himself smiling.

'Is it what you expected?' asked Boucher.

'If the contents of the envelopes are accurate, more than I expected,' replied Joel.

'Do you want to open them?

'No, no. They need to be opened in sterile conditions, and by a scientist, not me. How can I get these to England?' Joel asked in a matter of fact way.

'I'm afraid you can't,' said Boucher. 'These belong to the deceased's family or perhaps the court, or even the police. I suggest Frederick will be able to advise what is possible and what is not.'

'Joseph, if I may call you that, I'm very concerned these exhibits remain secure. I won't tell anyone. I know you won't either, but I am conscious some people may be interested in what I'm doing here and, from what you said, may not like it. I wouldn't want to lose this box and its contents without having the opportunity to have them examined.'

'I understand.' Joseph Boucher turned and opened the door. 'Hector,' he shouted down the corridor. Hector came out of an alcove and back into the room. 'Hector, this box may be very useful for me. Do you think you could reseal it and place it somewhere only you could find it? If you understand me, Hector?'

'I understand perfectly,' said Hector.

Joel intervened, 'Will it be kept at the same temperature it has been kept at over the years?'

'Oh yes, Doctor,' said Hector, 'the very same.'

'Thank you so much, Hector. Please, if anyone asks what I was doing down here, say I was showing a colleague around the basement area with a view to some improvements.'

'I understand, Doctor Boucher.' With this, Joel and Joseph Boucher left the archive and returned via the labyrinth to Dr Boucher's office. They barely spoke on the way back.

Once in the office, Boucher asked, 'Is it a significant discovery?'

Joel responded, 'It could be, it could be. I need to talk to Mr Weisner.' He was excited but trying to remain calm. 'Thank you so much for your help. Hector won't get into trouble if people come asking questions, will he?'

'You've met Hector. He is very resilient, very conservative and can be very stubborn. The box is safe here, believe me.' Boucher showed Joel out of the building, where once again Joel thanked him for his help and hoped to see him soon.

'Oh, I think we're eating together at Frederick's tonight. Hasn't he told you yet?' Dr Boucher said laughing. Joel joined in.

Chapter Eight

Joel got into his cab, which he'd called from Boucher's office, and was driven away deep in thought. When he arrived back at the office there was no reply from the buzzer, and he took the opportunity to have a walk around the business district again. He also revisited the Crimson café, which he was developing a liking for, particularly its food.

As he walked into the cafe he saw Marta sitting at a table with a man. She hadn't seen Joel, and so he made his way to the opposite side of the cafe and placed himself in the window seat looking on to the pavement; the same seat he'd sat at when he first spoke to Marta. He ordered a smoked salmon and cream cheese bagel, coffee and water, and then read the newspaper he bought outside. The newspaper was full of the inadequacies of the South African Police Service. Joel considered the British police, and particularly the Met, got a hard time sometimes, but nothing like this tirade. The SAPS hadn't endured the allegations of cash for stories the United Kingdom police had, but they certainly had their problems: allegations of corruption, extra judicial killings and flawed investigations, to mention just a few.

It seemed to Joel the SAPS was run along militaristic lines; even the ranks were military. He was reading a story of the trial of two police officers accused of murdering a young black woman who refused their offer of a lift. The two had taken her off the street, and her burnt body was found three days later in an alley. There were plenty of witnesses on the street who saw the woman being abducted, but few were willing to give evidence, and those who did give evidence had been placed in the Witness Protection Programme. The fact one officer was white and one black made the story very newsworthy, Joel thought, and the investigating officer, Detective Sergeant Jean Van Gil, was getting a tough time from both defence advocates. So it's the same the world over! deliberated Joel.

The defence advocates were alleging the investigating officer had threatened the witnesses, and they also said his boss was to give evidence on the defendants' behalf. Joel couldn't wait to read about it tomorrow. He was so engrossed he didn't notice Marta standing beside him.

'Hello, Joel,' she said.

'Oh hi, Marta, how are you?' he replied.

'Good thanks.'

Joel noticed the man Marta had been talking to standing beside her. 'Joel, can I introduce Jean Van Gil? He's an old friend.'

'Not Detective Sergeant Van Gil, by any chance?' said Joel.

The man blushed. Marta said, 'I see you've been reading that rubbish, Joel,' pointing to the copy of the Cape Times on his table.

'I was just thinking the world is the same all over. The workers get the blame.' Joel held his hand out to Van Gil. 'Hi, I'm Joel Grant, good to meet you. I hope your boss got a hard time this morning,' he said, indicating the newspaper on the table, as Marta had.

'Yes, I think he did. I understand the judge has kept him in over lunch,' said his fellow detective.

'Bloody hell, Marta, you don't even give witnesses bail here?' All three laughed.

'He seems to have got confused in his evidence,' Van Gil commented. 'One of the accused is also the son of a friend of his.'

'The village, Joel, the village' Marta said.

'I'm sorry, I must get back to court.' Van Gil kissed Marta and shook Joel's hand again. 'Good luck, Detective Sergeant Grant.' He turned and walked out of the cafe towards the court.

'That was a coincidence,' said Joel.

'Not really,' answered Marta. 'I was just asking Jean about police evidence storage. I noticed he was giving evidence at court and suggested lunch. I've known him since school, and his wife is my closest friend. He should be far more senior, but he keeps upsetting his bosses. Bit like you really.' She stopped and left her words hanging in the air. 'Come on, let's get back to the office.'

They paid their bills and walked to the office as Marta described the building architecture and people of the district. When they were back Joel said, 'Come on, Marta, what did your friend tell you? I'm dying to know.'

'Well, he told me how precise he is in handling his exhibits and making sure the evidence chain is not broken. He is careful to use only people who have been trained properly and who he has seen working the system. He says the system is very tight.'

'You know what I'm talking about, Marta. What about historical inquiries? Sorry, old cases. What happens to the exhibits? Do they destroy them? Do they keep them? What do they do with them?' Joel was flushed with the morning's success, and thought he'd have solved the case by dinner – well, maybe breakfast. 'Come on, Marta, stop teasing.'

'Well, Jean says it depends,' she parried.

'On what, Marta? You're playing with me.'

'Well, you would think you could solve this case by dinner. That's the way you're behaving.' Good Heavens, could she read his mind? He hoped not, otherwise he would really get in trouble.

'Calm down, Joel, it really does depend on the detective, the police station, the families. It's all very random. You need to speak to Papa, he'll know what to do.'

'It seems your father is certainly the man to know around here.'

Marta laughed. 'Yes, it seems that way. That's why you're having dinner with him again tonight. Aren't you? Or hasn't he told you yet?'

'Joseph Boucher told me. It's kind of him.'

'OK, I'll pick you up same time as last night. Now off you go. I've got work to do.' She leant forward and kissed him on the lips. Joel returned the kiss, holding her around the waist and pulling her into him. This woman really excites me, he concluded.

Joel left, walked back to the hotel and promptly fell asleep.

He woke up with a jolt. The hotel room phone was ringing. He looked at the clock, it was still only 4.30pm and picked up the phone: it was Robert.

'Hello, Joel, how are you?'

'I was fine until I was rudely woken by someone ringing me, Robert,' Joel said pointedly. 'I said I'd ring you at the weekend.'

'I know, Joel, but I've had a telephone call from Matthew to see how I was and asking if I was going up to town for dinner. He has some sort of legal do in the next few weeks. I nearly told him you were in Cape Town, but thought you wouldn't be happy. I did think he or George could open some doors for you, though. I can ask him if you want me to?'

'No!' Joel said with a firmness which surprised him. 'I'm sorry, Robert, but I've just woken up. You know this place. Every time I meet someone I'm surprised about how Budleigh-like it is. I really don't want too many people knowing I'm here and what I'm doing. Once people like George get to know, no matter how helpful he may be he is, as you said, so well connected. Politicians would get involved and the next thing you know my bosses would start asking questions about what I'm doing. That will certainly not help. They probably think I've flipped anyway. I know the Corfields are virtually family and victims in their own right, but the time is just not right.'

'All right. I just thought they could help as a family.'

'Robert, there will come a time when I'm sure we will need their help, but not just at the moment. You know Matthew barely sees his father. I'm also not sure what impact this could have upon that already strained relationship.'

'OK, Joel, I get the message loud and clear. How are things going, anyway, while I'm on?'

'Any excuse to ring. That's what this was, wasn't it, Robert?'

'No, no, honestly.'

'Well, I'm still researching,' Joel told him. 'Nothing spectacular at the moment, but I always thought it would be like that.' The last thing Joel was going to do was mention to Robert the exhibits he'd found earlier. His friend would explode with excitement. 'I promise to give you a full update on Friday.'

'OK,' said Robert, sounding down. He'd rung up like an excited bunny, but was now like a deflated balloon. Joel felt sorry for him. Robert's heart and soul were in this inquiry; come to think of it, so were Joel's. Robert and Joel agreed to speak again at the same time on Friday, Joel thanked him for ringing and checking things, he thought Robert felt a little better.

Joel looked at the time and thought he should shower quickly if he was not going to be late. He felt so much better when he came out, still elated at his find at the hospital, he dressed quickly and made his way down to meet Marta. She was waiting and looking as gorgeous as she had done the day before, again in a short dress and high heels, which made her legs look incredible. She kissed him on both cheeks and whispered, 'You never know who's watching.' He understood, and they both got in the car before speeding off to her father's house.

Annette and Frederick greeted the pair warmly. 'Ah, Joel, you met Joseph earlier. This is his wife, Dee,' said Frederick, indicating the Bouchers who were standing nearby. Joel shook the hands of Dr and Mrs Boucher.

Dee Boucher said, 'I've heard a lot about you over the last thirty-six hours, you're making quite an impact on Cape Town,' glancing sideways at Marta as she spoke.

'Oh, I don't know about that,' said Joel airily.

Annette interrupted, 'What would you like to drink, Marta? We're having a Sundowner. Your father insisted, again!'

'What are we celebrating, Papa?' Marta asked.

'Nothing at the moment, but I'm hopeful. Joel, will you have the same?'

Joel said he would, and everyone joined in a toast to 'new developments' proposed by Frederick Weisner.

A little later, after disappearing for a moment, Annette emerged from the dining room saying dinner was ready. All six sat down at the table, Frederick at the top with Joel and Marta next to him, and Annette at the bottom next to Joseph and Dee Boucher.

'Now, Joel, I want you to tell what you have found and what you think we should do next. Please do not worry about omitting any detail. We all have strong dispositions, it's important we are sighted on everything and the possibilities.'

Joel went through what he'd found at the hospital and said he would like to take the exhibits back to the United Kingdom to have them examined, but he would also like to find out if the police had any further evidence. He mentioned his brief meeting with Jean Van Gil earlier.

'Marta, you should know better than to speak to Jean about this issue,' Weisner admonished. 'That boy is already very unpopular with many of his so-called colleagues because of the current case. If they find him poking around in this it could be very serious for him.'

'I wasn't asking him to do anything, I was only asking him to explain the handling of exhibits and whether the police were likely still to have them after all this time.'

'Nevertheless, that young man has enough problems. Keep him out of it.'

Joel interjected, 'I have to say I did find his explanations most useful, but I really rely upon you for the next steps regarding the police, the hospital and any opportunities to speak to Kem and his family.'

'OK, I take your point, Joel. Now let's deal with the exhibits from the hospital first. Joseph are they safe?'

'Certainly,' assured Joseph.

'And Dee, what will you need from me to get hold of the exhibits?'

Dee? thought Joel. What's she got to do with it? Marta saw Joel's puzzled look and explained, 'Joel, Dee is the hospital's legal adviser.'

'Well, technically they belong to the family of the deceased if the police investigation has finished,' replied Dee.

'It has,' said Weisner, 'until we start asking questions. Then they could reopen it to obstruct us, unless we get the exhibits quickly.'

'Well, in that case I will need a document signed by the deceased's next of kin, then I can release the exhibits immediately,' answered Dee.

'You will need to get them out of the country quickly,' said Annette. 'Whether Kem is guilty or innocent, the police won't like you taking them out of the country. They haven't changed that much.'

'You're absolutely right, dear.' This was the first time Joel had ever heard Weisner speak to Annette in such an affectionate way. No one around the table was surprised, nor did they bother to look for a reaction from Joel. He was, however, more surprised by the suspicion which was around the table, but paranoia seemed to be everywhere at the moment.

'Good. Joel, I will draft a letter from Jessica's father to me if you could please ask him to consider, amend where necessary and return it to us as soon as possible. When can you do this?'

'When will the letter be ready?' asked Joel.

'We'll deal with that in a moment. This tart is delicious, Annette.'

Joel had quite forgotten to start eating, and he took this as a gentle reminder to start from Weisner. He managed to take a mouthful of the asparagus and cheese tart when Annette said, 'Joel, do you really think you'll find any evidence after all this time?'

'I really don't know, but back home many cases have been solved by the re-examination of exhibits using new techniques. There have also been a number of miscarriages rectified by looking again at the exhibits.'

'To answer your question, Joel, we can draft the letter following dinner. The UK is behind us time-wise, isn't it?

Joel nodded.

'Good. Now the police exhibits,' continued Weisner, 'as soon as the hospital exhibits are out of the country, we will get a letter from Kem releasing his property to me for transmission to his family. Marta, you should go and see Thembi tomorrow and ask her permission to send his clothing away for examination. Sorry, you two,' Weisner looked at the Bouchers, 'Thembi is Kem's sister. I will then serve a letter on the prosecutor, who will agree to the exhibits being returned to the family. We will then go to the police station where we will be handed the exhibits. Marta, if we think there is going to be a problem you and Joel will travel to Jo'burg where you will courier the police exhibits to the UK. Otherwise we'll send them from here. Now is everyone clear?'

Everyone around the table was stunned at the apparent completeness of Weisner's plans. 'I have a couple of questions,' Marta said.

'Me too,' joined in Joel.

'I'm sure you do, but should we get our next course first? Otherwise I will get into trouble for spoiling dinner.'

'Again!' said Annette. She then served springbok fillets.

Marta asked, 'Papa, would Joel be happy about the involvement of Kem's family at this stage?'

Weisner said, with a glint in his eye, 'But, dear, you've already been trying to see them, haven't you?'

Joel jumped in to help Marta. 'I don't think they know what it's about, do they, Marta?' Marta shook her head. 'But if things are going to move as fast as you say, Frederick, the time may be right now,' added Joel helpfully.

'Good, it's agreed. Tomorrow morning, Marta, try to see Thembi again.' Joel suspected Weisner knew Marta had not tried to speak to Thembi yet, but things had worked out.

'Papa, how do you know the prosecutor and the police will just agree to handing over the exhibits?'

'Why would they refuse? The case is now twenty years old. Kem is unlikely to get out of prison any time soon as he continually denies the offence, and they will be pleased to get rid of them, I suspect, if they still have them.'

'But,' added Joel, 'we've all accepted the prosecutor and the police would not want the exhibits to go out of South Africa and we've got strategies to deal with this, yet you seem so confident they will acquiesce and give you permission and the exhibits there and then. I hope I'm not being negative, but isn't our strategy optimistic?'

'Ah, Joel, we were talking about the institutions: the prosecutor and the police. There are many in those institutions who are very good people. Like you, they share a desire for the search for the truth, or, as far as we are concerned, the Du Toit and De Wit factor.' Joel knew a little Dutch but couldn't fathom out what Weisner was getting at. Everyone else around the table chuckled.

'I'm sorry, I don't understand,' said Joel.

Marta said, 'Peter Du Toit is a senior prosecutor and Thomas De Wit is a senior police officer in charge of Wynberg police station.'

'Do they know what you are doing, Frederick?' asked Annette, just beating Joel to the same question.

'Not in any detail, but they are aware I am preparing a request to them regarding certain exhibits,' replied Weisner.

'You old fox.' Joseph laughed.

'Not so much of the old,' protested Frederick.

Joel looked around the table. He thought it reminded him of a council-of-war, and said so. Once again Annette jumped in and remarked, 'Just like the old days.' The others nodded.

'How will you get the letter of release from Kem?' asked Marta.

'I'm going to see him tomorrow. I pulled a few strings and said I needed an urgent consultation, which is perfectly true,' said Weisner. 'I thought about trying to get you in on the visit, Joel, but it would cause too much interest and curiosity, which we don't need at the moment.'

'OK,' said Joel, 'but could you ask him some questions for me please?'

'Better than that, Joel, you can drive me,' replied Weisner.

Chapter Nine

The group was in danger of overlooking the meal in their eagerness to plan the next steps. Joel took the hint when Weisner asked, 'How's the springbok? What do you think?'

'Delicious. You are a wonderful cook, Annette,' said Dee Boucher.

'How do you know Annette cooked it? It could have been Marimam, she's a good cook,' teased Weisner.

'I know, but I also know Annette-style. It's superb. You should open a restaurant, Annette.'

'I have one,' Annette laughed in response, looking directly at Weisner, 'with some particularly difficult customers!'

The rest of the meal was spent discussing couriers, forensic laboratories in the United Kingdom and the mechanics of the plan.

'So, Joel, how do we get the letter from your friend?' asked Frederick.

'I could ring him now, it's only eight o'clock there.'

'OK, does he have email?' asked Weisner.

'Yes,' said Joel.

'Good. Let's draft the letter first, and then you speak to him,' said Weisner.

'As the owner of this restaurant, I would remind you, dearest customer, you made a specific request for dessert and you're not doing anything until you've eaten it.'

Weisner threw his hands up and laughed 'I'm sorry, I surrender.' Annette then served up malva pudding with cream, Joel thinking he could get used to this South African cuisine, after which, Weisner suggested, 'Let's go and have some coffee and a liqueur.'

'Not for us, thanks,' said Joseph and Dee Boucher together. 'You've got work to do.'

'Nonsense,' said Annette. 'You must stay for a drink in any case. I insist, and so does Frederick!'

'Yes, yes, I insist,' said Frederick, holding up his hands. Everyone around the table chuckled at his mock subjugation.

Marta whispered, 'Let's draft this letter, it will save Papa a job. He's been busy today,' whilst the others went onto the veranda for a liqueur.

'He certainly has,' agreed Joel as he leant forward and kissed her neck.

'Come on, work,' Marta teased.

The letter was prepared in no time, and Marta took it to her father.

'I wondered what you two were up to. At least it was work,' Weisner said. Marta blushed as Annette winked at her. Weisner read the letter and nodded his head in approval. 'Very good. If you can just get rid of the two "that's", it will be fine.'

'What do you mean?' queried Joel.

'Papa has this thing about not using "that" in any written documents,' said Marta.

'It's for oral use only, never in writing. You know this, Marta.'

'You are such a pedant sometimes, Papa. Who cares?'

'I do, and so should you,' came the reply.

Joel looked at the letter. Weisner was right: 'that' was unnecessary, and he would have to remember *that!*

'One more thing,' added Weisner, 'I think it would be helpful if your friend could have his signature witnessed by a lawyer. It will help the prosecutor in the event of a challenge in relation to our inquiry.'

'I will give him a ring now,' said Joel.

'OK. Marta, can you please amend the letter and get ready to send it?' asked Weisner.

'Yes, Papa,' said Marta wearily.

Joel went to the telephone and called Robert.

'Joel, what's happened? Are you OK?' Robert was worried by Joel ringing him after their last conversation.

'I'm fine, no problems. Robert, I'm going to email you a draft letter, which I'd like you to consider. Once you're happy with the letter, can you sign it in front of a lawyer, ask them to endorse it, scan it and send it to Frederick Weisner? His address will be in the email.'

'OK, but what's the letter about?' asked Robert.

'We think we've found Jess's clothing in a hospital and I want to get it back to the UK for examination. It will cost though, Robert.'

'Money is not the issue. How will the re-examination help, Joel?'

Joel explained to Robert how scientific examination had advanced since Jess's death. It may not help, but he thought it was worth a try. Joel also mentioned he was trying to do the same thing with Kem's clothing.

Robert said, 'If you think it's worthwhile, so do I. The letter has just arrived. I'll have a look at it and take it round to William Goble. He will witness it.' Joel knew Goble, who was the senior partner in a firm of Exeter lawyers specialising in agricultural and land law. Joel had always thought he was a shrewd cookie.

'Please ask him not to tell anyone,' said Joel.

'Joel, he's my lawyer!'

'Fair point,' conceded Joel. 'Text me when you've replied.'

'Will do,' said Robert, 'this is the best news I've had for years.'

Joel thought about trying to bring Robert down, but knew it wouldn't do any good. 'Bye, Robert,' he said and hung up the phone.

Joel made a second call, this time to a friend who was a scientific support manager in the north of England. Joel often wondered why crime scene investigators, detectives who retired and come back as investigators and those who joined and trained directly as investigators, weren't called 'Detective'. Alistair Lang was one such person; he had forgotten more than some of the new CID chiefs, who made their move into the CID to get a tick in the box for the next rank and were called detectives, would ever know. Joel had mentioned the possibility of referring to investigators as 'Detective' to other colleagues, but they were very resistant to the idea. He worked out, in one of his more lucid moments, only 20 per cent of detectives of the rank of superintendent or above had spent longer than eighteen months in the CID, and some considerably less. These were some of the people against giving detective status to people like Ali, yet using it to describe themselves. Joel met Ali on an inquiry years ago, liked him tremendously and found they had similar views on life. Ali was bright, imaginative, fun, and he was also from Manchester!

'Hi Ali, it's Joel. How's things?'

'Ah, what can I do for Scotland Yard's best detective?'

Joel explained about Jessica's murder, what had happened, where he was and what he was doing. Ali said, ' It certainly sounds interesting. I take it there's nothing like the Criminal Cases Review Commission in South Africa?'

Joel confirmed there was not, Ali and Joel had met on a CCRC inquiry many years ago. Joel went on to tell Ali about the exhibits he had found and those he hoped to find, and asked if Ali would help.

'Bloody hell,' said Ali, 'that's a turn up. Of course I'll help. What sort of conditions were they stored in?

'It looked pretty dry and cool to me,' answered Joel.

'Well there could be a chance we may find some DNA. Have you got any samples from the defendant?'

'I'm hoping to get them from the police in the next couple of days.'

'No, I mean blood or buccal swabs.'

'Not yet. I'm just surprised I've got something. What else should we be looking for, Ali?

'Well DNA is the main thing: hers, the defendant or the suspect's and anyone else's really.'

'I have to say, Ali, the methods and practices here, particularly twenty years ago, were not good.'

'Don't forget, Joel, neither were they here!'

'Where should I send the stuff, Ali? Who's the best?'

'Mmmm, I'll have a think. It's not who's the best because they're all pretty good, it's who's got the capacity, and cost. It won't be cheap, Joel.'

'I know. I've told my friend Robert, Jessica's father. I need to get the exhibits out of the country and I want to keep the evidence chain to a minimum, so if you could, please give me some ideas, Ali.'

'I'll ring around now. It's late, but the main three labs owe me and I'll find out what the score is.'

'That's great. Email me the details. Ali, can I ask you another favour?'

'Go on,' said Ali slowly.

'Do you think you could knock up a submission form for me? You know what they will need and the incremental steps we will have to go through. After all, it is interesting, isn't it?'

'All right, Joel, I'm already hooked. No more stroking needed. I'll sort something out when I've spoken to the labs. Do you want me to send it to your normal email?'

Joel was just about to say yes when he had second thoughts. He didn't really know why, but he asked Ali to send the email to Marta at her father's email address.

'Ali, you're a star, thanks so much.'

'No problem, it's a real diversion.'

Joel put down the phone and returned to the veranda. It was now 11pm.

'We thought we'd lost you, Joel,' said Joseph, who was enjoying a glass of brandy. 'Can I get you a drink?' he added.

'Please. The wine we had with dinner was lovely, if there's any left.'

'Oh I think we can manage that,' said Weisner as he got up, walked into the house and returned holding a bottle of Chenin Blanc and a new glass. 'What news of your friend?'

'He's thrilled and has already picked up the email.'

'Yes, Marta told us.'

'He's looking at it and going to see his lawyer who lives around the corner from him,' added Joel.

'I'm glad I don't live around the corner from my client,' said Dee, who had clearly been enjoying the liqueurs and wine too!

'He's going to text me when he's sent the reply. I've also spoken to a scientist friend, that's why I was so long. He's making some enquiries and will send some advice on Frederick's email for Marta's attention.'

'For Marta's attention? What's wrong with me?' Weisner quipped.

'I thought we were going to be busy tomorrow, Frederick,' Joel replied, 'division of labour and all that. Anyway, Marta will be collecting the hospital exhibits.'

'Very good point, Joel. We'll make an attorney out of you yet.'

Joel didn't respond. He didn't need to, everyone could read his mind.

They all relaxed and enjoyed the liqueurs until Joel received a text from Robert.

Email sent!

Joel said, 'You have an email, Frederick.' Weisner then stood up and disappeared into the office.

While Frederick was away, Annette said to Marta and Joel, 'You two are up early in the morning. You must stay here tonight and leave first thing, Joel.'

'I haven't got a change of clothing.'

Annette said, 'Don't worry, we can sort that out. You could always borrow some of Frederick's.' Everyone laughed, and Joel, who was considerably larger than Frederick, grinned.

'I think I may need a slightly bigger size than Frederick.'

'I was only joking, Joel. It's not a problem.'

Frederick returned to the room, smiling. 'I like your friend Robert and I haven't even met him. Not only for his speedy response, his ability to get a lawyer at this time of night, but most of all for his knowledge of the English language.'

Everyone looked puzzled. Weisner then read from the email.

Joel, I hope the attached will do. If it needs amending please just send it back. William and I are having a drink. I particularly liked the tracked changes where "that" has been excluded. William and I send our compliments to the editor.

'Hah, told you, didn't I? Did you say Robert was a journalist, Joel? Used to work for the BBC, didn't he? And supported by a lawyer!'

Marta butted in, 'Sometimes, Papa, you can be insufferable, and you know it.'

Everyone laughed, and Joseph said, 'On *that* note it's time we left.'

'No, no, it's fine to use in conversation,' said Weisner.

'All right, Frederick, you've made your point,' Annette interjected.

The Bouchers said goodnight, and left saying, 'May see you tomorrow, Marta.'

'Maybe, you never know,' retorted Marta.

Annette said, 'Joel and Marta are staying here tonight, Frederick. The guest room is made up for Joel and I'll arrange for his clothes to be washed. Just leave them outside the door, Joel, I'll take care of it.'

'No really, I can do it,' argued Joel.

'Nonsense! I won't hear of naked men walking around the house at night. What would the neighbours think?' said Annette. Joel looked around. The house was in its own grounds surrounded by high walls – there were no neighbours!

'Good point, Annette. Come on, you two, off to bed. Up at six, Joel, OK?' Weisner asked.

'Yes, that's fine. How far is the prison?'

'Three hundred miles,' replied Weisner. 'Now you know why you're driving! Goodnight, you two.'

Weisner left, and Annette said, 'Come on, Joel, I'll show you to your room. Goodnight, Marta.'

The room was light, airy and spotlessly clean. 'Just put your clothes outside,' said Annette, 'there are pyjamas in the drawer.'

'My goodness, this is wonderful. I thought I would have to sleep naked.'

'That was for Frederick's benefit, Joel. He likes you a lot, but there are some things he doesn't need to know. Goodnight, see you in the morning.' She turned and walked out the door.

Heavens, people here can read minds, Joel thought. He took his clothes off, put them outside the door and had a hot shower. He was exhausted but his mind was racing. After the shower he climbed into bed. He usually slept naked, but thought he'd better wear the pyjamas in case of spot checks. As soon as his weary head touched the pillow, Joel was asleep.

Asleep, until he felt someone slip into bed with him and whisper, 'Hello, Joel.'

'Marta!'

Chapter Ten

When Joel woke at 5.45am, Marta was gone. He had no idea what time she left. They had made love, too tired to talk, and drifted into the night, relaxed and unwound. He hoped no one noticed or heard them during the night; he really liked Frederick and Annette, and didn't want to upset them or fall out with them.

Joel threw off the sheets, looked for his clothes and remembered he'd put them outside the door to be washed. He opened the door and there in a neat pile were the clothes he had worn the previous evening, cleaned and ironed. He took the clothes into his room and, after a reviving shower, emerged five minutes later to Annette's voice telling him she had left some coffee outside the door and breakfast was ready when he was. Didn't this woman ever sleep? thought Joel. He hoped so!

He brought the coffee back into the room and checked his phone. There was a text from Ali, which simply said:

> If you can't get swabs, use cotton buds, take a few samples and store them separately. Check emails. Ali

Cotton buds. I wonder if Annette has any, Joel thought. He took his coffee into the kitchen, which was a hive of activity. People were eating, talking, washing and cooking, all under the watchful eye of Annette, Frederick and Marta were already there.

'Morning, Joel, did you sleep OK?' said Annette. Marta and Frederick also joined in saying good morning, along with the other members of the working household who were in the kitchen.

'Morning. Great thanks,' replied Joel.

'Sit down, sit down. What do you want for breakfast – eggs, muffins, croissants?' Annette asked.

'I'm not really hungry at the moment. Do you think I could check my email please? I should have one from my scientist friend.'

'Nonsense, you must eat,' said Annette. 'You won't be eating for a while. Isn't that right Frederick?'

Weisner looked up, and in a resigned tone, indicating to Joel it would be best to eat, he said, 'You're absolutely right, dear.'

Joel sat down. 'Does he eat eggs, Marta?' Annette said.

'Think so,' she replied.

'What about an omelette? That will do him, do you think, with some toast?'

'Yes, that will be fine,' Marta said indifferently.

Frederick looked at Joel and remarked, 'Just like last night, go with the flow, Joel, go with the flow.'

Before Joel knew it, Marimam, who worked in the kitchen, had replenished his coffee, followed two minutes later by a most delicious vegetable and cheese omelette and toast, which Joel really appreciated despite his earlier comments.

'I'll use my iPad to check for the email, Joel,' Marta said.

'Marta, let the man eat for goodness sake,' Annette scolded. Weisner looked at Joel and shrugged his shoulders.

'It's all right, I really need to check it before we leave,' Joel said.

'Don't you try and protect her, she's a big girl,' said Annette smiling at Marta as she spoke.

'I know, but it would really help me to be able to read the email to everyone so we all know what Ali expects.'

'Oh, all right, you are a guest.' Annette gave in.

Joel opened the email and read it out aloud.

Joel,

Hope you're enjoying the sun!!

I've been in touch with my contacts at the labs and I think it would be best to use Cellmark. Their lab is: PO box 265, Abingdon, Oxfordshire OX14 1YX.

Address it for the personal attention: Dr Steve Webb.

Cellmark have the capacity and experience at the moment. I have spoken to Steve and he will be expecting the package. They will go through the exhibits incrementally to keep cost down. I reckon if he examines everything it will be in the region of £5K but I will keep my finger on the pulse and try to get a better deal.

I have attached a draft submission form, but you will have to list each exhibit. I hope the narrative I have written covers the offence and facts. As you know, this should accompany the exhibits. Steve will need DNA from the deceased or her family. Did you say her father lives in Devon? If so perhaps you could send me his details. I'll speak to him and sort out the best way forward.

I will send you a text in case you don't see this, but if you can't use buccal swabs, try and get some hair. You know what to do, just pull some out. They would prefer head hair, but if there isn't any, pubic will do. I will be on my mobile all day, if there are any issues, otherwise good luck.
All the best,
Ali.

Joel opened the attachment and quickly scanned the submission form, which was an extremely accurate account of the facts and their needs.

'What are buccal swabs?' queried Annette.

'They collect cells taken from the inside of the mouth,' said Joel. 'They are then examined, and you can get someone's DNA from them. I don't suppose there are any scientists on the way to the prison, are there, Frederick? We could do with some sample packs.'

Frederick thought for a moment. 'We could go to Cape Town University, but it's ten minutes north out of our way, and I'm not sure what time anyone will be in. If we're not at the prison on time they are likely to cancel the visit, which would be a disaster.' Joel remembered passing the University on the way to Frederick's home.

'I hope Kem's not bald,' said Annette, causing the men to wince and the women to chuckle.

'Do you have any cotton wool buds?' Joel asked the assembled throng.

'You mean the type for make up?' asked Marta.

'Yeah, that's right. We can use those, Ali said in his text.'

'I have some in my room,' Marta said, getting up to go and fetch them.

'I don't suppose for one moment you have any test tubes or freezer bags? Preferably both.'

'Mmmmm – Marta, Marta,' Frederick shouted after her.

Marta returned holding an unopened packet of cotton wool buds. 'Yes, Papa, I was only in my room.'

'I'm sorry, dear. Do you still have your chemistry sets? Marta was going to be a scientist at one point, Joel, but she saw the light and became an attorney.' Weisner had a familiar twinkle in his eye.

'You know she does, Frederick, you keep looking at them,' Annette interjected. 'It wasn't only Marta who wanted to be a scientist, was it?'

'Marta, there are some unused test tubes and bungs in the top set, I think,' Weisner said as he looked around, acknowledging Annette's assertion. 'Could you bring them in, please?'

The council of war was in session again! Marta returned with five test tubes and five rubber bungs, and Joel saw the cotton wool buds would fit in easily. Then he remembered a simple, crucial problem. Would they be able to get the swabs in and out of the prison?

'Frederick, are you searched when you go in and out of the prison?'

'Of course,' Frederick said, 'why?'

'What will the authorities say about this lot?' He indicated the test tubes, etcetera.

'They are my property. I will take five in and come out with five. If there are any problems I will create a fuss, they don't like that. Anyway I will also take a sample of *head* hair. Annette, could I have some freezer bags please?' Annette was ahead of him and was already coming back to the table, freezer bags in hand.

'How many do we need, Joel?' said Marta.

'One to hold the test tubes and one for each mouth swab, five swabs I think, and two for the hair samples. It may seem another silly question, but do you have any latex gloves?'

Frederick shook his head, 'I'm afraid not Joel.'

'Of course we have, don't we, Marimam? Please get the pack for Joel,' said Annette.

'Why on earth do you two have latex gloves?' asked Frederick.

'Cooking, Mr Frederick,' Marimam said practically.

When all the items were spread on the table, Joel continued, 'now we need some small labels.' Marimam was at the drawer in no time and pulling out assorted labels of various sizes.

'Now, Frederick, I want you to write five labels: b1, b2, b3, b4, b5, and place them on the test tubes,' instructed Joel. 'Then place a bud in the tube, seal it with a bung and put it in one of the bags marked in the same way. Put your gloves on first. Marta, could you please write labels HH1 and HH2 and put them on each of the other two bags?'

When all the tasks were complete, Joel said, 'Frederick, another naïve question, do you know how to take samples?'

'Remind me, Joel,' Weisner said smiling, as everyone else did. Joel explained Weisner should put his gloves on, take out each bud, rub around Kem's cheek, put it in the tube, seal the tube and place everything in the bag. This process needed to be repeated five times on different areas of the cheeks. The head samples should be tugged, including the root, from different parts of the head and placed in the bags as with the buds. Frederick should then place his gloves in the remaining bag and seal it.

'Can you show me how to take the samples?' Weisner requested.

'Of course, who's going to be the guinea pig?'

'I suppose it's me,' offered Marta.

Joel told Marta to open her mouth, put on a spare pair of gloves and rubbed the swab on the inside of her left cheek. 'Just like that,' said Joel, 'and then place it in the tube, which goes in the bag.' He put the swab in the refuse bin.

'What about the hair?' queried Weisner.

'You're not doing that on me, Joel, it will hurt,' said Marta.

'It's OK. Just take hold of about ten pieces of hair and pull, then do the same again. We can go through it any number of times in the car, Frederick.'

'OK,' agreed Frederick. 'Now what about the samples from the hospital?'

'Marta, if you take gloves, scissors, a large roll of brown paper and some Sellotape – is that what you call it here?' Marta nodded. 'What I'd like you to do is wrap the entire parcel in brown paper and place the submission form, which you should complete using the same words as are on the exhibits, together with a witness statement saying where you got the exhibits from on top of the parcel, then wrap it again in another layer of brown paper. Don't put an address label on it until you are out of the hospital. You will need some help, it's a big box.'

'Annette, could Marimam help me?' Marta asked. Marimam was beaming.

'Of course, dear. You don't mind, do you, Marimam?'

'Oh no, not at all,' Marimam responded triumphantly.

'When you've done that, take the box to the couriers – presumably DHL have an office – and send it to the lab. You will have to complete a customs form. What will you put on it?'

'Simply, legal exhibits. The customs here won't be a problem now, but what about in the UK?'

'I'll text Ali, he'll know what to do. Marta, when you've handed the parcel over, could you please text Ali and give him the reference number?'

Marta nodded.

'Joel, we must leave in ten minutes. Are you happy with everything?' Frederick asked.

'Yes. I ask you all the same question?' Everyone nodded. 'I must send some texts before we leave.'

Joel went to his room, sending a long text to Ali asking him to speak to Cellmark re customs and to expect a text from Marta. He also gave him Robert's contact details. Then he texted Robert, telling him to expect a call from Ali re samples, signing off with a Latin phrase he learnt on a CID course a long time ago: *veritas vos liberabit* – the truth shall set you free.

Frederick knocked on the door. 'Are you ready Joel? We need to go.'

Chapter Eleven

It was 7.05am when Weisner and Joel left the house. They both wished Marta and Marimam good luck, and Joel thanked Annette for her hospitality once again. Marta whispered in his ear, 'It was a good job there was not an instant DNA test in the house, there would have been some interesting results from my swab.' Joel told her he had no idea what she was talking about, and they both smiled.

'I thought I was driving today?' Joel said.

'Do you have a South African licence?'

'No, but I thought it would be OK,' replied Joel.

'And you a police officer! It's all right for a hire car but not our company's car, and we don't want to get into trouble, do we?'

'So what time will we get to the prison?' Joel was a little unsure whether to call him Mr Weisner or Frederick when they were alone in the car. The answer became instantly clear.

'Less than an hour, Joel, that's all.'

'You said it was 300 miles away.'

'Joel, I was teasing you again. It may as well be, though. Pollsmoor prison is in a different place to most of South Africa, a very dark and evil place. Haven't you heard of it? There have been a number of TV programmes about it, some by British film makers.'

Joel hadn't heard of it or seen it on TV. He actually watched little television when in the United Kingdom, and particularly didn't watch TV programmes about law and order. He answered, 'No, never heard of it.' Weisner then spent the remainder of the journey telling him about the prison, it's history, the gangsterism and violence.

Three things were puzzling Joel after Frederick's description of the prison. One, if it was so violent, how on earth were they going to let Frederick in with the glass test tubes? Two, how was he physically going to get access to Kem to get the samples? And three, how had Kem survived in such a tough environment? He posed those questions to Weisner

'It all depends, Joel. I'm known at the prison, and while there are well over a thousand staff there, they tend to stay in the same jobs. I therefore know the people I am dealing with. They will take my bag from me and escort me to the legal visits' area, where they will give it back to me. Whether they let me retain the test tubes will depend on who else is having visits and the atmosphere in that part of the prison. If they don't, I will simply place the buds directly in the bag and also obtain the hair samples, not forgetting, of course, I have to ask Kem to sign a letter of release for his clothing.'

In all the other activity, Joel had forgotten about the letter. Weisner clearly hadn't and had even thought through a contingency plan about the buccal swabs. He was one smart cookie, Joel thought.

Weisner continued, 'During legal visits, I can generally wangle direct access to my clients, providing there are no other great security fears. If I can't do that, then I will require the guards to do it, telling them it is for the court – which, of course, it is. They won't like doing it, and will no doubt try and facilitate my request.

'How has Kem survived? Well despite everything, he is tough! He has also proved invaluable to the numbers and the guards.'

'The numbers?' Joel queried.

'Yes, the number gangs: Twenty-six, Twenty-seven, Twenty-eight. These are the people who really run the prison. Kem obtained his LLB whilst in prison and is able to negotiate and arbitrate to a certain extent. It could be dangerous, but he has wonderful diplomacy skills and is a survivor. He is respected by the gang generals and the guards, so he is to a certain extent protected, but it is nevertheless a very dangerous path he treads.'

'How do you think he will take the request for samples?'

'He is a lawyer now, Joel. He may not be fully qualified, but he has considerably more legal experience than some of my partners by dealing with contract, tort, estate law, criminal law and arbitration on a daily basis. Please don't tell Marta that I agree with her on that point, it will make my life insufferable.' Weisner laughed. 'He will realise what is happening without the need for any deep and meaningful conversations, but above all he will remain calm. He has had many false dawns.' They were just driving out of affluent Tokaei and through the prison entrance barrier where they were checked into the car park.

Weisner said, 'Well, here goes. I may be gone for some time, I hope you've got something to read.'

'I haven't really, but I've got plenty to think about. Good luck.'

Weisner turned and walked towards what looked like a guard house. Joel watched him go into the prison, remembering the graphic descriptions he had heard of the violence which took place behind those walls; descriptions of torture, corruption, rape and murder for starters. His mind then drifted to Marta, and not just how she would be doing at the hospital.

Across Cape Town, Ms Marta Weisner and her assistant Ms Marimam Ndlovu entered the main doorway of Groote Schuur Hospital. Marta spoke to the receptionist, who was the same one Joel had spoken to the previous day.

'My name is Marta Weisner and this is my assistant, Ms Ndlovu. We are from Weisner and Co, the attorneys. I would like to speak to your Head of Administration, Dr Boucher. I have some forms to serve on him. It may be wise for your in-house lawyer to be in our meeting.'

'I'll see if Dr Boucher is available,' responded the receptionist.

Marta said, in her most lawyerly tone, 'If he's not, I wish to see your chief executive and your lawyer.' She turned away, and Marimam followed her to the waiting area where they sat down. The receptionist was on the phone right away. Marta suspected she knew the firm's name and would do all she could rather than disturb the chief executive. Anyway, Joseph and Dee were expecting them.

The receptionist came from behind the desk and asked Marta to follow her to Dr Boucher's office. She guided them down a marigold painted corridor then knocked on a glass-panelled door, which was marked 'Dr Joseph Boucher, Head of Administration'.

'I have Dr Boucher's visitors,' she said.

A voice from behind the door said, 'Please bring them in.'

The secretary opened the door, allowing the two legal eagles to go in, and closed it immediately after them. She didn't want to get involved or even know why two high-powered attorneys were visiting Joseph Boucher at this time of the morning with no appointment.

'Hi, Marta,' came the greeting from the middle-aged black woman sitting behind the desk.

'Hi, Joy, how are you? Do you know Marimam? She works with Papa as well.' 'I don't think we've met. Hello there,' said Joy, and Marimam returned the greeting. Marta and Joy had met at a number of parties at the Bouchers, and it came as no surprise when Joy said, 'Joseph mentioned you may visit. Go straight through, legal is in there already. Do you want a drink?'

'No thanks, Joy, I don't think we'll be long,' said Marta as she and Marimam went into the inner office.

Joseph greeted Marta like an old friend, which of course she was. 'Marta, Marimam, can I introduce you to Peit Meyer? He's from our legal department. Apparently our head of legal is off on some conference or other!' He laughed.

Marta thought it was wise of Dee not to be there in the room. She said, 'Mr Meyer, your hospital has custody and control of some property belonging to one of my firm's clients who lives in England. This is a letter from him requesting the immediate release of the property. You will note it is endorsed by his lawyer in England, and this is a letter from my firm outlining our request.'

The hospital lawyer read the documents, apparently carefully and deliberately, then looked up and said, 'Well this is all in order. If we have them we can release them. Do we have them, Joseph?'

'Let me see, twenty years ago – I'll search on the computer. If it's all in order, Piet?'

'Absolutely,' said Meyer. 'If you don't need me anymore, I need to get back to the office.' Everyone thanked him for his help. No one had yet queried or noticed the artists' carrying case being toted by Marimam, which contained all the things Joel listed earlier.

When Meyer left, Joseph picked the phone up and spoke to someone called Hector, asking him to bring the box from yesterday to the research room. Joseph then said, 'Come on,' and walked out of the back door to his office, leading the two women through the marigold painted labyrinth of stairways and corridors. A short while later they arrived at an open door, the entrance to a sparsely furnished room, where a man, presumably Hector, was placing a large box on the table.

'Ah Hector, good man,' Boucher said. 'These ladies have come to take the box off our hands.' Hector looked at them suspiciously. 'It's OK, Hector, they are associates of Dr Grant who visited yesterday.' Hector looked relieved. He thought he was going to have to challenge the women, given what Dr Boucher had told him the day before.

'Now what do we do, Marta?' asked Boucher, at which point both women set to work while the men watched. Opening the artists' case and removing its contents wearing latex gloves, they endorsed the document sent from England with the words on each exhibit label. They wrapped the box once as though it was a present then, as directed, placed the submissions form and a hand written statement from Marta in an envelope. The parcel was then re-wrapped, and again for good measure.

Joseph then asked, 'Where are you parked, Marta?'

'At the back of the hospital.'

'Good. Hector, show the ladies out of the back door.' Hector nodded, but not before he produced a receipt from his pocket for the large box, reference arc/2345/bd.

'Well remembered, Hector, good man. Where would I be without you?

Marta thanked Joseph. 'Say goodbye to Joy, won't you?' she added. Marta had borrowed Annette's station wagon and Hector carried the box to the car, placing it in the back.

'Thank you, Hector, you've been a great help.'

'It's a pleasure, Miss,' he replied, adding, 'I never believed Kem Siblisi was guilty,' as he walked away. Marta and Marimam looked at each other.

By 1pm the parcel had been handed over to DHL in Cape Town and Marta texted Joel's friend Ali as she had been asked.

Joel, meanwhile, was still daydreaming in the prison car park. After some further reflections regarding Marta, his relationship with her and what would happen when he was back in the United Kingdom, Joel's mind returned to concentrate on what she was doing at the hospital. He had no worries there. Marta knew what she was doing; she was a good lawyer. Very good, he thought.

His mind drifted again, this time thinking about the turmoil Robert would be going through by himself in Budleigh, bursting to share his newfound knowledge with others, particularly Matthew and his father. Joel felt this was entirely understandable but, as with the Siblisi family, the time had to be right. He was comforted in a small way now Robert had spoken to William Goble. He had no doubt Robert would continue to keep William updated, and therefore the lawyer would be Robert's release valve for all his pent up frustration at not being directly involved and, even worse, not being in control!

Earlier the same morning, back in the United Kingdom, Robert checked his emails and texts for any developments and was just going to see William Goble when the phone rang. A voice said, 'Could I speak to Robert Bennet please?' It was a male voice, with an accent not too dissimilar to Joel's.

'This is Robert Bennet, how can I help?'

The voice continued, 'Good morning, Mr Bennet, my name is Alistair Lang. I'm a friend of Joel Grant. Did he mention I would be ringing?'

'Oh yes, it's Ali, isn't it? Please call me Robert. How can I help?'

Ali asked Robert what Joel had told him, ever cautious not to say something inappropriate, which might upset him and then explained what Joel had said the previous evening.

Ali continued, 'Robert, I'm going to have to ask you some fairly sensitive and no doubt distressing questions, which I would prefer to ask you face to face, but...'

Robert interrupted, 'Where are you, Ali?'

'I live in Cheshire, just outside of Manchester.'

Robert said, 'Look, Ali, this has been tearing me apart for twenty odd years. I could be with you by – it is ten now – four o'clock this afternoon, if it's OK with you?'

'Robert, I really don't want to drag you half way up the country. I could ask the questions on the phone. It's just, well, you are the victim, and I would like to be in a position to support you when asking them.'

'There is no problem at all. Anyway I like Cheshire. Can you send me directions?' They agreed to meet at 4.30pm, and the rest of the conversation was taken up with Ali giving Robert his home address and telephone number.

Joel suddenly felt very stiff sitting in Frederick's car and glanced at his watch. It was 1.30pm; where had the morning gone? He must have drifted off. Where on earth was Frederick? Joel got out of the car to stretch his legs, checking his mobile phone and walking around the car park. A few minutes later he became aware of two guards striding towards him. He thought they wouldn't want to speak to him. They did!

'What are you doing here, man?' said one of the guards in an openly aggressive way. Joel was about to answer with a quip but remembered he was in South Africa, in the grounds of a prison.

He said, 'I'm sorry, am I doing something wrong? I'm just waiting for my friend who is making a legal visit.' Joel thought the inclusion of 'legal' might help calm the guards.

'You English?' said the second guard.

'That's right. I'm with Frederick Weisner, the lawyer.'

'You're not supposed to be here using the phone, this is a protected area,' guard two continued.

'I'm sorry,' Joel said in his most conciliatory tone. 'Mr Weisner went into the prison for his visit and left me here. I'm sorry if I've done something wrong, I had no idea.' At that precise moment, Joel saw Frederick hurrying across the car park towards them. 'Here's Mr Weisner now.' Neither guard turned around, instead continuing to watch Joel.

Frederick saw the guards with Joel, and when he was within shouting distance he called, 'Gentlemen, what has my young English friend done? I hope you can understand his accent, I have real problems. You would think they'd teach them how to speak properly, wouldn't you?'

Frederick was almost with them when Joel noticed a smile break out on one of the guards' faces. 'You're right there, Mr Weisner, but he shouldn't be here using the phone when you're in the prison.'

'Entirely my fault, I'm afraid. I jumped out of the car frightened I would miss my visit, and forgot to warn him about his phone and wandering around. Is that what he's been up to?'

'That's about it,' said the 'speaking' guard. 'We were just about to take him in, but now you're here he can exit with you. Please remember next time, Mr Weisner.'

'Oh, there won't be a next time. He's only here a short while and we're going down town for his holiday shopping now. I'm so sorry to have caused you this inconvenience. Come, Joel, back in the car before you cause these gentlemen any more problems. Thank you for being so patient and for keeping us safe, gentlemen. Good afternoon.'

'Goodbye, gentlemen,' added Joel.

Guard two said, 'Not a problem, good afternoon.' Guard number one did not speak.

Joel and Frederick got in the car and made their way to the exit. 'That was fortunate,' Frederick said. 'The one who didn't speak is ex-SAPS and a thug. I was partially responsible for him leaving the police. Did you mention you were waiting for me?'

Joel confirmed he had, and added he thought it would help. Frederick looked at him and said, 'I think you've just had a lucky escape. Van Wisents, the guard, would have loved to get one of my friends in the guard room with the remand prisoners. Very lucky indeed.'

They negotiated the exit from the car park with no further incident.

Joel was silent, thinking about what Frederick had just said together with his earlier description of the prison regime. Joel forgot for a moment why he had been waiting in the car park and automatically checked for texts on his phone again, there were two: one from Robert, the other from Ali.

Robert's text said he had spoken to Ali and was seeing him at 4.30pm. Joel was a little puzzled. They lived hundreds of miles apart, and he couldn't see them meeting half way if Ali was going to take some samples, but then he thought, why not? The answer to the conundrum came when he read the text from Ali. Ali explained he had spoken to Robert, who volunteered to drive to Cheshire to allow Ali to take the samples. Ali's text also said he had received a message from Marta. The parcel was with the couriers and he was speaking to Cellmark re customs' clearance.

Joel burst into life. 'Part one complete, Frederick. The parcel is with the couriers. Part two is underway. Robert is giving his samples today, but more importantly, part three. How did it go? I'm dying to know. How did it go, Frederick?'

'Well, thank you. Very well indeed. Kem was able to negotiate a side room without "in room" supervision. I explained to the author-ities what I was going to do and then was able to explain to Kem what was happening. I've got your samples and my letter. It is all systems go. Have you heard from Marta? Is that how you know about the couriers?'

'Not directly, but I know the parcel is with the couriers because my friend in England texted me.' Joel felt the need to explain to Frederick why he had been checking his texts and not enquiring how things had gone in the prison.

'Very good, very good. Now if we go back to the office we can get Marta and Marimam to parcel these up and get them out of the country as well.'

'It would be better if we did the wrapping, parcelling and delivery to the couriers, Frederick, if you didn't mind. I don't want anyone to be in a position to allege we cross-contaminated any of the exhibits. I saw the exhibits yesterday but I didn't touch them with my bare hands.'

'Very good point, Joel, we'll make a detective out of you yet. We'll go to our main office and deal with the matter there.'

On the car journey there was little in the way of conversation, both men thinking through the next stage of the investigation. Joel was again wondering about Kem, the mild mannered servant who had survived twenty years in one of the toughest prison regimes in the world and was able to arrange a private room to meet with his solicitor. Was Kem the innocent he was being portrayed to be? It worried Joel, but he snapped out of it when his phone rang. It was Marta.

'Hi Joel, it's Marta. Are you with Papa?'

'Yes, he's driving.' Joel turned to Frederick and said, 'Marta.' Frederick nodded in acknowledgment.

'We've dropped the material at the courier,' Marta told them.

'We know, Ali texted me from the UK.'

'Was Papa successful at the prison?'

'Very,' said Joel. 'We're just on the way to the main office to parcel the exhibits up and send them off. I'll ask your father what time we will be back at his office.'

Weisner replied, 'About 4.30pm. Can she arrange for Thembi Siblisi to be there so we can get stage four into action?'

'Did you get that, Marta?' Joel asked.

'Loud and clear. See you later.'

Joel said goodbye, recognising they were not too far from the Business District. He really was getting to know the area.

Chapter Twelve

A short while later they entered the underground car park off Bree Street. Instead of going to Frederick's office, they went into the corporate HQ of Weisner and Co the way Marta had described what seemed like months ago, but in reality was only two days ago. The lift went to the fifth floor and they walked out into a luxurious foyer area, where the receptionists seemed genuinely shocked to see Frederick.

The senior receptionist, whom Frederick referred to as Constance, was the most flustered by their unexpected presence, particularly when Frederick asked to use a meeting room and for a lap top and printer. Constance said the boardroom was free and showed them in, telling them she was going to get their equipment. After ten minutes Frederick asked Joel to enquire where their equipment was, and when Joel went back to the receptionist he heard Constance talking on the phone.

'Yes, with a Mr Grant. I think he has an Irish accent.'

Constance looked up with some surprise, temporarily broke off the conversation and said the computer was on the way. Joel returned to the office and told Frederick what had happened. He was not surprised.

'Ahh, Constance, so predictable. We will have a visitor shortly,' he said, unpacking the exhibits from his bag, which was more like a doctor's Gladstone bag than the lawyer's case on wheels which most in the United Kingdom seemed to prefer. 'Don't speak. Let me deal with it, you just type the relevant documentation.'

There was a knock at the door and three people came into the room, two carrying a laptop, portable printer and the stationery Joel had requested. The third person was not carrying anything, but was tanned, slim and wearing what Joel adjudged to be a very expensive suit.

The two men placed the computer and printer on the table and set it up, observed by Joel. The third man said, 'Frederick, to what do we owe this pleasure? It's not often we can prise you out of your cabana across the road.' He spoke with an Australian accent, Joel took an instant dislike to him and what he thought was a patronising comment.

'Oh hello, Todd, nice to see you,' Frederick answered. 'I just need a little space for one of my cases.'

'Oh, which one?' queried the man.

'You wouldn't know it, Todd, it's a foreign historical case.'

'Ah yes, I understand your associate is Irish. Good afternoon.' The man inclined his head towards Joel.

'Mr Grant, this is Todd Pennard, one of the firm's partners – in fact the managing partner now.' Pennard nodded, clearly annoyed Frederick added managing partner as an apparent afterthought.

Joel responded with a simple, 'Good afternoon.' He never took his eyes from the two other men who were setting up the computer.

'So why are Weisner and Co involved in Ireland? I wasn't aware we had clients there.'

'Oh Todd, we have clients everywhere, some quite, quite old now.' Frederick hoped Todd would assume the case was something to do with the 'troubles' in Ireland and would backtrack to avoid any connection with it. He was right.

'Goodness, Frederick, I thought all that nonsense had ended. We must watch our reputation, don't forget our English heritage client base. Aspects of Irish litigation won't be popular with some of them.' Todd then raised his voice and said, 'Where do you come from, Mr Grant?'

'I was born in the South and went to University in the North,' answered Joel.

'How interesting. I know Ireland, I used to live there. Did you go to Queens?'

Frederick jumped in to prevent any further questions, 'Oh don't worry, Todd, this won't affect our English client base at all.'

'Good, good, – well, nice to meet you, Mr Grant. Frederick, always a pleasure. Will you be at the next board meeting?'

'Oh, I expect so,' Frederick responded, 'I expect so.'

Pennard left the room, followed by the two others who closed the door behind them.

'Now, Mr Grant, to work.' Frederick held his finger to his mouth and wrote on a piece of paper: *walls have ears, speak as little as possible.*

'Now if you would kindly write the narrative and cost plan,' Frederick winked at Joel, 'I will get on sorting my material out.'

The work in the boardroom continued for the next hour or so.

Little was said other than the occasional, 'Thank you, Mr Grant' or 'It's a pleasure, Mr Weisner,' but a number of notes were passed. When they finished, they collected all their materials, together with the computer and printer, and exited the boardroom towards the lift.

Frederick said, 'Thank you for your help, ladies, good afternoon.'

Constance rose from behind her desk. 'Oh, Mr Weisner, if you could leave the laptop and printer I will ensure they go back to IT.'

Frederick quickly responded, 'Don't worry, Constance, I rather like them. I think I'll trial them. If you could please let IT know, it would be very kind, thank you.' The lift arrived. Frederick and Joel got in and went straight to the basement, put their goods in the car boot and drove to the local DHL office. They went through the formalities and the second package of the day, as far as they knew anyway, was on its way to Cellmark in the United Kingdom. Joel texted Ali to let him know it was sent.

When Joel raised the non-speaking in the boardroom, Frederick did not engage. 'Later, Joel,' he said and closed the conversation abruptly. Joel knew not to raise it again. Frederick would do so when he was ready. The pair travelled back to the underground car park with Frederick talking about how he built the company from humble beginnings to become one of the most influential law firms in the Western Cape, but how the company was now becoming part of the system and not necessarily challenging the system. To be in the premier league of lawyers he knew he should have moved to Jo'burg, but he had chosen the less pressured life on the Cape. He told the story in such a matter of fact way; there wasn't a conceited bone in his body.

They walked back to Frederick's office, continuing general conversation about the firm, the country, the future. They found Marta and Marimam talking to another woman – it was Thembi Siblisi. Marta introduced Joel. Thembi clearly knew all about him and smiled broadly. Frederick showed her the letter signed by Kem and she confirmed it had all been explained. Marta then showed her father a letter she had drafted from Thembi to the Office of the Prosecutor and the Commissioner of Police.

'Are you content with this letter, Ms Siblisi?' Frederick asked.

'Very,' said Thembi. 'Your daughter has been through it with me, Mr Weisner.'

'After reading it,' he added, 'if you are content could you please sign it? Marta, if you could please witness it?'

Both women did as they were asked, then Thembi said to Joel, 'Mr Grant, will my brother be free?'

Not wishing to hold out false hope, Joel replied, 'Everyone in this room very much hopes so, but there is still much to do.'

'I understand. Thank you for what you are doing, you are all most kind.' At this the woman got up and left.

When she had gone, Frederick said, 'Marimam, why are you still here? Annette will be angry with me.'

Marimam, who did not look in the least concerned, said, 'I'm enjoying it Mr Frederick and Ms Annette said it was all right. Marta spoke to her.'

'Did she indeed, and when did it become appropriate to enjoy yourself at work?'

He looked serious, then everyone burst out laughing. This reminded Joel of someone he used to work for who always said, 'It is a serious business, policing, but let's have some fun along the way.' It was all too easy to forget this back in the United Kingdom, where policing was becoming as politicised as in parts of the United States of America. Joel made a mental note to reinforce the work–life–fun balance when he got back to the United Kingdom.

The little group of four then went into Frederick's room and talked about their next challenge: trying to get hold of Kem's clothing. They suspected it was going to be at Wynberg police station if it was going to be anywhere, but persuading the police to look for it, let alone physically getting hold of it, wouldn't be easy. Frederick undertook to speak to Prosecutor Du Toit and Police Chief De Wit again, but gaining access to police stores was a different matter. Joel resolved to try his luck using what he described as his 'police charm' the following morning.

Frederick then sat at the computer and wrote two letters to Messrs Du Toit and De Wit, which he would personally deliver the following morning.

'Okay, let's call it a day,' Frederick said. 'Joel, I want you at Wynberg police station at 9am tomorrow morning. I will give you copies of these letters and my own letter to 'Whom it May Concern' later. Marimam, what does Ms Annette have for dinner tonight? We're hungry. Joel, you'll join us, won't you? Of course you will.'

Marimam replied, 'She said she thought Mr Joel would be coming.'

Joel said, 'I'll be fine, I'll eat at the hotel. I've got to go and get changed.'

85

'Nonsense. Marta, can you pick him up at, let's say, 6.30pm? We'll eat a little later tonight,' Frederick said firmly.

'Certainly, Papa. Do you want a lift to the hotel now, Joel? I have to go to my flat to change as well.' Joel nodded.

'Good, that's settled. See you around 7pm. Come on, Marimam, let's go and face Ms Annette.' Before they knew it, Frederick and Marimam were out of the door and on their way.

'I got the feeling you didn't want to join us tonight. Is it me?' Marta asked.

Joel walked over to her, held her waist and kissed her. She returned the kiss and they started touching each other's bodies. Joel pulled away and said, 'Does that answer your question, Counsellor?'

Marta said, 'I think so.'

'I just don't want to be a burden on your family.'

'You're no burden. It's a long time since I've seen Papa so engaged, and Marimam, well, she's like a women possessed. Let's get locked up.'

The two made their way out into the car park and Marta's Audi, unaware there was a BMW7 Series about to leave at the same time. The person at the wheel was a tall, slim, suntanned lawyer who spoke with an Australian accent.

Chapter Thirteen

Marta dropped Joel at his hotel and reminded him she would be back at 6.30pm. 'No time for a sleep,' she said, but Joel thought there was time for a nap. When he got into his room he set the alarm for fifteen minutes and quickly fell asleep. Joel had a great ability to 'cat nap', or 'power nap' as it had become known. For him it was a great reviver. He had learnt how to survive with little sleep and short bursts of rest a long time ago when he was at University, and he'd refined his skills in the police to a high art form. It was a talent he was particularly proud of, and one greatly admired by colleagues and friends.

The alarm went off, as set, fifteen minutes later, and Joel got into the shower, where he also shaved. He discovered this was a time saver in the mornings when he was in a hurry, and after the first cuts and finding an odd tuft of facial hair remaining, he had refined this skill too. In the shower Joel considered his efficiency in getting ready, but then he thought everyone must have personal short cuts – although Sarah didn't. This was strange because of the life she had led as an investment banker, working long hours from very early in the morning to catch the Hang Seng or late at night for the close of the Dow. Nevertheless she was always perfectly made-up, even now she was running her shop in Budleigh. Sarah, mmm Sarah. Joel had put her to the back of his mind; he reconciled this by thinking he was too busy with the inquiry, but in the peace and relaxation of the shower he knew it was because of Marta. He was beginning to really like her, but was it the proverbial holiday romance? He didn't know, only time would tell. Time, thought Joel. Oh shit, what time was it? He got out of the shower and saw it was 6.10pm. Plenty of time, he thought. He wanted to FaceTime his children in Canada, but would have to make do with a phone call.

*

It was early morning where they lived in Western Canada, and he knew they were off school on a public holiday. He missed his children – he missed them a lot. He kept in touch via email, text, FaceTime, Skype, but it was not the same. He so wanted to hold them and be physically present for them, but this had been prevented by his ex-wife and her departure to Canada.

Joel had thought he loved his ex-wife Margo when they were initially together. He now realised it hadn't been love, it was need. Joel needed someone to come home to, and she needed someone to have babies with. Joel mulled over what sounded like a really chauvinist thought, and then dismissed it without reservation. It was true, he concluded, when she took their children to Canada, he had hated her. He still hated her.

Joel rang the children's mother. 'Hello, Margo, it's Joel. Can I speak to the children, please?'

'No you can't, they're out,' she snapped.

'At this time of the morning?' Joel was sceptical.

'Are you calling me a liar?' she shouted down the phone. Joel wondered which audience in Canada she was trying to impress.

'Look, when would be a good time to speak to them?' Joel said evenly.

'Try at lunchtime, they'll be here.' She hung up before Joel had time to talk about his possible trip to see the children. How he loathed her, he thought. He'd try and talk to them at their lunchtime, failing which he'd email her. Email was OK, but he always had to compose his emails to Margo very carefully.

He sent a quick text message to Phoebe, his daughter. While he didn't necessarily agree with her mother's decision to give her a mobile phone at an early age, it proved invaluable for keeping in touch with the children, much to the chagrin of his ex-wife.

Joel dressed and went downstairs. Marta was already there waiting. 'Come on,' she urged. No kiss, no cuddle.

They got in her car. As they drove away, she said, 'I've had a phone call from Todd Pennard. You didn't tell me you and Papa had come across him in the office today.'

'I didn't want to mention it because your father seemed paranoid after meeting Pennard. I thought he might mention it tonight. What did Pennard say?'

'He asked about you, the Irishman Mr Grant, and the fact I had

88

been seen around town with you. He saw us leaving the office tonight! Were you a new boyfriend as well as my father's collaborator? Were you a lawyer? What was the case you were working on? What it had to do with Groote Schuur Hospital? Why I visited the hospital earlier? You know, just a general sort of chat.'

'How does he know about the hospital?' Joel asked. 'We only had a brief chat with him in the office and your father told him nothing. What did you tell him, Marta?'

'The same. I said I was merely being friendly to a visitor. I knew you were a researcher of some kind, but Father told me not to discuss the case with you. It was historical and with European connections. I didn't know you were Irish?' she added.

'I'm not,' he said. 'What did you say about the hospital?'

'I told him the truth: Papa had asked me to collect a box, which I did, and that was that.'

'Do you get many calls from Pennard?' Joel asked.

'Not now,' Marta said. 'He was interested in me for other reasons. When I returned from working abroad he tried to persuade me he was a power for good and was going to influence the other partners to allow me to join the firm and train. He was actually doing quite the opposite. He's a predatory shit.'

'So why the call?' repeated Joel.

'He's also a control freak. He will want to know all about you and what you're up to with Papa, or more to the point what Papa is up to. He's frightened of Papa and the influence he still has over the firm. Normally he's quite content to leave Papa to the meet and greet the client role, but now he's found out about you and seen both of you in the Corporate HQ it will have flustered him. I don't know why, as on the surface he is supremely confident. I suspect he's up to something. I don't know what, but it won't be pleasant.'

The rest of the journey was spent reflecting on the day's events and they were soon at Frederick's home, being ushered into the drawing room by Annette. 'He's on the phone. He's hardly been off it since he got home,' she said, indicating Frederick's home office.

Annette disappeared and returned with two glasses of chilled Sauvignon Blanc. Marta said, 'Aren't you drinking, Annette?'

'I've got a gin and tonic through there,' she replied, pointing at the kitchen. 'I'll get it. Did you meet Todd Pennard today, Joel? He rang before and said he'd met Frederick with an Irishman in the office today.

I don't like that man, he's slippery.' Joel and Marta looked at each other and told Annette what happened earlier.

Frederick appeared at the doorway. 'Let's eat, we've got a lot to talk about.'

All four of them sat at the kitchen table eating pasta and fish. Joel was starving. Frederick told them he had spoken to Du Toit and De Wit. He would visit them in the morning and give them his letters, which he had already prepared. He would see the prosecutor at eight and the police chief at eight-thirty. Joel would go to Wynberg police station at nine armed with a third letter, also written by Frederick, who pushed a copy over the table for him and Marta to read. Annette thought for a moment about objecting, Joel noticed, but didn't say anything.

The letter set out the basic facts of Jess's murder and the arrest, conviction and imprisonment of Kem Siblisi. It stated further information had become available and because of technical advances he, Frederick, now wished the clothes of the convicted prisoner to be examined forensically. There was no mention of where the examination would take place. The letter went on to say Joel Grant was acting as agent for Weisner and Co, and they would be grateful if all possible assistance could be given to him to facilitate his task. It ended with the usual diplomatic utterances of 'Please be assured of our...' Joel had never seen this in a legal letter before; he'd seen it in letters from and to embassies, but not elsewhere.

Frederick must have seen the look on Joel's face, and said, 'The last part is just about stroking the officer in charge of the police station, making him feel important, for, despite the wishes of his boss, it is he who can help or hinder us.' Joel nodded.

'What happens if we can't get Kem's clothing, either because they won't let us or because they can't find it?' asked Marta.

'It's not crucial. We have samples for his DNA, and I suspect there will have been contact between them that evening anyway.' Marta looked at Joel. 'Don't forget they were celebrating his acceptance on the correspondence course for access to complete the law degree at London, and knowing Jess, she may have hugged him.' Marta now understood and nodded. 'The most important samples were Jess's, but it would be nice to get Kem's to complete the picture.'

'Yes, I understand,' said Frederick. 'Is there anything else we need, Joel?'

Joel thought for a moment and said, 'I would like a copy of Kem's arrest picture to take back, and perhaps a statement from Thembi about him being left handed. These too are not essential, but when putting everything together would help with an overall assessment. It would also be handy if we could research any crime that took place in the area around the Corfields' house say six months before and after Jess's death.'

Frederick looked at his daughter and said, 'Marta, could you sort those out while Joel is at the police station please?'

'Of course, Papa, although I think the crime data may take longer,' she replied.

'Now, Joel, when are you going back to the UK?' said Frederick. It had been the unasked question. Marta looked down at the table – Annette was watching her reaction. 'Is your work here finished? I say this not because we want to get rid of you, but you must have things to do in the UK, and you are beginning to become of interest to others, which is not helpful to our inquiry.'

'I've never liked Pennard,' Annette interjected.

'Shh! As you have just heard, Joel, the managing partner of my firm is not well liked in this household. In fact, I have heard him described as a shit.' Frederick looked at Marta, who smiled broadly. 'I should explain my behaviour in the office. The boardroom has listening devices in – not for any nefarious reasons, but it helps sometimes in negotiations when they are on the record. Todd Pennard I suspect, but can't prove, uses the listening devices to keep a grip or control of the firm. You may ask why is it tolerated? Simply better the devil you know. I suspect Todd will have listened to our work, and do you remember Constance saying she would return the computer and printer to IT? I suspect the request originated from Pennard.

'The next question you will be asking is "Why?" It's not just he's concerned about what I'm up to, but Pennard deals in information. It is his commodity of choice. Bizarre I know for a lawyer. In fairness the information he trades is generally nothing to do with the firm directly. It's not surprising given his background: he's an ex-US State Department diplomat and legal counsel.'

Joel was surprised. 'How can that be? He's Australian.'

'Ah, he speaks with a mid Pacific accent because he lived there and spent a considerable time on missions in the region.

Chapter Fourteen

Over the rest of dinner Frederick talked extensively about Pennard: how he grew up in New England, the only child of two highly successful Boston lawyers. His mother was a leading criminal defence attorney who was regularly in the media promoting her clients' cases to the detriment of the district attorney's cases, and his father was a corporate lawyer representing some of the biggest firms in the country. While New York, Washington, London and politics were attractive, the Pennards were essentially New Englanders. Rather like Parisians and unlike the traditionally politically active Bostonians, when asked why they did not leave and further their careers elsewhere, had said, 'Leave New England? Why?' Joel had visited New England a number of times; he understood.

They were Democrats, but their son developed different political views. Pennard's parents, Todd (like father, like son) and Brenda, paid for the best education for their son. He declined Harvard in favour of Stanford, which disappointed his parents who were both alumni and, in the North American tradition, had donated considerable sums over the years to their alma mater. Pennard Junior then spent a year in Heidelberg, studying international law and German. He was a gifted linguist.

After his year abroad and training at one of the big US law firms, according to his CV, Pennard again departed from the norm and joined the diplomatic service, serving in US Embassies in Jakarta, Vienna, Manila, London, Bogota and Pretoria. 'An eclectic list of postings,' Frederick remarked.

However, Pennard was no diplomatic lawyer, Frederick worked out over the years. He was a Central Intelligence Agency operative who had clearly served in some politically sensitive missions. Pennard never admitted being ex-CIA, despite Frederick putting it to him directly.

This was interesting in itself, because Frederick had met many others who worked for the Agency and who had shown no reluctance to talk about who they worked for, although there was a reticence about what they had done.

Pennard's last posting had been in Pretoria where he met and married his South African wife Delores, who was the daughter of a leading South African lawyer, Hank de Bose. Keeping it in the legal family, thought Joel.

Just prior to Pennard's marriage, Frederick was approached by three of his partners, who were friends of de Bose, suggesting they take on Pennard who would qualify to practise with the firm. Frederick and the others met Pennard, who was bright, articulate and could speak Afrikaans, Xhosa and Zulu. According to Frederick, while Pennard was qualified at the American bar and in international law, he was also well versed in South African law and could argue his case very well.

After the meeting, the four partners talked. Frederick's colleagues were even more enthusiastic. Frederick was convinced about Pennard's abilities, but suspicious about his career and politics. Frederick's colleagues mentioned Frederick's desire to broaden the workforce. He had been working hard to employ black trainees in the law firm, but some of his partners were not as keen. It was not a threat, Frederick thought, just a reminder about how in a partnership the support of others was essential.

Pennard was staunchly supportive of the current US Republican administration and spoke disdainfully about the previous Democratic Government. Frederick wondered why such a politically astute and clearly well connected Republican wanted to settle in the 'backwater' of South Africa rather than take up some highly influential position in the US government. He found out later it was Pennard's desire for independent wealth rather than his parents', who, in any case, had given much of theirs away. Of course, being married to a foreign national may not have enhanced his administrative or political career in the United States.

Frederick said he persuaded himself the firm needed alternative views and Pennard could certainly give them. He was offered a position, which he accepted and done well for the firm, attracting some major clients.

Marta interrupted the monologue. 'That's nonsense, Papa, and you know it. Pennard may have made the introduction, but it was your name and the name of the firm which attracted them. Pennard is a classic wheeler dealer, that's all.'

'Marta, Marta, I know you don't like him or his politics, but he is also an accomplished lawyer and you know it deep down.'

'Hmmph,' grumbled Marta.

'But how did you work out he was CIA?' asked Joel.

'Elementary, my dear Dr Grant, elementary.'

Frederick continued to outline Pennard's CV, showing no apparent service within the State Department in Washington, which was strange for a lawyer. Posting upon posting to 'interesting' places. Over the years, Pennard had talked in some detail about the countries he worked in and the places he visited in them. Why would a State Department lawyer visit the region of Caqueta in Columbia, the Eue Valley in Peru, Sana'a in Yemen, not to mention Baghdad, Kabul, Belfast and Dublin? And everyone knew Vienna was 'spy central' during the Cold War. All places Pennard talked openly about visiting and serving on missions.

But it was also the people he knew. He was – is – very well connected, not just to the great and the good of the legal profession in South Africa and the United States, but his commercial contacts too. 'It seems to me,' Frederick said, 'spying is as much about the commercial interests of the developed and developing world as about their military or counter terrorism efforts, only the emphasis shifts from time to time.' Frederick recounted by way of example the fuss in Paris when the French expelled some US diplomats amid allegations of meddling in the French wine industry. 'Well it's a good story at least. Todd Pennard has always been interested in the Stellenbosch wine area,' Frederick added.

Annette intervened, 'That's because he likes the stuff so much.' Everyone laughed.

'And then, there is the final piece in the jigsaw: his close and long friendship with George Corfield, who was, of course, also a spy before he became successful in minerals.'

'What do you mean?' asked Joel.

'Well, I suppose it is guilt by association,' said Frederick. 'Not evidence, just suspicion…'

Marta interrupted him and said, 'If Pennard is such a good friend of George Corfield, why isn't George a client of the firm?'

'A good question, Marta. From a commercial point of view Corfield would have been an important client.' Joel was still considering Frederick's commentary re Pennard. It was like a history lecture tonight; Frederick the Professor, with the students listening carefully, questioning from time to time.

'At one partners' meeting,' Frederick continued,' Henri Vesper did ask Pennard why Corfield did not use our firm. Pennard was unequivocal in his view: George Corfield was a personal friend and it would be quite wrong to have him as a client. Vesper pointed out Pennard need have nothing to do with the account, but Pennard was having none of it and closed the conversation. It has never been mentioned again, but of course the fact Corfield used de Bose, Pennard's father-in-law, was not lost on the other partners!'

Marta said, 'I didn't know all that. How long has he been here altogether, Papa?'

'Years and years. He left the diplomatic service just at the end of Apartheid.'

'Was he with your firm at the time of Jess's death,' asked Joel.

'Let me think…yes, almost certainly. Why do you ask, Joel?' replied Frederick.

'I don't know. It was something Marta said earlier about him being a predatory male,' said Joel. 'I'm just thinking out loud.'

'Now it's you who isn't basing their thoughts on evidence,' Frederick said gently to Joel. 'I just don't want anyone to start taking an undue interest in what we are doing, and it looks like Pennard has started, so, Joel, when are you going back to the UK?'

'I think it really depends on what happens tomorrow. If I can get Kem's clothing it would be great, if not I may have to stay.'

'As much as I like you around, whether you get the clothing tomorrow or not is an irrelevance. I suggest, in fact I insist, you do your work tomorrow then you spend a couple of days relaxing. Marta, do you think you could take Joel down to Knysna for me? It would be a shame for Joel to go back not having rested and Knysna is just the place on the coast to go and relax. After all that's why he's here.' He winked at Joel, who had forgotten he'd told Frederick about his 'illness'.

Annette joined in, 'That's a wonderful idea, Frederick. They could stay with Simon and Maureen, who have always got plenty of room.'

'There, then it's settled.'

'Oh no it's not,' interjected Marta. 'No one asked me about my diary, whether I can spare the time to be a tourist guide, chauffeur and travel agent.'

'Well can you do it, Marta?' Frederick said. 'If not Annette and I can do it certainly, can't we, dear?'

'What does Joel want to be saddled with us for, Frederick?' scoffed

Annette. 'Marta, give them a ring now, see if they're about. Come on, the number's on the table in your father's office.'

Marta got up and walked slowly into the office. While she was out, Frederick said to Joel, 'It is for the best, Joel. Pennard is not a nice person and I really don't want him poking around.'

'He was a spy and probably still is,' concurred Annette. 'Getting Marta out of this will help as well, Joel, it really will. It will help us.'

'I understand, but I do find Pennard intriguing,' said Joel. 'I would love to know where he was when Jess was killed.'

Marta returned to the room. 'They're at home and will be delighted to see us.'

'Good, it's settled. Let's have a drink,' said Frederick, 'it could be your last night in Cape Town, Joel, so champagne I think to celebrate everything you have achieved.'

'Everything *we* have achieved,' Joel emphasised.

'I'll have half a glass, I'm the chauffeur,' said Marta.

The next hour was spent chatting about the history of South Africa and the South African justice system. At ten, Marta said, 'We'd better go. If I have a long drive tomorrow, I will need to get a good night's sleep.' Joel said goodbye to Frederick, Annette and other assorted members of the household who still happened to be around, including Marimam, then got into Marta's car and left.

Marta didn't say anything for a couple of minutes, then, 'I hate it when they make assumptions about my life, I really do.'

Joel responded, 'I don't think they were making assumptions. I think they were being kind to me and presumed you might want to do the same. Look, if you really don't want to go, it doesn't matter. I'll go back to the UK tomorrow night. Just drop me at the hotel and I'll get a taxi to the police station in the morning.'

'Fine! If that's what you want, it's not a problem.'

The journey to the hotel was silent and quick, Joel got out of the car, simply saying, 'Goodnight, Marta, thanks for the lift.'

Marta said a tight-lipped, 'Goodnight,' and drove away.

Chapter Fifteen

Joel went straight to his room; it was time to ring the children. The room looked more or less the same as he'd left it earlier, but he noticed the bed had been moved slightly, the impressions in the carpet were in different places. His papers had also been rearranged and moved, and the bathroom door was slightly more open than it usually was. His rucksack was still locked in the safe. He thought it could have been the cleaners, but he concluded it wasn't; they were more formulaic. The room had been searched, but not by true professionals who would have ensured everything was replaced in exactly the same way. Or was it professionals who were passing him a message? he wondered.

He picked the phone up and dialled the children. His daughter Phoebe answered the phone, and without any introduction said, 'Speak.'

Joel said, 'Speak? What sort of greeting is that?'

'Hey, Dad, I knew it would be you. You texted me, remember?'

Joel wondered if their mother had bothered to mention the fact he'd rung earlier. He had a very good conversation with Phoebe, and then with Will, his son, who wasn't as confident as Phoebe on the phone, or generally. Joel mentioned he was going to try and get out to see them, which caused excitement. How he missed them, but he thought he must email their mother now to prevent her from making any plans to frustrate his contact. He ended his chat with the children almost in tears; what a change from earlier in the evening when things looked so good.

Joel put the phone down and tapped out a quick message, saying to their mother he was going to try and get out to see the children in their next school holiday. A carefully crafted holding message, he thought as he lay on the bed and noticed one of the paintings was askew, as was a mirror. He concluded his room had definitely been searched.

His mobile vibrated. It was a message from Robert which read:

> Saw Ali, nice guy, everything sorted. Good luck. R

Well, at least something was going right, Joel thought. It was followed almost immediately by a text from Ali.

> Joel met Robert, good guy. Now have full picture. Will speak to lab am. When you back? Ali

Joel was just about to send a response saying he was leaving tomorrow night when there was a knock at his door. He looked through the security spy hole, thinking it might be his earlier uninvited guests. It wasn't, it was Marta. He opened the door, and she walked straight in and kissed him hard on the lips.

'I'm sorry, I'm sorry,' she whispered, 'it was just the realisation you would be leaving. I knew it would happen, but I put it out of my mind until earlier. I'm sorry, Joel, what must you think?'

Joel took hold of her and kissed her back, saying, 'I think a lot, Marta. I think a lot about you.' Then he suddenly remembered his room search. This time it was his turn to put his finger to his mouth and take her across to the desk where he tore off a piece of the hotel paper and wrote:

> Room has been searched, don't know it they left anything, hidden tape/camera.

Marta was startled. She wrote, you must tell Papa. I will ring him and tell him you phoned me. Stay here! She said casually, 'I'm just going to check my car, Joel, see you in a minute,' and left the room.

What seemed like moments later his mobile rang. It was Frederick. 'Joel, Marta is coming to get you. Pack, check out, she will collect you. No questions, just do it.' The phone went dead. Joel respected Frederick in all sorts of ways, and if he was saying get out, he must have a reason. Joel started to throw things in his bag when there was another knock on the door. He looked through the hole: it was Marta. Joel let her in. They didn't speak; she sat on the bed as Joel finished packing, then they were out of the room in a flash.

The hotel receptionist was surprised at the sudden check out but quickly sorted the final receipt, the bill having been paid in advance by Robert. Marta and Joel got into the car and Marta drove away, again quickly but this time aggressively, continuously checking her mirrors. Joel did the same through the wing mirrors. They both agreed they were not being followed so she drove straight to her father's house, where they were greeted by Annette and Frederick in their dressing gowns. Joel explained what he had found and Frederick insisted they should stay, get some sleep and discuss what to do in the morning. They all agreed it was a good plan, and once again Joel found himself in his borrowed pyjamas.

The door opened and closed quietly. Marta slipped into bed beside him.

'Hello, darling,' she said, 'this could be our last night together.'

Joel whispered, 'I do hope not,' as his hands touched her body and he began to kiss her. He could feel she was tense and gently stroked her, kissing her, blowing her ear and licking her delicious tasting body. She seemed to be relaxing, he thought. Now was not the time for talking through the night; now was the time for each of them to benefit from their lovemaking, relaxing and enjoying being pampered and loved. They made love for a long time, gently and carefully, fulfilling each other's needs before falling off to sleep. Well, this was Joel's recollection, because when he woke to Annette's soft call, 'Joel, there is coffee outside the door for you,' Marta had once again gone.

As he had done the previous morning, he collected his coffee, showered and dressed. He walked into the kitchen to find a very similar scene once again, and said good morning to everyone. It was like déjà vu, except Annette didn't ask him what he wanted for breakfast. She just told him to sit down, and Marimam almost instantaneously placed a vegetable and cheese omelette with toast in front of him. Annette said, 'You seemed to enjoy it yesterday,' and smiled. Joel thanked her, telling her how delicious it was. Frederick and Marta were tucking into some sort of porridge.

'Sleep all right after last night's activities?' Frederick asked. Joel assumed he was talking about the room search.

'Yes. I took a little time to get off, but slept very soundly, thanks,' Joel replied. Frederick then rehearsed what he was going to do. He no longer wanted Joel to go to the police station; he would do that himself. If the clothes were there he would put them in the big brown bag Joel had asked for. If they were not he would try to find out what had happened to them.

Frederick said, 'Joel, I know you will think we are being over cautious but you must return to the UK tonight. This is a wonderful country with many wonderful people, but there are also a few very bad people. We, as established trouble-makers, are relatively safe; you, as a foreigner poking around, could be hurt badly. We cannot afford for that to happen, not only for your own sake but for our search for the truth, so I want you to stay here during the day and get the eight o'clock flight tonight back to London. Marta and I will go to work and will see you back here at four this afternoon. Try and get some sun in the garden, but stay in the grounds. Annette is in charge.'

'So what's different?' said Marta, as she and Annette exchanged smiles.

'Good, it's settled. Come, Marta, you're working with me today. Watch and learn, my girl, watch and learn.'

'Oh dear, Marta, it's going to be one of those days,' said Annette, rolling her eyes.

Marta kissed Annette and Joel goodbye, followed by Frederick who gave a quick handshake to Joel and a kiss to Annette, then they were off in Marta's car.

Annette poured Joel some more coffee and said, 'He was serious. Sit in the garden, relax. If you need to send any emails use the office.' Joel thanked Annette, explaining he needed to book his flight. This proved relatively painless, and he then wandered out to the veranda where he sat down and thought about what he had to do. He made a mental list, and returned to the office where he emailed Ali and Robert from Marta's account to say he would be returning over the weekend. He thought better of emailing Sarah and went to his room to dial her number. He rang her at his house, then at the shop. It was nine in the United Kingdom; she should have been there. He rang her mobile and left a message, and thought he'd better text her just in case.

Joel went back out onto the veranda and relaxed with a glass of orange juice. He noticed one of the workers, Afua, repairing a wall. It was just like one of his walls back home in Budleigh, stones and mortar. Before he knew it, Joel was standing beside Afua, who looked up at him somewhat quizzically. Joel said, 'Hi, Afua, I have a wall like this at home. Do you mind if I help you so I can learn how to repair my wall?'

Afua was pleased with Joel's interest, but did say, 'I could come to England with you and do the repairs.'

Joel responded, 'I'm not sure Mr Frederick or Marimam would be too happy with that.' They both smiled. Joel knew Afua and Marimam were an item, but did not know how much of an item.

Joel and Afua worked together for about two hours. Annette noticed them working and thought it would help relax Joel, but also tire him out for his flight. She had visited the United Kingdom a couple of times and found it best to try to sleep on the plane rather than watch the films or drink the night away, as Frederick tended to do.

Afua stopped for lunch, which was salad, cold meats and home-made breads, and they both got cleaned up before going to eat. Annette announced Joel had worked enough and ordered him to take a shower so his clothes could be cleaned. She didn't want the customs officers thinking they'd been making him work while he was in South Africa.

As usual, Joel did what he was told by Annette. He then checked his mobile: still no response from Sarah. Strange, he thought. The rest of the afternoon was spent watching Sky TV and finding out what else was happening in the world. Unfortunately, as usual there was trouble in the Middle East.

Marta and Frederick returned shortly before 4pm. Things had gone well with the prosecutor and the police chief who, of course, had been expecting their visitors. Not quite so well at the police station operational level, though. Despite the De Wit call to the station commander, the man made them wait an hour before meeting with them in his 'plush, body odour riddled office,' as Marta described it. He read Frederick's letter carefully before saying, 'Why are you bothering, Mr Weisner? I remember this case, he's as guilty as sin.'

Marta also described how the commander totally failed to acknowledge her or her presence. Anyway, he did find a sergeant in charge of exhibits, who said if the exhibits still existed they would have been stored at the new storage facility. They spent two hours going through ledger after ledger before the sergeant disclosed there were thirty others to go through. There had been no back-record conversion onto a computer. Frederick then stood up, according to Marta, and said to the police officer, 'Good. Thank you, Sergeant, I will see you tomorrow morning at the same time and will spend two hours each day going through the records until I find what I want.'

The sergeant was stunned. Frederick added, 'Same time tomorrow, then. Please tell your chief, I expect he'll want to know,' at which they left, got in Marta's car and both laughed out loud – as indeed everyone did when the account was related in the kitchen.

Annette and her band of helpers had prepared food, and they sat and ate there and then. There was a chicken curry dish, which Joel thought had a slight lemon flavour. Annette explained she had learnt it from a friend who lived in Durban. It was delicious. Frederick concluded it was better for Marta to take Joel to the airport than him; she was a quicker driver, and if he went it may attract more attention from the police, or whoever. Joel thanked everyone for all their help and hospitality, and said he would, of course, keep them informed of developments. He once again said his goodbyes to the Weisner household.

Marta drove to the airport quickly as usual. They talked about keeping in touch but, like Joel, Marta wondered if he might just think it was a holiday type romance. For her it wasn't; it was much, much more. She stopped at the airport and said she wouldn't come in for the same reasons her father had mentioned, but in reality it was because she didn't want Joel to see her upset.

They kissed and held each other in the car like a young couple on their first passionate date, before Joel said he had to go. He promised he'd text her when he got to Heathrow and got out of the car, took his bags from the boot and kissed Marta for the last time through the car window. He said, 'Goodbye,' turned and walked towards the terminal door. For some reason he looked back and saw her wipe her eyes through the open car window. He started to walk back, but she waved and drove off, not just quickly but like a bullet.

Joel considered ringing her but thought it would make matters worse. He went to the desk; no issues with security and passport control. He had been expecting problems, but instead was quickly walking into the business lounge. An hour or so later, after a couple of glasses of champagne, he took his seat on the plane. He checked his phone: no message from Sarah.

He sent Marta a message.

Thank you for being there, for being the delight you are my beautiful African princess. Joel xxx

Chapter Sixteen

Joel switched his phone off, accepted another glass of champagne before take-off and was asleep before the plane reached cruising altitude.

Joel immediately thought the jolt which woke him was an "s the k", but he remembered he'd checked the cabin before going to sleep: there wasn't one! He realised it had been a loss in cabin pressure. While a few things tipped on the floor, which the crew was now scurrying around collecting up, there was no real damage. He checked the flight planner and saw they were passing over central Africa and crossing the Equator. He thought he'd get up, stretch his legs and have a drink of water. Joel had missed dinner on the plane; the large meal cooked earlier by Annette, followed by the snacks he'd eaten in the lounge at the airport would keep him going. He had a drink of water and a walk around for a little while, talking to some other travellers who were visiting the United Kingdom for the first time and were debating going to the Globe Theatre or Stratford on their Shakespearean adventure. Joel loved Shakespeare's work; it had been a passion in earlier years and he had thought about trying to become an actor. He had become a detective instead, in many ways quite similar!

He persuaded the travellers whilst they were in the United Kingdom it would make sense to sample both places, they weren't too far apart in South African terms and, while both Shakespearean, were very different. He felt like a tourist guide, and after returning to his seat, via the galley for some more water and fruit, he quickly snapped out of it by watching *Shameless* on the comedy channel. Joel loved *Shameless*, a series about a Manchester family; it reminded him so much of his time in the city.

Joel watched the programme and wondered why was he becoming so sentimental. He then remembered he always did on flights; he thought it was because, while he was in the safest form of transport, he still felt slightly vulnerable. He reflected on his brief visit to South Africa; much had happened in a short time, but his focus returned to the question of why his hotel room had been searched, by whom? And why it caused Frederick Weisner to get him out of the country so urgently?

What was it all about? Joel's speculation threw up many theories, but none particularly added up, lying on his flat bed seat, at 36,000 feet in the sky, watching *Shameless*. This subconsciously reassured him; there was not a great deal to worry about: only his return to work, facing the consequences of his court evidence and, of course, the wrath of Sarah. Joel was now asleep.

He was woken again, this time by the cabin light being switched on with an announcement breakfast would be served shortly. He was amazed at how well he slept, and this meant he would be able to hit the ground running when he got to Heathrow. Unlike many people, Joel liked airline food, particularly Business Class food. He declined a further alcoholic drink in favour of orange juice and water to wash down his scrambled eggs, bacon and sausage. Just what he needed!

The plane landed on schedule and Joel switched his phone on. There were two messages, one from Marta saying:

No, thank you JG, my Irish revolutionary! Mxxx

The second message was from Sarah, asking Joel to phone her when he landed. Oh dear, thought Joel, and the Coldplay song *Trouble* entered his consciousness. The song summed up what had happened over the last five days: he felt he was in the middle of a spider's web unable to get out.

Joel showered at the airport before sending Marta a text:

The eagle has landed.

Then he phoned Sarah. The ring tone sounded as though she was out of the country. He was right again as Sarah confirmed she was in Paris when she answered the phone. Sarah was due home tonight and pressed Joel on when he was coming back to Budleigh Salterton. She was unhappy when he said he anticipated getting further sick leave and accused him of always having something to sort out, but never himself.

She had a way with words which metaphorically dug the knife in! Sarah passed on messages from Billy, Suzy and Fiona who all wanted him to phone on his return. Duty done, she told him she was in the middle of something and had to go. Joel wondered what was so pressing on a Saturday morning in Paris, but his speculation was cut short as he turned his attention to dealing with the urgent phone calls.

First he rang Suzy, who was in the park with her children. She told him all hell had broken loose in the last twenty-four hours. The Guvn'r had been called to the Yard, and questions were being asked by the Commissioner's Office about who Joel was, who was he working for and what he was doing. South Africa had complained about his presence there, and she heard they were going to deport him. He thanked Suzy and phoned Billy, who was still in someone's bed. Goodness knows whose, thought Joel. Billy recounted a similar story, in a slightly more expressive way.

Then, the Guvn'r.

Fiona Henderson was with people when he phoned as he heard her excuse herself. About thirty seconds later she was back on the phone, 'Joel, where the fuck are you?' She was clearly no longer with whomever they were.

'I'm back in the UK, Guvn'r.'

'Joel, you have a problem, and I'm not talking about what you left me with at the Old Bailey.' Joel wondered how the case ended up, but she was now in full flow. With a voice which could strip paint, Fiona described how she was summoned to town the previous day to be met by the AC, the Head of Professional Standards and a civil servant, who grilled her about what Joel was up to in South Africa. She could only tell the truth, which was he was off sick and gone to South Africa for a break. The civil servant told her Joel had virtually caused a diplomatic incident and some very powerful people in South Africa wanted him deported. Joel quipped they were a bit late, which did not go down well with Fiona, who insisted he was at her house at midday for a meeting.

Fiona Henderson lived in Harrow, so he decided to go to his flat and dump his bags first. He caught the Heathrow Express; he could have used the Tube for free, but en route changed his mind about going to his flat and put his bags into the left luggage at Paddington. He didn't know why as he had plenty of time, but he too was becoming paranoid. In any case he could jump on the Bakerloo line at Paddington straight up to Headstone Lane, which he did after a coffee.

The Guvn'r lived in a substantial five bedroom detached redbrick house about half a mile from the Tube. Joel had dropped her off a few times. She said she was paying for it with the help of her parents, who were both medics in Edinburgh. There had been no need for her to tell him this, but he supposed it was her way of demonstrating she wasn't on the take to pay for it.

As Joel walked from the Tube station it was quiet. He didn't know why he kept looking for evidence of anyone watching him. He was still in South African mode – he didn't see anyone.

The door was answered by the Guvn'r, who ushered him straight through the entrance hall and kitchen into a conservatory at the back of the house. She told him her parents were in the house but would not bother them. They sat down in the conservatory, which overlooked a terraced area and well-tended garden. Fiona launched into her comments.

'Somebody on high is after your blood. This part of the conversation is off the record, if that's OK, then we'll have to have a more formal chat.'

Joel nodded.

Fiona told Joel she wanted to talk at her house as she didn't know what was happening, and she suspected the civil servant at the meeting in the Yard was a spy. The key issue was what was going on.

'A DS goes sick and buggers off to South Africa. That's not international news. What were you doing, Joel? The truth!'

He then told the story of Jess's death, and while he was in South Africa Robert had asked him just to make a few enquiries about it, which he had done with the papers and lawyers.

In formal mode, Fiona moved on to tell Joel he would now be on administration duties and have no direct contact with the public. Joel said it would drive him nuts, but despite his protests Fiona said it was a directive from the AC and she was surprised he hadn't been suspended. She added, 'I suspect some sort of report will come from South Africa. If there is nothing in it, fine. If there is something, you'll have to deal with it. But in the interim keep your nose clean, and watch what you say on the phone.'

So that's why she wanted me to come here, thought Joel. She suspects my phone is hooked up. When he asked Fiona why his phone would be 'on', she simply shrugged and told him the reason she had brought him to her house was to inform him he would be on admin duties and under investigation for what he had done in South Africa while he was off sick.

Walking to the door, Joel turned to face Henderson and thanked her.

'Well, just remember that the next time you're looking to drop someone in it at the Bailey,' she said. Joel asked her to tell him what had happened. Fiona recounted Whitaker had been given a public dressing down by the judge. She had been dragged in; said she was responsible for Joel's supervision and if there were issues she would deal with them. More importantly, the trial had ended, the Judge and Counsel agreed it was not necessary to wait for Joel to return to duty: a wise decision in her view. The jury convicted the lot, and with sentencing next month it was a good result all round.

Joel welcomed the news, which was a great result, and said, 'All's well that ends well,' winked at his DCI, turned and walked away before she could say a thing. He didn't look back, but he suspected Fiona might have been mouthing something at him.

On his walk to the Tube he sent a text to Sarah saying he'd speak to her in the morning, and switched his phone off when he reached the Headstone Road Tube station. Again he thought he was being ultra cautious, but better to be safe, and it certainly relaxed him. At Paddington he collected his bags and booked into the Hilton beside the station. He went straight to his room, ordered chicken Caesar salad and a beer, and watched some TV before falling asleep. He checked again on the way to the hotel to see if he was being followed and hadn't seen anything out of the ordinary, but what was ordinary? It's London, for God's sake, he thought.

Joel was up about ten the following morning and made his way to his flat by Tube. He concluded if he was going to be followed he had nothing to hide, at the moment. As he left the Tube at Highbury and Islington he phoned Sarah, but there was no reply.

When he got back into the flat it seemed as though he'd never been away and he soon got down to doing his laundry, which Joel strangely found relaxing and certainly not a burden. He FaceTimed his children, who were both on good form, and then went out to do some shopping. He wasn't aware of being followed and didn't test it by anti-surveillance; he would leave that until it was needed.

After shopping, Joel walked into the 'nick', which was only fifteen minutes from the flat. It was deserted. The Sunday duty CID were either in the cells interviewing or at a shooting which happened at one o'clock in a pub, he learnt from the duty officer. Joel was glad, as he didn't want to have to chat about where he'd been at the moment; the duty officer was far too busy to ask. Joel checked his emails and found there was nothing desperate so, after an hour, he went back to the flat and had an early night, ready for the following morning.

Chapter Seventeen

Joel was pissed off. He mulled over what had happened: he'd returned from South Africa, gone back to work and been placed on restricted duties, which meant he couldn't do any real police work. He was desk bound. This was because the authorities were looking into his absence from work.

Joel complained to the Police Federation over the way he had been dealt with. They were unsympathetic and, like Fiona, said he was lucky not to be suspended. What was the point of paying his subscription every month when they would not even support him? Joel thought about cancelling his subscription, but knew in his heart of hearts he may need legal advice in the future and didn't want to be left without any insurance. Anyway he was going to the doctor's tonight and would get signed off sick with 'fatigue'. He'd make sure she wrote fatigue, not stress. This way his employers may feel a little more vulnerable, and in his current position he needed them to feel this way. Despite his break in South Africa, Joel still felt genuinely very tired, and was beginning to think there might be an underlying issue.

When 4pm came Joel was out of the office like a shot, which was unlike him. He normally had to be dragged out, and usually to the pub. He left work and went straight to see his doctor, whom he had been with since joining the Met. Strangely everyone he spoke to always moaned when they went to the doctor, it was never the same one, but Dr Lloyd always saw him. She didn't like the police, but liked Joel for some reason. Joel thought it was because he once criticised the Government for not supporting health workers, as if he was going to say anything else when she was going to stick a needle in his backside!

He explained how he felt. Dr Lloyd examined him and took some blood for tests. She then said she was going to sign him off for four weeks; she suspected he just needed a rest.

'Take it easy though, Joel, get down to the West Country. It's not Wales but it's close.' Dr Lloyd not only had a Welsh name, but he suspected she was a Welsh spy sent to watch and report back on the English.

'See you in a few weeks, Doc.'

'I'm serious, Joel, take it easy,' said the Welsh Mata Hari.

'Thanks again,' replied Joel as he walked out of the door to see Fiona Henderson sitting in the waiting room.

'What are you doing here?' she said to him.

'Don't you know about medical confidentiality?' 'I'm seriously ill as it happens, and by the way here's my certificate.'

The DCI looked at the paper and said out loud, 'Fatigue? You?'

'I didn't realise you were medically qualified, Fiona,' said a Welsh voice from behind Joel. Henderson went bright red. Dr Lloyd was her doctor too; she must not have changed when she moved. Wise choice, Dr Lloyd was a good GP, thought Joel.

'You'd better come in, Fiona.' Dr Lloyd turned, followed by the chastened DCI. Joel whispered to Fiona as she passed him, 'Is she going to examine you to see if she can find a heart?'

Henderson didn't respond and she rarely swore, but the look he got from her clearly said, 'Fuck off, Joel,' as she walked into the consulting room. Joel wondered why she was seeing the doctor. She did look after herself, so perhaps it was a sports injury or something.

Joel walked down the street still thinking about what was the matter with his DCI. She wasn't a sickly person, but then again neither was he. Mmm, anyway it was a stroke of luck her being there. He didn't have to go back into work.

What to do next?

Joel rang Mark Brutus, his psychologist friend. 'The Brute', as Joel called him, was actually a genial, mild mannered clinical psychologist whom Joel met at university, and who was now based at the Institute of Psychiatry. Sometimes the police called him in for help on interview techniques and profiling.

Joel asked The Brute if he wanted to meet up for a drink and a chat. He slipped into the conversation he had been to South Africa and wanted The Brute's help to understand some of what he'd found there. He also mentioned his visits to the doctor, which wasn't at all like him.

'OK, but I can't see you until seven. Where?'

'What about Aubin and Randall in Brewer Street? We can watch the wonders of Soho go by,' suggested Joel.

'OK, see you there, if you're not too tired by then!'

'Fuck off,' said Joel amicably and finished the call.

The Brute was a great guy; not only one of the brightest people Joel knew but he also had a wonderful talent for getting to the nub of a complex issue very quickly. This was part of the reason Joel wanted to meet him to chat through his thoughts.

Two and a half hours to fill, thought Joel. I'm not starting drinking now, I'll be pissed by eight o'clock and forget all the nuggets The Brute will give me. The casino, there's the answer. Joel had a fondness for playing blackjack and was not one to pass up the opportunity to indulge his interest.

As Joel sat in the back of the cab, he looked at his watch. It was 7.05pm. He rang Aubin and Randall.

'Hi Juliette, it's Joel – is my friend Le Brute there?'

'The quiet one?' asked Juliette.

'Yes, that's him. What's he drinking?'

'Perrier and a café.'

'I'll be there in ten minutes. Give him a bottle of Veuve Clicquot and two glasses, I'll sort the bill out when I get there.'

'*Oui*, I will tell him.'

Joel fancied Juliette, who was the most attractive member of the entire staff at Randall and Aubin. She was from Mons, twenty-five, slender with long, dark hair, and as well as looking good was excellent at her job. She remembered names and was always attentive, unlike some of her male colleagues. Joel had never quite sorted out whether she was interested in him, but Sarah knew he fancied her and teased him about his 'Continental liaison'. Fat chance.

Juliette took the champagne to Brute's table and opened it.

'Would you like me to pour?' she asked.

'No, no, there must be some mistake. I never ordered this.' Brutus had been in Aubin and Randall on a couple of occasions with Joel, and while he had drunk champagne it was always the house champagne, which was very good but certainly not Veuve Clicquot!

'Monsieur Joel ordered it.'

Brute knew Joel fancied this Belgian woman; what was he playing at? Showing off?

'Where is he?' he queried.

'He is on his way. Ten minutes he say,' replied Juliette.

'Pour away, then, I'll start without him!' Juliette poured a glass and put the bottle back in the cooler.

'I'll bring some more olives and bread,' she said, noting le Brute had already eaten those she had given him with his coffee and water.

A cab pulled up and out jumped Joel, who walked straight in and kissed Juliette on the cheek three times. 'I believe the Dutch got this right, you know, it allows me to kiss the most attractive woman in the restaurant not just twice, but three times.'

'Joel,' clucked Juliette, 'you are terrible. Your friend is waiting.' And she pointed to Brute who was sitting in the corner watching life in Brewer Street. Juliette followed Joel across and poured out his drink.

'This is a bit flash, Joel,' said Brute. 'Your private work must be paying well, or are you just trying to impress mademoiselle?'

'I'm not getting paid for it. I've just won £1,000 at the casino.' Joel then relived his exploits while he ordered zucchini frites and a seafood platter to share with his friend. During the next hour or so, Joel recounted Robert's story and his experiences in South Africa, including his ignominious return to work earlier in the day. Brute had met Robert a number of times but never discussed Jess's death. He listened intently while tucking into his food, savouring the champagne combined with the fresh seafood.

'Sounds intriguing. Is the family she was marrying into originally from South Africa?'

As Joel was talking he looked around the restaurant, a casually dressed couple had arrived and sat very close to where Brute and he were enjoying their food. Not too close, thought Joel, just close. They were ignoring them completely and ordered for themselves, but Joel thought, Watchers, there would be others, as well. He said quietly to Brute, 'Try to keep your voice down. There are others listening.' Brute spoke quietly anyway, but dropped his voice a couple of decibels. Joel then answered his question.

He explained the Corfield family were originally from England and settled in South Africa some years ago, but Matthew returned to the United Kingdom after Jessica's death to train as a barrister. Brute had heard of Matthew and actually given talks at his chambers about the use of psychology in investigation and advocacy. Joel was a little concerned about a barrister learning psychology. He himself once dabbled with it and learnt hypnosis. He told Brute he tried it on a suspect and Brute had been furious, saying it would cause all sorts of complications. Joel's response was quite straightforward.

'It did cause complications when I brought him out of it and I knew all about the job!'

Brute agreed to look at the events for Joel, which was particularly useful as he had a South African research student working with him. Joel asked Brute to see if he could find out anything about the local crime patterns. He was a little concerned about Brute's South African assistant because of 'the village' experience in Cape Town, but was reassured when he discovered she was from near Johannesburg at the other end of the country.

After finishing the champagne, Joel and Brute left in separate cabs, having agreed they would speak the following day after Brute had spoken to his PhD student. Joel couldn't see anyone following him, but suspected they were out there.

Chapter Eighteen

Joel got back to his flat around 10.30pm having phoned Sarah to tell her all his news. She was happy he was going to Budleigh Salterton the following day to spend some time with her. He went straight to bed ready to make an early start, as usual falling straight to sleep.

Joel thought the phone was his alarm clock, reached over and tried to switch it off but then realised what it was. Sleepily, Joel answered. 'Hello?'

'Is that Joel Grant? This is Somerset and Devon Fire and Rescue control room.'

'Yes, I'm Joel Grant,' said Joel, still not properly awake.

'Mr Grant, there's been a fire at Fueze in Budleigh Salterton and the occupant, Sarah Cheatam, has asked us to ring you. Ms Cheatam is fine, but she's about to be taken to the Royal Devon and Exeter hospital for a check-up. She asked us to let you know.'

'I'm sorry, I'm half asleep. There's been a fire and Sarah's being taken to hospital?'

'Yes, that's right,' said the operator. 'There's nothing to worry about, it's only for a check-up.'

'How did the fire start?' asked Joel.

'Our crews are still at the scene, but it looks like rubbish at the front of the shop caught fire. We don't know how at the moment. The fire investigation team is en route.'

'Thank you for letting me know. I'm in London, I'll make my way down. I don't suppose you have the number for the hospital, do you?' Joel always kept a pen and paper beside his bed. It was a habit he found useful when getting work calls in the middle of the night.

'Just a moment.' The operator gave Joel the number and said, 'She is just getting in the ambulance now, so leave it for an hour or so I would think.'

He said, 'Thanks very much for ringing, I really appreciate it.'

'It's a pleasure, Mr Grant, goodnight,' the operator replied.

'Goodnight,' said Joel as he wrote the time, 4.03am, on the piece of paper: another habit.

Joel got up and showered. He didn't bother to pack properly, just put some extra clothes in his bag then cooked himself a bacon and egg sandwich, made strong black coffee and drank some orange juice. He really didn't want the sandwich, but thought he ought to eat and felt a lot better for it. He looked at the clock: it was still a little early to ring the hospital so he'd phone later. Joel went down to his car, a diesel Golf, and set off for Devon. This was the only time he used a car really – to, from and around Devon. If he didn't have the house in Budleigh, he probably wouldn't bother with a car.

He drove out of London and reached the M25/M4 by 6am. He phoned the hospital and spoke to Accident and Emergency. A staff nurse told him Sarah was with a doctor and to ring back in an hour. He noticed vehicle lights in the distance behind him travelling at the same speed, but they were a long, long way back so he thought little of it.

The motorway was quiet and Joel was soon cruising at 90mph. The lights of the car he had seen earlier had gone. He reached Swindon around 6.45am and rang the hospital again. This time another staff nurse, who checked who he was, said they were keeping Sarah in for observations and she was en route to a ward. Joel thanked the nurse and didn't alert him to the fact he was on the way. He thought he'd be in Exeter, all being well, shortly before 9am. Joel was wide-awake, constantly looking in his mirrors for police cars, but fortunately there weren't any. This was interspersed with thoughts about how the fire had started.

He had moaned a number of times about Sarah leaving cardboard and tissue paper from clothes packaging and other rubbish out over-night but she ignored him. That's probably what happened: they had somehow caught fire. Perhaps he wouldn't mention it when he saw her, though!

Joel arrived at the hospital, as he'd expected, shortly before 9am and went straight to Accident and Emergency. While the nurse said earlier Sarah was on her way to the ward, he'd lots of experience of hospitals and their acute bed shortages, and found many victims of crime in A and E cubicles and corridors long after their admission by doctors.

However, on this occasion his suspicion wasn't justified. Sarah was in the Culm Ward, and when he arrived he was told she was in a side room. Joel explained what had happened and asked if it would be possible to see Sarah. The nurse checked with the Sister, who said Sarah was awake and he could have ten minutes with her. He walked into the side room and saw, in addition to being wired up to an array of machinery, she was wearing an oxygen mask. When she saw him she smiled. He leant over her and kissed her on the forehead.

'How are you feeling?' he asked.

She smiled again and said, 'I'm fine. Have you just driven down? What time is it?'

'It's about nine. Does your mother know?'

'No, she'll only worry. I was in the flat, Joel. I didn't smell the smoke until I heard the sirens. Joel, I know you were always telling me about the rubbish. I should have listened.'

'It doesn't matter about that, as long as you are OK. That's all that matters.'

She reached out and squeezed his hand, and said, 'Thanks.' Not the sort of welcome home you were expecting.' They smiled at each other.

'Joel, I want out of here. I'm fine, really,' Sarah said. ' I'm going to have to sort the shop out, it will be a real mess. I have been decorating it.'

'It doesn't matter about the shop, I can get that organised,' he said, but he knew Sarah would want to be discharged at the first opportunity, which he presumed would be later in the day, all being well. 'What do you want me to bring in for you?'

'If you can, bring me some clothes, pyjamas, slippers and a dressing gown from your house. Those at the flat will reek of smoke. Oh, and my make-up, brush and toothbrush.'

Joel noticed her eyes were closing, and said, 'OK, get some sleep. I'll see you later.'

She opened her eyes and said softly, 'Thanks for coming, Joel, I wasn't sure you would.'

'Don't be silly,' he told her as he leant forward and kissed her on the head. Sarah's eyes closed again.

Joel went back to see the Sister and said Sarah was sleepy. The Sister thought this was a good sign. She told him the doctor would be around during the morning, but visiting time was in the afternoon. When Joel asked if it was OK to bring some of Sarah's things in, she smiled in agreement. He thanked her and returned to the car, having a mild panic when he walked past someone paying for parking at a meter until he remembered he had paid when he arrived.

Budleigh was only half-an-hour from the hospital on a good run, but Joel thought it would take longer in the morning traffic. It did. When he arrived in the town he went straight to the shop on the corner of High Street. It had been a hardware shop before Sarah bought it, and now it looked like a hardware shop again with large wooden boards in the windows masking the fire damage. He parked his car in the car park over the road and could smell the fire when he got out. Walking up to the shop, he saw the front door was padlocked and all the debris had been swept away. There were large scorch marks in the doorway. Joel went next door to Molly and Alan, the greengrocers.

As he walked through the door, Molly said, 'She's had a lucky escape, Joel, a lesson for us all I think. Have you been to the hospital? How is she?'

'She's fine, thanks Molly, hopefully out later today.' Joel was conscious the customers in the shop had stopped shopping and were listening too. They were probably all locals so it was just as well they heard the fact Sarah was fine, rather than the rumour mill, which would probably have her dead by now. 'Do you know what happened, Molly?' Joel enquired.

'Rubbish caught fire, that what's the fire brigade and police say. We all do it, Joel, but with us it would have just been a few roast veg, not all Sarah's lovely clothes.'

'Nobody knows how it started, but they think cigarettes or something,' added Alan.

'At four in the morning?' Joel sounded doubtful.

'Joel, there's all sorts around on this street at night. All sorts.' Everyone in the shop, except Joel, nodded in agreement.

'Do you know who's got the key for the padlock?' Joel asked.

'Police, I expect,' said Alan. 'You'll have to go Exmouth, though, that's where they'll have it.' Joel knew the local police station wasn't open to the public any more, part of the Government's cost cutting, although in reality it didn't get many visitors. It did give the local people a lot of confidence, however. He could not understand it, but with the closures of banks, post offices and shops over the years it was natural, he supposed.

One of the customers piped up, 'I've just seen Lesley going in the police station. She parked the car outside, she might be able to help.'

Joel thanked him and said he would try. The shoppers and shopkeepers all asked him to pass on their best wishes to Sarah, which he said he would. This was one of the nice things about living in Devon: people still cared.

Joel knew Lesley was one of the police and community support officers. PCSOs had virtually become the face of policing in many communities in towns, cities and villages. Joel felt they were very good, but too much was thrown on them. They were expected to be police without the powers or training. He pressed the bell and Lesley answered the door. Joel had known the public to be turned away from police stations because they weren't open to callers and the officers inside thought it was beneath them to deal with the public, but he knew this was not the case in Budleigh.

After hearing who he was and what he was after, Lesley asked him to come into the station and made a telephone call which confirmed the keys were in Exmouth police station. As long as he got there by 2pm he could have them. Another victim of the Government's cuts!

Joel asked Lesley if she knew what had happened. She said she had just arrived and heard from locals it was probably a discarded cigarette. Lesley wasn't having any of this and suggested he speak to the fire investigation people who she thought were good. On the way back to the car, Joel overheard a conversation between two locals and a reporter from *The Herald*. They too were not convinced about the theory of a cigarette starting the fire at four in the morning.

Joel really wanted to have a good look at the scene, but not while the reporter was around so he went on to his house. It seemed a little strange to be there after being away for nearly a month, but he thought he'd better get used to it. He would probably be spending a lot more time here over the next few weeks. While he was driving down earlier in the morning he found himself thinking again about Fiona Henderson and seeing her at the doctors. He would give her a ring on the pretext of telling her he was in Devon while he was on the sick. It was now eleven o'clock, as good a time as any to ring her. He phoned her mobile, Fiona answered right away.

'Hello, Guvn'r, it's Joel. Can you speak?'

'Go on, Joel, how is the fatigue?' she asked in an unusually formal way.

'Guvn'r, I'm in Devon. Sarah's shop and flat caught fire last night and she was taken to hospital. I travelled down overnight.'

'I am sorry to hear that. How is she?'

'She's fine. The doctor is looking at her this morning, I'll find out more later.'

'OK, keep me in touch.' Fiona asked how he was, and was he looking after himself as well as Sarah now. She also said some people had been asking about him. Code for Professional Standards, thought Joel.

'Well you know where I am if they want to talk to me. How are you, Guvn'r?'

Fiona was surprised by this enquiry from Joel, it wasn't like him. 'What do you mean?' she said sharply.

'You know what I mean, the doc's. You're as fit as a butchers dog, what's up?'

'Oh, nothing serious, only a few tests I need to have, that's all.'

'What sort of tests?' Joel enquired.

'Joel, I don't understand this surprising but very caring interest on my behalf *on the phone*.' With a slight emphasis on "on the phone" she was telling him to be careful what he said again.

'OK, Guvn'r, but if you need a break I can recommend east Devon, and we've got plenty of room.'

'Really, Joel, I'm fine. You get yourself sorted and look after Sarah.'

Joel considered his conversation, which was probably the most decent he'd had with Fiona for a long, long time. Fiona was thinking the same. The warning was odd; something was happening around him and he had no idea what. He was starting to get the distinct impression someone was 'looking at him'. He didn't know who; he didn't know why – the only possible answer was his visit to South Africa.

Chapter Nineteen

Joel phoned the hospital, and the staff nurse told him the doctors' rounds had been delayed until early afternoon but they were very happy with Sarah's progress. Joel said he'd bring her clothes in at visiting time. He said it as though he was talking to a third party on the line, something people who suspected they were subject to eavesdropping sometimes did. He didn't know why, but they did.

There was a knock at his door. He looked out of a bedroom window and saw it was Robert. Joel put some shoes and a coat on, deliberately left his mobile phone in the bedroom and opened the door.

Robert said, 'Joel, I'm sorry about Sarah. I've just heard.'

Joel took Robert by the arm and said, 'Let's walk.' Robert didn't complain, but was a little stunned by Joel's behaviour. Joel led Robert to the edge of town, along the footpath past the golf course and on to the coastal path. On the walk Joel told Robert he thought he was possibly being watched or his calls listened to, or both. He didn't know by whom or why, but he told Robert to be careful too in case it was about South Africa. Robert considered saying it was outrageous, but thought better of it.

Joel also asked Robert if the exhibits had arrived. They had not. For some reason they were in Accra, due to arrive in the United Kingdom tomorrow. Robert confirmed this sometimes happened with international cargo for very innocent reasons, and Joel remembered watching afternoon TV, months ago, where uncollected air cargo was being auctioned off. This strangely reassured him.

Joel asked Robert to go into Exeter and buy him a pay-as-you-go phone. He told Robert to watch and see if he was being followed and to text Ali, but not to contact Joel until he got a new number. Robert asked Joel what was going on, and Joel told him very genuinely he didn't know but they all had to be careful. Robert and Joel now walked along the path back into town, and the only people they saw were women golfers and a couple of hikers. Joel didn't think they were followed.

Leaving Robert in the town centre, Joel went back to the house, put Sarah's things in a bag and set off for Exmouth police station. He considered using his grandfather's Morris Minor Traveller, which he kept maintained, to confuse any followers, but thought there was no point. If he was being watched, they would know where he was going. He'd keep the Traveller in reserve.

At the police station, Joel explained who he was and was handed the keys for the padlock and a copy of the work sheet from the boarding up firm. The inquiry officer asked who the bill should be sent to. Joel intended telling the officer to send it to him, but thought Professional Standards may try and suggest he was involved in running a business. He gave Sarah's name and address; he was getting even more suspicious.

After the police station, he went to the hospital via the supermarket, which was just around the corner from the hospital, to pick up some shopping. Parking in hospitals at visiting times was never easy, despite the exorbitant car parking fees. Joel eventually found somewhere to park, paid the meter and made his way to Culm Ward again. He went straight to the nursing station as he was early for visiting and asked the Sister, who was the same one he had seen earlier, if he could leave Sarah's things for her. The Sister said there was no need as the doctor had discharged Sarah and she could go home. The Sister said she would take the bag in and he should wait in the day room.

Half-an-hour later Sarah came from the ward with the Sister. She looked tired, but had showered and made herself up as though she was going for a night out. The Sister explained Sarah was to take things easy; she had an inhaler to help her breathe, and if there were any problems they were to call an ambulance, which would bring her straight back. Joel and Sarah thanked her and made their way to the car, with Sarah asking all sorts of questions about insurance cover, causation of the fire and what would happen now.

When they got home, Sarah said she needed to lie down. Joel realised it was probably still the effect of whatever they'd given her in hospital and general exhaustion.

Joel was desperate to look around the shop to try and find out what had happened, but Sarah had gone to bed and he couldn't leave her alone. He thought about ringing the fire service and speaking to the fire investigators, but reconsidered, he'd give them another day or so. Anyway he wanted to look at the damage himself. He busied himself around the house, including slipping through the internal door into the garage to make sure the Traveller was still working. It started first time. He had deliberately parked the Golf on the drive away from the garage door so he could get the Traveller out without starting or moving the Golf, just in case any 'extra electrical equipment' had been fitted to it recently. He could always use Sarah's Range Rover, but it had cost a fortune and he didn't trust himself. He always saw its purchase at nearly £100,000 as her umbilical cord to banking.

Sarah got up about 5pm, but was still a little groggy and wasn't really hungry. She said she wanted to go and see the shop but Joel told her there was no point, and anyway it would be dark, he didn't mention it would be dark at anytime because of the boards over the windows. Joel suggested she phone her mother, who would be wondering where she was, and her friend Rosemary, who was a banker. Sarah hadn't really been up to it earlier, but was now.

Joel was getting hungry and poured himself a gin and tonic to suppress his appetite. Not surprisingly Sarah only wanted water; she was still coughing from the smoke inhalation. There was a knock at the door; Joel went to answer it and found Robert.

'Is Sarah home? Is she OK?'

'Yes, come in.'

'No, no, I won't disturb you. It's your first night home.' He looked around behind him, pulled a package from under his coat and said, 'I've told Ali, he understands.'

Understands what? thought Joel. I wish I did.

'Give me a ring tomorrow, bye.' Robert was off down the drive as quickly as he had arrived. To the observer the visit would have looked furtive – just what Joel didn't want.

Joel came back into the house and went to the bedroom to sort the phone out. He sent the same text to Marta, Ali, Billy and Robert:

From JG. Don't use other number, may be compromised. I will ring you. Only use this in emergency.

He hoped the others' phones weren't being intercepted. He couldn't see it – or could he? It would probably cause all sorts of turmoil in those who received the message, except Robert, but it would stop them ringing him. He debated texting the Guvn'r, but thought it may cause her problems.

Joel went downstairs and Sarah asked who had been at the door, when he told her it was Robert who wanted to know how she was doing, she looked surprised. Joel made some pasta and they spent the rest of the evening talking about his trip to South Africa, the fire and finally Sarah's trip to Paris. Sarah bought a lot of her clothes from Paris, which was one of the reasons the shop was so successful. She also spent her time visiting the sights. No matter how many times Sarah visited Paris, she still liked to go to the Louvre, the Bois de Boulogne, the Elysées, Montmartre and the Courtier areas around the Eighth, Nineth and Tenth Arrondissement. She loved the pace, the style, the ambiance, and would dearly like to live there. She felt the visit to Paris had recharged her batteries and this is why she started to redecorate. Sarah was someone who was usually quite methodical and thoughtful, so Joel found it odd.

They went to bed about ten o'clock. It was the first time they had slept together for a couple of weeks, and while they continued to talk, mainly about the shop, the fire and the clearing up, they drifted off to sleep without making love, again!

It was 6am the following morning when Joel woke up. He switched on his new mobile to see if there were any messages. There weren't. Sarah was still fast asleep when he went out for a run a little later and he left her a note in case she was worried. Joel followed the same route he had walked the previous day, again looking around to see if there were any strangers in the town, but he didn't see any. Back at the house he had a shower after which he started to make coffee, but he could hear Sarah coughing and went up to see if she was OK. She said she was and asked him to get into bed with her. Joel forgot about the coffee, jumped in the bed and they made love for the first time in over two weeks. Joel fell asleep with Sarah lying awake beside him.

Around 8.30am Joel woke and heard Sarah in the shower. He got up and asked her what she wanted for breakfast. She said she wasn't really hungry, but Joel insisted she had a croissant. Sarah was desperate to visit the shop so they dressed and made their way into the town. As they passed Alan and Molly's, they were waved in by Molly. Concern showing on her face, she said, 'Sarah, how are you?' Sarah confirmed she was fine after having a night in hospital and now a night at home.

Alan, who was serving a customer at the other side of the shop, shouted across, 'I said to Joel yesterday it would have been someone smoking and throwing a cigarette down with all those paint tins and things.'

Joel said, 'Paint tins? What paint tins?'

'I put the paint tins out as well, Joel, the ones I had been using to decorate.'

'Oh,' he said, now having a better understanding of how the fire had taken light so quickly and so ferociously.

Sarah said to Alan and Molly, 'We are just going to have a look round to see the extent of the damage.'

Alan added, 'The smell has almost gone, but goodness knows what it's like in there.' Sarah and Joel said cheerio and walked around to the shop. Joel had brought a powerful torch with him from his house as he anticipated it would be pitch black in the shop. It was. He had also told Sarah to put some old clothes on, because going into burnt buildings left a lasting smell on clothes. He'd had to have a number of suits dry-cleaned as a result of visiting fatal fires in London.

Joel looked at the seat of the fire; it had clearly been quite ferocious and intense. They saw the front door had been badly burnt when they removed the interim door and went inside. The fire looked as though it had quickly caught hold of the clothing with all its delicate fabric, and what hadn't been burnt was now black and covered in soot. Sarah started to cry. Joel held her arm in a comforting gesture and said, 'Don't worry, it can all be replaced.'

She said, 'But Joel, I had just painted the place. It looked so lovely.' They walked around the back and into Sarah's flat. The doors had been broken down by the fire service, but other than the smell of smoke and a little smoke damage the flat was fine. She looked outside and saw her car was still there, parked in the small garden area at the rear. There was debris in the garden but it was nowhere near the car.

They collected the clothes from the drawers, which were not particularly smoke damaged and Joel drove them to his house in the Range Rover. He parked the car in front of the Golf, but not in front of the garage. Sarah thought this was odd but didn't say anything to him. She spent the rest of the morning speaking to the loss adjuster whom she arranged to meet later at the shop. As she was doing this, Joel spoke to the fire service.

The fire investigator was very helpful. He said the seat of the fire had been where Joel had seen it, but he couldn't understand how it had been caused. A number of locals talked about a discarded cigarette, and while the investigator thought it could have been a potential cause, adding, a discarded cigarette usually remained alight for only two or three minutes without oxygen being drawn through it, he couldn't understand why someone would throw a cigarette in the doorway shortly before 4am. The investigator also confirmed the tins of paint were probably one of the reasons why the fire had been so intense, perhaps coupled with some thinners or meths which he suspected had also been present, although he couldn't find a container. He was certain there had been an accelerant other than paint.

Joel asked Sarah what she had put outside the shop. She remembered she had put some cardboard, tissues and papers together with the old paint tins. Joel asked about any thinners. Sarah said she had used meths to clean the brushes and the bottle was still in the storage area at the rear of the shop. Joel wondered where the accelerant for the fire had come from.

This was beginning to look odd. He began to think about CCTV in the town. There were signs but he'd never noticed any cameras, and the signs tended to be near car parks. He assumed they were designed to be deterrents, but he would make enquiries about it.

Joel asked Sarah if she wanted him to go with her to meet the loss adjuster. She said it wasn't necessary; she would go down and do it herself, so Joel said he would walk into town with her as he needed to get a few things from the shops. They separated when they reached the High Street, and all the way Joel was looking for buildings with CCTV cameras. He found none. He kissed Sarah goodbye and started to look into the shop and office windows, like any other local or tourist. Budleigh had a real variety of shops, from up-market clothes shops to pharmacies, butchers, bakers, pubs, restaurants and tourist shops. It was really an old fashioned seaside High Street and Joel liked it.

He spent the rest of the day visiting every building on and around the High Street in search of CCTV coverage of the street. He found no difficulty in accessing the CCTV in the shops and buildings when he explained who he was and what he was doing. The business people all said it could have been them; Joel didn't think so, though. The shops and firms had all placed their CCTV inside the buildings, which was completely understandable but meant when he reviewed the coverage the outside images through windows or doors were poor. Even the pubs only had internal coverage; very different from large cities and towns where CCTV covered all the entrances to pubs and nightclubs. There were no nightclubs in Budleigh.

While Joel was reviewing the coverage from the night of the fire in one of the clothes shops, he noticed at 3.55am a car being driven slowly down the High Street. He couldn't see what colour or make it was; in fact, he couldn't even see if it was a car, van or lorry, but it was a vehicle of some sort. Joel thought this was interesting, but could not get any better coverage from the other cameras around the town, which were of variable condition and quality.

There were only two main ways into Budleigh, one to the east and one to the west, and Joel thought he'd try his luck along those roads tomorrow, all being well. He was walking back home when he passed William Goble's house, The Oaks: a big imposing Georgian house just off the High Street. What Joel had not noticed before was it had a number of very discreet CCTV cameras around it. Joel walked up the driveway and rang the doorbell.

The door was answered by William. 'Hello, Joel, how are you? Terrible news about Sarah's shop. Is she ok?'

'She's fine thanks, William. I was going to come round to thank you for helping Robert, but there is something else I'd like to chat with you about if you have a minute?'

'Please come in,' said William and he led Joel through to a study overlooking the rear garden, which contained a swimming pool. 'Would you like a drink? Tea, coffee, perhaps a beer or gin?'

It was four o'clock, but Joel considered he'd worked hard and said, 'A gin would be welcome.' William disappeared for a moment and returned with two gin and tonics.

'Excellent. Now what can I do for you, Joel?'

'I have just noticed you have CCTV on your house.'

'Yes. It's a long and rather sad story.' William described how, because of some people he represented, animal rights activists threatened him about eighteen months ago. They found out where he lived because of a stupid MP, aided by an inadequate jaundiced 'troll' type person in Somerset who didn't like success. William couldn't understand it; he just been representing his clients, who themselves had been subject to arson attacks at their homes, but nevertheless the police said he was a target and persuaded him to have CCTV installed. Joel thought William wasn't finished with the MP, or the troll.

'But how can that help you?' asked William.

Joel explained about the fire, his suspicions and some of the fallout from his South African trip. He told William about the CCTV coverage in the town on which he'd seen a vehicle on the High Street about the time of the fire, and wondered if William's CCTV would show anything. He asked where the CCTV was monitored, and William told him it was a commercial company somewhere in Bristol who would alert the police about suspicious behaviour. Fortunately there hadn't been any.

'William, do you have the contact details for the company? I'll give them a ring and ask if I can go to review the footage, if you don't mind.'

'No need for that, old boy, come with me.' William took Joel through to the integral garage, where he saw what appeared to be a mini CCTV control room.

'The police describe this as "a safe room". I've got one upstairs as well, but this one has all the CCTV stuff and the monitors in. What do you think?'

'Amazing!' said Joel, looking at the coverage from eight cameras. He only noticed three earlier.

William sat down and asked Joel, 'Now when was the fire? Tuesday morning, wasn't it? What time?'

'About four in the morning.'

'OK, we'll review 3.30 to 4.30am.' William pressed a number of buttons. One by one each of the camera views came up on the monitors and showed fast forward images between the times chosen by William. The first four were of the rear of the house, and William stopped the camera to watch a deer nibbling at his rose bushes and a badger walking over his lawn.

'Bloody deer!' William muttered and continued.

The fifth and sixth cameras covered part of the High Street. There was no movement at all on the street except one car, which came from the direction of Exmouth. It was an old Nissan with 'Roxy Cabs' on the side. Joel didn't know many of the local taxi firms and he had never heard of Roxy Cabs. The car then turned into a side street. William continued to fast forward the recording. Shortly before 3.50am two men appeared from the same side street and went into the doorway of Sarah's shop. Joel thought they may have been trying to break in or having sex. Anyway, after a short time they exited the shop doorway and went around the corner again. Some three minutes later a strong glow emerged from the doorway and Joel could see a fire had started.

Joel looked at William. 'Very interesting,' he said. 'I don't suppose you can enhance this to see if we can get the car number, William?'

'Mmm, I think so, but could you do me a favour first, please? Our G and T s are dry. You'll find the gin in the drawing room, tonic in the fridge and ice in the freezer.'

Joel went to get the gin and tonics, and while he was doing it he thought about William. William was a real dab hand with the CCTV, and Joel wondered how much time he spent on it.

Joel returned to the garage. 'Good man, Joel, now let's have a look at this.' William had an image on the monitor showing the car and its registration plate: LL51 HYS.

'William, you're a star. That is brilliant.' Joel could have hugged him.

'Don't forget, Joel, they're only images,' cautioned William the lawyer. 'They could mean anything.'

'Yes, but it's a start, a good start. Thanks, William.'

They discussed how to retain the footage. William said he would run a copy off and ask the company to retain the coverage from 1am to 5am. They agreed this would be fine. Joel finished his G and T, thanked William again and almost ran home to tell Sarah. He looked at his watch: it was almost six and he wondered why Sarah hadn't rung. Then he remembered – his new habit of switching his phone off.

He walked through the door to be met by Sarah. 'So, you not only disappear to South Africa, you disappear in Budleigh as well. I've been ringing you since 4.30, where have you been? And you've been drinking, I can smell it!'

The elation drained from his body. He walked through into the lounge, sat down and said, 'Sarah, please sit down. I'll tell you what I've been doing,' and recounted what he had found out with William. After he finished his explanation, which took a good ten minutes, Sarah said, 'I'm sorry, Joel, I feel awful. I'm sorry.'

Joel rose from his seat, gave her a hug and said he understood. They spent the rest of the evening trying to think of reasons why anyone would deliberately set fire to the shop and talking about the insurance visit. Joel dismissed any connection between South Africa and Sarah.

Sarah said the loss adjuster was a bit stroppy because he felt she was to blame for leaving the materials out on the doorstep. She'd said this was normal custom and practice as the bin men came really early in the morning and everyone did exactly the same. She felt it was going to be a bit difficult. However, he did approve the ripping out and refurbishment of the shop: the argument would be over the price of the stock and the relative contributory negligence part of it. He also agreed for the flat to be redecorated and anything damaged in there to be replaced. Sarah was quite happy with this, but she was still suffering with her cough as they watched the TV and started thinking about contractors.

Chapter Twenty

The next morning Joel rang the police and asked to be put through to the CID covering Budleigh Salterton. He was eventually connected to a police station in Exeter, and explained the situation and the fact he had found CCTV footage of a car in the area at the time. The person he was talking to, whose name he elicited as Eliza Quarry, said, 'Because there wasn't enough evidence and it was clearly an accident, the police were not involved.'

Joel said, 'But you don't know whether there has been a crime because you haven't investigated it.'

Ms Quarry said dismissively, 'The police attended at the time, and according to the information it was a fire of discarded rubbish.' This did not satisfy Joel, who asked to be transferred to her supervisor. Bristling somewhat, she connected him with a DS Bennett. Joel explained the situation to the Detective Sergeant, who was probably not related to Robert, and he too said as there was no offence they would not view the material.

Joel followed up with, 'Well I'm making an allegation of arson. How are you going to investigate this offence?'

The DS became annoyed at Joel's attitude and pointed out he had no right to make an allegation. Joel explained as the partner of the person who owned the premises he had every right. This was a case of arson and he wanted to know what DS Bennett was going to do about it.

Again, DS Bennett became hostile and defensive.

Joel countered, 'Can I speak to your supervisor, please?

'There isn't anyone here. I am the supervisor in charge.'

Supervisor in charge! This guy's been watching too many American cop shows, thought Joel.

He tried again. He said he understood they might not have the capacity to look through the CCTV, but he had done so and found a car in the street plus two men going into the shop doorway at the same time the fire started. When the DS discovered Joel had not actually seen the men get out of the car and three minutes had elapsed before the fire started he said there was no evidence of arson.

Joel said, 'Are you going to check out this car number?'

The DS replied, 'No. There is no offence, no concrete connection with the vehicle and therefore I won't be doing it.'

Joel slammed the phone down. He wasn't very happy with this person. He picked up his new phone and rang Billy, who was looking after his flat. Having established Billy had not noticed anything suspicious, such as people hanging around or anything changed in the rooms, Joel told him he wanted a vehicle check.

'A vehicle check? What do you mean?' said Billy.

'I want you to check the following car: a blue Nissan, LL51 HYS. Sarah's shop has been fired and I suspect it was arson, but the local plod down here won't do anything about it.' Joel told Billy there had been a taxi from Roxy Cabs on the street a short while before the fire, but there was no trace of Roxy Cabs locally. Billy agreed to carry out the check, and then said, 'What's this about a new phone?'

'I know you think I may be mad, but I am sure there are people listening to my phone and I want you to use this number to contact me. Can you give the number to Suzy, but only to phone in an emergency?'

'OK, OK, Joel. No problem,' replied Billy.

Joel phoned Ali and asked if the exhibits had arrived. Ali explained they were due to arrive later in the afternoon. He had spoken to the lab; they'd had an influx over the last few days, and because of its historical nature Joel's case would be put on hold for a couple of days, unless, of course, he wanted to pay extra. Joel considered this, and thought while it was frustrating he completely understood it, and he certainly didn't want to involve any extra expense, even if it meant a few more days. It had already been twenty years. However, he would speak to Robert and Frederick about it.

The next phone call, with Robert, was not an easy one as he was annoyed at the delay. Joel worked hard to placate him and in the end he understood it, but was still irked. Joel rang Marta's number but there was no reply, which was strange. He then rang the office number directly through to Marta's desk. Again there was no response, so he left an answerphone message.

'Marta, this is Joel. Can you please tell your father that there has been a delay in relation to the exhibits. It's going to take longer than we thought – not too much longer, but a little while. I will email you and let you know the detail.' Joel wrote an email to Marta while Sarah was busy talking to the contractors, then thought twice about it. He'd send it from a new account at an internet café.

During the next few days Joel continued to watch out but didn't see anything. Carrying on with his new running regime, he thought through his trip to South Africa, Sarah and their relationship, the attack on her shop and the subsequent fallout, which had not brought them closer together. He began to wonder what their future, if any, looked like. Billy in the interim found out the car was in fact registered to Roxy Cars with an address, south of the Thames.

Chapter Twenty-One

The days in Budleigh passed quickly. Sarah was busy organising the shop, and one Sunday travelled to Bristol to see her friend Rosemary, who was visiting for the weekend, and stayed overnight. The next morning Joel was almost ready to go for a run when his 'throw away' phone rang. It could only be one of a small number of people; four or five maximum.

It was Marta. He knew from the tone of her voice something was wrong. 'Hi, Joel, bad news I'm afraid. Kem has been attacked in prison. He's in hospital, he's very ill. Papa and Thembi are with him.' Marta pumped out this information in a staccato fashion, almost like a machine gun.

'What happened, Marta?' Joel said, shocked. 'Tell me the detail.'

'The phone went at Papa's house sometime early this morning. It was Thembi. She told him her brother was being taken to hospital. The prison had phoned the hotel where she works and got a message to her, goodness knows how. Kem was taken to Groote Schuur Hospital. Thembi told Papa his condition was critical. Papa went to pick her up as she had gone to the prison and he took her to the hospital. Kem was in theatre, and as far as I know he still is. Papa rang the prison from the hospital and they said they were still investigating. They wouldn't tell him much other than Kem had been attacked and he was now in hospital, which of course Papa knew. That was where he was ringing in from, fools! He rang me at work and I'm on my way to the prison now to ask some questions.'

Joel said quickly, 'Shouldn't you leave that to your father, Marta?' He could feel her bristling, despite being 6,000 miles away.

'Not women's work, eh Joel?'

He apologised immediately; he had forgotten momentarily how Marta could get prickly when she felt patronised. He explained what he

132

meant was her father knew the prison and the people there. Mollified, Marta told Joel her father wanted to stay at the hospital to support Kem and his family. He was seriously concerned the explanations from the prison would start to change, so she had been to court and secured an order which meant the prison authorities would have to help whether they liked it or not. The court had been most sympathetic given the history of the prison, and she hoped the order might prove to be unnecessary, but they were prepared just in case.

Joel understood, but the prison was a dangerous place for anyone, as Kem had just found out. He was reassured to discover Marimam was with Marta. Those two together were more than a match for the South African Correctional Service, he thought.

Joel told Marta he would like to speak to her father when he was free and urged them to take care.

'We will,' came two voices in unison. 'Speak to you later,' added Marta.

The call ended, and Joel reflected how strange it was Kem had survived all those years free from attack, or so it would appear. Now he was attacked for the first time. Very strange, Joel mused.

Five minutes later Joel's phone rang again. He could hear it but couldn't find it. Then he realised he had slipped it into his jacket pocket after talking to Marta.

'Hello, Joel, it's Frederick Weisner calling from South Africa. How are you?'

This was typical of what he had learnt about Frederick: always clear, always concise. 'I'm fine, thank you. How are things there?' he asked. 'How is Kem? What happened?'

'Things are a lot better than they were, Joel. Kem's condition has stabilised, thank goodness. I have spoken to the surgeon. Kem was stabbed in the back and it punctured his perineal sac, which holds the heart. A few centimetres either way and he would have been dead. Fortunately it wasn't in the neck, which is the usual method in the prison, and when he was attacked there were other prisoners near him who knew him. They apparently stopped the attack and alerted the guards to get Kem to hospital, which they did relatively quickly. The prison hospital immediately realised it was too serious for them and arranged his transfer here.'

'Why now? It seems strange to me,' commented Joel.

'Yes, really strange, but I'm afraid the answers lie within the prison, not here, Joel. That's why Marta and Marimam are at the prison, asking that very question. Kem will be sedated for twenty-four hours. There is nothing you can do, Joel. Let's wait and see what comes of the prison investigations – the official one and the one being conducted by Weisner and Co.' Frederick then changed the subject. 'How are things going at your end, Joel? Slowly?'

Joel looked around. He wasn't sure why; he was on his own, for God's sake! 'Yes, that's right, Frederick. It's a difficult line,' he responded rather formally.

'Ah yes, I understand,' said Frederick. 'I have been in a similar position on many occasions over the years.' Frederick quickly grasped Joel's reluctance to talk about details even on this phone.

Frederick again switched subjects. 'Once I have heard from Marta, I will let you know what happened. No.' He stopped himself. 'She will ring you direct, far better than through a messenger. We will no doubt speak again soon.'

'If there is anything I can do, just let me know. I feel so helpless.'

'I know, Joel, but you concentrate on your end and let's see what our intrepid investigators come back with. Then we can reassess what's happening.'

'OK, I'm just trying to be the distant detective.'

'I know. Goodbye for the moment, Joel Grant.'

'Goodbye for the moment, Frederick Weisner.' The call ended.

Joel moved to his laptop and searched Cape News – nothing. He reminded himself what a violent place Pollsmoor Prison was, with spaces for four thousand prisoners but actually housing over seven thousand, including the numbers gangs.

After what seemed hours since Joel spoke to Frederick, he had heard nothing from Marta. In fact it was six hours; what could be taking them so long? The prison was only 25km out of Cape Town city centre, and Marta had her mobile with her. He thought about phoning Marta or Frederick, but remembered how much he himself hated being hassled when he was doing an investigation. It was the habit of some managers in the absence of information to enquire what was going on. Joel considered this was necessary for some who might be idling their time in the pub, cafe, gym or fornicating, but it wasn't dealing with the symptoms or the problem.

Being a detective was a responsible position. The very nature of the fact they did not wear uniform gave them greater freedom than their uniformed colleagues, freedom which shouldn't be abused by idleness. Joel told all his staff he trusted them, but if they let him down there would be no second chances. They all understood this, and during the last three years only one abused the trust. He was no longer in the CID. However, this philosophy was not applied by some of Joel's bosses, although funnily enough it was one Fiona Henderson had come to adopt over the years. Joel 'educated' his bosses in this philosophy, some subtly, some bluntly. It tended to be the inexperienced, insecure ones who adopted an 'interruptive style of management', and this certainly wasn't leadership, Joel thought. He'd leave Marta and Frederick alone.

Marta must have read his mind, again. His phone rang.

'Hi Joel, it's Marta,' said the voice on the other end.

'Good to hear from you, I was getting a little worried. Sorry, I couldn't help it knowing a little about Pollsmoor.'

'It's OK,' said Marta, 'Marimam and Papa are both here and you're on loudspeaker. We thought it would be better if Marimam and I ran through the story once to make sure it's consistent. Is that OK? I forgot to ask, can you talk?'

'Yes, no problem. Good idea, you two.'

'Right, I'll start. Marimam, you interrupt when you want, don't wait until the end, and Joel, if I drop into local colloquialism, stop me. I've heard some new words today.'

'Me too,' agreed Marimam.

Marta continued, 'We got to the prison all right, but it was then the problems started. That ex-policeman was there – the one you got fired, Papa.'

'Van Wisents?' Frederick queried.

'Yes, that's him. I made a deliberate note of his name,' said Marimam, chuckling. 'He didn't like it.'

Marta carried on, 'He said we couldn't go into the prison. It was a matter for the Department of Correction and SAPS, nothing to do with lawyers. He added spitefully, "The sister was here, speak to her. She'll tell you what happened."

'I informed him I was acting under judicial authority and showed him the court document. He ignored it, said it meant nothing to him, Papa. I thought it wouldn't, the ignorant pig, so I asked him directly if he was refusing to help us and give us the information we desired.

'The ignorant pig said, "That's right, you have no rights here."

'As I was still in the reception, I thought I'd better leave the grounds before I made any calls, so Marimam and I left the prison through the barriers, but still within sight. I phoned Jean Van Gil. Papa, it was a legitimate call, his police station covers the prison.'

Her father didn't comment. Not for the first time, Joel thought, she's good. She's very good. Marta continued, 'We returned to the reception area and a few minutes later Van Wisents was called to the phone and disappeared. Ten minutes later Jean Van Gil arrived. I told him, in the hearing of everyone in the reception area, that Van Wisents was obstructing me from carrying out the court's instructions and that I wanted him to be arrested.

Jean went to the reception counter and spoke to the people who had been listening to my monologue. He told them he wanted to see the director of the prison and Van Wisents immediately. Almost simultaneously a man appeared and introduced himself as the duty senior manager. Jean said something like, "Ms Weisner and her colleague are acting on behalf of Kem Siblisi and his family under judicial authority, and your office has obstructed them in the pursuance of their duties."

'The official said there must have been some confusion and that we were very welcome to make inquiries, and asked us into the prison. Jean said, "Your officer obstructed these people acting under judicial authority without just cause." Oh the language! You should have seen his face, Papa. Jean was very good. The prison manager said he knew you, Papa. His name is Bilson.'

Frederick confirmed he knew Bilson. 'He is a good man,' he added.

Marta took up the story again. 'Jean said, "You may help these people, but where is the officer who obstructed them? I need to take him to the judge." Marimam pointed behind the screens and said, "There he is." Jean said firmly, "Please ask him to come out here" which he did. Oh, and then the fun really started, didn't it, Marimam?'

Marimam took over, 'Mr Van Gil said he was a police detective from Diepriver police station and the two people with him were colleagues. He told Van Wisents he was arresting him for attempting to obstruct or defeat the course of justice and was taking him to see the judge who issued the documents earlier. He told Van Wisents to put his hands behind his back, which he did. The police handcuffed him, took his belt and the equipment attached to it, then comes the best part – his trousers fell down! Everyone in the reception area started to laugh, and do you know why, Mr Frederick, Mr Joel? He was wearing boxer shorts with pink hearts on them. Do you believe it? The people in reception were mostly from the townships, would you believe it, Mr Frederick? Everyone will know.'

Marta took over again. 'One of the detectives pulled the trousers up and put Van Wisents's hands on them to keep them up. Van Wisents was as red as a beetroot when taken away by Jean and his colleagues. Bilson allowed us to enter the prison. He took us to his office and asked what we wanted. I said, "To see the report of the incident, any statements made and details of the assailant."

'Bilson warned us some requests were easier than others, but asked if we would like him to give an overview of the prison regimes first to help us understand what may or may not have gone on. We said that would be very helpful, which it certainly proved to be. He told us the prison should house 4,000 prisoners, it actually has 7,000 today.

Wikipedia was accurate, thought Joel.

'The prisoners are housed in different blocks and sections. He said there are about 1,200 prison staff, and the prison is run with the cooperation of the "numbers" gangs. No matter how disturbing this is to the outside world, the gangs had been around a long time and are in every prison in South Africa. He was very open about them, and said post-Apartheid the gangs became more powerful as the guards could no longer get away with the arbitrary and cruel beatings, or even killings, which had taken place during Apartheid.'

'It is true,' interrupted Frederick. 'The NGOs and human rights groups regularly visit and check on the welfare of prisoners which certainly was not generally allowed previously, or if it was they were given partial, controlled access.'

'Anyway, there are three main gangs,' Marta continued, 'the Twenty-sixes, Twenty-sevens and Twenty-eights. Rather than go into the background, Joel, just have a look on the Internet if you want to understand their history. It's fascinating and horrific.'

'No problem, I had a look after visiting the prison with your father, and again today following the attack on Kem.'

'Those who don't join the gangs are fair game, it would appear. They're mistreated and sometimes taken into the gangs as "wifeys". You can imagine what that means.'

Joel could, graphically.

'Kem was not in a gang, but he had a privileged non-gang affiliated status among them all.'

'I have explained this to Joel,' Frederick added.

'What this meant in practice was that he was protected by all three gangs who sought his advice and guidance, not only in relation to internal prison disputes but also legal advice on issues on the outside world – property, tort, criminal and, increasingly, human rights issues. The prisoners sought Kem's advice before going to lawyers on the outside, and this status of Kem's seems to have been encouraged by the authorities.'

Joel could almost hear Frederick nodding.

'Kem didn't live in the blocks. He was in the remand centre: a special privilege because of his status. At night the guards effectively withdrew and the prisoners were put in communal cells in which about thirty prisoners sleep. Goodness knows what goes on in there. When the cells were unlocked about 6am, Kem got up and was talking to another prisoner when Mhkize came up behind him. He'd stabbed Kem in the back once, before other prisoners got hold of him. Kem was taken to the prison hospital, which thank goodness, knows how to deal with this type of incident and according to Bilson is not uncommon.

'All witnesses were taken to segregation, where they are still being interviewed by the police. I will read you extracts from the official report, which is not pleasant but describes what took place according to the officers and what they could glean.

'*At about…*'

Frederick interrupted, 'Why do they always say that? It's either at or about, it simply can't be "at about" for goodness sake.'

'Papa, we are not here to critique the grammar of someone writing something about a grave incident in the middle of the night. Too many of our colleagues do that, and you have said so on a regular basis. What do you call those who say with hindsight they "should have done this", they "should have done that"? The "shudders"?'

Whap! Joel thought.

'I'm sorry,' he responded, 'you are, of course, quite right, but it does annoy me.'

'As I was saying,' Marta continued assertively, '*at about 6.00 hours this morning the alarm was sounded in the remand centre, as we were unlocking. I called together officers Hlatshwag, Mphahlele, Myburgh and Dladla. We made our way into the area where there was a commotion and found the body of Kem Siblisi lying prostrate on the floor in a communal area. He was surrounded by four prisoners Ndlovu, Mtembi, Vilakazi and Ethrahim. There were others, but they were observing. We were allowed unhindered access. I saw there was a sharpened metal knife type object lying on the floor next to Siblisi. It was covered in blood. I seized the metal and put it in an exhibits bag.*

'*We immediately sought to render first aid and called for assistance from the medical team who attended a short while later. Siblisi was breathing but bleeding heavily, and we tried to stem the blood until the arrival of the medical staff that took over and removed him to the prison hospital.*

'*We separated the prisoners who had been close to Siblisi and asked them what had happened. They all reported Siblisi was talking to prisoner Kubheka when Mhkize came behind him and stabbed him in the back with the sharpened piece of metal we had found beside Siblisi. We asked where the assailant and Kubheka were and none of the prisoners said they knew. Team two joined us and proceeded to lock down the wing and we took the four to segregation. Kubheka was found in his cell. He said he had returned there when we entered. He confirmed the account given and quite openly blamed himself for not seeing Mhkize sooner. He said Mhkize had disappeared. Kubheka is in the Twenty-eights, Mhkize is in the Twenty-sixes.*

'*Upon searching the wing, Mhkize was found in the toilets with his trousers and underwear around his ankles and with stab wounds to his hands, feet and forehead. He was unconscious and we took him to the hospital. By this time Siblisi had been taken to Groote Schuur Hospital.*

'*Our inquiries indicate Mhkize was subject to "slow burn". He has been placed in protective custody. The Generals have sentenced him to death.* The report then goes on about the arrival of the police.'

Joel asked, 'What is slow burn?'

Frederick answered, 'Putting it bluntly, Joel, it's being raped by one or more people who are HIV positive. It means slow death. The gangs use it as a punishment, as they have with the stigmata type stabbings. It is just a signal. As we have heard, Mhkize and probably his family will be killed in due course, but they may let him let him live for a while.'

My God, that's horrific, thought Joel.

'Thank you, Marta and Marimam, a most clear account. Were you allowed to interview the witnesses?' asked Frederick.

'No,' replied Marta. 'As we said, they are in segregation and the police are interviewing them.'

'What did you find out about Mhkize, the attacker?'

'Bilson allowed us to look at his file,' Marta said. 'He comes from the Cape Flats, Guguletu Township, NY 171 Street. He is thirty-eight years old and has been in and out of prison most of his life. He is, as the report said, a member of the Twenty-sixes, which also dominate parts of his township. He was on remand for robbery and burglary. Bilson explained Kem's attack had already caused other disturbances with the Twenty-sevens and Twenty-eights demanding Twenty-sixes' blood.

'I anticipated this,' said Frederick, 'it always happens. Thembi has issued a statement on Kem's and the family's behalf pleading with the Generals not to take any more vengeance in Kem's name. I sent it through to the prison. It's written in Xhosa, English, African Zulu and Fanigalore – well, we've tried to write Fanigalore, but it's a spoken language really.'

'I've never heard of Fanigalore,' said Joel.

Frederick explained, 'It's the language of the gangs, a spoken mixture of languages. It was originally used in the mines to enable the workers and the owners to communicate. I'm not sure how much the message will be listened to but we have tried. It is what Kem would have expected from us.'

Joel didn't like the way Frederick phrased the last sentence. 'Is Kem OK?'

'Yes! I'm sorry, I've just realised the way I said that. He is still heavily sedated but stable at the moment. I have spoken to the hospital and he will not be moved without me knowing. The prison authorities have a habit of taking prisoners back to the prison hospital as soon as they can to save the extra cost of their guards being in the general hospital.

We must go to the township. I will go with Afua and his friend Fenyang, it will be a break for them from working at the house,' said Frederick decisively.

'Papa, it will be too dangerous,' said Marta.

'Not for us,' responded Frederick, 'but I fear it will be for the Mhkize family. Joel, is there anything else we should be doing?'

Joel paused before asking, 'Marta, did Jean say who was investigating the case?'

'Not their names, but they are from Jean's police station,' she replied.

'Try and make early contact with them. Make sure they understand you are not a threat to them, you just need help and in turn may be able to help them. I know it sounds obvious, but they will have heard what happened to Van Wisents and you need to get to them fast. Despite Jean's involvement they will be suspicious.'

'That's a good point, Joel, thank you,' acknowledged Frederick.

'Frederick, are you sure you will be safe?'

'I will be perfectly safe. In township terms, in parts it is more developed than most. You will have passed it on the way in from the airport. I have been there many times over the years, and with Afua and Fenyang I will be very safe. OK, that's it for the moment. Joel, we will keep you informed of Kem's condition and any other developments.'

Everyone said goodbye, and Joel was left with his mind spinning once again at what was going on. This South African experience was certainly a rollercoaster. It was also somewhat bizarre.

Chapter Twenty-Two

Frederick, Afua and Fenyang travelled along the N2 towards the airport. There always seemed to be roadworks every time Frederick drove along this road, so he turned off the N2 at the Modderdam Road exit and headed for Kipfontein Road, which was more or less parallel with the motorway.

It was relatively easy to find what they suspected was Mhkize's home; they followed the smoke! They found the house still smouldering and it looked as though it had been set alight some hours ago. They drove straight past what remained of it. People were gathered nearby, talking and looking into the car, a white man driving two black men in a township being a strange sight even today. Someone in the crowd shouted, 'It's Weisner, the lawyer.' Frederick didn't see the caller, but he thought he recognised the face of one of his clients in the crowd.

The crowd began to cheer, wave and dance. Frederick waved back but did not stop; some of the crowd were obviously intoxicated, and no matter how good-natured they seemed, things could change dramatically and quickly in these situations when alcohol, and goodness knows what else, had been consumed.

Frederick drove to the home of another client: a member of the Twenty-six gang, Letsego Shabangu. He was their leader in the township. They arrived at the house, which was surrounded by aggressive looking young men. As Frederick stopped the car, Fenyang said, 'Let's just sit here for a moment, Mr Frederick, let them have a look at us. Let's put our hands on the dashboard.' As Afua put his hands on the back of the seat, Frederick thought this was sound advice.

Some of the men were very close to the car, until a man came out of the house, looked into the car, beamed broadly and walked over, barking out instructions to the men as he did. The men visibly relaxed, moved back from the car and also smiled.

Frederick smiled back at the man, and said to his companions in the car, 'It's OK, let's get out,' which they did.

'Mr Frederick, good to see you,' drawled the fit tattooed man of about thirty-five. He held out his hand and shook Frederick's with the grip of a vice.

'Letsego, it is good to see you too. Might I introduce my companions, Afua and Fenyang.'

Letsego Shabangu looked at them, and said with a lift of his eyebrow, 'Minders, Mr Frederick? You don't need minders here, you are our friend.'

'They are my companions, Letsego. May I introduce them? This is Letsego Shabangu, a former client of mine.' Frederick felt it important Letsego, and particularly his men, saw everyone as friends. The gang leader looked at the two suspiciously, but held his hand out and shook theirs.

'Letsego, we have just come past the house of Tebego Mhkize. It has been burned. Where are his family?' queried Frederick.

'Aaah, I thought you'd come because of that shit. He has caused us a real problem. The others are demanding blood from us because of him. Pollsmoor has already had Twenty-six blood spilt, but they want more. I now understand the letter, which went round the prison. That is your work, Mr Frederick?'

'It was the wish of my client, Kem Siblisi, and his family. I merely facilitated it.'

'I know The Doc, he is a good man. He has helped my brothers many times. How is he, Mr Frederick?'

'He is still very ill, but stable. Can we talk somewhere, Letsego?'

'Here is best, where my brothers can listen to what is being said.' Frederick understood: Shabangu was playing tactics. There was little doubt in his mind some of the Twenty-sixes would think attack was the best form of defence and would want blood before their own was taken. Frederick suspected this was why any conversation needed to be held in earshot of the others, to involve them.

'The Doc, is that what Kem is called?' said a surprised Frederick. 'All these years and I never knew this.'

'That is how he is known. A great mind, Mr Frederick, I hope he lives.'

'So do I! Letsego, where are the Mhkize family?'

'Gone,' Shabangu replied firmly.

Frederick didn't like the sound of this, and pressed, 'Gone? Where, Letsego?'

'They all left yesterday. His wife, mother, children, sisters and their families – about fifteen. No one knew anything. The first I knew was last night. I suspected something, but not this.'

'Do you know where they have gone, Letsego?'

'Not yet,' he replied, 'but we will. We will find them, if the others don't first.'

'This is all very strange. What do you think?' asked Frederick.

'The wife and mother visited him two days ago,' Shabangu said. 'That was when the plan was hatched. He was going to plead guilty to robbery and grievous assault, then changed his mind a while ago. He said his lawyers told him to plead not guilty. They said they could get him off.'

'Where was the robbery, Letsego?'

'In a house in Edgemead. He attacked the woman and was caught there by the husband and staff. He was beaten. God knows how he thought he was going to get off with it.'

'Do you know his lawyers?' Frederick queried.

'Not you, Mr Frederick?' came the quick reply.

'I don't know, Letsego. I hope not, given what you've said. But why the attack in prison? Why Kem? What for?' Frederick shook his head slowly.

'Money. What else?' Shabangu explained. 'He has been paid by someone to do this and the family knew. They may not have known what was going to happen, but they knew something and it was arranged for them to get out. "The Insect" pleaded not guilty so he stayed in the remand centre with The Doc.'

'But who would pay to kill Kem? He was the voice of reason in the prison.'

'At first I thought it was the others, the Twenty-sevens and Twenty-eights, trying to clear us out, joining forces against us. I thought they had turned Mhkize, and our elimination in the prison could be one of the consequences, but a truck early in the morning? Not them. It is not the way they operate. This used to happen before, Mr Frederick, you know.'

Frederick knew what he was talking about. During Apartheid, when informers were identified, their families were moved overnight. A truck would arrive, the family and all their belongings would be put into it and driven away to a new life, far away. Unfortunately, some were tracked down and suffered horrendous consequences. As Frederick witnessed earlier, their homes were always burnt as a visible warning to anyone who thought about informing, indicating the informers would also be burnt – probably 'necklaced'. Frederick would never forget the graphic TV footage of car tyres filled with petrol being placed round people's necks; it was horrendous.

'The SAPS? Is that what you're saying, Letsego?'

He nodded solemnly.

'But why? Kem was not a danger to them,' said Frederick.

'Ah, don't forget there are still those in SAPS who have a lot to hide. The Doc advised many of my brothers on how to identify and sue those who hadn't gone to the Truth and Reconciliation Commission. He was not popular with some. He chased them, hunted them, and they knew it was him.'

Good Heavens, thought Frederick. He didn't know any of this, and had never thought of Kem as the Simon Wiesenthal of Apartheid.

'Letsego, you have given me a lot to think about,' said Frederick. 'It has been most enlightening. Is there any way I can help?'

'No, Mr Frederick, you have already done what you can. More blood will be spilled, it is just how much.'

The four shook hands and Frederick thanked Shabangu again, making a point of thanking the other gang members who had been listening intently. He gave his card to the leader, 'Just in case you've lost my numbers, Letsego,' who smiled and winked at Frederick as he returned to the house, followed by the group of men.

The three companions got into the car and drove off. Not a word was said. It didn't need to be. What they had heard was very worrying; very worrying indeed. Virtual silence continued all the way back into the city. Even when they passed the enormous sewage farm at Kewtown, where usually everyone remarked on the stink, nothing was said.

Joel was still in shock at the news from South Africa when the house door opened and Sarah walked in. She came into the kitchen where she found Joel prepping a meal.

'Hi, Joel, how are you?' she asked as she kissed him.

'Good, thanks, how's things in "Brissle"?' he asked in his best Bristolian.

'Rosemary wants me to go and stay with her for a few days in London, but I'm concerned about you being down here by yourself.'

Joel thought this was just the excuse he needed to get back to London and visit the taxi firm. It would also be a diversion from thinking about Kem.

'I'll come to London as well and sort my flat. There are loads of jobs need doing while you're at Rosemary's.'

'I don't want you going out on the town,' said Sarah suspiciously.

'No I won't, promise. Don't forget I'm sick, and Dr Lloyd would only want me to be in contact with "She who must be obeyed" at work.'

'*She* has been very supportive of you, not like some of the men who just want rid of you. Although, I wish they would retire you.'

'Retire? How many times have I got to say it? I am not retiring.'

'I'm not talking about *retiring* retiring,' said Sarah. 'You could start a new career.'

'Shop-keeping in Budleigh?' Joel quipped.

'Of course not. Teaching? Training? You'd be good at it.'

'Maybe. Come on, let's get packed,' Joel said, ending the conversation.

While packing, Joel's thoughts wandered back to the events in South Africa. He had been wondering more and more whether the fire was related.

Joel and Sarah went to bed, fell asleep and set out early the following morning. The A303 was surprisingly quiet, but the sooner it was made into a dual carriage way all the way to London the better. They arrived in London about ten. Joel dropped Sarah at Rosemary's in Canary Wharf, where he parked the Range Rover and went straight to his flat in a cab. There was a mountain of mail, but it could all wait. He had been planning his activities during the night and on the drive up. He did, however, have a quick look round the flat; everything seemed OK. He'd asked Billy to keep an eye on it, and looking at the spare bedroom he found Billy had been keeping a *very close* eye on it. Joel wondered who Billy had been entertaining, but thought it was too big a question to consider without the benefit of a large drink or two. Billy would not be difficult to pin down: he was a chatterbox.

Joel had a shower, dressed, switched off his phones and headed off to Sutton. He could have caught the overground to Clapham Junction, but as he was walking he became convinced he was being followed. He had considered this, and the contingency plans he'd thought through the previous night in bed kicked into action. Joel took the Tube to Oxford Circus; he didn't use his Oyster card, which was a bind but he thought it was better. It proved invaluable because, while waiting to buy his ticket, he saw two people he'd spotted near his flat walking into the station.

He jumped on the Tube and went to Oxford Circus, where he got off, walked slowly through Soho to Trafalgar Square, and then turned up Charing Cross Road. As he did so he was carefully looking at buildings and windows for reflections. He concluded he was definitely being followed. He continued right up the road until he reached Foyles bookshop, one of his favourite haunts, and walked round the store. He didn't buy anything; he normally couldn't resist. He then went out of the side door into Manette Street, turned left into Greek Street and back into Soho.

He walked towards Leicester Square and went straight to the Odeon. The first programme started a little earlier at 12.10pm, and the adverts would barely have finished. He walked straight in, bought his ticket and went into the cinema, where he was the first customer. He took his coat and tracksuit bottoms off, placed them in the plastic bag he had in his pocket, opened the fire exit, which activated the alarm, and calmly walked out of the cinema into Charing Cross Road through the gate he had earlier seen was open. He looked completely different, wearing a green light anorak and black cords as opposed to the blue overcoat and grey tracksuit bottoms. To complete his new outfit he put on a green Baseball cap.

Joel mingled with the tourists, making his way towards Charing Cross station. At the station he walked inside and waited: no one was following. He bought a ticket and went to Clapham Junction, where he again waited to see if he was being followed, he decided he wasn't, before catching the train to Sutton.

As he walked into the Roxy Cars office, the young women behind the counter said, barely looking up, 'No taxis for half an hour.'

Joel explained he didn't want a taxi, he wanted to talk to the owner.

'Not in today,' said the chewing gum machine/radio operator. 'Echo five, when you've finished with Yvonne go to 5 Newbury Gardens. Pick up a Sarah for Excelsior Bingo.' Not his Sarah, Joel smiled inwardly. He wondered if she'd ever played bingo, and realised investment banking was a bit like bingo really!

Joel noticed a man slipping out the back door of the taxi office, trying to look invisible.

'Ok,' said Joel to the helpful operator.

'Who should I say was asking?'

Joel simply said, 'You know who's asking!' It seemed to be part of the curriculum at some schools to learn how to spot a cop.

Joel turned left out of the taxi office, then left again. He thought he'd find an alley giving access to the rear of the shops and the flats above. He was right. The figure from the taxi firm came scuttling down the alley and virtually bumped into Joel.

'Hello,' said Joel. 'Why am I so unpopular?'

'Nothing to do with you, Guvn'r, just stepped out for some fresh air,' said the man from the taxi office.

'LL51 AYS, a Nissan in blue, who did you sell it to?' asked Joel.

The man looked stunned. 'Oh, is that all?' Joel wondered what this little chap had been up to make him so relieved it was purely a car enquiry. 'That one went to the scrapper, they all do.'

'Which one?'

'Ron Weston's in Croydon. It's where I get rid of them all.'

'Does he scrap them or sell them on?'

'That's his business. I get a good price, that's what I'm interested in.'

'OK. I'm going see Mr Weston, and if I get the slightest inkling he's been tipped off I'll be back, in numbers, with the taxman. Don't suppose "Beautiful" on the radio should be missing so much school, either.'

'What do you mean? She's eighteen,' said Mr Taxi, a little too defensively, thought Joel.

'Maybe in bed she is. Live in the flat above, does she?' At this Joel left, pretty confident he had hit the taxi man's weak spot. Mr Taxi wouldn't have been bothered about being turned over on a whim, even by the HMRC, but Joel spotted something in his weakness around the girl – who was clearly not his daughter.

Chapter Twenty-Three

Weston's Yard was a big place, surrounded by what appeared to be steel shutters on which 'Keep Out, Dogs' was written on every side. The place was full of cars and car parts in various states of cannibalisation from the assorted vehicles. Lines of radiators, engine blocks and wheels seemed to be the predominant articles. Also in the yard were various items of scrapping equipment, including two very large crushers, one of which was crushing what looked like the shell of a new Ford.

However, Joel was not interested in potentially stolen cars. When he walked into the yard he quickly found evidence of the dogs by stepping in their faeces, then they appeared: two snarling German shepherds with long, unkempt coats.

'Keep still, they won't touch,' came a voice from the portakabin beside the entrance of the yard. Despite this, Joel never took his eyes off the snarlers. One he thought he could deal with, but two at one time? Mmm.

'Snoot, Tosh, come here,' continued the same voice, and the dogs ran to the portakabin. A figure appeared from the door and chained the dogs to a couple of engine blocks.

Ron Weston was the figure who emerged from the doorway. 'What can I do for you?' he asked. He was about five foot seven inches tall and the same wide, but he wasn't fat; it was muscle. Joel thought he looked like a rugby hooker. He had a shock of blond hair and wore khaki overalls, stained in oil. He appeared sixty, but was probably a little younger.

'Don't just stand there, get some fucking work done,' he shouted to two other figures who were standing talking in another part of the yard. They too had the shock of blond hair: clearly Westons. I wonder, just wonder, if their middle name is Boris or Johnson, thought Joel mischievously.

Turning to Joel, Weston said, 'Fucking rigor mortis will set in if they stand still any longer. What do you want, son? Old bill?' Despite Joel being dressed casually and carrying his plastic bag, Weston had still clocked him.

'Yes, that's right, Joel Grant. I am making some inquiries about a car you bought from Roxy Cars. LL51 AYS.'

'I buy all their old cars. Not from round here, are you, son? When was it? Last one I bought was about three weeks ago. Come into the office, I'll have a look.' Joel was pleasantly surprised by Weston's openness.

Weston began to pore through books, which were in copperplate handwriting, no computers here thought Joel, when a voice cut in.

'Get your filthy hand off my books.'

'The Missus,' announced Weston.

'I've told you not to touch those books. You stick to metal and oil. What are you doing?' asked Mrs Weston, equally blonde and similar in height but slimmer than her husband, who had just walked into the portakabin.

'The *officer*,' Weston said, emphasising the word, Joel thought, 'wants to know about one of Roxy's cars we bought. What was the number again, son?'

Joel repeated, 'LL51 AYS. They sold it to you a few weeks ago.'

'I remember,' said Mrs Weston without any reference to her beloved ledgers. 'You sold it to those two wasters who live in Argyllshire Street above the drycleaners shop. What are they called?'

'Beavis and Butthead as far as I am concerned,' said Ron Weston. 'Where they got three hundred quid from I don't know.'

'Yes, here we are. Richard Gilles, 131a Argyllshire Street,' said The Missus.

'Do you know if they still have it?' Joel asked.

The Missus then explained they had taken the car back from Gilles a matter of days later and scrapped it. She asked Joel if the car was needed as evidence, he told them it had been used in an arson attack in Devon and it would have been good to be able to examine it. The Westons clearly assumed Joel was from Devon, which may have accounted for his somewhat relaxed dress, but when he explained he was actually from Islington, they became even more confused.

Mrs Weston asked Joel if he would like a tea. He was very grateful after his exploits in the West End. The next hour flew by. Joel enjoyed talking to people; he enjoyed listening to people more, which was why he became a detective. The Westons liked to talk; they were interesting people who had grown up locally and become childhood sweethearts before Ron left to join the army because there was no work locally. After the army, the Westons set up what Joel thought must have been the straightest scrap metal business he had ever come across, and had rebuffed the local underworld who tried to extort money from them. Ron, he learnt, had a reputation as a 'tough cookie'. Joel noted, but made no comment, when The Missus made a throwaway comment about still having to pay rent.

Ron Weston threw a glance at his wife, who immediately changed the subject to Ron's days in the army and how she had missed him. Despite his tough exterior, Ron had clearly felt the same, and while he enjoyed his time in the army, he was essentially a home bird and missed South London. The Missus said Ron travelled all over the world when he was in the army, but she stayed in South London. She didn't want to go and live in Herefordshire which was another option.

Joel asked, 'Were you in a particular regiment, Ron?' he knew Herefordshire was the HQ of the SAS.

He coloured slightly, and before he could give another warning glance to his wife, she said, 'Yes, he was in the SAS.' When Ron did give 'the look', she got up from her seat, walked to the door and said, 'I'll just make the boys a drink.' Nothing further needed to be said.

Joel witnessed just how uncomfortable Ron became around his military history and didn't delve any further. There was one issue Joel did want to delve into, though. He said, 'Ron, I know we've just met, but "the rent"? Are you paying the local police?'

For the third time, Ron coloured and said he didn't want any trouble. Joel reassured him he wasn't in trouble and pressed him again. Ron said he would not give evidence or confirm it outside the room, but yes he was paying the local DCI. He said there were a number of businesses in the area who were giving some in the CID 'a drink'. It served for a quiet life.

Joel understood what 'the drink' meant. It was a bribe to keep corrupt local police sweet. What he couldn't understand was why a character like Ron would ever pay the gangsters in uniform when he rebuffed the approaches of other gangsters in the area. However, Ron explained the DCI arrested one of his sons on a trumped up handling charge and demanded £1,000 for the charge to be dropped. Ron paid, and a monthly 'drink' had then been demanded which Ron was also paying. He reiterated he would not confirm it to anyone else. Joel accepted this, but he had no intention of ignoring it.

As Joel left the yard he considered going to Argyllshire Street, but it was too late to pay a visit to Beavis and Butthead. Joel always paid visits to nighthawks between eleven in the morning and midday, when they were invariably just waking up.

He went back to his flat and started on the little jobs he was supposed to be doing. It was still only 7pm. Sarah rang to ask about his progress, but it was really to check if he was there, he thought. He told her he had just taken one of the window frames to pieces to fix the sash cord. He hoped it sounded sufficiently complicated to keep him in all night. It worked: Sarah said she was very impressed and was going out for dinner with Rosemary.

Joel said, 'Don't worry about me, I'll just get a kebab.'

'Oh I won't worry. When was the last time you ate a kebab? I bet it was years ago, it certainly hasn't been while we've been together.' Joel regretted telling her some time ago about a drunken incident involving a kebab when he was a student in Manchester. More ammunition for her, he thought grimly, but did not rise to her dig.

Joel had already decided what he was going to do for the rest of the evening. On the way back from the Westons', Joel had phoned Piers Messenger on his throwaway phone. Piers was a DI in the 'rubber heels' or the Professional Standards Directorate as they were better known,

He preferred 'rubber heels', which had its origins in the sixties and seventies – presumably because they used to sneak about quietly.

In fairness, they enjoyed some notable successes, which had been because of the people in the department at the time. Joel was in for a short time, and he viewed his contribution as part of one of their notable successes. Most detectives hated bent cops and liked investigating them, despite politicians and popular media coverage giving the public the opposite impression. Joel thought pro rata the level of police corruption was considerably less than in politics, but one bent cop was one too many.

Joel had a theory about police corruption: like a lot of policing it was cyclical, the same issues recurring on a regular basis, always with a different response because the police had not learnt the lessons from the last time. A Commissioner would come along and attack the corruption head on, but they would be succeeded by one who wasn't keen on the inevitable poor publicity it brought. The new Commissioner would ignore it and therefore allow its growth, leaving the next Commissioner an enormous problem. Joel thought the current Commissioner had inherited a festering corruption problem.

He arranged to meet Piers in Islington at 8pm, explaining he thought he was being followed. Piers told him he was being ridiculous.

Piers arrived dead on 8pm. Joel had ordered a bottle of Sancerre and started on his first glass, which he raised in greeting to Piers.

'Hi, Joel, how's it going? I see you're in the shit again,' said Piers without preamble, which was Piers' natural straightforward style. 'Aren't you on the sick?'

'Yes, fatigue,' said Joel.

'Fatigue? Must be all the air miles you've been collecting,' Piers retorted.

'How do you know I've been travelling?'

'It was mentioned the other morning at daily briefing. We've been asked from on high, with a push from FCO or someone, to look at you. The Guvn'r was having none of it, though. She told them straight, "Joel Grant may be a maverick, but he's not bent. If you want us to divert resources from corruption inquiries, I want it in writing."'

'Bloody hell, I didn't realise she really thought that about me,' said a surprised Joel.

'Course you didn't because you think the world is against you. She might have knocked them back, but don't be surprised if someone has a look at you, Joel.'

'Who?' He never dreamed of mentioning his conversation with Fiona Henderson; it wouldn't be fair to either of them.

'Your guess, but some ambitious soul will,' responded Piers.

'But you said I was being ridiculous,' recalled Joel.

'For the benefit of any listeners, and I told the Guvn'r I was seeing you. She said there was no problem, but seriously watch yourself.'

Joel poured Piers a drink and told him the tale of the Westons and the local CID. Piers asked Joel what he was doing talking to them, but Joel told him it was best he didn't know.

Piers said he was sympathetic but the Westons would have to agree to cooperate. Joel said there was no way they would do so, even though Ron was ex-Special Forces.

'What do you mean, ex-Special Forces?' queried Piers.

'Yeah, the old man was in the SAS apparently.' Joel had left this part to the end, and said, 'Weren't you in Special Forces, Piers?' Joel knew full well Piers had been a captain in the Army, the Scottish Borderers and then the SAS. It was not only because of Piers's current job Joel thought of him, it was also because of his previous life.

'Is this guy called Ron? Ron Weston?' asked Piers.

'Yeah, that's him.'

'Ron Weston MBE, I think, if I'm not mistaken,' Piers continued.

'Yeah.' Joel didn't know about the MBE. 'Here is his card.' He handed Piers Ron Weston's business card.

'Mmm, you say he's paying the CID? I'm surprised they're still alive,' commented Piers.

'What do you mean?'

'Ron Weston is a name, not just anyone,' Piers explained. 'His reputation is legend. He was one of the toughest troopers ever to come out of Hereford. They still talk about him. I had no idea where he was – I'm certain very few do! I think we can help the Westons, surgery, I think. Not on them, but on our so called colleagues.'

Joel was hopeful the Weston family would be £200 a month better off very soon, very soon indeed. Piers was just the man, and his Guvn'r would be up for a bit of skulduggery if it ripped a vipers nest apart!

They had almost finished their bottle, thought about another but didn't. Piers promised to let Joel know what was to be done in respect of the Westons.

When he left the pub, Joel looked around and didn't immediately notice anything odd on Upper Street as he walked towards Highbury. Then he turned into the Sutton estate, where he tucked himself in a doorway behind the wall. He noticed a man and woman come into the estate a minute or so after him, followed by another man on his own. They made a good pretence of being lost, but Joel clocked them: they were watchers. As he stood still a door opened behind him and a voice from inside said, 'What you up to Mr Grant, skulking around like a villain?'

Joel looked back and realised he was a few yards away from Viney Tatellis's shop, an Italian deli which Joel used from time to time to buy bread and pesto. Joel had known Viney since he'd been in the police, and had helped him out from time to time when his sons went off the path Viney wanted them to tread. Viney was always very grateful and often didn't want to take any money from Joel for his food. Joel always insisted on paying; it was a matter of principle with him. He knew Viney had little spare money, and what he did have he spent on his children, one of whom was on the books of Arsenal. Joel thought it was a shame he hadn't signed on for Man U.

Viney said, 'Come in. They're looking for you, I think.'

Joel didn't need asking twice and was inside the shop in a flash. 'Thanks, Viney, can I go out the back door?'

'They're all over, Joel. Sit down, let them wear themselves out. What about some food?'

At this point Mrs Tatellis came through. 'Joel, good to see you. Viney, why haven't you offered him a drink?' Viney knew better than to answer back and said Joel was staying for something to eat as well.

While it was late, the Tatellis' always had something to eat late at night. They had eaten their main meal with the family, but invariably had some bread, cheese, olives, pesto and a glass of wine around this time of night. Joel thanked them and tucked into his food and a tasty Chianti.

The next hour was spent talking about the family and business; not a mention of what Joel had been up to earlier. Mrs T went upstairs to check on the children about 10.30pm, and when she returned she said, 'Gone, all gone.'

Joel thought he had better explain, and said, 'I think…'

He was interrupted by Viney, who said, 'Joel, no explanations necessary. We don't need any. We know you, you're our friend and it's good to eat with friends. Now, out the back door just in case. There were about ten of them, Joel, all shapes and sizes.' He smiled and handed Joel some photographs he'd taken. Joel looked at them. They were clearly pictures of the surveillance team, and Joel knew where he'd be sending them with his complaint, when the time was right.

Joel said, 'Thank you,' to the Tatellis' and went back onto the estate. He saw no signs of life, other than the pubs, which were all quiet. He thought about going back to his flat, but supposed they would be watching for him, whoever 'they' were. He jumped in a cab and asked to be taken to The Eagle on City Road. On his way he texted Billy on the 'throw away' phone, saying:

Eagle ASAP, don't bring phone, watch your back.

Billy lived five minutes' walk from The Eagle, and Joel knew if he was in the area he'd be there. As Joel didn't get a reply he thought Billy was already in the pub.

Billy was in the pub when Joel arrived. He looked around to see who else was there. It was not a pub either of them used regularly, so the chances of a random check by watchers was unlikely. The pub was just around the corner from Shoreditch police station and there was a group of local police officers drinking at the bar. Billy knew them.

Billy said, 'Seems clear. What's the problem, Joel?'

Joel explained the recent events, and asked Billy, 'Do you still have that mate who's a motorcycle courier, Billy?'

'Zoot, yeah, he's a busy lad. Very popular, always gets there on time.'

'Do you think he could do me a favour?' asked Joel.

'Yeah, no problems,' replied Billy. 'You want something delivered? Where? He's the boy.'

'Not exactly,' said Joel, and went on to explain what he wanted Zoot to do.

Joel didn't hang around in the pub, and warned Billy to be careful and only phone Joel in exceptional circumstances. Joel would phone him if necessary.

The two left the pub about eleven. Joel went to a late night Tesco's, and then to the Travelodge in Kings Cross; paying in cash. He had work to do the following morning and wasn't going to risk going to the flat and allowing the watchers to 'reconnect' with him. He slept very well.

Chapter Twenty-Four

Piers went in early the following morning to research the CID at Belmont Gardens, the police station covering the Westons' scrap yard. Later he went to the departmental meeting; much of the time was spent recounting the weekend's debacles, where members of the Metropolitan Police had allegedly assaulted, stolen from or, more often than not, just been stupid with Londoners, as the Mayor used to like saying. Of course, it wasn't just Londoners but the millions of people who visited the capital each year and who came across the Met. Mostly for the good, Piers believed, but in his current job he invariably heard of the worst.

At the end of the meeting, the Guvn'r asked if anyone wanted to talk about anything else. She was a good boss, always keen to involve everyone.

'I have something,' piped up Piers. 'It's the local CID ripping off a scrap merchant down in BG,' Piers explained what he knew to the others at the meeting.

DCS Liz Campbell asked, 'Is there an intelligence package, Piers?'

'No, I'd prefer to keep this tight.'

Det Supt Yellop, who was Head of Intelligence, burst in, 'Are you saying you don't trust my staff?'

Piers replied, 'Three of your team used to work in the CID at Belmont Gardens. I have no reason to doubt them, but they will still have friends there and you know how people talk. Anyway, this should be a quick hit.'

'I trust all my people and you should too,' Yellop retorted.

Mmm, thought Piers. 'I've said I have no doubts, Guvn'r, but you know, better than I, it's best to keep some work really tight.' Piers didn't need to spell out an embarrassing incident one month ago where one of the analysts in the Intel Department, who was sleeping with a DS from a district, happened to tell him she was working on a job with Greek connections. The DS was based in Green Lane, North London, and the analyst thought there would be no harm telling him. She didn't give away the details, but little did she know her lover was a friend of one of the targets. When talking on the phone, the target asked how the DS's 'bird in the spies' was doing. The DS blurted out she was doing well and getting some international travel out of it.

'Very nice,' said the target, 'furthest I get is south of the river.'

The boyfriend then added his girlfriend was going back and forth to Greece. The hairs on the back of the target's neck bristled; he suspected they were looking at him, which, of course, they were. He had formed a relationship with some club owners who were keen to get sex workers into the United Kingdom from the Balkans, also using them as drug mules to ensure value for money. They were trafficked through Greece. The target was on a retainer from the gangsters, keeping his eyes and ears open and supplying intelligence where he could. What neither the target or the boyfriend realised was their conversation was being monitored.

To prevent alarming the target any further, the analyst remained in post. She was quietly being isolated and given long term strategic work, and would eventually be moved into a less sensitive post, developing policy for the Mayor or something similar, but not until the target had been dealt with.

Everyone knew what Piers was alluding to, but nobody mentioned it.

'So what have you got in mind for our colleagues in BG?' said the Guvn'r.

'How do you know about this?' interrupted the Yellop, clearly pissed off.

'I know Weston, the owner of the business, by reputation. He will not, under any circumstances, give evidence.'

'What sort of reputation does he have then?' jibed the Head of Intel.

'He is one of the bravest members of the armed forces to have served during the seventies/eighties.'

'Ah, so it's the old boys' network, just the sort of thing we should be looking at.'

'Were you born a prick or did you grow into one?' Piers retorted, regretting it immediately.

'Piers, less of it. Danny, let him finish.' Piers would not normally have attacked a senior officer in these circumstances, but he knew his boss had no time for the Head of Intel and thought he needed a slap.

'I'm sorry, *Sir*,' Piers said to Yellop without a hint of contrition, then continued, the local DCI, Magnus, goes to collect his money at the end of each month, anywhere from the twenty-first to the thirtieth. It is already the nineteenth, so anytime now. That's why I said it should be a quick piece of work. If I'm right, he'll take the rest of the snakes out for a drink and they'll sort out their monthly takings. I think they use the Pilgrims on Strand Street, run by Billy Granger who used to be in here.'

Again Yellop glared at Piers. Granger had also been in Intel, and left overnight following the failure to find £50,000 which had gone missing from the property store. Granger was suspended for a long time, but it could not be proved and he quietly left on retirement. Death by a thousand slashes, thought Piers.

'So we put an op on the scrapyard when Magnus visits and an op on the pub to make the best use of our team. I suspect they'll go to the pub with Mr Granger, do the split, get drunk and go their separate ways.'

'And what do we do then, just grab them and hope for the best?' sneered Yellop.

'With a twist,' said Piers. 'Because there is no Tube or overland, these idiots use their cars. They strut around the place as though they own it, inside and outside the nick. They all live within fifteen miles of the nick and drink and drive on a regular basis, so all we do is wait until they leave one by one, have Traffic plotted on their routes home, nick them and search them, their houses and their offices. We will find money and, with luck, bank accounts. They'll all go to court, be banned and then sacked.'

'Yeah, but we haven't got them for corruption,' argued DCS Campbell.

'Probably not, but we will have ripped the heart out of a corrupt office and put out a very strong message across the Met,' suggested Piers. 'This is the worst case scenario as I said, but given the arrogance this lot show, I think we'll get a lot more.'

'And how do you know they'll be sacked, if, and I say if, they are driving drunk?' said Det Supt Yellop sarcastically.

'We'll just have to make sure we have a hanging panel to adjudicate on them,' said Piers.

DCS Campbell thought for a moment, asked the others if they had anything to add, and then said, 'I'm sorry, Piers, but there are too many other jobs. We just can't afford the resources. You'll have to get Weston to give evidence.'

'There is no way he will,' Piers exploded, 'so we are just going to let these bastards screw a guy who's trying make a living and let them rip off the rest of their district.'

'Well, we'll have to see if we can get some more Intel. Danny, can you see what you can do?' she requested.

'Will do,' said Yellop.

'OK. I'm sorry, Piers, but I want all your team to go to help the West Midlands with their request for an independent look at the traffic and recovery firms. You're our resident mongoose, you should sort that in a couple of weeks. Get up there tomorrow.' She handed him a file of papers marked 'West Midlands Police'.

'OK, anything else? No? OK, tomorrow! Danny, four weeks report back on BG please.' The meeting ended.

'So we're prepared to send my team to the West Mids, but not to deal with this lot on the doorstep. What would the Mayor think of that?' retorted Piers.

'You keep out of politics, Piers, I'll deal with any fallout,' DCS Campbell said firmly. 'We have had lots of help from the provinces in the past, it's about time we paid them back. Now get on with it.'

As they were leaving, Yellop collared Piers. 'Don't you ever talk to me again like that.'

'I said I'm sorry, Sir.'

'The Guvn'r has got you pegged,' said Danny. 'Fucking mongoose, hah! Don't hurry back, wanker.'

Piers was sick of Yellop. He moved close where no one else could hear, and whispered, 'The thing about the mongoose is he will rip a snake apart and chew it up. You fuck with me and I'll come after you.'

'You can't say that to me,' Yellop said, almost pleading.

'Say what, Guvn'r?' said Piers as he walked away into the team office.

'I'm going to see her about you. You're history, fucking history,' shouted Yellop.

Typical response from him, thought Piers. 'See her'? He would never say anything to Piers, but Yellop clearly resented having a female boss. Chauvinist pig.

Fifteen minutes later Piers's phone rang. It was his boss. 'Get in here, now,' she ordered.

Piers walked to the DCS's office to be met by Yellop emerging with a smirk on his face. Piers knocked on the door and went in.

DCS Campbell stood up and looked out of the window for a moment before turning round and saying, 'Piers, you can't go around threatening superintendents. It's just not on.'

'He's an incompetent imbecile,' muttered Piers.

'That's not for you to worry about. You've made it really difficult for me, Piers. I'll have to do something about you. You're going to have to leave the office.'

'What?' said Piers aghast. 'You'd get rid of me because of him? I don't believe this.'

'I'm sorry, Piers, I have no alternative. If I don't support him, it will look very odd. Anyway your time working with the West Midlands may cool things off short term.'

'Tipton, here we come,' mouthed Piers.

'What's Tipton when it's about?'

'It's a town in the Black Country,' replied Piers.

'Odd place to mention, Piers, what's wrong with Birmingham?'

'Odd? I tell you what's odd,' Piers blurted out in a most un-Piers-like fashion, 'you keeping him here. You know he's rubbish and all you do is protect him. Everyone thinks he's rubbish except you.'

'I run this office, not you or any other of the would-be democrats out there. This is not a democracy, clear?'

'I'm sorry, Ma'am, but why do you keep him?'

'Piers, shut up. You're moving when you've finished in Tipton.' The DCS was getting annoyed.

'What, for upsetting a superintendent?' replied Piers.

'That's about it. You're going to leave here today with your team and travel to RAF Odium where you will see Gary Wilson. He will brief you.'

'I know you don't know where Tipton is, Guvn'r, but it's a long way from Odium, and isn't Mr Wilson abroad at the moment?' Detective Superintendent Gary Wilson had been sent to do an inquiry in the High Commission in Dakar about six weeks ago, and as far as Piers was concerned he was still out there.

'Don't mention anything about Gary to anyone. Tell your team Odium is a secure briefing environment before leaving for the West Mids. And you will need some traffic expertise for the inquiry. Do you know anyone trustworthy in there?'

'Yes I do. Are you still serious about me leaving?' pleaded Piers.

'Yes. I don't know where, HR will know. Your career needs further development.'

161

'Aah, the kiss of death, eh? Career development.'

'Oh grow up, Piers, it's for your own good.'

'Yes, yes. Tell me one thing, Guvn'r, are you looking at him?' Piers asked.

'Piers, don't be so silly. Go and enjoy getting reacquainted with Tipton. And apologise to Danny.'

'I have done.'

'I don't think threatening to rip him apart is an apology. Do it now! And get out,' she said firmly.

Piers left the room; he knew he had pissed off his boss, which was most unlike him. He went straight to see Yellop, said he was sorry and told him he was moving after the West Midlands job.

Yellop said, 'That will teach you, you puffed up twat, don't fuck with me.'

For a moment Piers thought about hitting him, then realised it was unwise to say the least. Anyway he had work to do, telling his team about their banishment to the Black Country – well, the West Midlands – and to make a phone call to a traffic inspector he knew. But what was this to do with Gary Wilson?

Piers called the team meeting for 3pm.

'I'm sorry people but because of our considerable successes we have been selected to work in the West Midlands. We won't be back for at least a fortnight. Does that cause anyone any problems?'

'Problems, Guvn'r? We'll earn a fortune,' said one of the assembled throng.

'Yes, but despite that, if anyone does have any problems see me after this. Otherwise I want everyone to go home, pack and I will see you at RAF Odium at 9pm where you will be briefed fully on the job.'

'Are we flying up there, Guvn'r?' said one of the office wags.

'Yes, you'll be flying through Tipton International Airport, better known as the M3, M40, M42, M6. Now get home, and don't be late.'

The meeting was brief, and just under six hours later everyone made it to Odium and gathered in a briefing room. Piers arrived early and had already spoken to Det Supt Wilson. There were some strange looks when an senior RAF Officer, who treated them like VIPs, escorted an Inspector and Sergeant from Traffic into the briefing. More mysterious still was when Piers greeted them as the long lost friends they were! All four had served together.

Piers explained the operation to the assembled throng. They were not going to the West Midlands but were to investigate the activities of DCI Magnus and a number of his team in the CID at Belmont Gardens. Piers explained it was very sensitive as other inquiries were linked in, but as far as anyone was concerned they were in the West Midlands. They would be housed at Odium for the next two weeks at least.

Piers allocated the work. 'We have to keep this tight, really tight,' he continually stressed. 'If you feel you need some more help, say so. I'll arrange it, don't try and get it yourself.'

Piers outlined the plan, then added, 'Tom and Gordon,' indicating the traffic cops, 'will be responsible for organising the stopping of the cars at an appropriate place and seeing whether our targets have been drinking. If they have they will be arrested, taken to predetermined police stations, searched and interviewed.

'As soon as all of them have been arrested, the search of their offices will begin, then their houses. We're looking for anything: numbers, cash, documents. I suspect we may find drugs, but more of that nearer the time.'

'What happens if they blow negative?' asked one of the team.

'That's a possibility. They may be cautious, so we'll have to make judgement at the time. Worst case they will be allowed to go on their way and hopefully we will have enough to arrest them later when we've searched their offices.'

'Arrested? What for, Guvn'r?' enquired one of the DCs.

'Well, here we have five plus detectives,' detailed Piers, 'all probably with large amounts of cash on them, all having met up in a pub run by a bent ex-cop who is still on bail. I think we've got enough for suspicion to corrupt, prevent, steal, handle…whatever.'

'Got you, Guvn'r,' said the same DC. He understood, so did every-one else.

'Everyone clear? Yep?' said Piers. 'OK, it starts tomorrow, 7am, here. Let's go.'

Everyone, except the two traffic officers and Piers, filed out of the briefing and to their rooms in luxurious Odium.

The inspector said, 'I take it you want them all nicked, Piers?'

'If you could. If they've been in that pub, I reckon we'll have enough on a search even with a negative blow.'

'No problem, boss, they're as good as in the cells,' said Gordon.

'Thanks, guys, I appreciate it. Thanks again for dropping everything to help.'

Piers left the room. Everyone was standing in huddles in the corridor, and someone shouted, 'Is it right, Guvn'r, you're on the move?'

'Yes, at the end of the month,' he responded, 'so let's make this job a great leaving present for me.'

'It should be that twat Yellop who is on the move, not you.'

They had clearly heard. Piers said, 'Less of it. It's about time someone realised my potential and developed my career.' Everyone burst out laughing, but the resentment was still evident.

Chapter Twenty-Five

The following morning Joel once again made his way to South London. He hated wearing the same clothes two days running and had managed to buy some socks, underpants and a shirt from his earlier visit to Tesco. He was still watching for followers, but was aware they may be running around the M25!

131a Argyllshire Street was above a dry cleaners' shop as described by Mrs Weston, and when Joel didn't get an answer to his knock he eased open the door to the flat, which was unlocked. It was dry but it certainly wasn't clean. Walking straight into a narrow hallway with four doors leading from it, Joel realised he had been in similar flats countless times before: the layout was different; the smell was the same.

As he walked down the corridor, Joel opened the doors. Kitchen, mmm, better close the door, he thought. Same with the bathroom, where a mobile phone lay precariously on the cistern, and the bedroom. It wasn't until he came to what could loosely be described as the living room was there any sign of life. Under a filthy duvet on the equally filthy sofa lay two bodies, one male, one female. Joel shook the bodies and the female woke up first.

'Police,' announced Joel, 'do you live here?'

'No way, Mister, I just came here for a fuck last night. Didn't get it with this sad bastard – he's so full of shit, I'm surprised he's still alive.' The female was about twenty with long, dark hair, a stud in her nose and was quite pretty, despite her rude awakening.

'Who is he?' asked Joel.

'Aren't you supposed to know? You're the cop!' the girl challenged.

'Don't get cheeky or you may end up where this one's likely to go. What's his name?' asked Joel.

'Calls himself Wildo, God knows why. His real name's Richard – he's a real dick, if you get me.' The girl was getting out from under the duvet as she replied; she was only wearing her pants.

Joel wasn't a snob, but he abhorred the street talk phrase, 'Do you get me?' It was irritating; very irritating at 11.30 in the morning, he thought.

'OK, get yourself sorted and get going,' Joel snapped at her.

'What you going to do with him? Nick him?' the girl asked with a cheeky smile.

'No, just a quiet word with him, and his mate who lives with him.'

'Not anymore he doesn't. You're gonna have a problem talking to that one,' the girl blurted out as she put her top on.

'Why?'

''Cause he's dead. Died about ten days ago. This idiot survived. They were both full of gear, I think they'd robbed a dealer. Is that why you're here?'

'On your way, little girl, I just need to talk to your friend,' Joel said, trying to wake the comatose body on the sofa.

'You could fuck me if you want to. I wouldn't charge. He won't notice.'

'That's very kind of you, but I've just partaken,' answered Joel.

'Fuck off then,' said the girl as she flounced out of the flat, slamming the front door. Joel felt quite flattered for a moment being propositioned by a twenty-year-old, but when his attention refocused on her partner of choice last night, he didn't feel so flattered all of a sudden.

Joel spent ten minutes trying to raise Wildo, until the sleeping mess suddenly sat up and vomited across the room. It was as though he had just been brought back to life. He looked at Joel and said, 'Who the fuck are you?'

Joel used a line he'd been dying to use for years. 'I'm your worst nightmare, Wildo. Just when you thought things couldn't get worse, I enter your life and they have.' Joel thought, I've got at least three films in the sentence. Wonder if it worked.

Wildo tried to get up but collapsed back onto the sofa. 'What do you want? Search the place, I haven't got anything.' He may have been partially out of it, but Wildo clearly identified Joel as a cop. He had probably been to the same school as the young woman in the taxi office.

'I'm here to talk to you about your trip to Devon.'

'Never been to Devon,' replied Wildo quickly.

'That's why your friend died,' said Joel. 'He'd never been to Devon either.' It was a risk, but Joel thought it was a risk worth taking. 'That's why your gear was crap. You were meant to die as well, no trace.'

'Shit, man, Jancey wouldn't give us duff gear, he's a mate.'

'Jancey, mmm. Did he ask you to visit Devon?'

'I'm saying fuck all. You can't nick me, I've got no gear here.'

'But what about Jancey?' pressed Joel.

'Did he send you here? What have you done with him? Is he back inside? I know he's on licence, you blackmailing bastard,' accused Wildo.

'Jancey is nice and safe, not like you.' Joel was not telling any untruths as far as he was aware.

Wildo was still confused following his night out and was no match for Joel's straightforward questions and subtle innuendo. 'He gave us the money for the car, we only did what he told us.'

'And what do *you* say he told you exactly?' queried Joel.

'Just go down, smash the shop up and he'd give us three grams each, plus the car,' replied Wildo.

'So what did you do?'

'Went down. Crete thought it would be easier to use petrol, only we didn't have any, the car was fucking diesel. So we had to buy some paraffin on the way down, did the job and fucked off. No worries until Crete died and you turned up. Have you got Jancey banged up?'

'Not yet,' said Joel, 'not yet. It would be best if you didn't talk to Jancey for a while. I think he may be a little angry with you, particularly if I have to nick him on breach of licence on your say so. Whether I can prove it or not, he'll be away.'

'You bastard.'

Wildo lunged towards Joel, who took hold of him round the throat and spat out, 'If you want to continue living round here, I would seriously think twice about telling Jancey you've been talking to me. If you do, either he or I will come after you. Catch 22.'

'Catch 22, what the fuck's that?' Wildo queried.

'Never mind. You keep your mouth shut, you haven't seen me, OK?'

'OK. Who are you, anyway?'

'The Masked Avenger,' Joel responded. He was getting into these film quotes. Wildo was as confused as the condition of the flat.

'Billy, it's Joel.' Joel was outside the flat on Argyllshire Street and knew he would have to move fast. Despite his threats to Wildo, Joel thought he may try and contact his dealer, who was probably far more important than some random cop. Joel would have a little time, though; Wildo was bound to fall asleep again, and it would take him some time to find his phone in the toilet. It probably wouldn't work anyway; Joel noticed on the way out 'Madam' must have dropped it down the loo. Love scorned, thought Joel.

'Hi Joel, how's the fatigue?' responded Billy sarcastically.

'Fuck off. Are you at work? Can you talk?' asked Joel.

'Yeah, no problem, everyone is out,' Billy said as he looked around the office.

'Can you do me an Intel check now, quick?'

'What is it?' said Billy, with no challenge to his colleague as to the legitimacy of the check.

'I want to find a drug dealer, down Sutton way, with the street name Jancey. I think it's spelled Juliet, Alpha, November, Charlie, Echo, Yankee.' Joel could hear Billy typing away on the other end.

A minute later Billy came back. 'Got him. Leonard Alfred Jancer, also known as Jancey and Jana Man, born 15.4.77. Last known address 564 Wilton House. Form for dealing, possession of imitation firearm, and he's on licence for the dealing.'

'Great, thanks Billy. Got to hurry, I'll explain later. Did you see Zoot?'

'Yes, he's got matters in hand,' replied Billy.

'Ta-ra, see you.' Joel hung up quickly. He didn't know, but he suspected Wilton House was one of the blocks of flats he'd seen on the way into Merton, not far from Wildo's flat. He had to move even quicker than he'd thought, despite Wildo's wet phone.

Joel was correct. Wilton House was among the blocks of small, well-maintained housing association flats he'd seen. From the outside they looked as though they were built in the seventies.

Joel went to the communal entrance just as a sprightly old lady was coming out, and he held the door open for her. Despite this, she challenged him.

'You don't live in here. What you up to?'

'That's quite right, Madam, I'm here to see a Mr Jancer in 564,' responded Joel.

'That waster. Are you police?'

'That's right, Madam.'

'Have a look in the flower pot outside his door, that's all I'll say,' said the woman with a slight sniff.

'Are you a neighbour?' asked Joel.

'All I'm saying is look in the flower pot,' repeated the woman as she walked off towards the main road.

It was a piece of luck meeting her, thought Joel. Wilton House was a small block, five floors high and only four flats on each floor, despite the number system. Joel used the stairs, gently opened the door at the top and crept onto the landing. As he did so, the door of 562 opened. An old man popped his head out of the door, pointed at one of four plant pots on the landing, said, 'That one' and closed the door as quietly as he opened it.

Joel thought, the tricky old bird has phoned her old man. God, I could do with these two in Islington. Joel had always dreamt of having an army of elderly people riding on the Tube, buses and trains, listening out for the chance loose conversation travelling criminals make. They would then ring in the Intelligence, the villains would have no idea where it had come from, game, set and match! He thought the idea, while mirroring elements of the Stazi, still had some merit.

Joel went to the plant pot, took one of the obligatory latex gloves from his pocket and pulled the foliage to one side. Well, well, well, Joel thought, a bag of white powder, a handgun, a lock knife and a door key. The plant pot was opposite 564, not next to it. Nevertheless, the siting of this stash so close to his flat indicated a degree of confidence, if not arrogance, on Jancey's behalf. Joel went back to the staircase and made another phone call to Billy, then returned to the landing and knocked at the door. He'd considered using the key, but determined on a straightforward strategy as far as Jancey was concerned.

A voice from behind the door asked who was there. Joel said, 'Police, Offender Management. Spot check.' Well it was true, Joel justified to himself.

The door opened, but not before the unlocking of two locks, two bolts being drawn back and a chain being removed. Joel moved in quickly. There was only one person in the flat, which was small, well kept and had two bedrooms. Fortunately all the doors were open, and Joel could see no one else in the flat.

'Hello, Lawrence, how are you?' said Joel without introducing himself.

'I'm fine, man, what's this? A shakedown? I'm clean, man, why the hassle?' Jancey was a broad-shouldered black man, six foot in height and looking as though he could have been a handful. Joel didn't want to have to fight him.

'I understand you've been keeping some bad company, Lawrence,' said Joel. 'The prison population already has enough people in without adding you to it.'

'I'm just keeping myself to myself, don't want any prison time, man,' replied Jancey.

'Well, Lawrence, you have been doing people favours, haven't you? What about Wildo? He did a job for you, didn't he? And, of course, his friend Crete, who is sadly no longer with us. Just having talked to them should get you back inside.'

'What you talking about, man? I don't know them, what's your problem? I ain't done nothing.' Jancey was clearly agitated.

'The problem is, Lawrence – and I know it wasn't your idea, you're just the piggy in the middle – those two did a job for you. Who asked you, Lawrence? It would be unfortunate if you had to go back to Wandsworth, with no chance of an open prison, now wouldn't it?'

'Hey, man, what's your game? I thought you were Offender Management.' Jancey was becoming suspicious.

'Oh, I am,' replied Joel. 'I really am. I just want to make sure prisons are full of the "right" people, not those who have been duped. Now, Lawrence, who asked you to get Wildo and Crete?'

'You promise you won't revoke my licence for talking to them?' pleaded Jancey.

'I promise as long as you're telling me the truth,' Joel reassured him.

'Ok, it was Bunny, from The Lancet in Croydon. He owns the place, or says he does. He gave me the address and said he wanted some woman warned. Those two idiots just decided to firebomb the place.'

'Why?' Joel queried.

'I don't know. She and her boyfriend were causing trouble for some friends of Bunny's.'

'Which friends?'

'Come on, man, Bunny is very well connected. All sorts go in his club.'

'OK, but if you've told me lies, I'll be back.'

'Honest, man, I'm telling the truth. I'm not doing anything, I'm clean. I just want a job,' whined Jancey.

That's not what the contents of the flowerpot indicate, thought Joel, but he replied, 'OK, but remember if it's lies I'll be back.'

'Hey, man, you're not going to front up Bunny, are you? He'll do me.' Jancey sounded frightened by the sudden realisation of what he had said.

'No, no, no, Lawrence, that's not how it works. Be lucky, Lawrence, be lucky.'

Joel left the flat quickly before Jancey had further time to think about his Offender Management Manager and walked down the stairs. As he was leaving, he confirmed there was no CCTV in the hallway, which was unusual for housing associations nowadays.

Who should he meet but the old lady again as he was walking away from the flats.

'Find what you wanted, Officer?' she queried.

'Yes, thank you, your friend was very helpful,' he replied.

'He's no friend of mine, he's my husband,' she muttered and walked off.

Joel said, 'Might be best if you keep off the landing for an hour or so.' The old woman turned back, nodded her thanks and continued on her way.

Joel walked around the corner to a side street, where he phoned Billy for the third time today and simply said, 'The coast is clear.' He also arranged to see him for breakfast the following morning.

Seven minutes later, a transit van arrived at Wilton house. Five of its occupants went in the front entrance, one went to the back and another stayed with the van.

The five made their way to the fifth floor, photographed the hallway and burst down the door of 564, which the occupant had failed to secure properly. Jancey denied any knowledge of the plant pot or its contents. The occupants of 562 confirmed it was their plant pot, but knew nothing about the non-vegetable matter. The raiders were sure they'd find DNA and fingerprints belonging to Jancey on the contents.

Jancey was in a state of confusion. He'd just had a visit from Offender Management; now the police had found his stash. They couldn't be connected or his Offender Manager would have revoked his licence there and then, wouldn't he?

Sarah had been distant for a while. Joel surmised it was because of the fire, the business or Joel's visit to South Africa, or a combination of all three, but her vagueness was strange.

They arranged to meet at Trader Vics, a buzzy, popular restaurant in the basement of the Hilton Hotel in Park Lane, at 7pm. She had stayed with Rosemary while Joel was 'doing the flat up', and causing a little trouble in South London, of course. Joel was relaxed about Sarah staying with Rosemary, it would be good for her, and also allowed him to continue with his own little tasks.

When Joel arrived in the restaurant Sarah was already there, drinking what appeared to be a martini. Joel ordered a beer. They greeted each other with a kiss on the cheek more akin to acquaintances than lovers, even though they had spoken every day since they returned to London.

Before going into the restaurant, Sarah blurted out, 'I've got something to say…Joel, I'm thinking of going back to banking.' Joel had expected some news, but this was not it. He knew Sarah had disliked banking, and now was not exactly a good time to go into this arena after everything which had been written about 'fat cat' bankers and how they had destroyed businesses and damaged most of the world's developed economies.

Joel remarked, 'It seems to me a lot of bankers couldn't lie straight in bed, a bit like those politicians who are now criticising them, and you want to join that lot?

Sarah argued the banking world was changing for the better and told him she had been offered a position as a partner in Behrens Bank in the City. They were desperate to demonstrate transparency and equality of opportunity, with none of the chauvinistic nepotism, which had been there for years.

'Oh, but it's OK for feminist nepotism is it? When was the job advertised? Very transparent!'

'Joel, stop playing the detective and looking for something which isn't there.' Sarah glared at him. 'You know how it operates.'

'Course I do, it just seems such a contradiction from your opening. Anyway, a detective is what I am. A seeker of facts, motives and the truth – it's what I do.'

Ignoring his negativity, Sarah reiterated it was a great opportunity and she even had a buyer for the shop in Budleigh Salterton. She simply wanted his agreement and support. Joel realised what he said wouldn't make any difference. He had long ago discovered the only person Sarah cared about was Sarah, this event just brought it to the surface. It might have been different if they had any children, although he suspected not even then. Sarah did not see it would change anything as the two of them would be in London, but he knew the reality: the hours she would have to work and the returning home shattered. He reminded her he also worked weekends and they would hardly see each other. Despite Sarah promising it would be good for them, he understood this was the way she tried to reconcile her selfishness.

'Sarah, you've made up your mind. You know you always put

yourself first, so just get on with it.' There, he'd said it: it was out. She stared at him. Fortunately they were called through to their table where the steaks were served. They ate their food, washed down by a shared rum log, which was a porcelain log filled with rum punch, drunk through two very long straws. Joel loved them.

The conversation over dinner was polite but distant, with both asking about various people they knew and then turning to the shop sale. Sarah explained while he was in South Africa she visited Paris to take a prospective buyer around some of her contacts. Any thoughts the sale was because of his trip to South Africa quickly vanished. This meant she had been thinking about it for a while.

They finished their meal and caught a cab to the flat. Sarah was impressed by what Joel had achieved in what seemed like a short time. In reality it was all cosmetic.

She said, 'Now you've done it up we could put in on the market, add the money to come from the shop and get somewhere bigger.'

'Don't you mean somewhere nearer the City?' Joel snapped. Sarah's face turned to permafrost. He continued, 'This place is fine, I'm not moving anywhere.'

The conversation went dramatically downhill from there, partly fuelled by the alcohol but mostly by their frustration with each other. They came to the joint conclusion there was little future in their relationship, which seemed to lighten the tone of the conversation considerably. Without rancour they agreed to go their own separate ways, Sarah returning to banking and Joel staying in London. And this was the end of the conversation for the night. No goodnight pleasantries, no goodnight kiss. They both pretended to slip seamlessly off to sleep, but in reality they were both thinking; thinking very hard but a little relieved the conversation had taken place.

Chapter Twenty-Six

Frederick was in his office, having arrived at the usual time, and enjoying his coffee when Marta phoned to tell him there was a caller on the line who wanted to speak to him but would not give a name or say what it was about. She and Frederick were used to this sort of call, given the type of cases they became involved in.

Frederick asked Marta to put the call through, and said, 'Good morning, this is Frederick Weisner. How can I help you?'

The caller answered, 'My name is Francois Pienaar I have some information for you.'

Frederick immediately recognised the voice and the irony of the name they had chosen. It was Letsego Shabangu.

'Good morning, Mr Pienaar. I recall meeting you some time ago.' Frederick was deliberately vague about when they had met; clearly Letsego was suspicious of telephone conversations, and Frederick wanted to indicate he understood his cautiousness and didn't want to do anything to expose his identity.

'Yes, it was difficult to talk openly, but I wanted to tell you something else. The Insect has been very active for over twenty years in his attacks on houses, including in the Constantia area, before being caught this time.

Despite his nom-de-plume, Letsego was cross-coding: switching from English to Xhosa. Frederick could readily understand what he was trying to say, literally and subliminally. Letsego was telling him the reason Kem may have been attacked was because Tebego Mhkize broke into the homes of the wealthy, and may have been responsible for the break in at the Corfields' home and Jessica's death.

'I understand, Mr Pienaar, that is very useful,' Frederick said solicitously. 'I am grateful, I hope things are calm for you at the moment.'

'They are better. People understand what has gone on, but we are always careful. Goodbye, Mr Frederick.' And the conversation ended as quickly as it had started. Frederick looked up and saw Marta standing at the door.

'What was that about, Papa?' she asked.

'An interesting development, Marta. Can you please get me all the information we have collected on Tebego Mhkize?'

'You have it, Papa, it's in your file,' she replied.

'Of course, now where is it?' As usual, despite the paper taking over his office, which Marta constantly threatened to 'tidy up' when he was out, he went straight to a bundle of papers and found the file on Mhkize. 'Ahh, here we are,' he said as he laid it on his desk and recounted the conversation which had just taken place.

As they looked through the files, they reminded themselves of Mhkize's criminal history. He began committing crime when he was thirteen, or at least had begun being caught when he was thirteen. The crimes were of a relatively minor nature and they tended to be associated with breaches of the Pass Laws. What became evident from the file was Mhkize was a traveller, but unlike many of the people who lived in the townships and travelled to work, he travelled to commit crime in traditionally white areas, where his very presence at the time must have caused suspicion among the residents. A highly risky activity.

He was regularly arrested and imprisoned for thefts from shops: running in, grabbing something and running out, or burglary in shops and warehouses at night. These crimes were coupled with local violent and drugs' offences. Nothing about burglaries or robberies in houses appeared in the files, despite Letsego's information, but both Frederick and Marta concluded Mhkize was about at night.

They looked through the scant information, searching for associates. There was little historical information, but one name came up three times: Charl Majola from Guguletu.

Frederick said, 'Marta, are you still in touch with Andrica Greef?'

'Papa, you know I am. You know full well she is married to Jean Van Gil.'

'Of course. Perhaps we should invite them and her parents for dinner. What do you think?'

'Papa, what are you up to?' Marta said suspiciously.

'Oh, nothing, just Jean has excellent current knowledge of Guguletu, and Andrica's father was a detective there twenty or so years ago.'

Marta had forgotten about Andi's father, a retired police officer who, according to Frederick, was very similar to Jean: incorruptible and honest. She now understood her father's request.

'OK, but should I tell them they will be quizzed over dinner?' Marta asked.

'Why not?' said Frederick, but Marta had already gone into her office and he was left thinking about today's twist in the Kem Siblisi inquiry.

Joel was up early the following morning. It was like getting ready for work, except he was still 'sick'. He showered, dressed and peeped in the spare bedroom. Sarah was still asleep, or looked like it. He left a note. *Have to go out, see a man about a job, backlater, J.* No kisses, no greeting, a note to a colleague or perhaps a friend, Brute would have assessed.

Joel had arranged to meet Billy for breakfast. He left the flat, caught the Tube into Victoria, walked down to New Scotland Yard, jumped back on the Tube to Monument at St James Park and returned to the Angel on the Northern line, just in time to join Billy at eight when the Breakfast Club in Camden Passage opened. He was beginning to enjoy pissing his watchers off – a lot!

Billy arrived about 8.15am, joined him in a cup of tea and slipped Joel his mobile under the table, as discreetly as he could. They ordered breakfast; he went for the full English while Joel preferred the more understated bacon and egg sandwich. Billy explained he gave Zoot Joel's phone and he had taken it everywhere he went yesterday. Zoot switched it on when he was in the Chelmsford area for about two hours, then switched it off until he reached Slough, when he switched it on again for a couple of hours. Zoot then travelled into Central London where he kept it on until 4pm before switching it off and calling at Billy's to return it. Joel asked Billy to pass on his thanks to Zoot and they smiled at each other, picturing the hapless surveillance teams sprinting across London. Joel was, for once in recent times, grateful for his habit of taking his phone with him everywhere, even if it was switched off.

Joel and Billy glanced around the café looking for watchers. Joel thought he had spotted two earlier on his trip into NSY, and there were a couple of likely suspects enjoying their breakfasts. Joel and Billy suddenly got up, leaving their half eaten food, paid the bill and walked around Islington, laughing about the poor watchers who not only would be frazzled yesterday trying to track down Joel, or rather his phone, but were now having to leave their breakfast. Joel and Billy walked on to Upper Street where they went into another cafe and re-ordered the same meal.

'I feel a bit like a restaurant critic,' joked Billy.

'Me too,' concurred Joel. 'I would give this seven out of ten and the BC eight. What do you think, Mr Gill?'

'Who the fuck is Mr Gill?' asked Billy.

'AA GILL the critic, you plonker,' Joel responded. He could get used to this life. Rather like hobbits, the pair finished their second breakfast and walked out into Upper Street.

As they were walking back towards the Tube station, Joel said, 'Billy, I'm going to Canada to see my children, if the "Belial" will let me.' Billy knew the person Joel was talking about. 'While I'm away, have a discrete look at a guy called Bunny who runs or owns the Lancet Club in Croydon. Don't do it until I'm out of the country, but if anything happens I asked you to do it because it's connected with the fire – which it is. Remember, Billy, be careful.'

Billy replied, 'No problem, Joel, just let me know when you are back.'

The pair shook hands, and as Billy went off to work, Joel walked back into the café where he had a tea, switched on his phone and transcribed a draft letter to his ex-wife into an email, which he sent from his phone. He didn't care who read it.

As it went, he thought about his children. He missed Phoebe and Will enormously. His ex-wife was like Sarah in many ways: ambitious, confident, motivated and selfish! Why did he always go for women like this? Then he thought of Marta. She wasn't at all like it. She was confident, yes, but cared about others, whose thoughts and feelings she always seemed to put before her own. Perhaps his taste in women was changing, probably maturing.

Margo enjoyed a successful career in local government and the health service before she went to Canada. Joel wanted children; so did Margo, but despite his shifts, it was Joel who generally dropped the children off and picked them up from nursery, school, friends' houses, wherever, while Margo was at work, at a function or elsewhere.

She had moved jobs quite a lot over the years Joel had known her. A particularly nasty trait he noticed in Margo over the years was she always thought she could do a better job than her boss. Many people think they can do a better job than their bosses, including Joel sometimes, but with Margo, it was only a question of time before she would tell Joel so. On a number of occasions she undermined her bosses with the non-executive directors or politicians, or accidentally missed them out of the loop in an initiative for which she would seek the glory. This resulted in her premature departure from jobs on three occasions, invariably with compromise agreements and pay-offs, which just seemed to disappear into the ether. Joel had never been driven by money or individual ambition, and it was only during the subsequent divorce hearings he realised money had disappeared. Despite his ace detective ability, the length of time prevented him from finding where it had gone.

He was constantly surprised how Margo managed to get another job. Invariably it was through her connections, which she exploited brazenly, but he was still surprised. Her reputation, personal and professional, couldn't have been good.

Joel and Margo had drifted apart, and when she said she wanted to separate, it was not a surprise. In fact it was a relief. The knowing glances from friends and her nights away 'working' had worn thin. The timing, however, was a surprise. She was once again out of work. The children were Joel's only concern and because Margo was out of work, she was looking after them as she had done during her other bouts of enforced unemployment.

She wanted to take the children with her. What could he do? He was in full time employment, she was not. Joel made the agonising decision it was better for the children to have one full-time parent rather than a part-time one: him. He hated himself for being in this position, but the legal advice confirmed his fears. A court would be more likely to grant her custody, residence, whatever it was called, given the current circumstances. The actual divorce and financial settlement took their toll, and while Margo's earning potential was considerable she played the dutiful mother card for all it was worth. The court accepted it and it cost Joel a fortune. Financially he could live with it, but emotionally it cost him.

At the hearing, he learnt of another bombshell: Margo wanted to move to Canada and take the children with her. She had a Canadian boyfriend, someone she worked with in London. This hit Joel very hard, and while he could have fought it, the advice was he was more likely than not to lose a very long, protracted and financially expensive court case. It would have been different if Joel had retired, but he thought this was not an option. He had to work to provide for the children.

Seeing no way through the mess without affecting the children, Joel hoped the Canadian experience would be like an adventure for them and so reluctantly agreed. He had never forgiven his ex-wife and never would: she treated the children as chattels, which she had stolen from him.

Joel never wished his life away, but at this time he did wish for retirement so he could challenge the Belial as he called her, an old Hebrew word, literally meaning the devil. He was also left with considerable debt from the sale of the house she had desired: a big country house to which he had capitulated. Now she had fucked off, he had to sort out the debt. It was a tough period for Joel, but he got through it with friends like Brute helping him.

Stop plotting revenge, he admonished himself.

Surprisingly she came back in response to his email almost instantaneously saying she felt it was a great idea and the children would love it. Did he want to stay at the house? There was a guest apartment in the grounds. Joel knew this, but declined her 'very kind offer' and said he wanted to hire an RV. Joel was suspicious of her reaction: he had learnt to be so, the hard way.

Joel went to a travel agent he had used before who was always very helpful. He considered booking the trip himself, but given the timescales he needed some professional help. In any case, if he organised it he would probably end up in 'Deliverance' country. He could hear the banjos playing in his head as he thought it! By four o'clock in the afternoon everything was booked: flight, RV and campsites. He felt exhilarated.

Joel FaceTimed the children during the evening. They were very excited at the prospect of their father coming, but also about exploring in an RV. They had been away for weekends with their friends and warned their father about the dangers of bears. Bears? Oh my God, it's worse than South Africa with those bloody baboons. It'll be OK, thought Joel. He was also excited. FaceTime was good, but not the real thing.

When he got back to the flat Sarah had gone and left a fairly functionary note saying she would collect her things during the following weeks. Joel thought it was good he was going to be out of the way.

He phoned Fiona Henderson to let her know where he was going, and to emphasise he was going to see the children and his trip had nothing to do with anything else. She knew how much Joel missed his children and thought the break would be good for him, but privately she was concerned about the impact of leaving them again in Canada might have upon him.

Chapter Twenty-Seven

Things moved quickly over the next few days for Piers's team identifying the patterns of the targets, when they left home, where they parked their cars, which routes they took home. The surveillance teams also established five of the CID, including the DCI, were very active, visiting clubs, pubs, shops and restaurants. Magnus actually paid a visit to the Westons the weekend the operation began.

Joel flew on the Saturday, and the day after he was in the Rockies with the children. They were having a wonderful time and the children took great delight teaching their father about the do's and do nots of camping in the Canadian part of the Rocky Mountains. Well, camping was a euphemism; while the RV was a tin can on wheels, it had every luxury – TV, PlayStation, a fridge bigger than the one in Joel's flat and beds to die for. He was also spending a lot of time thinking.

Piers phoned Joel in Canada and asked him to speak to Ron. Joel had invested in yet another phone on his arrival in the country and sent the number to Piers and his other collaborators in the United Kingdom and South Africa. The call was a diversion from his thoughts.

'Hi, Ron, it's Joel Grant from Islington.'

'Hello, son, how's it going?' said Ron cheerily.

'How's it going with you more to the point? You've had a visit.'

'Yes, he was here. Cheeky bastard wanted £500, said it was the holiday fund. I haggled and got away with four. He said next month it's going up permanently to three.'

'Well, we'll see about that,' replied Joel.

'You watching the place, son?'

'Not me, but some friends of ours. They're looking after you now,' replied Joel.

'I'm grateful, son, but you know I won't give evidence.'

'We know that, Ron, you just carry on and forget I rang.'

'OK, son,' said Ron, and Joel hung up then rang Piers and related the story.

'Cheeky bastard,' said Piers.

'That's what Ron said.'

'It does explain why they haven't had the meeting,' said Piers, with a special thought in the back of his mind, 'they're collecting their holiday money. We could be on big style, Joel.'

'I do hope so. Let me know, won't you?'

'Of course,' said Piers.

Piers thought the job was going very well. The team was working long hours, and while the trip to and from Odium was a bind and needed extra drivers, they were buoyant. None of them noticed another team who were based on the other side of the camp; also police officers, but with Midlands accents.

Two days later Piers received a call from one of the watchers. Rigby and Taylor had just gone into the pub as Magnus was tidying his desk. After Magnus paid the early visit to Weston's Yard, Piers set up an observation point on the CID office and was monitoring phone traffic, although they quickly discovered Magnus and his henchmen only used the phones for legitimate business.

Piers was then told Magnus had left the office, but had turned to go in the opposite direction from the pub. Piers was not too alarmed; Magnus always parked his car round the corner from the pub and was using a different route for some reason. He told the team not to follow him. Sure enough, twenty minutes later Magnus arrived at the pub to join the other four who had all reached it by now, including one DS who was on 'lates' and should have been working, but this didn't seem to bother him.

To have placed one of the team in the pub would have been too risky, not only because, despite his arrogant behaviour, Magnus was wily and would be on the lookout, but also Granger, the pub owner, knew many of the surveillance team who had worked with him prior to his departure. Three long and tortuous hours later, all five of the targeted team were seen leaving the pub together. Piers thought this typified the conceit he and his team had witnessed. The surveillance team identified a CID car parked up two streets away and assumed it had been driven by the late turn DS.

Sure enough, they were right. The DS went to the car, got in and was making his way in the opposite direction from the police station.

He was still under surveillance, and Piers allowed it to continue to see where he was going. It quickly became evident he was making his way through two other police districts to his home, in the police car. The traffic car, which was discreetly tagging on the end of the surveillance team, was called forward and stopped the car.

DS Evans said he was a police officer on a delicate job. He was: taking his money home. The traffic officers breathalysed him; he failed to blow it properly, and was arrested with three thousand pounds in his pocket. One down, a satisfied Piers thought when he got the news in his control room at Odium.

Three of the others were arrested and found to be over the limit. They too had three thousand pounds in cash on them. Four down; Piers ticked them off his list. It was going better than he could have dreamt.

Magnus on leaving the pub was being cautious, very cautious, but having taken an unusual route, including going down dead-ends and walking into local shops, he eventually got into his car and started driving. Piers made another call to Tom, the traffic inspector.

'He's yours, Tom.'

Two minutes later DCI James Magnus was being stopped and asked to blow into a breathalyser.

'Don't you know who I am? I'm DCI Magnus from Belmont Gardens CID.'

'That's fine, Sir,' said the traffic sergeant, indicating the breathalyser device. 'If you wouldn't mind just blowing in this, Sir.'

'I'll have your job for this, you Scots bastard,' Magnus spluttered and pushed the device away.

'I think that's a refusal, Gordon,' said the inspector who was standing just behind his sergeant.

Magnus tried to push the sergeant out of the way and make a run for it. The sergeant grabbed him by the arm to stop him when Magnus turned around and took a swing at him. Gordon ducked in enough time to see his inspector's fist going over his head and hitting Magnus on the jaw, causing him to fall on his bottom.

'Thanks, Sir,' said Gordon.

'My pleasure,' answered Tom, knowing the entire incident was being videoed by a third colleague.

'Let's get him up,' said Tom. As they did, Magnus dropped something on the pavement; it was an envelope.

'What's in that?' asked the inspector.

'What?' said Magnus.

'That envelope.'

'Don't know what you're talking about,' said Magnus aggressively. 'Are you trying to fit me up for that as well as assaulting me and falsely arresting me?'

'Handcuff him, Gordon, we don't want anything else falling from his pockets or further attempts to assault you.' Tom, the inspector, looked around. Their third colleague nodded: he'd got it all on film.

'I'll film the whole scene as well, Sir, and we'll get someone to guard it while CSI come out,' said the evidence gatherer from Piers' team. The subsequent examination of the envelope found only Magnus's prints.

Magnus was then taken to Belgravia police station, but not before Tom made a discrete call to Piers to tell him of the arrest. Once Piers received the call he then rang Det Supt Gary Wilson. Within fifteen minutes The Pilgrims was being raided by a specially briefed SPG search team, and Billy Granger, the ex-police licensee, was arrested.

Almost simultaneously, Det Supt Danny Yellop was leaving the Tube at Mill Hill near his home when two men and a woman approached him. They spoke in West Midlands accents, identified themselves as police and arrested Yellop for corruption and misconduct in a public office. They found five thousand pounds in his pockets.

Piers also made a call to Joel and left a message saying, 'It's done, they're finished!'

The next forty-eight hours were frenetic for Piers and his team: searching, researching and making further arrests.

The first full debrief of the team came at nine, two days later. It was opened by the Commissioner herself, saying a major strike against corruption had been achieved because of the actions of those in the room, and those who were still busy throughout London continuing the investigation. She wanted to thank everyone personally for what they had done.

She handed over to DCS Campbell, who also said her thanks not only to her own officers, but also to the West Midlands team who had been working away for months supporting an undercover operation, which struck at the heart of her own command. She explained how suspicions developed over the activities of Yellop and his associates, and for the first time she revealed the fact a commander and chief superintendent had also been arrested. The search of Yellop's home revealed forty thousand in cash and the deeds of property in Cornwall.

The Magnus search was more illuminating: twenty thousand pounds, two Rolex Oysters and, more importantly, from his desk drawer a ledger of payments which had been received and payments made. Not in the copperplate writing of Mrs Weston, but all held on a handy iPad, police issue. He had made the notes, it was thought, for no other reason than to blackmail the senior officers and those who would become senior officers as their careers progressed. Also found was reference to a safety deposit box in central London which, when searched, revealed a further £100,000, jewellery, a kilo of cocaine and the deeds to a flat in Chelsea. When visited, the flat revealed Magnus's other life: it was the home of a twenty-five year old Cuban jazz singer whom Magnus had befriended and fallen in love with.

Another important search took place in The Pilgrims Arms where, to everyone's surprise, £50,000 was found still in its MPS bag!

Quite a haul!

The DCS said all those arrested on the first night would be appearing in court this morning, when they would hopefully be remanded in custody, which happened. All except the DS who had been on duty had gone 'No comment'. The DCS announced for the first time the conversations in The Pilgrims Arms had been monitored and recorded, they were illuminating. She also divulged the reason for the hike in the demands made was because Yellop had warned Magnus of the possibility of an impending operation against him,

The team visited a number of businesses in Croydon, Sutton and Merton over the following days, and the extent of the corruption became ever clearer. The team had cooperation from some, but not from others who were still frightened of the possible repercussions from the police. One of the local chief superintendents was removed from post and new personnel were drafted into the CID over the following weeks.

It had been gut wrenching for Joel to leave the children with their mother after ten days, but they were back at school the following day. Joel discovered her boyfriend was no longer there. He had departed and was now living in Quebec. God, thought Joel, he really wanted to get away. The Belial had spent the time he was with the children looking for work. Not entirely successfully, Joel established.

As Joel relaxed on the overnight plane to the United Kingdom, he thought about the children. Perhaps he would retire. It would be expensive in terms of his pension, but the last few weeks had opened his mind. There was another life outside the police, however much he enjoyed it.

The steward interrupted his reverie. 'Another drink, Sir?'

Joel looked around and noticed an "s the k" two seats in front starting to wind up the irritation at being strapped in. 'Why not?' said Joel. 'Why not?'

While Joel was enjoying himself in Canada, others in London had not been enjoying themselves, as he found out when he picked up Piers's voicemail, and he toasted the Westons.

Chapter Twenty-Eight

The Commissioner was heading to her regular catch up meeting with the Home Secretary, accompanied by her Chief of Staff, Commander Eric Nugent.

The meetings took place in the Home Secretary's office, and usually the Permanent Secretary would accompany her, or more often the Director of Policing, her private secretary and at least one Special Political Adviser. On this occasion there were two. These meetings were a legacy of the days when the Home Secretary was primarily responsible for policing of London and before the Mayor's time. The Home Office still had an influence on policing, and meetings tended to concentrate on national security type issues.

Today was not going to be any different, thought the Commissioner, but she wanted to emphasise to the Home Secretary the success of the recent corruption investigation, despite the negative media coverage any such exposure brings. The Commissioner wanted the Home Secretary onside, praising the police, not castigating them for letting it happen.

The meetings were generally short, no longer than an hour, and went along the usual lines of dialogue between the Home Secretary and the Commissioner, with the occasional prompts and interventions by the Home Secretary's Advisers.

The Home Secretary opened after the formal greetings. 'I think everyone knows each other, don't they?' Everyone nodded. 'Over to you, Commissioner.'

The Commissioner welcomed this no nonsense approach to meetings. She outlined some of the threats and events which had already taken place, and those due to happen in the next ten days or so. The Security Service would provide similar briefings, but this briefing concentrated on the practicalities.

After the normal business, the Commissioner continued, 'Home

Secretary, I know we spoke briefly on the telephone regarding the recent corruption operation, but I really wanted to emphasise the intelligence regarding it came from within the Met, and with the assistance of additional resources from the West Midlands it was organised and executed by the Met. It is without doubt a major blow against corruption.'

'Yes, I totally agree, Commissioner. It sounds a very significant operation and I am with you in terms of the impact it will have. I see the Mayor has been talking.'

'Yes, he's very happy as well.'

'I'm sure he is, but he doesn't have to answer the difficult questions in the House.'

'I think he knows that, Home Secretary.' She smiled. 'But I would stress this is a good news story. I will ensure you get a note later today, which will fully brief you.' Eric, her Chief of Staff, nodded, acknowledging it would be on its way later.

'I'm grateful, Commissioner,' the Home Secretary said. 'Now is there anything else?'

Katherine Thornley, one of the SPADs, said nothing up to this point. She was fairly new, and came from a background in TV news, directly into the Home Office via party HQ and her own PR firm. 'If I may, Home Secretary, you mentioned corruption, Commissioner. One of your officers has been to South Africa, upsetting the Government and some influential people there. He is now conducting anti-surveillance techniques here in the UK while on sick leave. This surely must be a matter for your complaints people?'

Individual cases were rarely discussed at these meetings and the Commissioner could see the Director of Policing fidgeting in his seat.

The Commissioner, in her relaxed and gentle manner, replied, 'Of course it is, Katherine, and I'm sure they are.'

The smug spin doctor continued, 'But they are not, Commissioner. Hydra have had to do it and are investigating him.'

'Hydra?' queried the Commissioner in the same calm non-threatening manner. 'What is the nature of the allegations against the officer?'

By this time the Director of Policing was desperate to attract the SPAD's attention.

'As I said, he's been upsetting influential people in South Africa,' repeated Thornley.

'Upsetting people? Is that what Hydra are about, investigating people who upset people? I seem to recall when you set up Hydra,

Home Secretary, it was to tackle the top echelons of criminality here and abroad.'

The Home Secretary had only seen the Commissioner annoyed once before in a meeting. She did not want it to be repeated.

'I'm sure it's a bit more than that, Katherine,' appeased the Home Secretary. The SPAD took the hint from her boss.

'And how do you know about this, Katherine?' persisted the Commissioner.

Despite the hint, she couldn't help herself. 'I was at a meeting with AC Bobbin and DAC Dennis at the Yard a couple of weeks ago and saw the detective's superior officer. I was told later you could not do anything because of lack of resources, so I just happened to mention it to the Director General, Gwyn Oliver at one of our briefings. The officer was actually seen having a meeting with an Inspector from the Professional Standards Department,' Thornley added, in an apparent attempt to justify the involvement of Hydra.

While the Commissioner was furious, she couldn't believe the naivety, or was it arrogance, of the SPAD. She suspected the arrogance. The Commissioner had always feared the operational direction of Hydra could be influenced politically, particularly in its early days. It would appear this was proof of them being tasked by a Political Adviser, if not the Secretary of State herself, and a Director General who was weak and keen to please.

The Director of Policing looked as though he was about to collapse. The colour drained from his face and the Home Secretary was only a couple of shades behind him. 'I'm sure this can all be explained, Linda,' said the Home Secretary, who never called the Commissioner by name in meetings.

The Commissioner responded, with a steely glare, 'This is a very serious matter, Home Secretary, one for which the public, the Met and the individual deserve an explanation. The officer may have done something wrong, but two wrongs do not make a right, and what appears to have happened is a very grave wrong. Who is the officer concerned?'

All eyes were now focused on Thornley. 'Grant', she said, 'Detective Sergeant Joel Grant from Islington.'

The Commissioner slowly turned to the Home Secretary and said quietly, 'Home Secretary, there is another matter of the utmost sensitivity I would like to brief you on, but because of what has been said about Hydra I can only do this with Ms Thornley not being in the room.'

The Director of Policing tried, 'Commissioner, Katherine has been vetted to the highest level. I don't think your request is appropriate.'

The Commissioner ignored him and spoke directly to the Home Secretary, saying, 'I can assure you, Home Secretary, my request is entirely appropriate in the circumstances.'

The Home Secretary replied, 'This is rather extreme, Commissioner.'

'I accept that, Home Secretary,' the Commissioner responded in a matter of fact way and with no intention of elaboration.

The Home Secretary turned to Katherine Thornley and said, 'Katherine, could you please excuse us for a moment? I'm sure we can sort this out, if you could just wait outside for a minute. I'm sorry.' Thornley stood up, looked directly at the door and walked straight out of the office. The Director of Policing seemed as though he was about to explode.

'Home Secretary, Joel Grant was the officer who single-handedly identified the corruption network we talked about earlier. We should be talking about rewarding him, not secretly launching an ill-thought through spying operation against him. This, of course, explains why he met with Professional Standards and why he was cautious.'

The Commissioner decided she was going to make the Home Secretary squirm. She knew the Home Secretary would try and come up with excuses, and the Commissioner felt it important to fire the first, hopefully fatal, shot. 'Your investigation,' she said pointedly to the Home Secretary, 'could have jeopardised the whole corruption inquiry. Home Secretary, I'm now going to see the Director General of Hydra and I shall be asking for an explanation.' She turned to the Director of Policing and said, 'I would be grateful for full disclosure of all documentation and decision notes on this matter.'

The Director of Policing had regained some of his colouring. 'That's a matter for the Home Secretary, but would you like me to speak to the Director General for you? I know him quite well.'

The Commissioner replied, 'I think it would be unwise for you or anyone else from the Home Office to speak to Mr Oliver about this matter, most unwise.' She turned to the Home Secretary and continued, 'Your official has said the release of documentation is a matter for you, Home Secretary. Will you release the documents?' Eric Nugent, the Chief of Staff, while making frantic notes was enjoying watching the Home Office suffer. Too many times they had run rough shod over the police. The Commissioner had them on the ropes and seemed to be enjoying it.

'Of course, Linda, we will release whatever we can,' said the Home Secretary.

'Subject to legal advice, of course,' muttered the Director of Policing.

'I hope I don't have to resort to law, Home Secretary,' stated the Commissioner.

'No, no, it's only Hubert being cautious,' the Home Secretary said as she fired a warning glance at her Director of Policing. 'We will, of course, help in whatever way we can. Now, Detective Sergeant Grant, how were you proposing to recognise him?'

The Commissioner thought you're quite a piece of work, Home Secretary, trying to get the issue back on track, but holding back. She said, 'That's something for another day, Home Secretary, and for the record Joel Grant's involvement is known to very few outside this room, including, it would appear, Hydra personnel. I hope it remains so.'

Everyone nodded furiously.

'Is there anything else, Home Secretary?' the Commissioner asked.

'I think not, Commissioner, I think not,' the Home Secretary responded.

'In that case, good morning.' The Commissioner got up from her chair, turned and left the room in metaphoric tatters. She walked straight past Thornley, who was still sitting in the outer office, then made her way out of the Home Office, greeting people as though she didn't have a care in the world.

As the Commissioner was due to go to a meeting in the City, her car was waiting outside the Home Office. She sat in the front, and said, 'The Yard please, Jack,' to her driver, an ex PC who had worked with her for years.

She turned to her Chief of Staff and said, 'I'll ring the office and postpone the City meeting. I can go on later.' She didn't like letting people down. 'Get hold of that idiot Oliver and ask him to my office ASAP. Can you also track down AC Bobbin and DAC Dennis and ask them to my office after I've seen Gwyn Oliver?'

Jack knew the Commissioner was pissed off. The Chief of Staff had seen the Commissioner angry before, but not this angry.

The Commissioner heard the conversation from the back of the car. The Director General of Hydra was out of the country and his deputy was due at a meeting with the Home Secretary in an hour. She heard her Chief of Staff say to the private secretary on the other end of the phone, 'That would be fine, he can call and see her on his way, please. It will only take five minutes. She feels it's not appropriate to speak about it on the phone. Yes, it's an operational matter, twenty minutes will be fine.' The Commissioner thought they were clearly asking what it was about.

The Chief of Staff finished on the phone. 'Well done, Eric, you did well,' the Commissioner said. 'I take it he is away?'

'He's in Italy, Commissioner,' Eric responded.

They had just arrived at the Yard and they went straight to the Commissioner's office. 'I may as well see the AC and DAC now. Ask them to come up, please,' said the Commissioner to her Staff Officer, Pam Styles.

Five minutes later, AC Bobbin and DAC Dennis were in the Commissioner's office. She asked her Chief of Staff to stay.

'Hello Callum, hello William,' she said.

Both men answered, 'Good afternoon, Commissioner,' almost comically in unison, like schoolchildren.

The Commissioner opened, 'I understand you had a meeting recently with Katherine Thornley.'

The AC took the lead, 'Yes that's right, Commissioner, but it was a meeting including Katherine. We all three met DCI Henderson from Islington about a rogue DS and what he had been up to in South Africa. We said we'd have a look at him, but we didn't have capacity to do anything. When we checked with DCS Campbell, Head of Professional Standards, she told us she would not divert resources without written orders. I think she used to work with the officer, whose name was Grant, I think.'

The AC looked at the DAC, who confirmed, 'DS Joel Grant, Commissioner.'

The AC continued, 'I told Katherine and she said she was owed a couple of favours by Hydra, and we left it with her. I think the recent operation in South London has shown how important it is to root out corruption. I stand by my decision, Commissioner.'

'And what decision was that?' asked the Commissioner.

'To speak to DCI Henderson.'

The Commissioner continued in the same charming style she displayed earlier. 'And what has DS Grant been up to? I know Liz Campbell, it wouldn't make any difference to her whether she worked with Grant or not.'

'He's a real rogue, Commissioner. He dropped his DCI in trouble with a judge at the Old Bailey, went sick, buzzed off to South Africa and started making inquiries about a murder down there which happened twenty years ago. He upset the government, and some people got hold of Katherine to tell her and she told us.'

'OK, I see. And who are these people Katherine knows?' asked the Commissioner.

'I don't know their names, just they are influential,' replied Bobbin.

'And how does Katherine know these people?' asked the Commissioner.

'Just through contacts, Commissioner.' The AC didn't like the way the conversation was going.

The Commissioner continued, 'And what sort of contacts are they? Was it an official government approach through the FCO?'

'Not at that stage, although it may come to that, she told us. They were just people she knows who complained to her.'

'Have we had an official complaint in the intervening period, Callum?'

'No, Commissioner,' said the beleaguered AC.

'Has DS Grant received discipline notices?' asked the Commissioner. The Chief of Staff thought, my God, she is going for the jugular.

'Well that's a matter for others,' he responded.

Oh dear, thought the Chief of Staff, his boss wouldn't like that. 'Slopey shoulders' never went down well.

'And do you know what Katherine Thornley's job is at the Home Office?' interrogated the Commissioner.

'She's one of the Home Secretary's advisers.'

'Yes, quite right, but she's not just an adviser, is she, Callum? She's a Special Political Adviser, a SPAD! She is a political activist, a member of the Party, and you interviewed one of my DCIs with her?'

The two men's faces now resembled the colour the Director of Policing had gone earlier. The DAC intervened, 'I wouldn't say we interviewed her, Commissioner.'

'What was it then?' she asked.

'It was more like a chat,' said the DAC weakly. Oh dear, Eric thought once more.

'So two of the Metropolitan Police's most senior officers sit down with a Special Political Adviser to the Home Secretary and have a *chat* with a DCI about one of my Detective Sergeants, who is subsequently put under surveillance by Hydra. Thank God I've got Liz Campbell in charge of Professional Standards, otherwise it would have completely destroyed a major operation.' The Chief of Staff noticed the two men seemed to have gone even paler.

The Commissioner continued, 'This has very serious implications. I want separate reports from you both by three giving me your accounts of what took place. Three o'clock, you'd better get on with it. Oh, and don't bother speaking to Ms Thornley again.' She'd presumed because of the comments they had received a call or text from Thornley. Looking at their reaction, her presumption was right.

The two men needed no further invitation to leave the office.

The Commissioner's PA rang. 'Mr Walkden from Hydra is here, Commissioner,' she said.

The Commissioner asked the Chief of Staff to collect him. He asked the Commissioner if she wanted him to stay for that meeting as well. She did. Good, thought the Chief of Staff.

The Deputy Director General of Hydra walked into the room. The Commissioner said, 'Arthur, good of you to come at such short notice. It's very good of you, I won't keep you long. How are you?'

'My pleasure, Commissioner. I'm fine, how are you?' The Deputy Director General had worked with the Commissioner a long time ago, and had reckoned then she would be the Commissioner one day.

'Arthur, do you know Katherine Thornley?' the Commissioner asked.
'The SPAD?'
'Yes, that's right,' said the Commissioner. 'What dealings do Hydra have with her?'

'Just the usual, really. She attends the meetings with the Home Secretary, she's fairly new, fairly full of her own self importance.' The Deputy Director General felt safe in being frank with the Commissioner.

'Would it surprise you, Arthur, if I told you that, as a result of Ms Thornley's involvement with Hydra, you targeted one of my officers for what looks to me like no good reason?'

Arthur Walkden was taken aback. 'Who was it, Commissioner? When? What for?

'DS Joel Grant from Islington, within the last few weeks according to my sources, because Mr Grant apparently had the audacity to upset someone in South Africa.'

The DDG read her; he knew the Commissioner wanted to know if it was true and wanted to know now. 'Commissioner, if you wouldn't mind, can I make a quick phone call and see if I can shed some light on this here and now to prevent any unnecessary escalation? It sounds odd to me.'

'It is odd, Arthur. Please feel free,' replied the Commissioner.

The DDG made a phone call; the Commissioner could only hear one side. 'Kevin, it's Arthur. I will be brief and circumspect. Operation against a Met DS? That's him. What was it about? Why did we get it? Who authorised it? Which team? OK, tell no one about this call, and I mean no one.'

He ended the call.

'I'm sorry, Commissioner, it was us. DS Joel Grant from Islington, I've heard of him but don't know him. It was something to do with corruption. I need to do more digging and speak to some people. If you could please give me a little time.'

'Who authorised it, Arthur?' She looked straight at him as she said it.

'It looks like the Director General, but I need to check. You know what it's like, things happen in my name all the time.'

'Please do let me know, Arthur. You are going to see the Home Secretary now?'

'That's right, Commissioner. Does she know about this?'

'Yes, we discussed it this morning.'

'Commissioner, I do not intend to talk to anyone about this matter until I have more information, and that includes the Home Secretary,' stated the DDG.

'She will want to talk about it, Arthur,' warned the Commissioner.

'My Staff Officer will ring her private secretary now and say I will not discuss this issue with her, and if she does raise it the meeting will have to be adjourned,' said the DDG resolutely.

'Adjourned, Arthur?' queried the Commissioner.

'Adjourned for legal advice, Commissioner. This stinks,' said the DDG. 'Thank you for telling me, I'm sorry if Hydra has embarrassed you. Grant isn't corrupt from what I know, but I have been wrong before.'

'Thank you, Arthur. If you could let me know what your inquiries reveal?'

'Of course, I will ring you this afternoon. Thank you, Commissioner.' Knowing the meeting had ended, the DDG left.

'What do you think of that?' enquired the Commissioner.

Eric Nugent said, 'Well, it was pretty impressive.' Unlike the previous meeting, he thought to himself, 'I hadn't met Mr Walden before, but I've heard of him.'

'Arthur and I go way back. No backward postings for him or trips to the Inspectorate to help his networking, just hard work. I somehow feel he may be the next DG of Hydra, or hopefully Deputy Commissioner, but I feel a spell on secondment as an AC would be good for both of us in the interim. I think AC Bobbin and DAC Dennis need their careers developed, perhaps to the HMI or the College of Policing!'

The Chief of Staff knew the current Deputy Commissioner was leaving in six months; he liked the way the Commissioner was thinking.

Chapter Twenty-Nine

The DDG's meeting with the Home Secretary went well. She did not ask about the corruption inquiry; the DDG's staff office had phoned ahead and spoken to the Home Secretary's private office. Interestingly, Katherine Thornley was not at the meeting, nor was the Director of Policing. The Home Secretary had her private secretary and another senior civil servant there.

After the meeting with the Home Secretary, Arthur rang the DG, who was in Italy, and told him about his conversation with the Commissioner. The DG went quiet after Arthur briefed him, and Arthur asked him directly, 'Did you authorise the surveillance, Gwyn?'

'Well I wouldn't say I authorised it. I passed it to Richard Lister to deal with. I think you'd better speak to him, Arthur.' Arthur could tell the DG was backtracking, which was typical of the man, and thought he'd apply a little more pressure.

'Are you going to ring the Commissioner, Gwyn?'

'I'm back tomorrow. I'll pop in and see her then, I think,' the DG responded.

'If you don't mind me saying so, Gwyn, I suggest you at least give her a ring. This has serious implications for our relationship and our Constitutional position.'

'Yes, I know, but the Home Secretary didn't mention it to you so it can't be that serious.'

The DDG in exasperation replied, 'But I told you, Gwyn, I'd made it clear I wouldn't talk about it.'

'Well, that wouldn't have stopped her. I'll speak to the Commissioner tomorrow. OK, Arthur, thanks for the call. Got to go, bye.'

Pompous arse, the DDG thought as he made his way to HQ to speak to Richard Lister, the Head of Operations. It had always surprised Arthur how different the DG and he were despite going to the same school in the North East, albeit several years apart, and then Universities a stone's throw from each other.

En route he made a call to the Commissioner's office and spoke to Eric Nugent. The Commissioner was at her meeting in the City. He told Eric the Home Secretary did not mention the issue and he had spoken to the DG who would speak to the Commissioner tomorrow. Arthur added, 'I know she will not like it, but he's in Italy and is adamant he will speak to her personally tomorrow.'

The Chief of Staff read between the lines, something he was becoming quite good at doing, and said, 'I understand, Sir, thank you for trying.' The DDG said he was still attempting to get to the bottom of the authorisation and would speak to the Commissioner when he had done so.

Nugent knew the Commissioner would be unhappy with the Director General's response, but be it on his own head.

Richard Lister was a shrewd investigator, who had a similar background to the DDG, albeit not in the Met. When the DDG came in to see him, he was not surprised; he had been tipped off following the DDG's phone call earlier.

'Hello, Richard, how are things?'

'Better than with you, I suspect,' responded the Head of Operations. 'I heard about your phone call earlier and where you were. 'I know you told Kevin not to tell anyone, but he thought we'd better get the paperwork.'

'What happened, Richard? I understand you authorised the op against Joel Grant.'

'That's not strictly true, Arthur,' replied the Head of Ops as he opened a file on his desk. 'I think you'd better read these documents,' and he handed the file to the DDG, who sat down and started to read.

'Coffee?' asked Lister.

'Please.' Lister left the room to make the coffee and to let Walden read the file, which was comprehensive. It contained a number of documents, but the killer document was a file note compiled by Lister and another senior colleague, Brian Withers, following a meeting with the DG. The document read:

We were called to an urgent meeting with the DG at 4pm today. The DG said he had personal intelligence that a detective sergeant in the MPS was corrupt and in league with South African criminals while he was on sick leave. The DS was Joel Grant from Islington. The DG said this was a matter of national security as it also involved South African political activists. Grant had travelled to SA without authority on the pretext of investigating a murder that took place years ago and his motives were extremely suspect. The DG wanted us, under the personal command of BW, to put Grant under surveillance to establish his corrupt networks and co-conspirators.

RL asked what the classification of the intelligence was and the DG said A1. RL queried whether this wasn't a job for the Met Professional Standards. The DG said they couldn't be trusted as Grant had worked in there in the past.

RL also asked, as it was national security shouldn't the CT Command take it on? The DG dismissed this and said the Home Secretary had asked us to do it and we would.

RL asked what was the exact nature of the allegation against Grant. The DG said he was corrupt, he had been trying to make contact with criminals, visited prisoners and we needed to find out who else was involved. This job was a great opportunity for Hydra.

BW asked if he could see the source documents. The DG said no, they were highly sensitive and he was the conduit. No one else should know, not even the DDG when he returned from leave. The DG said the Home Office had confirmed the telephone intercept application could be signed this evening.

RL said he found this very odd. The DG lost his temper and said, 'I am giving you a direct command. No one outside the investigative team knows about this, clear?'

We then returned to my office and made this note. RL instructed BW that all authorities for surveillance should be forwarded to the DG's office for his signature.

As Arthur was reading the documents the phone in Lister's office rang. Arthur answered it.

'Arthur Walkden, can I help?'

The voice on the other end was Lister's PA. 'Oh I'm sorry, Arthur, I was after Richard. I've got the DG for him.'

Arthur thought this might happen, and said, 'If you could please tell the DG Richard is in a meeting with me, and does he want you to interrupt?'

A moment later the PA came back with a reply. 'The DG said it's OK, he'll see Richard tomorrow.' I bet he did, thought Arthur.

The other documents in the file were surveillance authorities and intercept applications signed by the DG, which Arthur felt were vague to say the least. They included phrases like, 'A source known personally to the DG' and 'The DG indicates the veracity of the intelligence cannot be doubted and is A1'. Arthur could see Lister and Withers had clearly not been comfortable with the op.

When Lister returned to the office with the coffee, Arthur said, 'Why did you let him do it, Richard?'

Lister responded, 'We were left with no alternative. You've read the file note, he was adamant. I thought he was going to explode at one point, and we were told specifically not to tell anyone, including you. I presumed because it was A1 the spooks had got it from Intercept or SIGINT and passed it on. The DG was on a real high with it.'

'Do you know Grant?' asked the DDG.

'Not personally, but we know a lot about him now,' replied Lister.

'And is he corrupt?' asked Arthur.

'I would say no, but he's tricky, very tricky. Good detective.'

'A bit like you then, Richard,' the DDG responded.

'We are on him now. He's just returned from a visit to Canada to see his kids.'

'Please tell me we didn't operate in Canada or get the RCMP involved?'

'I took the decision, Arthur, not to involve anyone else.'

'I'm taking a copy of this file with me. I know protocol says copies can't leave this environment, but this is an extremely serious matter and I need to have these documents readily available. Could you please copy them for me, Richard?'

Lister did this immediately, then returned and asked, 'What's going to happen now, Arthur?'

'I don't know, but it's going to be a real shit storm. I know that. Richard, please do another file note. As of this moment the operation is cancelled. All surveillance authorities are cancelled, and we call the dogs off on my authorisation. Please have it typed up and I will sign it before I see the Commissioner again.'

Arthur took the copy file and walked slowly to his office. He ruminated about the document he was carrying and the conversation he'd had earlier in the day with the Commissioner. In ordinary circumstances he would have gone to the Home Office for advice; on this occasion it was impossible. He called his legal adviser and asked her to come to his office.'

'What's it about?' she said. 'Do I need to bring anything with me?'

'Only your best and most clear brain, Wilma,' he replied heavily.

Two minutes later the legal adviser was in the DDG's office. She was a diminutive birdlike figure with an enormous intellect. Arthur told her of the day's events and the background he had discovered. He finished by saying he was asking advice as her client, but also as a senior manager of the organisation.

The legal adviser took a deep breath, and said, 'I can only advise you as your lawyer, and the situation is clear. I think the full facts need to be disclosed to the Commissioner, she has the investigation. You cannot go to the Home Office. You could go to the Attorney General, but my advice is to go straight to the Commissioner who asked you the question in the first place.'

'Thanks Wilma, I will do that. As always I will follow your advice.' They both smiled. There had been a number of occasions when Arthur had said he heard her advice and thanked her, but then done something different, saying it was only advice.

As the legal adviser was leaving, she turned and said, 'Arthur, as a senior manager in this organisation, my advice would be the same.'

'I recognise that, Wilma, thanks again,' he responded and picked up the phone to the Commissioner's office.

At seven he was back in the Commissioner's office, where she was with her Chief of Staff going through the following morning's work. She offered him a coffee, which he declined saying he didn't need any more caffeine and asked for water. The Commissioner asked, although she didn't need to, 'Would you mind if Eric stayed, Arthur?'

Arthur said, 'Not at all. Has the DG been in touch, Commissioner?'

A terse, 'No,' was the response. Arthur hoped following the DG's abortive phone call to Richard Lister he might have had second thoughts. Unfortunately not.

'In that case, Commissioner, I need to share the contents of this file with you,' said Arthur. He handed her the file he had taken from Lister's office earlier. The Commissioner read all of the documents carefully then closed the file.

'Well, Arthur, I am grateful to you for alerting me to the contents of this dossier. I am not asking for any comment other than whether you believe the authors of this file note?'

'The DG told me earlier Richard Lister authorised the surveillance. The documents tell a different story. I have spoken to Lister as well – his account is plausible. In short, Commissioner, I believe him. You will have noted the operation has been cancelled forthwith.'

'I did. Thank you, Arthur, may I retain these documents?'

'That is the reason I brought a copy Commissioner.'

'Thank you, Arthur. I realise this is difficult for you, but may I ring you if I need any further clarification?'

Arthur admired her different approach; the DG would just have told him to get on with it. She was a class act. 'Of course, anything I can do to help. I am so sorry for this embarrassment, Commissioner.'

'You have nothing to be embarrassed about, Arthur, thank you. Eric, could you ask Tony Silvers to pop up? He's expecting the call.' Arthur left the office and made his way out of the building. He knew Silvers was the Commissioner's Legal Director.

The Commissioner looked at her desk and re-read a document she had read shortly before her meeting with Arthur Walkden. It was a Home Office email:

Katherine Thornley, who has worked in the Home Office on second-ment as an adviser for the last six months, will be leaving the department to resume leading her public relations firm. Katherine will not be replaced immediately, and her work will be distributed among other staff who will be in touch with stakeholders in the near future.

The Commissioner thought what wasn't said was more interesting than what was said in the email: No thank you, no message of good wishes for the future. In particular there was no mention of her having been adviser to the Home Secretary. She was being burnt in the hope it would all fall on her shoulders, and the Commissioner knew this would not be the last resignation regarding this matter.

Chapter Thirty

As Joel drifted in and out of sleep on his flight home he was aware of a chorus of French people talking a few seats away. Is chorus the correct collective noun? he thought. Perhaps not, but it should be.

Joel's mind continued to wander, this time to Kem and to South Africa. He considered he might have made a grave error in concentrating on Kem being innocent; he had become carried away with it, concentrating on the significant scientific developments which had taken place over the years. He had not, he felt, paid enough attention to the whodunnit aspect. Who *had* killed Jess?

His annoyance at himself lessened when he forensically analysed the total ongoing process he had been through: his briefing by Robert; reading the case papers in South Africa; reviewing the media and talking to people. What Joel was doing was what any good investigator does: review their findings and challenge their assumptions from different perspectives as they went along – the search for the truth.

As he sat there he speculated. If the murderer wasn't Kem, who could it be? Who was around at the time?

What about Virginia, Matthew's mother? Perhaps a jealous mother? But jealous of what? A new, attractive woman in the household? But from what Joel could determine, Virginia had loved Jess and viewed her as the daughter she'd never had. She was also glad, he recalled Robert telling him, Matthew had fallen for an English woman, not a South African of whatever colour! Motive – zero, so perhaps not Virginia.

George, the wealthy businessman? But again, what was his motive? He wouldn't be jealous in the same way Virginia could have been. As far as Joel had seen, George had been delighted by Matthew's choice of potential life partner. He was very successful, and popular among the chattering classes of white South African society, Joel wondered why would George murder Jess? A possible motive: predatory male with his future daughter in law – not unknown, but unlikely. Also, Joel thought, as far as he could remember George was not a big man, and certainly didn't have large forearms like the murderer at the Bailey.

Matthew? Hmm, Matthew. He'd loved Jess, this much was evident, virtually from the first time they had met. They lived together for three years, just got engaged, planning their wedding and the rest of their life together. It surely couldn't have been Matthew, Joel thought. But was it Joel's friendship for the guy or logic discounting him? Matthew had a slight build like his father, and there was certainly no history of violence in the relationship. Jess would have jettisoned him right away – literally, thought Joel. Yes, she could handle herself. He recalled her taking on some robbers as she was getting off the Tube, whacking one so hard she knocked him out while his mates ran off. No, no domestic violence.

What about another member of staff? He wondered where the police file was – if there was one. He had seen the prosecution case but not the file. He wondered what other inquiries they had made. He feared the police had made their minds up it was Kem who was responsible and had paid no attention to the other possible scenarios. From his limited experience, it seemed to Joel house staff tended to stay with families for years, if not generations. Perhaps the majority were still around, but the police file was the start.

Then the most likely alternative scenario: intruders. A burglary gone wrong; an assault gone further than anticipated; a sexual attack with a predetermined outcome. The police would have discounted these options at a very early stage, if they had been examined at all. The Corfields lived in a secure compound, but it would not have been the first secure compound in South Africa to be broken into without the offenders being caught. Joel's mind wanderered tangentially as he wondered if Marta had been successful in finding the file, or crime data regarding attacks at similar houses in the Constantia area. He was not hopeful of either, particularly the details of other offences.

Joel thought, even in the United Kingdom it would have been difficult, if not impossible, to find such details. Files would have been destroyed, and only the metadata retained. Additionally, recording practices varied considerably across the United Kingdom, never mind in South Africa; for example, attempted burglaries would sometimes be recorded as criminal damage. This was plain stupid to Joel; if you wanted to identify patterns of offending, offenders and better still, predict accurate, timely data was essential. It tended to be the lazy, inept or simply incompetent managers who manipulated crime figures, but Joel always thought of crime classification as an art, not a science as others did.

Upon reflection, Joel had covered the bases. His annoyance with himself was just a momentary crisis of confidence; a symptom of his high flying and alcohol consumption, he concluded.

He started to relax, but for some reason Matthew returned to the forefront of his mind. Matthew was supposed to have been away for the weekend, and had not been due to return until the morning after Jess was found dead. In fact, he arrived back early, about an hour after Jess's body had been found. So he had been in the Cape Town area when Jess was killed, but there was still no motive Joel could find in his deliberations. Where had Matthew been? Joel remembered Matthew had been to see a friend who lived in Port Elizabeth over 350 miles away, but didn't know any more. He suspected the police didn't know either, as there was no reference to it in the prosecution. Once again, Joel considered what he thought the police mindset could have been on the night. They had their suspect, who had been seen running away; they didn't need anything else.

Why would Matthew murder Jess? He loved her, for fuck's sake. But there was something. Joel began to consider Matthew's life since Jess's murder.

Matthew adopted London as his home and he rarely returned to South Africa, in fact, he seldom talked about his parents or South Africa when he and Joel met. Joel found this curious because Matthew and Jess had constantly talked about Africa, and it wouldn't have surprised him if they had made their home there, but perhaps it was an understandable reaction to what had happened in the past.

Matthew had enjoyed a successful pupillage back in London, and been offered a place in chambers in the Temple; in Paper Buildings to be exact. He worked hard and specialised in criminal and administrative law, whilst also developing a reputation around human rights work. This in particular brought him work representing and challenging government policies and departments.

In time Matthew became a part-time judge. Given how much Matthew and Joel had argued dogmatically over the years, Matthew becoming a judge amused Joel, although he did privately concede Matthew would be extremely good at it. As Joel contemplated Matthew, the suspect, he dismissed his negative thoughts about his friend – in fact, his good friend.

He once again drifted off, only waking as the plane prepared for landing. He'd missed his breakfast. Most unsatisfactory, he thought, but not a squeak out of the "s the k"!

As Joel collected his hand baggage from the overhead locker, he wondered again what sort of reception he would get at Immigration. It had been a recurring and haunting theme during the flight. He made his way from the plane towards the Border Force control points. Surprisingly the queues were not long and it only took him fifteen minutes to reach the point where he was at the front of the queue. As he stood in line, he was watching behind the control points for any sign of cops. He didn't see any, but they could be waiting in one of the offices. He was surprised they hadn't snaffled him as he got off the plane and taken him down the steps to a waiting car!

He was called forward, held his passport open and handed it to the officer, who looked at it, looked at Joel, scanned it, handed it back and said, 'Thank you, Sir.' Joel just stood there; he didn't move.

The officer said, 'That's all, Sir, thank you.'

Joel said, 'Oh, I'm sorry. I've been daydreaming, sorry to trouble you,' and walked on to collect his bag from the carousel.

His next thought was they'd get Customs to grab him, but he walked through unhindered and caught the Heathrow Express to Paddington. He walked outside the station and took a cab to the flat. Throughout the journey Joel was on the lookout for watchers. He didn't see any, but he put it down to being too relaxed after his holiday. They're there, he concluded.

When he got to the flat, he sent a text to everyone with the simple message:

The eagle has landed.

He'd wait to see who reached him first. He was still a little tired and thought he would have a nap.

Barely three minutes later Robert rang. He told Joel he had been in regular contact with Ali and things were moving slowly; too slowly for Robert. He hoped Joel didn't mind but he'd also kept Frederick Weisner in the loop about the exhibits. Joel said he didn't mind in the slightest, it was a nice thing to do.

The call ended, Joel contemplated. It hadn't been Robert ringing up to brief him on progress, it had been Robert the worried surrogate father. It was sweet of him.

The phone rang again almost immediately: it was Marta. She sent a couple of emails when he was away, mainly briefing him about Kem's condition, but now said, 'I just need to hear your voice, Joel. I know it's pathetic, but I needed it.'

Joel recounted his tales of bear spotting and living in his luxurious tin can. He said, 'It's great to hear your voice too, Marta.' They talked for five minutes and she said her father had prepared a letter for him, which he would email.

Joel suspected and surmised the watchers may have this phone as well now. Marta asked him if it would be safe. He said, 'As long as your father is happy with the contents being read by others,' he was doing it again, talking to the listeners.

Marta said, 'It's a letter from Papa to Robert, his client. Once you are happy with it could you send it? It is subject to legal professional privilege, so I hope no one else does think about reading it!' Once again Joel thought how sharp she was. He wouldn't have been surprised if she had read the Regulation of Investigatory Powers Act, which covered looking at people's mail, and he hoped the listeners had too. Marta then said, 'I miss you so much, Joel.'

'I miss you too.' The call ended and Joel put the phone down. He spent the rest of the morning working on the flat and dozing. It wasn't in a bad state; it just needed some care and attention, which Joel had failed to give over the years.

Shortly after two the phone rang: it was Billy. Before he had a chance to speak, Joel asked, 'Are you at work, Billy?' which he confirmed he was. 'Camden Passage at 2.30, OK?'

Billy replied, 'OK.' When he arrived, Joel explained he thought his 'throw-away' phone might be compromised.

Billy gave his update in a matter of fact formal police-like way. 'Bunny, whose real name is Reginald Alan Husband, runs the Lancet Club in Croydon. He is thirty-four and lives in Croydon with what looks like his partner and two children. He has no previous convictions, and there was no intelligence on him other than the club was used by the Cooper family. Their OCG is of interest to Hydra. I'm not surprised, given their reputation,' he added. Joel wondered about calling a law enforcement organisation Hydra, but it now seemed apt: it was a multi headed creature in organisational terms.

'The Lancet Club itself is legitimate, or so it seems,' Billy continued. 'There are two licences for the place according to the local authority.

One held by Bunny and the other by Cantact Ltd, the owners.' Rosie, Billy's current girlfriend from crime support, had done a check for him, and Cantact Ltd had their registered offices in Bishopsgate. 'Rosie hasn't done any more searches on Cantact Ltd just in case.'

Billy added the only other thing was Ferguson Childs, who was an Intelligence Detective Sergeant in Croydon, had said Bunny was supposed to be ex-army, in fact ex-Special Forces, and had worked in Iraq. Joel thought, Special Forces, again. Just how many people in South London weren't ex-Special Forces? pondered Joel. He thanked Billy and said he'd better return to work otherwise they'd have him for extended lunch breaks. They both chuckled and Billy set off.

Joel went to a telephone box, dialled the Met general number and asked to be put through to Piers.

'Hello,' said the voice on the other end.

'Piers, it's Joel, can you talk?'

'Yes, of course. How's the fatigue?'

'Oh, fuck off.' Joel was getting very tired of hearing this line. If he was going to be signed off again, he'd ask Dr Lloyd for something different, and liked the idea of a 'strained groin as a result of over-exertion', which would cause a few wry smiles in the admin at the nick.

'How are things?' asked Joel.

'Very good, it's all coming together well. It looks like a really strong case already.'

'Good one,' said Joel. Without further pleasantries, he said, 'Piers, from your background again, have you ever heard of someone called Bunny Husband? His full name is Reginald Alan Husband, he's about thirty-four and supposed to be ex-SF.'

'Name doesn't ring a bell at all. Bunny Husband? Mmm, no, but I'll ask around though. Is this to do with your fire?'

'Course it is. He's the one who was supposed to have set it up, but on paper he's legit.'

'You sure about your source?' enquired Piers.

'I think so.' But Joel started to doubt whether Jancey was as frightened as he'd thought he was.

'OK, I'll get back to you when I've spoken to a few people.' Then quite out of the blue, Piers said, 'See you had another success in the last couple of days.'

'What do you mean?' queried Joel. He had no idea what Piers was talking about.

'The DG of Hydra and that Home Office adviser going,' explained Piers.

Joel had to think for a moment and then remembered the article he had read in *The Standard* on the Heathrow Express. 'I didn't catch them shagging, and it certainly wasn't a ménage a trois, if that's what you're thinking. What's it got to do with me?' asked Joel.

'Think about it, Joel, you're supposed to be the ace detective!'

'Come on, Piers, give me a clue,' pleaded Joel.

'Can't say. I'll get back to you on Bunny. Take care.' The phone call ended.

Joel was intrigued. What had two high profile resignations got to do with him? He could only think they were somehow in trouble because of the inquiries he had made in SA, but it really didn't add up.

Joel went to the Internet café he had been using on Upper Street and read the email Frederick sent him. It was brief and to the point, summarising the South African inquiries for his client, Robert Bennet. Kem continued to improve and they were pursuing their search for his clothing and crime data with the police, but were not hopeful. Frederick included a scanned photo of Kem, taken when he was arrested, and a statement, as requested, from Thembi, stating Kem was left handed.

Very interesting, Joel thought. They had established Mhkize, Kem's attacker, was responsible for attacks in Constantia at the time of Jessica's death. Finally, Frederick confirmed conclusively Todd Pennard was in the United States at the time of Jessica's death. Joel forwarded the letter to Robert and said if he wanted to discuss anything to contact him. He also asked Robert to forward it to Brute, if he was happy to do so.

Chapter Thirty-One

Leaving the Internet café, Joel was again veering towards Jessica's death being as a result of an attack by burglars or robbers, and Mhkize was up there as a star suspect. For some entirely random reason his mind then switched to Fiona Henderson. He thought he'd ring her and see how she was. Henderson answered the phone in a hushed voice.

'Hello, Guvn'r, it's Joel. Can you talk?'

'I'm in a waiting room. Just a minute, Joel, I'll go outside.' A few seconds later, she said, 'OK I can talk now. How are you?'

'How are you, more to the point?'

'I'm fine, why do you ask?'

'Guvn'r, you're in a waiting room, for God's sake. Even a CID trainee could work out you're in a hospital or something.'

'If you're that clever, Joel Grant, you'd better get back to work,' she snapped.

'Come on, Fiona, I am concerned. If you don't want to talk about it fair enough, but there are people who are worried about you. You should know that.'

'I'm sorry for snapping at you. It's a difficult time, and having my parents around doesn't help.'

'Look,' said Joel, 'let's meet and have a drink. Take the afternoon off and don't go back in, you need to chill a little. Where are you?'

'Harley Street,' said Henderson. 'I must admit I'm tempted.'

'What time are you going to be finished there?'

'About 3.30, all being well.'

'OK, do you know Randall and Aubin in Brewer Street?'

'The fish place?'

'Yeah, that's right. I'll see you there at four.'

'OK, Joel, but I don't want the third degree about how I am. I just need a break today,' Henderson added.

'No problem,' said Joel. Fat chance, he thought. They said goodbye, knowing they would see each other very soon.

Joel thought it was all very 'un-Hendersonish' to accede so quickly. There was clearly something serious going on. Joel thought of a cunning plan to divert her while he 'interrogated' her in the bar, then made another phone call as he walked to the flat where he quickly showered and went on to Brewer Street.

When Joel arrived at Randall and Aubin, Fiona was standing outside – always a tricky thing to do in some parts of Soho. Joel went up to her and kissed her.

'Hello, darling, how much for a good time?'

'Nice to see you too,' said Fiona, bristling at the thought she might look like a sex worker.

They went inside the restaurant, and Joel said, 'Can you drink?'

'Of course I can, as long as I take it easy. I'm told my liver is in prime condition.'

'Only asking,' said Joel, ordering a bottle of the house champagne from the waiter who'd just joined them. It was quiet, and unfortunately Juliette was not in.

'So what is wrong with you then?' asked Joel.

'I see all the training in the Diplomatic Corps is really showing dividends Joel!' Fiona smiled for the first time, probably in a while, thought Joel.

'Well?' he repeated.

'Well,' she said, 'I have a Hemochromatosis, which means I have too much iron in my blood. I have to have blood drained out of me once a month. If I don't, I could get heart or liver failure, hence the tests on my liver, and no jokes about drinking too much Iron Bru as a child. It also means white wine only, so champagne is fine!'

'I'm sorry Fiona. Does that mean you can still work?'

'Oh yes, providing I stick to the regime, and what else could I do with two parents who are medics? That's what the visits to Harley Street are about.'

The champagne arrived and the waiter poured them each a glass.

'I not going to say cheers,' said Joel. 'Good luck.'

'Thanks, Joel,' said Fiona and they touched glasses.

'What are you going to do then? You mentioned your parents, what have they got to say?'

'They have too bloody much to say. That's been half the problem with them sticking their noses in, saying I should go up to Scotland to be treated. I would do if the specialist was up there, but it's just their inherent belief medical care in Scotland is the best, and of course they aren't prejudiced, are they?'

'Fair enough, but they are doctors and they are your parents,' Joel responded.

'Yeah, but they're not specialists. Dr Lloyd recognised the problem, but also realised she couldn't do anything herself so referred me to a specialist in Harley Street. I'm staying there.'

'Have you told your parents about your decision?' Joel queried.

'No, not yet. That's why I'm here, Dutch courage.'

'And I thought it was my charm and wit,' joked Joel.

'Excuse me while I go to the toilet to be sick.' She laughed. He joined in. They spent some time talking about Fiona's parents and their attempts to control what they considered to be their wayward child who had chosen the police over academia, and Joel's time with his children. Joel also touched upon the resignation of the Director General of Hydra and the adviser, but Fiona, who was usually very well connected, said she hadn't seen the article or heard any gossip. Joel didn't mention Thornley's name as he'd forgotten it, nor did he relate the news to Fiona's conversation with the AC, DAC and the 'spy' at the Yard some weeks ago. Had he done, things may have become a little clearer.

Joel said in a serious tone, 'Fiona, what's Iron Bru?'

'Goodness, I forgot you were a southerner. Clearly your education in Manchester was not as complete as it should have been. Having said that, it's still quite a way from Scotland. You're a Man United supporter, aren't you?

Joel said, 'yeeesss,' somewhat quizzically.

'Well, what's Alex Ferguson's drink of choice?'

'I don't go drinking with him regularly, but I would have thought whisky or red wine.'

'You're probably right, but it should be Iron Bru, the stuff girders are made of.'

'Fiona, is this blood thing affecting you in other ways? Are you feeling OK?'

'Oh Joel, Iron Bru is a fizzy drink, very popular in Scotland and the North. It's advertising slogan was "The stuff girders are made from", hence my quip about drinking too much as a child, although my parents never approved of the stuff. Far too plebeian.'

'Ah, I see, I understand now. Does this mean I can start calling you Iron Woman? I always thought there was something of the Mrs T in you.'

'No it fucking doesn't, and I don't want to hear anyone else saying it. I will hold you personally responsible, do you follow me?'

'Okay, I follow you. I'll follow you anywhere, it must be your magnetic attraction.' He laughed.

'Joel, I'm warning you,' she said sternly.

In a lull, Fiona excused herself to answer a telephone call outside. Joel had been looking for watchers but didn't see any signs. Strange, he thought, his mind working overtime on iron jokes. Although he knew it was serious, Joel thought he'd help by lightening the worry, but then he realised Fiona may not appreciate it as much as others.

Unusually Joel hadn't noticed, but Juliette had come in. She was on a later shift, and while Fiona was outside she came across to Joel and they kissed. 'New girlfriend, Joel?' she asked.

Joel laughed. He explained Fiona was his boss, which for some reason amused Juliette. When Fiona returned they agreed they were peckish, and were about to order when Brute's large frame bustled through the doorway. He waved at Joel and made his way over. When he joined them Joel explained the man was a friend of his, Mark Brutus. Fiona immediately recognised the name, and said, 'Dr Mark Brutus, the clinical psychologist?'

Brute blushed, said nothing and shook Fiona's hand.

'There, told you. You are famous, Brute. Everyone knows you,' said Joel.

'Oh behave, Joel. Could you please excuse me? I just need to pop to the loo.'

'Okay. Do you want a platter to eat? Juliette's on her way back.'

'Sounds good to me,' replied Brute.

Juliette was stopped by some customers on her way to the table, and Fiona said, 'Oh great, thanks Joel. Thought you'd have me psychoanalysed? Thought I was losing it?'

'Brute and I go way back. We were at Uni together, so don't be silly. I know even the great Brute couldn't help you! We needed to catch up about South African stuff and I owe him a meal. Don't be so bloody sensitive, but watch him if he stares in your eyes – he's trying to hypnotise you!' They both burst out laughing as Juliette and Brute returned to the table.

Joel ordered food, and Brute started chatting about his research assistant who was working with him on Joel's "South African mystery", as he put it. He confirmed he'd received an email from Robert. Joel asked Brute to talk about the general stuff as he didn't want to compromise Fiona, she thanked him, but said she was already compromised. However, Joel was adamant they get their SA business over with, then he and Brute would talk in more detail in the morning.

'Before you go to court, representing the good guys this time,' joked Joel.

Brute, ever ready to defend his independence, launched into a defence which had the desired effect of moving him away from South Africa.

Brute and Fiona were getting on really well, Joel noticed. There was still half of the third bottle of champers left, so he thought he'd make his excuses and leave. It had never entered his mind he might end up as a match-maker with these two, but it certainly looked an interesting proposition.

'Right, my friends, I'm off. I have things to do,' Joel said, lying. 'Fiona, watch his eyes. Remember what I said about hypnosis!'

'Joel, you're retiring early, aren't you? And you're the hypnotist, not me,' retorted Brute.

'What do you mean?' asked Fiona.

'I'll get the bill. Don't worry, your turn next time. Look after yourselves, you two. Speak in the morning, Bruto, OK?'

'OK, thanks Joel.'

Fiona leant over and kissed Joel. 'Thanks, Joel, this is just what I needed.'

Joel left the restaurant after paying the bill and saying cheerio to Juliette. As he left he saw Fiona and Brute talking intently. Fiona was shaking her head from side to side in apparent disbelief and laughing uncontrollably. Joel suspected the topic might have been the antics of a certain hypnotist!

Chapter Thirty-Two

Joel walked through Soho to Oxford Circus where he caught the number 73 bus back to Islington. The streets and the bus were quiet; nobody joined him on the top deck.

He sat on the aisle seat and slumped down in an effort to prevent being seen by anyone watching from a following vehicle. If he was spotted on the phone and there was no activity on his ordinary phone, the watchers would get even more suspicious, if they didn't already know his other number. He phoned Robert, who was keen to hear of any news.

'You got my email. Thanks for forwarding it to Brute. I've just seen him and we will talk again tomorrow. Things are moving along. No news from Ali and the exhibits.'

Robert for once had news for Joel, 'Didn't Ali tell you? I took Jessica's Aunt Louise to see him and she gave a blood sample as well. He said the lab needed it for mitochondrial DNA. Apparently it's only passed through the female line or something like that. Anyway it all went well.'

Joel was puzzled for a moment why Ali hadn't spoken to him, then remembered he had told everyone only to contact him if it was essential. Joel understood the need for the blood in order to correctly identify Jess's clothing.

'Ali said you would understand what he was doing,' added Robert.

Joel replied, 'Yes, I understand. Robert, I need you to do me a favour. I want you to do a Companies House search on a firm called Cantact Ltd. C-A-N-T-A-C-T. They have their registered offices in Bishopsgate in the City. I think the address must be an accountant's or lawyer's,' Joel added. He didn't want to mention his concerns about being followed; he thought Robert would make this assumption. He continued, 'I think you have to register online, and I didn't want to do it in my name and leave a trace.'

Robert said, 'Don't worry, I'll get one of my old chums to do it.'

'Old chums?' queried Joel.

'Yes, at the Beeb. They use Companies House searches all the time to track people down.'

One to remember there, thought Joel, but then recognised it would never affect him anyway. 'That's great, how long will it take?'

'Depends how many they've got. For something like this they'll add it to a batch. Shouldn't take long, though.'

'Great,' said Joel. 'All quiet in Budleigh?'

'Positively catatonic,' said Robert. 'No fires, but someone saw a dolphin off the coast the other day and it caused great excitement. I saw Sarah down at the beach, she looked well.'

'I'll be down myself soon, Robert, I will keep you in touch and contact you probably at the weekend.' Joel was determined not to engage regarding Sarah.

'OK, Joel, I've got the hint, again! Speak soon, bye.' The conversation ended just in time for Joel to put his phone in his pocket as a young couple bounded up the stairs, having got on at Euston. Watchers? surmised Joel. He remembered Euston Towers used to be the base for the Security Service watchers. Although he realised they'd moved, he still thought, how apt.

The rest of the journey passed without incident. Joel got off the bus in Islington and walked to his flat, unaware whether or not anyone was following him, the couple had stayed on the bus. He went straight to bed as he was tired and emotional – Joel speak for drunk!

In bed, Joel looked at his phone and saw he had a text from Matthew, saying it was his turn for dinner and how about Windows at the Hilton on Park Lane at eight the following night? Joel replied:

Great see you there.

Joel phoned Brute at nine the following morning and asked what time he had got home. Brute said he and Fiona left shortly after Joel; he added he quite liked Fiona and she was nothing like Joel had described her. Joel conceded he'd probably been a little harsh in respect of Fiona. Brute asked Joel to go to the Institute to meet and chat with him and Ifu, his research assistant, he thought it was an excellent idea and a distraction from mundane housekeeping tasks in the flat. They settled on eleven.

Joel found himself heading for South London once again. This time he wasn't bothered about any watchers and used the overland direct to Denmark Hill. In fact he rather liked the idea of them following him to the Institute of Psychiatry; they would probably think he was going for treatment.

Joel arrived at the station shortly before eleven and walked straight to the Henry Wellcome Building where Brute had his office. Joel had been to the building before to see Brute, but still went to reception to ask for him. Brute came down quickly and they went in the lift to his third floor office. Ifu was already in the office, and Brute introduced her.

Brute opened up by saying they had not produced a report as it would take a long time, but they were willing to share what they had found with Joel, although Brute repeated it was fairly limited given the dearth of information. Joel asked if he could make notes. Both Ifu and Brute nodded and Joel delved into his rucksack for his notebook.

Over the next hour or so Ifu and Brute, mostly Ifu, outlined the information they had been given, what they found in their research, where it was found and what their conclusions were. They also produced pen pictures of the main characters, which Joel thought was novel but interesting nevertheless.

The summary of their research was, as Ifu put it, inconclusive, but what it did was reassure Joel he wasn't missing anything, which was one of the main reasons he had asked Brute, and subsequently Ifu, to help. Joel asked his psychologists if he could buy them lunch and, quite bluntly, how much he owed them. It was Ifu who jumped in first, saying he didn't owe her anything; it was part of her research and she was delighted to help. Brute nodded in the background, but added lunch would be nice. The trio left the IoP and went to The Phoenix, a gastro pub, which looked like a station – because it used to be one. They all had burgers and beer before Joel took the train back north to Islington.

Travelling back, Joel rehearsed in his mind what he'd been told, particularly the pen pictures which Ifu had summarised. It was the first time he found out Jess's Masters dissertation had covered the impact of the mining industry on the cultures and development of indigenous peoples in the Vaal River Valley. Ifu was amazed at the access Jess had been given, but it was clear from Jess's acknowledgments at the beginning of the script George Corfield was instrumental in facilitating this.

It was not an entirely supportive document in respect of the mine owners, Ifu said. As Corfield appeared only to have been involved in mining for a relatively short time, he clearly hadn't been bothered, Joel thought. His opinion of George Corfield went up considerably after hearing of his support for Jess.

Ifu added Jess's dissertation was not published at the time and oringinally was only available to view within SOAS. She concluded this was probably because of the concerns of the miners and their families about possible identification and repercussions, although it could have been following representations by the mining industry. Ifu doubted this, so did Joel. They wouldn't have seen it. Ifu also disclosed she came from the Vaal valley and found the dissertation fascinating.

Joel was grateful Ifu's and Brute's research helped him to know a little more about the culture of the place, but there were no bolts of lightning. Returning to the flat, not even looking for watchers on the way, he felt exhausted and fell asleep; beer at lunchtime did this to him.

He got up at six, showered and set out for the West End on the Tube. On the way Ali sent Joel a text, which simply said:

Can we talk?

Windows was a posh restaurant and bar on the top floor of the Hilton, Park Lane. After his recent visit with Sarah, Joel thought, goodness, I'm becoming a regular. If anyone were following him, they would think he had a real taste for the high life – which, of course, he did! It was just he couldn't afford the prices most of the time.

Joel was not looking forward to the forthcoming chat with Matthew. He had asked Robert not to mention what was going on, which was difficult for Robert, although he knew very little of the detail and Joel thought it best for the moment. If Robert learnt everything which was going on, his journalistic training would kick in and he might go to the media. There may be a time to go to the press, but not at the moment. Some drawbridges were still down with the gates open, and the occupants had no idea Joel was hoping to get into the castles without being detected! Those castles were in South Africa. Joel once again reflected on his metaphors and thought it must be the actor in him. He smiled to himself.

Perhaps it would be better to speak to Ali after he had seen Matthew, just in case there was any news. It was going to be difficult enough to

217

keep shtum without more information he had to keep secret. Joel had considered telling Matthew. After all he was a victim and a friend, but something was stopping Joel.

Joel texted Ali:

Just going into something, can I ring later? Say 10ish?

Ali replied instantaneously:

No probs, will be up till 12 watching CSI.

Piss-taker, thought Joel as he walked through the doors of the Hilton and asked the concierge where he could find the Windows restaurant. He was directed to the lift, and told, 'Right to the top, Sir, the Twenty eighth floor.' Joel entered and joined another couple. They seemed familiar, and he wondered. The lift glided smoothly and swiftly to the top floor and the man gestured for Joel to leave first.

As he stepped out, a waiter greeted him and asked if he had a reservation.

Joel said, 'No, I'm joining a friend, Matthew Corfield.'

'Ah yes, Sir, Mr Corfield has arrived and is waiting in the bar.' It was the first time Joel had been in the place, and as he walked around, looking for Matthew, he was struck by the view. Although it was dark outside, the light show from what must have been Kensington and Chelsea was amazing. The variation, intensity and colours were spectacular.

He saw Matthew and walked over to him. 'Quite a view, Matty,' he said as they shook hands. Matthew hated being called 'Matty', and Joel was the only person who did so every now and again, deliberately, just to keep him grounded.

'Isn't it?' Matthew replied. 'Wait until you see it from the other side.' Joel thought the view was familiar and remembered why, it was similar to the Rainbow Rooms in the Rockefeller building in New York, which he mentioned to Matthew.

'Name dropper,' laughed Matthew. 'I presume you want some of this?' he added, pointing to the Veuve on the table.

'I don't suppose they serve bitter here? The nearest they have would be angostura bitters!'

'You know the Rainbow Rooms are closed now Joel?' Matthew said as the waiter poured Joel's drink.

'Never,' he replied. 'I've only been twice, but it was fantastic. Great for people spotting.'

'This place is as well,' said Matthew. 'You find potential Queens Counsel in here sometimes.'

Joel immediately recognised what Matthew was telling him. Matthew explained he had applied to become a QC, which was a long and slow process, having completed the sixty-seven page questionnaire and paid the not insubstantial £4,000 fee. He felt it was slightly early, but his head of chambers encouraged him to apply. If his application were successful he would learn about it on the following Maundy Thursday. Joel enquired what success would mean in practice. He personally had no doubt of the merit of Matthew's application.

Matthew said, 'It means my fees go up!' They both laughed. 'But nowadays in my area, because of legal aid cutbacks it means little other than the status. I hope I will be asked for advice on the more complicated cases before they go anywhere near the courts.'

'Presumably you can still be a recorder?' asked Joel.

'Oh certainly, I'll probably need the money.' Matthew grinned. 'I won't quite be on the breadline, despite this Government's best efforts. Though I should be careful, I have been getting quite a lot of work from them recently. I'm sitting at North London Crown Court this week and I heard through the grapevine about you causing James Whitaker some discomfort at the Bailey. You are quite the talk of the judiciary at the moment.'

They chose their food from the menu, and a short while later a waiter ushered them into the restaurant. As Matthew and Joel walked in, Joel looked out of the window at the stunning view of St. James, towards the City, and said to Matthew, 'I see what you mean.'

Their table was across the room from the couple Joel had been with in the lift. As they sat down, Joel said to Matthew, 'That guy over there, with the bald head and the women in green. I'm sure he's in the job you know, Matthew, his face looks so familiar.' Joel hadn't told Matthew of his suspicions about being followed; it would be too complicated to explain, for a variety of reasons.

Matthew looked across casually at the couple now tucking into their food. He turned to Joel, and said, 'I'm not surprised he looks familiar, Joel, he's Stirling Moss, the racing driver. For God's sake, you're supposed to be the detective!' They both looked at each other and laughed.

Joel and Matthew talked about old times and caught up on events in their lives over dinner. As they were drinking their coffees in the bar, Matthew commented, 'Joel, you haven't mentioned Sarah at all this evening.'

'No. we're going to go our separate ways, it's for the best, Matthew, we both agreed it was for the best.'

'Oh I'm sorry Joel, it makes my next news somewhat crass but there is something I need to share.' he said. 'I know we've never discussed it, but I've been living with someone for a number of years now. I know as an old friend you will find it odd that I've never mentioned it.'

Joel said, 'Matthew, despite being the nosey detective, people's private lives are their own. I've always felt strongly about privacy.'

'Well,' said Matthew, 'I'd like you to meet my partner because we're going to make it official. We're going to have a civil partnership ceremony and I'd like you to be one of our witnesses.'

Joel immediately grasped what Matthew was telling him, and just then a tall suntanned man walked across the room towards them. It was almost like a film script.

Matthew said, 'Here's Peter now.' The man went to Matthew and they hugged. 'Peter, this is Joel Grant. Joel, this is my partner, Peter Browne.' The two newly introduced men shook hands.

'Nice to meet you, Peter,' Joel said.

'And you, Joel. I've heard a lot about you from Matthew, I know you go back a long way.'

Joel noticed an accent when Peter spoke. A South African accent, stronger than what was left of Matthew's.

'I've only just told Joel about our plans, Peter, I think he's in shock.'

'Shock at being told one of my oldest friends in London may become a QC, then being asked to be a witness at a civil partnership, but most of all mistaking Stirling Moss for a cop. How will I live it down?'

Peter looked at Matthew and laughed. 'I'll explain later,' he said. 'I suppose I'd better fill you in on the details.'

'I'm all ears. What should we have to drink? Champagne, I think, my treat.'

They ordered the champagne, and Matthew explained the story so far, as he put it. The next hour was spent with Joel listening intently to the couple talk about their lives. At the end of the evening, Joel told Matthew, 'I'm delighted for you, for you both. You seem so happy together.'

'We are,' they replied in unison.

'Listen, I must go, but let me know the exact date as soon as you can. We poor shift workers have to plan ahead.'

Peter said, 'Don't forget I'm a shift worker too, Joel.'

'Mmm,' said Joel. Peter was a consultant vascular surgeon at Bart's and had rooms in Harley Street.

He hugged both men and told them to enjoy the rest of the evening.

Chapter Thirty-Three

Joel left the hotel and looked at his watch. It was 10.30pm: not too late to phone Ali, but tonight's revelation had complicated his mind, considerably. He needed to think it through – hearing all of Matthew's good news, Joel was concerned he didn't want to upset him by continuing to hide what he had been doing. It was a real dilemma. He texted Ali:

Still stuck, will ring am.

Joel caught a cab. He didn't trust himself on the Tube, he needed to clear his mind but he couldn't and began to assess what he'd been told: it was dramatic news. When he reached the flat he sat down with a large mug of Horlicks, his favourite bedtime drink. Joel found after a busy day he just needed to sit, relax and have a drink of Horlicks; it did wonders. He switched on the TV: oh no, CSI was on. Maybe Ali really did watch it. He switched over and found an episode of *M*A*S*H*, which he watched while trying to sort out what to do about Matthew.

Matthew, the QC – fine. Matthew, a bisexual man who was going to marry his long-term partner – fine. It was what else had been said which was concerning Joel.

Matthew and Peter had been friends since they were eleven, having met at school. They recounted their parents and friends described them as 'twins' because they were constantly together. They socialised with others in their school, but they were always close. At school, a boarding school in Johannesburg, they began a gay relationship, which they never told anyone about, not only because it was illegal but also because they didn't want anyone else to be part of what they thought was very special.

When Matthew announced he was going to study in the United Kingdom, Peter also applied to University in the United Kingdom and was offered a place to study medicine at Bristol, where Matthew had secured an offer. It was at this time Matthew's father became suspicious and confronted Matthew, who confessed everything to him. His father was appalled a son of his was a 'queer', as he called Matthew. George Corfield confronted Peter, and threatened to tell his parents about his sexuality if he went to Bristol as well.

Peter too came from a British family. His father had moved from Edinburgh to take up a senior post at Barclays in South Africa, and remained in the country when Barclays withdrew in 1986. Peter's parents were Presbyterians and very straight laced. Peter didn't want to upset them or cause any trouble, so withdrew from Bristol. Instead he went on to the University of Cape Town where he still studied medicine.

Matthew and Peter explained going to University, adopting the professions they had and being born in the United Kingdom saved them from conscription into the South African Defence Force and its infamous training camps. Like many young white South Africans, Matthew went to London and Peter to the United States to do further training, which also helped.

Despite the geography they managed initially to maintain their relationship, albeit from a distance but it was during this period Matthew met and fell in love with Jess. On a visit to South Africa he told Peter, who became upset at the prospect of losing Matthew, but said he understood. Matthew explained to Joel he had never told Jess about Peter, other than mentioning he had a friend called Peter who was training to be a medic. They had never met, or hadn't until the night she died.

When Matthew and Jess went to South Africa after their engagement, Jess said she wanted to meet Peter, and Matthew agreed to invite him to his parents' house. Matthew's mother knew nothing of his former relationship with Peter and she thought it was a wonderful idea. His father said nothing.

It was arranged Matthew would go to Port Elizabeth and collect Peter for a party, where other friends of the family would be invited to meet Jess. Matthew arranged to stay with Peter's parents for a couple of days while Jess got to know his parents, particularly his mother.

Matthew and Peter returned a day early, and Jess met Peter. Peter considered they got on well, until the early evening when they were having a drink. Matthew's father, who had been drinking heavily, made a remark about which bedroom Matthew had slept in when he was at

Peter's parents' house. Peter didn't respond, but George repeated his remark. Matthew then shouted at his father and told him to shut up. Peter left saying it was probably best if he went to his room.

Peter said Jess worked out what was going on and while Matthew was still arguing with his father, followed Peter to his room where she asked him to explain. Matthew's mother knew nothing of this as she was supervising the preparation for the party due to take place the following evening.

Peter told Jess he loved Matthew and didn't want him to marry her, but it was Matthew's decision. At this point Matthew came into the room to find them arguing about why Peter had come to the house when he knew it would be difficult for everyone. Jess felt it was completely wrong of him to do so.

Matthew recalled he was distraught at finding the two people he cared about most in the world arguing over him. He tried to placate Jess, but couldn't. She was incensed he had kept his relationship with Peter from her and simply walked out of the room. Peter realised it had been wrong for him to go to the house and followed Jess, whom he found in the library. He told her he was leaving immediately and he was sorry for causing so much trouble on what should have been a happy occasion. Peter said even today he still regretted going to Matthew's parents' house. Matthew reluctantly agreed Peter should leave and, without saying goodbye to anyone, he took Peter to a hotel and left him there. Peter stayed the night in Cape Town and returned to his parents' the following morning, which was when he found out about Jess's death.

After dropping Peter at the hotel, Matthew returned to the house and found Jess was dead.

Joel didn't ask any questions when these events were being relayed to him. He couldn't. Matthew and Peter were now firmly suspects, and he had gone into receive mode.

Matthew went on to explain the night effectively destroyed his relationship with his father, and he had rarely returned to South Africa or spoken to his father since. This at least explained something, Joel thought.

Peter and Matthew drifted apart following Jess's death, and they didn't see each other until ten years later when Peter came to London to present a paper at a conference. He read in the newspaper about the prosecution of some footballers for allegedly fixing matches, and noticed a barrister called Matthew Corfield was representing one of the footballers. Peter explained he went to the Old Bailey, sat in the visitors' gallery and watched Matthew at work, and realised he still cared enormously for him. Peter waited for Matthew after the case and they rekindled their friendship during his remaining days in London. Peter then decided to apply for a job and move to London. The paper he presented was widely acclaimed, and without a great deal of difficulty he was offered the position at Bart's.

When Peter came to live in London, Matthew recounted they saw a great deal of each other – well, as much as their busy careers would allow – and eventually Peter moved in with Matthew. They had been partners ever since.

Joel felt he had to say something, and asked if their parents knew they were partners and intended to have a civil partnership. Peter revealed his parents were dead. Matthew's parents were travelling and coming to the United Kingdom in the next month or so, and Matthew intended to tell them then.

Now, for the first time, Joel had alternative real live suspects with motives. Peter admitted he had seen Jess in the library, where she was found dead, before he left the house. He'd admitted he still felt strongly for Matthew, and as a medic would have the knowledge of the consequences of a sharp strike on the neck. Matthew also had the opportunity to kill Jess. She had just found out he was bisexual; she may have threatened to break off their engagement. Matthew may have become angry. Strangely, Matthew did not mention seeing Jess before he took Peter to the hotel. Joel found this odd, but then it could be they committed the murder, together. Whatever, Joel had some work to do – lots of it.

Chapter Thirty-Four

'Hi, Ali, sorry it's taken a while to get back to you. Life is just so complicated at the moment,' said Joel. 'Can you talk?' It was now Saturday morning, and Joel hoped Ali was at home and not at work.

'Yeah. No problem, Joel. Let me get my notes. Ah, here we are. I'll keep it simple. What you must appreciate is these are preliminary findings and we'll have to wait for the full report.'

'Got it.'

Ali started to go through his notes. 'There are no real breakthroughs at the moment other than in simple terms, the lab has established the samples from the hospital belonging to Jessica were mixed male and female. The dress and clothing samples were inconclusive, but the nail scrapings were highly likely to have come from a male of European heritage.'

Joel didn't say anything.

'Joel, are you there?'

'Yes, yes, I'm here. Can you just repeat what you said?'

Ali did this almost word for word.

'A European, Ali? Not a black African, how certain can they be?'

'I said I'd try and keep it simple, and I realise you know about DNA, but the facts are: 99.9 per cent of DNA is the same in everyone! It's the other 0.1 per cent, in fact less than that, which allows us to identify someone's DNA.'

He continued, 'We also share a lot of our DNA with plants and animals, but different geographical ethnic groups have different DNA. The lab was able to identify Jessica through the samples we obtained from her father and her aunt; they were able to predict which haplogroup the nail scrapings originate from. It's fairly certain it is Western European, but given the migration of Africans over the centuries throughout the world, there is still an unknown element.'

'What do you mean, Ali?' asked Joel.

'Well, you need to look at the slave trade and the way people were transported to the Americas and then abused by European slave owners and their white workers. The mixed heritage children who were born had DNA from at least two haplogroups; genetic groups which share the same ancestry, and over the years more and more people have been born with those groups in their DNA. I remember reading ten years ago about 60 per cent of African Americans probably have a European great or great-great grandfather. Do you understand what I mean?'

'Yes I think so,' said Joel. 'So that means the attacker was white?'

'Not necessarily,' said Ali. 'There are many reasons why tissue gets under nails. Think about it, Joel!'

Joel quickly grasped what Ali was hinting at. 'You mean in bed?'

'Trust you to come up with that, but yes, that's one way,' replied Ali. 'So they are still working on Kem's profile, and for some reason they are having difficulty with it. I think it's because it's in another part of the lab and is in the queue. It will be done soon, though.'

Joel noted Ali didn't tie himself down with definitive timescales; very wise, he thought.

'So you haven't found Kem's DNA on anything yet?'

'Joel, that's why I said at the beginning there are no real break-throughs. They still have a lot of material to examine on the dress and other clothes, separate traces, work them up, see if they match Kem's and then work up the other material they have found. Patience, Joel, patience.'

Over the years, Ali had learnt to manage the expectations of an investigator who may hear what they wanted to hear and start a course of action for which there was no justification. Normally Ali would not have given the preliminary findings before the full report other than in time crucial or very important cases, and this was such a case.

'Ali, thanks, but I have something to add to your deliberations,' said Joel, who then told Ali about his meeting with Matthew and Peter, and the significance of the disclosures they had unwittingly made.

This time it was Ali's turn to be quiet, until he uttered, 'Hmm, that's very interesting. We will need their DNA, you know that, Joel.'

Joel had been thinking about little else. How could he get it? Could he get it covertly? Should he get it covertly? Should he front them up? He didn't have an answer, and was relieved when Ali said, 'We don't need it yet. The lab staff still have to conclude their tests, and when they do we may not need their DNA after all! Although I think we will,' he added.

Joel said, 'I know. I've been thinking about how to get their DNA, but from what you say there's no great hurry.'

'Look at it this way: the lab still has a great deal of work to do, and from what you said they are hardly likely to leg it. If the lab had their DNA it would make it easier, but it's not essential, yet!'

Joel thought Ali was right; he invariably was. 'Thanks, Ali. Does Robert know what you've told me?'

'No, I thought I'd tell you first.'

'Can you do me a favour? Could you leave it until next week? He's actually seeing Matthew and Peter this evening. I suspect he will ring me over the weekend and I will suggest he contacts you for an update, but please try and keep him calm, Ali. I know you will.'

Joel considered telling Robert the news himself, but judged a scientist, Ali, could deliver it far more objectively and clearly.

'That's not a problem, Joel, I will be sensitive and careful in what I say.'

'Thanks, Ali, I'll let you know if Robert rings. Thanks again, pal!' They ended the call, and not for the first time in recent days Joel had a lot to think about.

He also considered phoning Marta and Frederick, but he needed to think about the way forward before he spoke to them. He needed to have a plan. He would send them an email update outlining Brute's research, mentioning he would ring them soon re the forensics.

Joel needed some fresh air, a run he thought, setting off ten minutes later, enjoying the next hour or so trotting through North and East London. Thinking things through, what would he tell Dr Lloyd? Did he want to go back to work? Should he go back to work? The answer was clear, wasn't it? He should return to work, but how could he then complete his investigation? He couldn't. The thought of leaving the police was still at the back of his mind, so the answer wasn't clear. Another week, or perhaps two, on the sick was the answer.

When Joel neared Victoria Park he came to a halt and looked around. Once again he could not see any watchers; perhaps they had stopped, or perhaps they were getting better. Joel's attention returned to who the watchers were. He was still certain he was being watched, he just didn't know who it was, or why. Piers said it wasn't Professional Standards, and Joel knew how difficult it was to get surveillance support for ordinary investigations from other parts of the Met. He couldn't think it would be one of the specialist teams, although Piers had mentioned the Foreign Office. It could be a counter terrorism type unit, but surely the same applied. Perhaps the security service? No, it couldn't be, could it? Fiona had mentioned the spook at the meeting, it could be them. Joel's mind was bouncing around like a tennis ball.

In reality, the only people who could be interested in him were from the Met. He went to South Africa on uncertificated sick, returned, then gone certificated sick, and the surveillance seemed to have started after the Guvn'r's meeting at the Yard. Well that's how it looked. If it wasn't any of the people he'd been thinking about, then who could it be? Got it, the press. He knew they paid private detectives and surveillance teams to look at people. They didn't need the authorisation police surveillance teams needed. Returning to the police, Joel wondered, from his own knowledge, whether there was enough information for them to watch him. He suspected they could make a case, but surely not for telephone intercept. There had been an AC at the meeting with the Guvn'r and they could authorise eavesdropping, but who authorised the spooks? He presumed their own hierarchy. He knew telephone intercept had to be authorised by the Home Secretary personally. No one within law enforcement or the Intelligence world would go to those lengths. No, it must be the Press.

His mind in turbo-drive, Joel's thoughts turned to why? It would not be the first time the media had been fed a story by the police, particularly the Guvn'rs. If they had been frustrated and unable to do an investigation themselves, perhaps they had thrown him to the wolves of Fleet Street. It could also have been the spook at the meeting: she could have done it.

Following the Leveson Inquiry the press appeared to have become far more careful with their investigative journalism, but there seemed to be a sustained attack on the police from some newspapers. Joel suspected this was fed by the Government, helped sometimes by the police themselves. He was sure a DS on the sick, going to South Africa and then undertaking private investigations while on full pay, would be just the stuff some of the newspapers would die for, let alone some in Government, to give the police another bashing. Bastards, thought Joel – not the press, but the people who had served him up.

Revenge was what he needed to concentrate on for the return run. He became conscious he was almost growling at people while he was running. However, on the way back he did calm down slightly, helped by remembering the recent opinion poll published on how the public viewed those in authority. It still had politicians right at the bottom, miles below the police and even journalists, but he recognised the police had some reputation problems to deal with, particularly at the top! It seemed, from his own lowly position, many in charge of the police were just concerned about themselves and their own profiles. The current Commissioner was one of the exceptions.

He still saw no signs of followers. Despite continually asking himself questions on the way back, he was firmly convinced it was the press who were watching him, and probably listening to him too. It had gone quiet recently, and he wondered if the investigation's findings might be in the Sunday newspapers tomorrow. Then he thought if they were going to print them they would at least have doorstepped him. There was still time.

Joel returned to the flat, showered, changed and left fifteen minutes later, looking for watchers. He didn't see anyone. He booked into the Travelodge at Kings Cross again; at least he would be able to get the papers early. He hadn't taken his iPad with him, just in case! As soon as he booked into the hotel, he left and walked up Euston Road towards the station. He phoned El Parador, a tapas restaurant on Eversholt Street, to see if they could squeeze him in; it was a popular restaurant. The deciding factor was he'd be able to spot people who were interested in him easier in El Parador rather than among the travellers in the Great Nepalese, which was also on Eversholt Road.

El Parador offered a table at 6pm when it opened. This suited him, but he still had a few hours to kill and continued his walk. He chose not to go to Somerstown on the right hand side of Euston Road; his gang of robbers was due to be sentenced soon and he really didn't want to run into any of their families. He thought he'd be OK on Eversholt Street, but not in the back streets. Instead he turned left into the University area and found himself walking past Great Ormond Street Hospital, and then the British Museum. Joel considered going into the museum, but he didn't need distracting at the moment. When Joel was worried about things, he would sometimes go to museums or galleries, 'just to clear his mind'. He found he could get lost in the exhibitions, but despite his thoughts being cluttered at this moment he needed to concentrate, not relax. He knew the museum would be a good place to watcher spot, but he hadn't seen much activity around the quiet streets and presumed they'd got what they wanted.

He found himself outside SOAS just off Russell Square in Thornhurgh Street. It was 5pm, a good time to phone Marta and her father while patrolling the streets of London searching for felons and footpads. Well you never know, he thought as he held his mobile tight to his ear in an effort to deter would-be snatchers.

He phoned Marta first, only to discover she was at her father's house having dinner. He said he didn't want to disturb their meal, and could hear Frederick and Annette in the background asking if he had any news. Joel told Marta he would ring back later. 'Would 10pm be too late?' He was conscious Frederick, at least, generally went to bed early.

Marta said it wouldn't be a problem as there were guests for dinner, then said, 'I think they may be here for some time,' and started to laugh.

It was agreed Joel would ring back later, after some Spanish food and wine. He continued his walk and loved reading the doorplates, trying to guess what secrets the buildings held.

He walked into Eversholt Street at six on the dot, and entered El Parador, the first customer of the evening. He ordered some Riba Guda and water to drink and at the same time what he wanted to eat: fillet steak goujons, smoked haddock goujons, stuffed peppers, spicy potatoes and their own variety of tortilla. It sounded a lot, Joel thought, but he hadn't eaten since his run and was starving. He liked Spanish food, particularly tapas where you could snack away in a bar or restaurant, watching the world go by. Still no obvious watchers, thought Joel as the restaurant began to fill up and he concentrated on his feast.

He looked at his watch and paid his bill, followed by a brisk walk down Eversholt Street back to the hotel, where he phoned Marta. She answered the phone almost immediately and said she would get her father, but ring Joel herself later. Frederick came to the phone and Joel explained there was no trace of a forensic link between Kem and Jessica, but there were traces of European heritage tissue in her nail scrapings. Joel tried to calm Frederick's excitement down by saying there were many reasons why this may not be significant, but he could tell his effort was only partially working.

Joel attempted to distract Frederick by telling him about Brute's findings, which had been greatly aided by his assistant from the Vaal River area. Frederick said for the first time, this was where Kem's family originally came from; they had moved to the Western Cape with the Corfields.

'There's something else I need to share with you,' Joel said, and recounted his meeting with Matthew Corfield, and later with both Matthew and Peter. The phone went quiet.

'Are you still there?' asked Joel.

'Yes, yes,' replied Frederick. 'Some more surprising news, Joel. On the one hand I'm happy for Matthew, but the events of the evening Jessica was killed and what you told us earlier are intriguing, are they not?'

Intriguing is one way to describe it, thought Joel. He said, 'I'm keeping an open mind, Frederick. Matthew doesn't know what I, or you, have been up to, and I'd like to keep it that way until we decide what would be the best way to approach it.' Joel then went on to explain the way he had considered getting samples from Matthew and Peter, but stressed until the current examination at the lab was completed there was no need to do anything. Marta and Frederick agreed.

'Did you get the letter from Papa, Joel?' Marta interjected.

'Yes, thanks. I forwarded it to Robert, who has shared it with Brute, the psychologist,' Joel replied.

'So in that case, Joel, things are moving on. Kem is still in hospital and is likely to remain there for some time. I think Marta's activities at the prison and the arrest of Van Wisents have fired a very timely shot in respect of the Department of Correction. There has been no pressure from that quarter.'

Joel asked about the Mhkize family. Frederick had learnt they travelled over 1,100 miles in the back of a truck and disappeared in Zimbabwe; awful, but better than what lay in wait for them back in South Africa. He added it was all very strange.

Frederick continued, 'Be assured, Joel Grant, the information you have shared with us this evening will go no further, despite the intense questioning which will follow shortly, led, of course, by my dearest Annette. Good luck in your endeavours.'

'And yours. I'm conscious I have given you a lot to think about this evening,' said Joel. As far as he recalled it was the first time Frederick had talked about Annette in such affectionate terms.

'You certainly have, Joel.' Marta's voice broke through his musings. 'Thanks for what you're doing,' she added. 'I will phone you if there are any significant developments from tonight.' The conversation was finished, and Joel could almost hear them thinking at the other end of the phone.

'Bye, everyone,' Joel added and the phone line went dead.

Joel wondered for a moment whether Marta's phone was being

intercepted, but by whom? He slipped off to sleep almost immediately. He didn't hear the phone ring at 10pm, 11pm or midnight.

Joel remained in his partially comatose state until 4.30am, when he woke, looked at his phone, saw the time then spotted the missed calls from a withheld number. He presumed it had been Marta. He looked at his messages, and sure enough there was one which simply read:

Tried to call no reply will try am. M x

Joel was annoyed with himself for not hearing the call, but then fell quickly back to sleep.

He woke again at six, dressed and walked across the road to Kings Cross Station, which was just springing to life. He amused himself by wizard spotting – after all, this was where the train to Hogwarts went from. Joel spotted a number of likely candidates, four in particular who were pretending to be a family returning from a holiday, but Joel knew what they really were – wizards looking for Platform nine and three quarters! He snapped back into reality and bought eight Sunday newspapers, to the surprise of the assistant who was more asleep than Joel. He also bought a coffee and returned to his temporary lair, arms full.

Looking through the newspapers, Joel could find nothing about a wayward globe trotting Detective Sergeant, which was how he felt the tabloids might have described him. Perhaps it wasn't the press after all and he'd have to readjust the target of his venom and potential revenge. Then he thought they, the press, weren't out of the woods yet. It could still be a Daily, but he'd be surprised.

He'd started reading, as opposed to scanning the papers, when his phone rang. As anticipated, it was Marta. She told him despite the brevity of their relationship in South Africa she missed him, and urged him to take some time and come back, perhaps go to Knysna this time. Joel liked the idea, but he had much to sort out in the United Kingdom. Then he would think about it. Marta mentioned her father and Annette were thinking about visiting the United Kingdom in a few months' time, and she was going to join them. This caused Joel some anxiety, but it was a long way off.

Joel remembered the business reason for the call and asked, 'What did you and your father glean over dinner?'

Marta said, 'Goodness, I'd quite forgotten about that. What we did confirm is the lack of useful data around both then and now. Jean's father-in-law Stefan remembered Jessica's murder and Kem's arrest. He wasn't involved, he was working in the townships. Put out of the way, Papa suspects.

'Anyway, he also remembers Mhkize and his partner in crime. He recalls them because they were suspected of robberies in people's homes away from the township, but nothing could ever be proved. Stefan said both of them were very violent whenever they were caught and always fought to get away, even from the most simple shop theft. They were certainly well capable of getting on to secure compounds.

'Jean provided further useful information: Charl Majola, Mhkize's crime partner, is also in Pollsmoor serving a sentence for housebreaking. Papa's going to go and see him.'

'Does he think he will get to see him?'

'Papa's going to talk to some people,' Marta responded.

'Aha,' said Joel. Why did that not surprise him.

'He will let you know,' Marta added. They ended the call, both saying how much they missed each other.

Chapter Thirty-Five

Joel was out running at seven the following morning, along the canal to Camden. It was quiet, only a few other runners and commuters walking to work, and nobody seemed out of place. He had an appointment to see Dr Lloyd, so when he returned to the flat he ate some porridge, showered and was at the surgery by 8.45am.

As usual the doctor was supportive. She asked what he had been doing and how he felt. He was somewhat circumspect and said resting and travelling, certainly not working. Dr Lloyd asked if he was ready to go back to work and Joel said he felt he needed a little more time, but was concerned about the label 'fatigue'. She told him not to be so sensitive and she certainly wasn't going to type in groin strain. Joel thought, what is it with some women? They can mind read!

Dr Lloyd gave Joel a certificate for two weeks, further evidence of her physic powers, and endorsed it, viral complications. She judged he was run down and the cause was probably viral. The blood test results indicated as much, but she was certainly not going to give him antibiotics. What he needed was rest. This would do, thought Joel.

He considered popping into work to drop off his certificate, but it would be the usual hectic Monday morning and he didn't want to get in the way. He had an envelope with him, addressed it to Fiona Henderson and posted it. He would ring her later. As he was walking back to the flat he thought he was being followed but remained indifferent, not anxious any more. He wasn't doing anything he shouldn't.

Next Joel sent a text message to Ali and asked if he was available for a call, maybe Skype, at 6pm. Almost instantaneously the reply came back: he was available. Joel responded by saying he was trying to get Frederick and Marta on the call as well. He would discuss it with them when they rang back. Back at his flat, Joel researched Skype and discovered he could have a conference call with up to twenty-five for free, providing it was just audio. He sent a message to Marta and Ali asking them to send their Skype addresses to him, and he would start the call at 5.50pm, United Kingdom time. He had not heard back from Marta but he assumed it would be OK.

Having stayed firmly behind the technological curve, Joel had to get to grips with Skype by practising making calls to Robert. He told Robert he wanted to have a three-way conversation on progress, and surprisingly Robert did not ask to take part. This pleased Joel; it would have been very difficult otherwise.

Robert did talk about his meeting with Matthew. He had been a little shocked, but was glad Matthew's life seemed to be coming together in all sorts of ways. Joel assumed Matthew had not gone into the history of his relationship with Peter, and certainly not the events of the night Jess was killed. Robert said Matthew also invited him to the civil partnership ceremony, and hoped his parents would be there too. George and Virginia were due to arrive soon and Matthew hoped they would be able to make the event. Joel did not envy Matthew the conversation with his father when he told George about Peter. If anything this put more pressure on Joel to get samples from Matthew and, more importantly in his mind, Peter.

Joel left the flat at 5.30pm and made his way to the Internet café on Upper Street. Nobody followed him in. It was surprisingly quiet.

When 5.50pm came, Joel started making his calls on Skype. He'd had no problem in the morning with Robert, but was not optimistic on a three-way international call. Surprisingly it worked first time. Joel had sent an agenda to the others: update re forensics; update from South Africa; update from the United Kingdom; next steps. He had done this in an attempt to organise the call as all four of them had information to give and questions to ask.

Joel asked Ali to start, and he went over what the lab had found. Just this evening he received a lab report confirming their findings of the nail scrapings originating from a male with European heritage. No other traces were found. The report added there were many reasons for the nail scrapings, and the absence of other samples could have been the result of the spontaneity of the attack, the length of time or a combination. In any case if there were people who were likely to have had contact with the deceased, samples should be obtained for elimination purposes, regardless of their ethnic origins.

Next it was Frederick's turn. He said he would probably repeat information people already knew, but he would do this to give a complete picture. This was nothing less than Joel expected. Following dinner on Saturday evening, Frederick and Marta had not wasted time. He visited Letsego Shabangu the following morning. The situation had been less volatile than on his last visit, and he asked Letsego if it would be possible to see Charl Majola who was also in the Twenty-sixes. Letsego agreed he would see what he could do. The same afternoon Frederick received a phone call from 'Mr Pienaar' who simply said all was in order for a family visit at nine the following day, and this was where he and Marta had been earlier. The family of Majola must have been due a visit, but Frederick took their place. He felt uncomfortable doing this, but when he arrived at the prison they were there and seemed keen to help. Letsego, thought Frederick!

The prison authorities, of course, knew Frederick and thought it was strange he was on a family visit, but he explained it was urgent. In any case, the visit was brief. Majola had clearly been told to cooperate, and confirmed he and Tebego Mhkize committed burglaries and robberies in the homes of the rich over the last twenty or so years. He was adamant he had not been involved in Jessica's death, but he knew Mhkize often went out by himself, although he never mentioned it to Mhkize then or subsequently. There was nothing else he could add. Frederick and Marta said they were inclined to believe his account, but it was interesting he didn't give Mhkize a clean bill of health. Frederick added they had failed to recover Kem's clothing from the police. Despite the initial resistance from the station commander, the exhibit sergeant had been very helpful. So helpful, in fact, Frederick and Marta were absolutely convinced the clothing was not there, and had probably been destroyed.

Frederick also said there were no crime data available from twenty years ago. In fact, data were still suspect today. He recalled there had been attacks on households by robbers in and around Cape Town at the time of Jess's death. This was an ever-present problem. Frederick added the robbers tended to sneak into the houses and avoid confrontation with the householders or their staff, but when challenged had no hesitation to use violence. Relatively few robbers were caught by the police and added in a slightly defensive manner, it was not just in South Africa. Joel thought, quite right.

Frederick explained Kem remained in hospital recovering well, but was still weak. He said there continued to be no pressure from the prison authorities to remove the guards, and the guards themselves were pleased with the situation. They preferred being in the hospital than Pollsmoor. Frederick did, however, anticipate a move to the prison hospital in the next six weeks.

The Mhkize family had definitely gone to Zimbabwe, and there the trail had gone cold. Frederick was glad to hear this because it hopefully meant the Numbers wouldn't be able to get to them. Marta had been in touch with the police investigation team, and Mhkize, who was still in protective custody, refused to cooperate with them. They had gleaned no further information from the prison or prisoners, but Frederick added this was not unusual.

Now it was Joel's turn. He recounted his conversation with Brute and Ifu and said he was trying to track down who had been following him and why, without success. He now suspected the media, meaning it probably had nothing to do with the investigation and suspected it was because he was on the sick and had travelled abroad. He had to explain to Marta and Frederick this was news in the English tabloid context, particularly at the moment. All understood. Curiously at this point Joel chose to mention he thought Skype was safe to talk on, although he had no idea whether it was or not or why he mentioned it.

'And so to the difficult part of the conversation,' said Joel. 'What to do next?'

After considerable discussion, the four agreed a number of actions. Frederick and Marta would commission an independent lawyer to try and see Mhkize; they would also see if they could trace his family. Ali would continue to update the lab, and Joel would approach Matthew and Peter for samples. Everyone offered suggestions about the best way to do this. They all discounted the covert route, and left it to Joel to decide upon the tactics. They all agreed Robert needed to be told. Despite Joel's belief he should do it, they determined Ali was the best person to impart the developments in an objective and scientific way.

The conference call ended with everyone agreeing to email updates unless they were particularly sensitive. Later in the evening Joel spoke to Robert and introduced the idea of him getting a scientific update from Ali, rather than Joel's abridged version. Robert jumped at the chance for another trip to Cheshire, and Joel left him about to phone Ali to make arrangements for the visit.

He phoned Matthew and said he would like to come and see him in Chambers the following day. Matthew asked what it was about and Joel just said he needed some help. They agreed 4.30pm, and Matthew suggested they could go for a drink afterwards. Joel accepted, but he wondered whether Matthew would ever want to go for a drink with him again once he'd said what he had been doing and what he wanted.

The next day Joel was aware of being followed as he made his way to Matthew's Chambers in Paper Buildings. He felt relaxed; at least he could talk in confidence here. He thought his watchers would wonder what he was doing visiting the Temple, which was a great place to spot watchers out of place in their comfortable but casual attire. Then he recalled he met Matthew and Peter at Windows. If he was being watched at the time, and dependent on the size of the surveillance team, they may have already been identified.

He gained access to the building via entry phone and went to the reception area, where he found a variety of people sitting around waiting: solicitors, clients and families by the look of them. This was the time, after the courts closed for the day, when barristers had their conferences. Joel introduced himself to the reception staff and told them he had an appointment with Matthew, who two minutes later bounded into the reception area and greeted Joel as a long lost friend.

Matthew took Joel to his room. As a senior, longstanding member of Chambers, unlike many barristers, he did not share with others. When Joel had visited barristers on business, the meetings were held in book-lined meeting rooms, furnished to a high standard. Matthew's room was well furnished but not as sumptuous as the other rooms, although it was much tidier than Frederick's.

As they sat down, one of the office staff brought in tea and biscuits, and Matthew said, 'And so, Mr Grant, please tell me in your own words how you came to be in possession of 200 stolen surfboards, seventy wetsuits and a pair of flippers in your two bedroomed flat in Islington, seventy miles from the nearest surfing beach?' They both laughed – the first and last time during the afternoon's discussion.

Joel took charge and started with the beginning and context of his recent exploits: Robert's constant concern regarding Jessica's death; the event at the Old Bailey; Joel's need to get away, then his trip to South Africa and his findings there. Matthew did not interrupt; he neither asked any points of clarification nor made any notes. He simply looked shocked. The events surrounding the fire at Sarah's shop and the follow up inquiries drew a gasp from Matthew. Concerned, Joel thought, about Sarah. After half an hour Matthew excused himself to go to the men's room, and while he was out the tea and biscuits were replenished.

Matthew returned, sat down and quite formally said, 'Please continue, Joel.' He did, telling Matthew about the attack on Kem in prison and the subsequent fallout. Joel also told Matthew about his suspicions regarding being followed, which elicited a rare intervention from Matthew. 'But why, Joel?'

Joel explained he had been told it wasn't the Met, or at any rate not the complaints people, but he suspected someone from Scotland Yard had fed to the press the fact he had gone sick in the middle of a trial and travelled to South Africa, Canada and Devon, seemingly enjoying himself at taxpayers' expense. Matthew completely got the current anti police stance in the media, some of which, he thought, seemed to go to extreme lengths to spice up and twist minor everyday mistakes into headline grabbing events. However, if they had been following Joel, Matthew said he would find it extraordinary.

Now for the crunch issue. Joel had mentioned the clothing he found but not the forensic results, so he began to outline them. He said there were no contact traces from Kem on Jessica's clothing, reminding Matthew of Locard's Principle, used widely by scientists and police officers, which Joel paraphrased as, 'Every contact leaves a trace'. There was, however, DNA, probably from a European male, on non-clothing samples. The realisation of what he was being told quickly dawned on Matthew; after all, he was an experienced trial lawyer and part time judge; he understood DNA.

'There can't be any samples,' Matthew pointed out. 'Jess was cremated, Joel, remember?' Joel deliberately had not said where the DNA had been found, and clearly Matthew hadn't thought it through yet. Joel explained there were samples which the police had taken, and Matthew, who had now gathered his thoughts, said, 'Well my DNA would have been on Jess. We kissed when I arrived back from bringing Peter to the house.'

'When was the last time you made love to Jess, Matthew?' Joel asked in a matter of fact but confident way.

'Oh God, she wasn't raped? Oh no, nothing was mentioned at the trial,' Matthew responded.

Joel quickly said Jessica had not been raped, and after Matthew composed himself a little asked if they'd had a fight during the evening.

'We had an argument, I told you, but I could never harm Jess. Never,

never, never. You know that, Joel.' He paused for a moment, the penny dropping. 'Joel, does this mean you want my DNA?'

Joel nodded. 'And Peter's,' he added more tentatively.

Matthew blanched. He clearly hadn't thought about Peter. 'Peter wouldn't harm anyone, Joel. You've met him, he saves lives, he doesn't end them.' Joel said he needed to ask him, and Matthew explained Peter was going to make his way to Chambers from Bart's, if he hadn't been told they were in a bar somewhere. He was due between 6pm and 6.30pm.

Matthew suddenly snapped into work mode and asked Joel where he needed to go to give his samples. Joel reached into his bag and explained he could take them now if Matthew agreed, which he did. As Joel finished, Matthew's phone rang. Peter had arrived early and Matthew asked for him to be shown up.

Matthew presumed Joel would want to speak to Peter alone, and after saying, 'Hello,' he left them in his room. Peter looked taken aback at the way Matthew simply said Joel had some questions to ask, and was even more shocked when Joel told him what it was about. Joel didn't go into the detail he had with Matthew; it wasn't necessary. He explained exhibits had been found with DNA on them, and Peter, the medic, also quickly grasped what Joel was talking about. He pointed out his only contact with Jess, as he could recall, had been to shake her hand, so his DNA may be present. Joel asked Peter if he could take samples from him.

Peter replied, 'Of course,' and reiterated he had touched Jess. Interesting, thought Joel, Peter hadn't referred to his visit to the library to talk to Jess, which he had mentioned at their first meeting in Windows.

Joel took the samples, then he and Peter went in search of Matthew, who was in a meeting room along the corridor. Joel explained he would get the samples sent first thing in the morning. He had already resolved he was taking them personally to the lab, and he didn't know how long it would take.

'Joel, we were going to go for a drink. I certainly need one,' Matthew announced.

'Thanks, Matthew, but you two have a lot to talk about and you don't need me. You would only be thinking I was watching and looking for reactions. Another time, I think.'

'Soon,' said Matthew and, along with Peter, thanked Joel for what he was doing. Joel left them still in shock, and once again joined his watchers as he travelled back to his flat. He wondered if he was attacked whether the watchers would come to his aid. He thought not.

On the way back he phoned Ali, recounted somewhat circumspectly what had taken place and said he would put the samples in the fridge and send them to the lab in the morning. Ali said he was seeing Robert in a couple of days and asked Joel if he should tell Robert about the samples being at the lab. Joel confirmed Robert needed to know and arranged to speak again when Ali had spoken to Robert. The conversation ended, and Joel sent Ali a text saying:

Will go to lab personally in morning.

Ali would realise Joel was being cautious around the watchers.

Joel ate a stir-fry and made some Horlicks as he watched another episode of late night $M*A*S*H$. The horrors and turmoil McIntyre and Pearce went through in Korea put his own issues into context.

Later, Joel looked at his phone. There was a text from Matthew, which he opened with more than a little trepidation. The text read:

We know 2day was very difficult for you J. If there was anyone we would want to find the truth, it's you. Tx for being so kind. It could have been so much different. M & P x

Joel was not surprised; this was the Matthew he knew. He hoped the Matthew twenty years ago had been the same person. Joel set his alarm, ready for his very early start, laid his clothes out and went to bed, falling quickly to sleep.

Chapter Thirty-Six

Joel's trip to Oxford went well but was tiring and after a long couple of days he was recovering in bed the following morning when the phone rang. It wasn't beside the bed, he'd misplaced it, again, and realised it was echoing down the corridor from the living room.

When Joel finally answered, a voice said, 'Hello, Joel, my name's Eric Nugent. I work on the eighth floor at NSY.'

Joel quickly came to. He didn't know the Yard well, but he knew many of the bosses worked on the eighth floor, including the Commissioner and her deputy.

'Good morning, Sir, what can I do for you?'

After apologising for disturbing him so early in the morning and enquiring after his health, the caller asked if Joel could pop in to see him at the Yard. Joel was confused. What the fuck was this? He wondered for a moment if it was a wind up, and said, 'Sir, I'm sorry, it's a really bad signal. Can I ring you back, please? What extension are you on?'

Sounding impressed with Joel's professional attitude, Eric Nugent gave him the number. Joel hung up and rang straight away to make sure he had some element of surprise. He presumed the caller would expect him to check the number out first, and he had surmised correctly as Eric commented on the speed of the returned call. Happy this was a legitimate number, Joel was more concerned to find out why Eric wanted to see him. He didn't get many invites to the Yard, let alone to the eighth Floor. Eric explained it was rather delicate and he would prefer to see Joel in person.

'Would I need to bring anyone with me? Lawyer? Police Federation?' asked Joel cautiously. Eric assured him there was nothing to worry about and they agreed to meet later in the morning.

Joel couldn't understand it, what was this all about? He picked the phone up and spoke to Fiona Henderson. He was circumspect, but told her what had happened. She didn't know what it could be; no one had been looking for him for days. Eric Nugent was a Commander and the Commissioner's Chief of Staff. She knew him and he seemed a good guy, but why he wanted to speak to a Detective Sergeant from Islington she had no idea.

Oh well, thought Joel, let's see what he wants. He showered and for the first time in what felt like ages put a suit and and lace up shoes on, it felt odd. After toast for breakfast he headed for Central London, conscious of potential followers. He arrived at St James' Park Tube station and had a coffee in Caffe Grana next to the Tube, watching the comings and goings out of the window of the café. A number of people he recognised walked past on their way to and from the Yard. Nobody saw him; he didn't want anyone to see him.

Joel went into the Yard, showed his warrant card and made his way to the eighth Floor. He arrived at 10.50am and asked for Commander Nugent. A tall, slim red-haired man about the same age as Joel appeared and introduced himself as Eric Nugent. He repeated it was good of Joel to come in so promptly, led him along a carpeted corridor and said the Commissioner had finished her meeting early so could see him now.

Joel stopped dead. 'The Commissioner?' he said, stunned.

'Yes, she wants to have a chat with you. I'm her Chief of Staff, that's why I rang.'

'But I thought *you* wanted to talk to me?' Joel managed to get out.

'No, no, come on.' Nugent walked through the outer office where everyone was busy, or trying to look busy. He knocked on the door and walked in, saying, 'Detective Sergeant Grant, Commissioner.'

The Commissioner rose from behind her desk, walked round it and shook Joel's hand, saying, 'Good to meet you, Joel. How are you? I've heard a lot about you. Please take a seat. Would you like a drink? Tea, coffee, water?'

Joel managed to ask for a coffee and was shown to a seat directly opposite the Commissioner. 'Now, Joel I suppose you are wondering what all this is about. Well, I'm sure Eric has told you there is nothing to worry about.'

Joel nodded his head, and at the same time was handed a coffee by the Chief of Staff.

'Cutting to the quick, Joel, when Jessica Bennet was murdered, was her home in London or Devon?

Joel thought, ah, it is about South Africa. 'She lived in Camden,

Commissioner. She had just moved from Chelsea.'

'And the Met have never investigated it as a Coroner's Inquiry?'

'No, Commissioner, I suppose because of an early arrest being made and then a conviction.'

'Is Kem Siblisi guilty?'

'I don't know,' said Joel honestly. 'I suspect not.'

'Joel, tell me what you've found out. Don't worry, just tell me.' Joel spent the next twenty minutes telling the Commissioner in the broadest terms what he had found, and to his surprise was soon in free flow.

The Commissioner said, 'Joel, I'm going to make you an offer. I want you to come and work here in my staff office.'

Joel looked at her quizzically, and thought, these are really restricted duties. They absolutely want to clip my wings.

She continued, 'Don't look so surprised. You're a bright, experienced, challenging detective, just what the service needs more of. Your first task will be to conduct an inquiry on behalf of HM Coroner into the death of Jessica Bennet. I spoke to the Coroner personally and, having listened to the facts as I knew them at the time, he asked us to conduct an inquiry, providing Jessica Bennet was a resident of North London. You will start as soon as you return from sick leave.'

'But… Commissioner, I'm not sure I'm the sort of person you want in here,' stammered Joel.

'Nonsense, you're just the sort of person I want,' she said in a tone which brooked no argument.

'Commissioner, in relation to Jess, I have discovered a personal friend of mine may be a suspect, and in reality I don't think it's correct for me to undertake an official investigation.'

'It wouldn't be if you were leading it, but you will be working with a Detective Superintendent.'

Oh, here it comes, thought Joel. Who is it going to be?

'Show them in please, Eric,' ordered the Commissioner. Joel hadn't been aware the Chief of Staff was still in the room. He opened the door and in walked Fiona wearing a beaming smile.

'Hello, Ma'am,' said Joel.

'Hello, Joel. I didn't know about this when we spoke earlier,' she said quickly.

'So, Detective Inspector Grant, can you work with this officer?' the Commissioner asked.

'Certainly, Commissioner, but I'm a DS not a DI.'

'When you came in you were a DS, you are now a DI. Congratulations, Joel.' She leant forward and shook his hand, followed by Eric Nugent and Fiona.

'Commissioner, I don't know what to say,' Joel said. 'Thank you so much, thank you. I won't let you down.'

'I know you won't. Fiona and Eric will brief you on what I want, but the first Tuesday you're back on duty I want you to come with me to a meeting.' Joel nodded. He didn't know which meeting, but presumed it would be with the South African High Commission or something.

'Thank you again, Commissioner,' Joel said as he, Fiona and Eric walked out of the room and into an office along the corridor.

The Commissioner felt good about what she'd just done – very good! There may be those who would challenge her decisions: she looked forward to those challenges.

'Please sit down, you two. I'll get more coffee,' said Eric Nugent and went down the corridor.

'Fiona, what the fuck is this all about? I don't understand,' demanded Joel.

'I got a call about 9am telling me to be here at 10.30 to see Eric Nugent, and was told not to tell anyone. I came and was whisked into the Commissioner's office and told I was being promoted to Professional Standards in charge of Intel, but beforehand I had to do a Coroner's Inquiry with you. I said I would be delighted, but it was a little odd being called down and promoted personally by the Commissioner, so I asked what the inquiry was.

'The Commissioner told me, "You and Joel Grant have shown you're worthy of promotion, and you will be working with him investigating the circumstances of the death of Jessica Bennet. Joel will be here soon, I want to talk to him too." With that I was shown into this office until I was called back in.'

Eric returned with the drinks. 'Well you two look in shock. Just relax and I'll tell a story for your ears only.' Eric recounted the meeting between the Home Secretary and the Commissioner and the subsequent fallout in some detail. Joel finally understood Piers's comments. Eric said the Commissioner had read their personal files and the surveillance logs. 'She felt you had both been very badly treated and asked me to tell you specifically you have a strong case to sue.' He handed them a letter signed by the Acting DG of Hydra.

The letter was an apology, stating they had both been subject to unwarranted surveillance, which amounted to a clear breach of their human rights. It had been ill conceived and wrong in law. The letter also contained a request from the DG to meet with them personally to apologise.

Joel said, 'So that's who was watching me?'

Fiona chipped in, 'I had no idea, no idea I was subject to surveillance. Do you know what they did?' Eric said he didn't, but Arthur Walkden could answer any questions.

'Sir, I think you should know I've written to the Investigatory Powers Tribunal complaining I was under surveillance without good reason,' Joel said.

'Don't worry about it, Joel, the Commissioner thought you might do that. She feels it's completely understandable, but she hopes Mr Walkden will go some way to helping explain.

Fiona looked at Joel and mouthed, 'My God!'

Eric quickly turned to practicalities. 'Joel, while in theory you will work from this floor, you will both continue to work at Islington while conducting this inquiry. It will not present any difficulties, the Borough Commander will make space for you on the top floor. In terms of reporting lines and cover, it's me. Don't hesitate – if you need anything, ask. The Commissioner is very interested in this, as you have witnessed.'

'Excuse me, Sir, and I don't want to cause any more trouble, but if you say Hydra are not following me, then who is?' asked Joel.

'What do you mean?' replied Eric.

'I was followed here today by a team. I counted about five of them,' added Joel. 'There's one out there now walking past the post office.' While talking to Fiona and waiting for Eric, Joel had been looking down on the Broadway and Caxton Street area from the office on the eighth floor. He pointed towards the post office on Broadway.

'The white woman walking across Caxton Street towards the Tube wearing the grey coat and black trousers.' All three of the occupants of the office were now looking down from their observation post, and watched as the woman stopped and began talking to a slightly overweight middle-aged white man, dressed in a dark suit. The woman continued to walk towards the Tube station entrance and the man began to walk slowly along Broadway.

'Are you sure, Joel?' Eric asked.

'I'm positive. The guy she's just talked to was in the Caffe Grana with me earlier.' Eric said he needed to make a few calls. He returned a few minutes later and asked Joel and Fiona if they could wait for a short time before leaving the Yard. As he did so he glanced out of the window and saw the man looking in the shop window opposite.

About five minutes later, the door of Eric's office was opened and a man walked in. 'Hello, Sir, I'm DI Messenger, we spoke a few minutes ago.' It was Piers.

'Come in, Mr Messenger. I think you know DI Grant. This is Detective Superintendent Henderson,' Eric said.

Piers looked at Joel, who shrugged his shoulders. 'It's just happened, Piers.'

'Congratulations, Joel, and you too, Ma'am,' Piers said.

Eric interrupted, 'There will be plenty of time for that later,' as he turned to the window. 'That's one of them there in the dark suit, outside St Ermin's.' Joel thought, God, I hope I'm right, although the Commander seemed to be convinced. Piers joined Eric at the window and made a call describing the man and the woman who had been around earlier.

He finished his call, and asked, 'Where are you going after you leave here, Joel? No offence, Ma'am, but I think they will be following Joel.' She nodded in agreement.

Joel hadn't really thought about it, and in the Commander's company wondered about mentioning it, but said, looking at Fiona, 'Well if my boss will get the afternoon off, I think we should go for a drink and a meal in Soho.'

Eric agreed. 'Excellent idea, and as your new Guvn'r, Fiona. Have the afternoon off.' Fiona for once was lost for words; events were happening so quickly today.

'Where exactly are you going, Joel?' Piers asked.

'Randal and Aubin on Brewer Street, I think,' replied Fiona. She was now back in control.

'If you can just wait until I call you, I reckon about another fifteen minutes!' quipped Piers as he left the room.

Joel turned to Eric and Fiona and articulated his thoughts. 'I hope I'm right.'

'I think you are,' concurred the others.

Twenty minutes later, Joel's phone rang. It was Piers who told him to leave the Yard and gave him specific directions where to walk. En route he'd get another phone call. Fiona and Joel thanked Eric Nugent as they left. He said they would no doubt speak later.

They followed Piers's instructions. As they were in front of what used to be Rochester Row police station, but was now flats, Joel's phone rang. He didn't recognise the voice, which told him there was a black cab coming up behind them. They were to wave it down and ask for Brewer Street. Joel ended the call, turned and, seeing a cab coming, flagged it down. When they were inside Fiona asked what was going on, and Joel pointed to the red light which indicated the driver could hear the conversation. The driver looked in his mirror at the same time.

'It's all right, Guvn'r, Mr Messenger sends his regards.' The cab was a surveillance vehicle. The driver asked them not to look out of the back window as they crossed West London, but he confirmed they were being followed.

The driver said, 'I'm going to drop you off in Romilley Street outside Kettners. Do you know it?' Both Joel and Fiona did. It was a great place, right in the middle of Soho, and a place they discovered they both loved.

The driver interrupted. 'Please don't go in, Ma'am.' He then gave Joel more walking directions, ending with, 'You'll get another call soon.'

Joel said, 'But I'll be going away from Brewer Street.' The driver told them not to worry, all would become clear.

Ten minutes later the taxi stopped outside Kettners. Joel ignored its magnetic pull, it would not be wise to mention magnetism to Fiona! Fiona exited the cab first and leant in, offering the driver a twenty pound note, which he took and gave her two five pound notes and ten pounds in coin change.

The driver said, 'Thanks, Guvn'r, see you when you start work.' The Met grapevine was working well, she thought.

Fiona and Joel followed their instructions, making their way to Oxford Circus, chatting away knowing they were in capable hands. When they turned left into Oxford Street, Joel's phone went again, and this time it was Piers.

'You're clear, Joel, we have your watchers. Speak later,' and the phone went dead. Joel told Fiona, and they made their way back into to Soho to Brewer Street and the delights of Randall and Aubin; both desperate to find out who had been following them.

They went into the restaurant and sat at the window watching the world, and Fiona ordered a bottle of Veuve. The champagne came and they toasted each other.

'Success,' they cried. Then Joel turned to Fiona and said, 'What

I can't understand is why this has happened, you didn't recommend me for promotion. Remember, the day before the Whitaker incident at the Bailey?'

'I remember it all too well, Joel, but I actually said I was thinking about your recommendation. You assumed I meant I wasn't going to recommend you and stormed off. I actually gave you a very good grade, despite, as you call it, the "Whitaker incident".'

As they were talking, a black cab stopped outside. Brute got out and went into the restaurant. He walked up to them, leant over, kissed Fiona on the cheek and said, 'Congratulations, darling.' He then took Joel's hand and shook it, saying, 'Congratulations, Joel, you deserve it.'

It wasn't often Joel was lost for words but he just stared at his companions, who explained they had been seeing each other since they met with Joel some weeks ago. Joel thought by the way they were interacting they had been doing a bit more than seeing each other.

The trio ordered some food and requested another glass for Brute. As creatures of habit they had the seafood platter and the zucchini frites, while filling Brute in on the detail of the day's events. As usual the food was delicious, and they were about to start on their second bottle of Veuve when Joel's phone rang. It was Piers.

Joel went outside to take the call. Given he was in Soho he didn't dawdle and look in the shop windows. He set off at a brisk pace, listening to Piers as he did.

Piers told him they had identified and arrested nine members of a surveillance team, including a motorcyclist, who were mostly ex military. He was confident they had the whole team. Joel, ever the detective, asked, 'What have they been arrested for?' Piers explained they had found Hydra documents on them, pictures of Joel and a plan of Joel's flat. He said they had been arrested initially on suspicion of theft of Hydra documents, but also on suspicion of conspiracy to commit burglary at Joel's flat. He said some of the team were so shocked at being arrested, they told the arrest teams they had been commissioned by Katherine Thornley, the former Special Adviser to the Home Secretary, on behalf of a national daily. Joel recognised the name this time, both in the context of Fiona's meeting at the Yard with the AC and DAC and his earlier conversation with Eric Nugent. Piers added they were now also going to be arrested on suspicion of conspiracy to cause a public nuisance, adding a team was on their way now to arrest Thornley. He suspected it would be a long night.

Piers asked if it would be OK to sweep Joel's flat for eavesdropping devices because of equipment they had found on his watchers earlier. Joel said it would be fine and thanked Piers for his help. Piers once again congratulated Joel adding it was a really interesting job and the team was loving it. Unless Piers needed any urgent information, they would speak again in the morning.

Joel thanked Piers again, and for the first time looked to see where he was: in Greek Street outside the Gay Hussar, which was famous for its use by politicians. Perhaps he should pop in to see if the Home Secretary was there and tell her the news about her Special Adviser. He snapped back into the real world and returned to Brewer Street, where he sat down and recounted to his fellow diners what he had been told.

Fiona summarised, 'You couldn't make it up.'

Chapter Thirty-Seven

Joel stayed in Randall and Aubin until 4pm when he left Fiona and Brute, who were about to order another bottle. He'd had enough and was feeling a little deflated, despite having had a highly successful day. Part of the reason he felt down was really selfish. He saw how much Fiona and Brute meant to each other, and felt he needed someone to be there with him. In the middle of London, he was lonely.

At the flat he undressed and crawled into bed. Tiredness had overtaken self-pity; lunchtime drinking was having its effect. He fell asleep, then woke with a start. His phone was ringing. He could hear it but couldn't find it again. Why did this often happen? Locating the phone beside the bed where it had fallen on the floor, he picked it up, answered and noticed it was 7.30pm. 'Hi, Joel, it's Robert.'

'Hi, Robert, how are you?' Joel replied.

'I'm fine. You sound half asleep. What have you been doing? I'm at Ali's, he's on the extension.'

Another voice spoke. 'Hi, Joel, you do sound as though you've just woken up.'

'Thanks, Ali, I have,' replied Joel.

Robert resumed, 'Ali's told me the whole story and the implications, Joel. Do you think it's Matthew or Peter, or both?'

Joel considered Robert's statement; he'd clearly thought the issue through. 'To quote a police spokesman, Robert, I'm keeping an open mind. However, when I saw them they were both very shocked, and if I was to go on my gut instinct, I'd say they didn't have anything to do with it.'

'But all the evidence points towards them, Joel,' Robert responded.

'No it doesn't, Robert. Some of the evidence indicates Jess had contact with a male with European heritage, probably violent contact, but we don't know. Let's wait for the results.' Joel thought he sounded sharp with Robert; he probably was a little.

'That's what Ali said. I don't want to believe either of them was involved, I really don't, but…'

Ali interrupted, 'I have explained to Robert some of the various scenarios and explanations, Joel, including the local burglars.'

Joel didn't elaborate on his conversations with Matthew and Peter regarding physical contact with Jess; it would only heighten Robert's suspicion. Ali's children could be heard in the background asking Robert when he was going to play Monopoly, before Ali ushered them away. Robert explained he was staying with Ali tonight, which Joel thought was a good idea. He considered not telling them about his promotion, but thought he would. Robert was an official victim and Joel was now officially investigating – well, he would be when he was back in work. He had agreed with Fiona to meet over the next couple of days and then go to brief the Coroner.

Robert was delighted. He congratulated Joel, as did Ali, but Robert asked what it meant in practice. Joel pointed out he would know more when he saw the Coroner on whose behalf they were investigating, but Fiona Henderson was the senior investigating officer and he was her deputy. The Commissioner was very supportive of the investigation. Joel didn't know why he added this, but thought it may alleviate some of Robert's concerns.

Robert asked, 'What does this mean for you? I have confidence in you. What's Superintendent Henderson like? Is she any good?'

Joel instinctively answered, 'She's one of the best detectives I know, Robert. She understands and cares about people. I like her as well.'

'High praise indeed,' said Ali.

'She's that good, Joel?'

'I think so,' answered Joel. 'Don't get me wrong, we have had our moments, as you know, Robert. She can be tough, but she's bright and fair. You'll like her. She and Brute appear to be an item,' he added.

'Well, it sounds promising, when can I meet her?' Robert asked. 'I'm travelling back through London and going to the theatre with William Goble, so I could meet her tomorrow or the day after.'

Joel remembered how he'd felt in South Africa when Frederick had asked Marta to arrange a meeting with Thembi. He didn't want to bounce Fiona into a meeting when she was still learning about the case, and replied, 'Let me see what she's up to, Robert. She is probably handing over her work.'

Robert said, 'I understand, but it would be an ideal opportunity. Just let me know.'

Joel said he'd speak to Fiona in the morning.

'Well I have an important game of Monopoly to play,' said Robert, adding, 'Well done, Joel, thanks for what you've done, and are doing. You're a star.'

Joel's emotions began to well up. He thanked Robert and said goodnight to him. Ali remained on the line for a moment, and said, 'Don't worry, Joel, he's fine. The children are seeing to that. Well done, see you soon, bye.' Ali was gone before Joel could reply.

Joel didn't know why Robert saying thank you had such a profound effect on him. It was probably fuelled by the alcohol and the highs of the day; only those very close to Joel knew how near to the surface his emotions could get. He wiped the tears from his eyes and went back to bed. He was asleep in no time.

Joel woke at 6am and went for a run to Camden. He felt deflated again, not looking for watchers anymore. Lost in his emotions, Joel suddenly remembered arranging to meet Suzy and Billy in the Breakfast Club at nine.

On the way down Upper Street Joel phoned Fiona and relayed his conversation with Robert. As expected, Fiona wasn't keen to meet Robert but understood his need and they agreed to meet him the following day. Joel sent a text to Robert to find out where he was staying and when he wanted to meet.

The response came back almost immediately.

Oriental Club, Stratford Place, 12 noon, lunch.

He's keen, thought Joel, forwarding the message to Fiona, adding he'd meet her at the front entrance of Bond Street Tube.

Billy and Suzy were both delighted at Joel's news as they sat down and enjoyed their full English. Billy, ever the opportunist, saw Fiona's move to complaints as a positive step in his career aspirations towards getting in Professional Standards. Suzy said she'd miss them, but Joel reminded her they hadn't gone yet and had a lot of work to do when he got back. He thought this would be in a week or so, dependent on Dr Lloyd.

Joel's phone rang: it was Piers. He was at Joel's flat and wanted to carry out his sweeping. Joel left Suzy and Billy with a promise to meet next week and walked back to his flat. He made Piers and his colleagues tea while they began carefully scanning the flat with what looked like ray guns. One of them turned the sofa upside down and was taking the bottom off.

Piers dangled a microchip type object in front of Joel. He explained the techies had found it on Joel's car. It was a surveillance beacon, which Piers thought would relate to a computer programme on the equipment they'd found in the watchers' offices in Finchley.

As they were talking, the technician, who was looking at the sofa, pulled out a small plastic box and explained it was a listening device, fairly low tech but effective. Joel thought about what they might have heard; he tended to make calls from the bedroom, and wondered if there was anything in there. Ten minutes later the techies found a similar device hidden in the same way under the base of the bed. They didn't find anything else, but Joel speculated about how the watchers had gained entry. He had good locks. Piers revealed they had found key making equipment and keys in the Finchley office, which they would need to test on Joel's door. Joel smiled to himself when he thought about Billy learning his bedroom activities may have been broadcast throughout North London.

Piers told Joel half the surveillance team were talking and being quite open. They really didn't think they'd done anything wrong. The others were keeping quiet for the moment, but there was a long way to go. Katherine Thornley had said absolutely nothing and didn't seem to like the idea of sitting in a cell. A partner from a big firm of lawyers, whom Joel had never heard of, turned up during the previous evening to represent her. They even came back at 8.30am to ask for her to be bailed to return for questioning later. The request had been politely refused; Piers knew the lawyer and said he was switched on and expensive.

The search was completed by midday, and Piers and his team left to go to Fiona's house to conduct another sweep. Joel lay on the bed and thought about what had taken place since the fateful day at the Bailey, he then busied himself around the flat and as usual found no difficulty in falling gently to sleep later in the evening.

The following morning Joel got up and saw he had a text from Fiona:

I'm all clear, see you later.

He hoped it meant Piers hadn't found any devices and it wasn't meant for Brute. This made him chuckle. They met as planned outside the Tube and walked across the road to the Oriental Club, which was an ornate, stylish building just off Oxford Street. Robert waited for them at the front door with William Goble and they went straight into the dining room, which was light, airy and very comfortable. It was reasonably busy with what looked like business people, and Joel did what he always did, tried to guess what business they were in.

Over lunch, which was roast beef for Robert and William and Indonesian chicken curry of the day for Fiona and Joel, Joel explained in some detail what he had found out since going to South Africa. He did this not only to fill Robert in on the details, but in reality it was the first time Fiona had heard the full story. He also told his audience about elements of his activities in South London. All three of his lunch companions were impressed by Joel's exploits, and Fiona led the questioning. She asked about motive, opportunity, the trial and the attack on Kem, then Robert asked about who Joel thought had searched his room, and was the press surveillance connected?

Joel answered the questions as completely as he could, but was not able to answer any of them definitively, only propose theories or, as the current vogue put it, hypothesise. He hoped Piers would have a breakthrough over the weekend regarding the surveillance. After pudding of apple pie and custard, the quartet retired to an upstairs drawing room where they ordered coffee.

Fiona excused herself and went to the bathroom. Joel suspected it was a tactical visit to allow Robert and William to pass any comments about her, which they did. They were impressed. Neither expected her to have the in-depth knowledge which Joel had, but the questions she had asked at the right times, in what Robert described as a relaxed, searching style were the things which really scored the points.

The coffee arrived, shortly followed by Fiona who was immediately asked by Robert what the next steps were. Fiona without hesitation said, 'As soon as Joel is back from sick leave we will visit the Coroner and hopefully get their approval to conduct an investigation into Jess's death.' It wasn't a murder investigation so much as an effort to find out the facts. They would interview witnesses wherever they were, and this included South Africa, at the Coroner's direction.

All eyes then fell on Joel, who announced, to some relief around the table, he was seeing his doctor on Monday with a view to returning to work on Tuesday. Fiona said she would try to see the Coroner on Tuesday, but Joel reminded her the Commissioner wanted him to go to a meeting on his first Tuesday back. This intrigued Robert and William as much as it had done Joel, who said he thought it was going to be with the South African High Commission.

As they were leaving the club, Joel went to the cupboard in the entrance where he had left his bag. He pulled a large buff envelope from his rucksack and handed it to Robert, telling him it was Jess's dissertation. Robert was grateful; he had read it in the draft stage but had never received an actual copy. This time it was Robert's turn to become emotional.

Fiona and Joel left the club and walked across the road to the Tube. Fiona confirmed her visit to the bathroom had been tactical, and Joel told her how impressed the others were with her. She was relieved but also pleased, and went on to say she thought giving Robert Jess's dissertation was kind and thoughtful. Was he mellowing? Joel didn't respond to her comment, kissed Fiona on the cheek and they agreed to speak on Monday.

Early on Monday morning Joel phoned Eric Nugent and told him, subject to his doctor's agreement, he would be available the following day if the Commissioner still wanted him to go to the meeting with her. Eric texted Joel back, confirming the meeting was at 11.30am but he should be at NSY at 8am for preparation. Joel confirmed this was OK, but was intrigued by the time set aside for a pre-read. He went straight to see Dr Lloyd, who was delighted by his promotion but still gave him a lecture about not working too hard. He promised he wouldn't.

During the evening Joel telephoned Marta, who was joined on the telephone by Frederick. Joel told them about the surveillance operation against him, and how he was starting work the following day, officially investigating the circumstances of Jessica's death. Frederick had clearly been thinking about the implications and asked how this would affect the flow of information. Joel said he had discussed it with his boss, Fiona and also Robert over lunch, and they both felt it was vital information continued to be shared as openly as it had been, but in a more formalised way. Frederick was relieved by what he heard, particularly when he knew Fiona and Joel were going to see the Coroner so promptly.

Chapter Thirty-Eight

It felt strange for Joel to get back into his work routine in the morning: showering, putting a suit on and wearing lace-up shoes for the second time in a week. His feet didn't like it and hadn't recovered from their previous outing. He wondered whether he should have tried to get a uniform, but in reality, when did he have time?

Joel arrived at NSY at 7.15am. Eric was already there and handed him a file of papers, which were headed "Home Office". Joel began to read through the papers: briefing notes for the Commissioner on a wide variety of current topics. He had just started when he heard a voice down the corridor say, 'Good morning, Commissioner.' A moment later a figure stood at the entrance to the office: it was the Commissioner.

Joel got up, and she said, 'Good morning, Joel, welcome. Good to see you.'

Joel replied, 'Thank you. Good morning, Commissioner.'

'We'll talk later about our meeting, please pop along about 10.55.'

'Yes, Commissioner,' replied Joel and the conversation ended. Pop along at 10.55 – relaxed but precise. He liked her style.

Joel resumed reading, then *popped* along as he had been asked. The Commissioner said they were going to see the Home Secretary for one of her regular meetings. Joel should make notes, and if asked any questions respond openly to them. Eric had already briefed him; he told Joel to write as much down as possible to help him record the content of the meeting and the Home Office officials would do the same.

They left the Yard at 11.05am. The Home Office was just five minutes around the corner, but the Commissioner liked to stop and chat to people as she walked along the streets. She was behaving as she wanted her staff to do: engaging with the public and listening to them. Eric came with them, but explained he wouldn't be coming into the meeting. This was Joel's area.

They went through the security and into the Home Secretary's outer office. At 11.30am the door opened and they were invited in. The inner office was neat and tidy; quite plush, thought Joel. They were invited to sit down by the Home Secretary, who introduced her team: the Director of Policing, her private secretary and a SPAD. The Commissioner introduced Joel as the newest member of her office, and Joel was aware of the Home Secretary and her officials noting his name.

The meeting went well, Joel thought. The Commissioner was really good, batting off what Joel considered were stupid and sometimes naive questions from the officials, particularly the SPAD who Joel had concluded was a self important prick. He considered momentarily his opinion may have been a little tainted because of Thornley but thought not, he was a pompous ass! When the Home Secretary asked if there was anything else, the Commissioner replied, 'I hope you got my note about Katherine Thornley, Home Secretary?'

'Yes, thank you, Commissioner,' replied the Home Secretary rather stiffly. Joel didn't believe the thank you was genuine for one moment. 'We have had a number of press inquiries already.'

'There will be additional charges, and others will be joining her in the dock,' continued the Commissioner.

'I understand,' the Home Secretary said, then looked directly at Joel. 'I would like to thank you, Mr Grant, for your efforts in exposing corruption in your own organisation. You were very brave, it must have been difficult for you.'

'It wasn't brave or difficult, Home Secretary. It's what 99.9 per cent of people in policing would have done,' Joel responded quietly.

'Oh come, surely that can't be true. I know I couldn't say that about the Home Office.' The Director of Policing looked perplexed.

Joel didn't like the Home Secretary. She was condescending and aloof. 'I'm afraid I must disagree. I know my colleagues. I know their standards and ethics. The activities of a few won't destroy the reputation of many.' Joel didn't know where the last comment had come from, but he was on a roll. 'Walking here this morning with the Commissioner, with her talking to members of the public, reminded me the vast majority of people love their police.'

'Yes, but look at the papers and what they say,' challenged the Home Secretary. Joel saw the Commissioner looking at him. One more comment, he thought.

'Yes the papers can highlight our inadequacies, but it's the personal interaction and support from the police which influences the public, not opinion columns, politicians or leaks.' Joel thought, oh my God, have I gone too far?

'Thank you, Mr Grant, I am sure you are right, although you sound like a police spokesman,' said the Home Secretary.

This really annoyed Joel, who retorted, 'I am a police spokesman, for the quarter of a million or so who work in policing. One more point, Home Secretary, why did you have my phone bugged?'

Everyone in the room, except the Commissioner, seemed surprised by the question. The Commissioner waited for a response which didn't come, so she said, 'Is there anything else, Home Secretary?'

'No, no, Commissioner, that's all, thank you,' said the flustered Home Secretary.

The Commissioner and Joel left the room and walked out of the building without saying a word to each other. Eric and Jack were waiting in the car to take the Commissioner to her next appointment. As soon as they drew away, Joel said, 'I am sorry, Commissioner, I shouldn't have said what I said. I think I had better stick to policing.'

The Commissioner replied, 'Nonsense, Joel, you said what I couldn't say because it would have been interpreted as defensiveness. What you said in there was great, and the final question was a killer. Well done, Joel.'

'You didn't seem surprised by the last question, Commissioner. Everyone else was,' commented Joel.

'No, I wasn't. You will have noticed, of course, you didn't get an answer. Tell Eric and Jack what you asked the Home Secretary, Joel.' He told them. There was no response apart from two wry smiles.

The Commissioner's mobile rang, and Joel recognised the voice of the Director of Policing. The Commissioner said little and listened intently. She then said, 'He is an innocent victim asking the person responsible for an explanation. Explanations and transparency are encouraged by me and, supposedly, by this Home Secretary. Perhaps the Investigatory Powers Tribunal will get the answer Mr Grant didn't.' The phone call ended and nobody else said anything.

Jack dropped the Commissioner and Eric at their next appointment in Lambeth, where they would be spending the rest of the day. The Commissioner asked Jack to take Joel back to the Yard. Joel didn't speak much on the way and explained to Jack he wasn't being ignorant, he was just thinking about what he had said. Then he remarked, 'She's bloody good, isn't she?'

'Who is?' queried Jack.

'The Commissioner, she is so sharp.'

Jack replied, 'I am biased, Guvn'r, but she is the best.'

Guvn'r? Jack was talking to him! Bloody hell, thought Joel.

They arrived at the Yard, and Joel went directly to the office to phone Fiona about their meeting with the Coroner. He didn't mention the meeting he had just come from; the only people who needed to know had been in the room at the time or in the car.

Joel spent the rest of the day getting to know the people who inhabited the eighth floor; the important people: personal assistants and staff officers. He waited until Eric came back, fearful the Commissioner might have changed her mind following his attack on the Home Secretary. She hadn't. Joel explained he was going to see the Coroner the following day. Fiona had already spoken to Eric. Joel went home tired and thoughtful, but satisfied. A good first day in his new job.

The next day Fiona and Joel went to see the Coroner, Dr Isos Lloyd-Thomas. He was a Welsh medic, unlike most Coroners who tended to be lawyers, so Fiona and Joel felt at home. They both independently wondered whether he was related to 'their' Dr Lloyd.

The meeting went well. The Commissioner had laid the foundations and explained some of the background. There were no potentially embarrassing questions about what had happened previously. Dr Lloyd-Thomas was satisfied with what had taken place, but emphasised it was now a Coroner's inquiry, not a police inquiry. Fiona and Joel were pleased with the clarity of this message. One thing did surprise Joel: DLT, as he was known in police circles, said he would pay for the analysis of all the exhibits. He said he wanted to control access to new information, and would be writing to Ali's Chief Constable, asking for his cooperation in allowing Ali to advise him. Joel thought the Coroner's reputation as a swift operator was certainly well earned.

The meeting lasted nearly two hours. DLT directed how he wanted the Inquiry to operate, which almost exactly matched the way Fiona and Joel had hoped themselves. They were to document everything which had taken place and obtain statements from the key players. They left the Coroner, reassured he was serious and on the case, and retired to their new office on the top floor of Islington police station to gather their thoughts. From there, Joel rang Ali.

Chapter Thirty-Nine

When Fiona and Joel met Robert at the Oriental Club they had already settled on Joel adopting the official family liaison role. Under normal circumstances the theorists would have frowned upon this, but Fiona considered continuity and welfare of the victims was vital, not rigid adherence to some pseudo-academic philosophy. Joel liked this approach; he liked it a lot.

Their next move was to visit Robert in Devon and take a formal statement from him, which would be vital to the Inquest in many ways: it would chart Jessica's life, her death and what had happened after her death. One person would normally be enough to take the statement, but Joel thought it would be a good idea for Fiona to come with him to further build a relationship with Robert. She readily agreed, and they set off after Joel confirmed Robert was available; in fact, he was available all week.

They arrived at Joel's house in Budleigh around 9pm, and were up bright and early the following morning. Fiona and Joel ate breakfast and walked to Robert's house as arranged. Fiona remarked en route, since moving from Islington she had forgotten how pleasant it was to walk to work rather than being crammed on the Tube, bus or train.

Robert greeted them and showed them into the breakfast room next to the kitchen. As they walked past Robert's study, Joel noticed there were papers scattered all over the floor and his desk. He didn't mention this, but thought it was strange. Robert was usually extremely tidy, which was exemplified by the state of the kitchen. Not a thing out of place. They sat down at the table, and Robert brought in a tray of coffee.

Joel thought how easy it was to listen to Robert relating the story of Jessica, from the moment she was born to how and when he had learnt of her death. By the time they finished this part of the story it was late afternoon, Joel had typed twenty-three pages on his laptop and there was still more to write. Fiona felt it was time to take a break, and Robert asked if they wanted to come to The Feathers where he was meeting William Goble at 5.30pm. They both agreed it was a good idea.

On the way to The Feathers, Fiona had started to tell Robert in more detail about their meeting with the Coroner. Joel noted Robert was uncomfortable about something and asked him if anything was the matter. Robert explained, while he was grateful for the Coroner offering to pay for the examination of the exhibits, he was concerned about losing control of the information he was getting from Ali and Joel. Fiona tried to reassure him, but Joel suspected he still had his doubts.

William Goble joined them as planned. Fiona seemed to enjoy learning about the trials and tribulations of the farming communities of Devon and South Somerset from William, who was critical of the Government for its lack of interest in the countryside, exemplified by the MP he had told Joel about. Joel also learnt something about Fiona. Her ancestors had been sheep farmers in the Borders between England and Scotland – Reivers, she called them. Joel remembered from his detective training course it was the Border Reivers who had invented blackmail. They would paint their chain mail black, go out at night, steal sheep and cattle and sell them back to the losers for a ransom. Tricky! Joel thought Fiona was tricky too: it must be in her genes!

The next morning everything went to plan. Robert continued his statement, covering what had happened since Jessica's death, the trial, his concerns about the conviction and how grateful he was to the people who had listened to his concerns. Just as Fiona and Joel were leaving, William Goble came strolling down the drive.

'Hello, you two. Good job you left when you did last night. I was led astray by Robert, and what's more he expects me to do some work for him now. Outrageous.'

Fiona and Joel said their goodbyes and drove back to London via the A303. Joel privately pondered what Robert was involving William in. After William's outbursts last night, Joel thought they could be writing an article on the countryside and the Government, but he suspected the work may be more to do with the sale of Robert's house. It was too large for one person, with five bedrooms and four reception rooms. Additionally, reliving Jessica's life and death was clearly taking its toll on him.

They arrived back in Islington at 6.15pm. Joel had a text from Billy, who was in the pub, asking if Fiona and Joel wanted to join him. Fiona said she had Brute coming for dinner. 'It must serious,' remarked Joel, deciding he would join Billy for a quick drink. Joel was walking along Tolpuddle Road towards Upper Street when he got a text from Ali. It simply said:

Call me, urgent.

Joel rang him straight away.

Ali explained he had sent the text two hours ago and had the preliminary results from the lab. The DNA was not Peter's, but it was very similar to Matthew's. This in itself was not surprising, given his relationship with Jessica, but it was not Matthew's DNA either. It looked as though it was a male relative. Ali asked if Matthew had any brothers. Joel said no, and the only male relatives he knew of were Matthew's father and three uncles. One uncle, an accountant, lived in Edinburgh, and the other two were abroad somewhere. They were not a close family so he would have to check their whereabouts with Matthew. Joel remembered George and Virginia were due in London any time. Ali said as a start he would need Matthew's father's DNA to compare with the sample. Joel thought about how he could handle this and told Ali he would call him tomorrow. He turned round, retracing his steps towards the police station, and sent a text to Billy saying something had come up.

In the office, Joel found Fiona still poring over documents. 'I thought you had a hot date.'

She looked up, surprised to see him back in the police station, and said, 'And I thought you were going for a drink.' She explained the police in Scotland had contacted Brute regarding a body they found buried in a shallow grave, and asked him to go and look at the scene with the other experts before it was disturbed. 'Just like a detective, he is on his way,' she added.

Joel told Fiona his news. He made some tea and they sat down for a 'what to do next' session. They concluded they needed to speak to Matthew before they did anything else. Joel rang him, but went straight to his voicemail and he did not leave a message.

Joel told Fiona he knew Matthew was an early riser and he could ring from six in the morning. Matthew definitely would be up by then. They agreed to get back to the nick at 6.30am, when Joel would ring Matthew in the hope they could go to his flat in St John's Wood before he left for his normal routine of the gym then Chambers. They both felt like a drink, but it could be a long day tomorrow and they would need their wits about them, so they went straight home.

Fiona and Joel were actually back in the office at 5.45am; neither had much sleep. Joel made the coffee and then the call. As he'd expected, Matthew was up and awake: they decided to tell Matthew it was about the samples but not the detail.

When Joel told him, Matthew asked quietly, 'Are you coming to arrest me, Joel?'

Joel reassured him he was not, but they needed to talk to him. Quite spontaneously, Matthew said, 'Peter's in the US, Joel.' He was obviously jumping to conclusions. Again Joel tried to reassure him, and told him they would be with him shortly, repeating there was nothing to worry about. Joel suddenly panicked; it wouldn't be the first time someone who was innocent had taken his own life in a fit of depression. He urged Fiona to move fast.

The journey from Islington to St John's Wood could have taken an hour or so during the rush hour, but at 6.15am the speeding police car did the journey in less than ten minutes. To Joel's relief Matthew opened the door.

'Thank God, I was worried about you.' Joel hugged Matthew who, like Fiona, was a little taken aback. Joel quickly introduced Fiona, and told Matthew the investigation was now an official Coroner's Inquiry. Matthew nodded in understanding. He showed them into the drawing room of the expensively furnished apartment on the fifth floor, with views of Lords Cricket Ground. He had made coffee.

Fiona explained the DNA results, and Matthew slowly said, 'My father, my fucking father.'

Fiona jumped straight in, and said, 'Matthew, there could be all sorts of reasons for these results, and I would stress they are preliminary. We mustn't jump to conclusions, but we do need to take samples from your father and any other male relatives. Joel said your parents were due to visit the UK at any time.'

Matthew repeated himself. 'My-own-fucking-father. He is here now, in London. I saw my parents the night before last. I told them about Peter, but they weren't as shocked as I expected. Then I told them about your Inquiry into Jess's death, Joel. My father knew about it as well. He said he heard from a lawyer friend in Cape Town.'

Pennard, concluded Joel.

Matthew continued, 'It was when I mentioned you had taken our DNA that I should have realised something. The bastard just changed the subject and said he and Mother needed to go. My mother was surprised, but ever the dutiful wife she followed his lead.'

Fiona said, 'How long are they in town for, Matthew?'

'They go back on Sunday. They have been away about a month, and he said they couldn't make the ceremony, which frankly didn't surprise me. I am seeing them again this evening, we're meeting at The Goring.'

'Are they staying in the hotel?' asked Fiona.

'They don't stay in hotels, they stay in a flat in Knightsbridge. Well, I suppose it's Belgravia really. It belongs to one of the companies my father is involved in. I don't know the exact address, I have only been to collect them twice over all the years they have been coming here. Strange, really.' Joel realised Matthew was continuing to place pieces of an imaginary jigsaw together. 'The flat is behind Harrods, in Hans Place. It's called Evertree Buildings. I don't know the flat number, but I could take you there.'

'That's OK, I think we will find it. Do your parents have a mobile phone they use in the UK?' Fiona asked.

Matthew replied, 'Yes, but I tried to ring them twice yesterday. It was switched off. They are the sort of people who only switch their phone on to make calls.'

Fiona and Joel finished their coffee and said they would go and see Matthew's parents a little later. Matthew asked what he should do if his parents rang. Fiona said, 'Ask them to ring Joel, you have got his number. We just need to talk to them. Please, Matthew, don't jump to any conclusions. We will also need to see your uncles as well.'

Matthew said he would find his uncles' addresses, and if his parents rang he would tell them to ring Joel, then he thanked them both for being so kind.

Joel said, 'If you need to talk any time, and I mean any time, ring me.' Matthew thanked him again and they left the flat.

Back in the car, Fiona asked Joel what he thought they had just experienced. Joel said it was difficult for him because Matthew was a friend, but he thought Matthew suspected his father of killing Jessica. Fiona confirmed she had the same feeling, but there were many possible explanations for the results, and really only George Corfield could help. It was still only 6.55am and they went to Belgravia police station to try and find the flat where the Corfields were staying.

266

They looked at the flats on Google Earth but found no further clues. The only solution was good old-fashioned police work: knocking on doors.

Joel's phone rang. It was Robert. Robert asked Joel if it was convenient to talk. He had William Goble with him, and would Joel mind if he put him on loudspeaker? They had something they both needed to talk about.

Joel told Robert he was with Fiona and would find an office to ring him back from a landline to allow everyone to listen and talk. He put the phone down, looked at Fiona and said, 'This is odd.'

'Very,' Fiona confirmed.

Chapter Forty

The Chief Superintendent's office was empty; they were out for the day. Joel rang Robert, who answered instantly. Everyone said good morning and Robert took the lead.

'I know you will think what we are about to tell you is bizarre, odd and probably downright mad, with us jumping to enormous conclusions, but if you could just bear with us while we tell you what we think we've found.'

Fiona and Joel said in unison, 'Go ahead.'

Robert outlined how he re-read Jess's dissertation, which Joel had given him, and remembered he still had all her research materials boxed up in the attic. He hadn't looked at them since Jess died, when he retrieved them from her flat for safekeeping. It was too painful to go through the papers then, but Robert explained reading the dissertation spurred him into looking at the background material. He said he was intrigued by the subject matter. As with all dissertations, Jess found a variety of potential future research topics, which she had neatly and comprehensively documented, not only in her dissertation but also in her notes.

One area, which intrigued Robert, was the mining of uranium as a by-product of gold in the Vaal River area during the 1970s and 1980s. He continued, 'Jess carried out substantial research into uranium mining because she had been told of the death of twenty villagers on the Vaal River from what looked like radiological poisoning during this period.

'There were no official records of the deaths other than oral testimonies. This was not surprising as national and local governments of the time were not interested in the deaths of black villagers. Jess suspected, but could not prove, the villagers had been involved in the smuggling of "yellow cake", which is basically purified uranium ore. It was taken out of the area into Mozambique, and she believed it was destined for onward transmission to Israel. She also suspected the same couriers were bringing equipment back into South Africa from Europe, the Far East and Israel for the covert South African nuclear industry. All this introspection was outlined in her papers.'

William Goble then came on and said Robert had asked him to help. He too read Jess's dissertation, and said, 'I found it fascinating, and my understanding was considerably helped by Jessica's meticulous note taking and organisational skills. I was sceptical at first. How, during Apartheid, could all this smuggling by black villagers go on? The answer to which both Robert and I were led was starkly illustrated in Jessica's material. The smugglers would travel through the tribal areas, and were afforded protection by the South African Government on whose behalf they were acting, by bringing machinery parts into the country. Jessica had taken oral testimonies to this effect from a number of those who survived.

'It all adds up. After the Yom Kippur war, most countries in Africa, except South Africa, cut off all links with Israel. South Africa itself was subject at the time to fuel blockades and had to develop other sources of power, nuclear being an option. Of course, nuclear weapons could be a by-product, which certainly Israel would develop and exploit. Hence the so-called "machinery imports" smuggled into South Africa. Jessica had identified some of the mining companies, machinery companies and agents she suspected of being involved. I wondered why she hadn't published her work, but being an academic, these were just her suspicions and she would have had to do a great deal more research in the area before she could publish.'

Robert resumed, saying, 'William and I have been looking at the material almost constantly and thanks to Tim Berners-Lee have been doing further research into Jessica's findings on the Internet. Since the fall of Apartheid, the extent of cooperation between Israel and South Africa is now on record, but we couldn't find anything about the dead villagers or smuggling other than it is still going on and people are regularly arrested.'

This explained the state of Robert's study Joel had noticed on his last visit. Fiona and Joel looked at each other; this was all very interesting, but what did it have to do with Jessica's murder? The phone went quiet.

Robert said, 'I can almost hear you thinking: interesting, but why this phone call? What is the issue?'

Joel replied, 'You're absolutely right there, Robert.'

'Cantact, Joel. Cantact Ltd, remember? Cantact Ltd was listed in Jessica's research notes as an agent who possibly facilitated smuggling machinery into South Africa, particularly from Germany and Israel. I know it's just a possibility, but it's interesting, Joel. Cantact!'

Fiona looked at Joel and mouthed 'Cantact?' at him.

'Fiona doesn't know the significance of Cantact, Robert.' Joel turned towards her, and said, 'They are the owners of a club in Croydon run by an ex-soldier who is the guy I suspect of organising the fire at Sarah's shop. I can't prove anything but, like Robert, I suspect.'

Fiona said, 'Is Cantact a public company, Robert?' looking at Joel at the same time.

'No. It's a private limited company. I asked for a search on the company and got the results overnight. There are four named directors whose addresses are the same as the company's in Bishopsgate.' He clearly had the documents in front of him and read out their names, 'William T Rother, Cynthia WA Rother, David J Davies and Simone Davies. Sounds like a family type firm to me. They have all been directors since 1980 when the company was formed.'

'Are you sure it's the same firm? Smuggling nuclear machinery into South Africa is a far cry from running a club in Croydon,' Fiona said doubtfully.

'We don't know,' replied William, 'but we suspect so.'

'I think we need to do further checks on Cantact,' Fiona said. 'Thank you, Robert, this is very interesting, very interesting. We will get someone on it.'

They said their goodbyes. Robert and William felt a little disappointed by the perceived lack of enthusiasm from the other end, but they shouldn't have done. For the first time, Fiona and Joel had a possible link from South Africa to London and the attack on Sarah's shop. They also felt a spark of excitement; pieces might be about to click into place, but they didn't want to jump to conclusions too quickly so Joel asked Billy to do more research on Cantact.

Fiona and Joel left Belgravia police station and walked the mile to Hans Place where they found Evertree Buildings, easily identifiable from what they had seen on Google Earth. It was an imposing red brick building, looking resplendent in the morning sunshine. They saw from the doorplate there were ten apartments in the building and a doorman was standing just inside the stained glass and oak front doors.

They walked up the stairs, through the doors and introduced

270

themselves to the doorman, asking if he knew the Corfields, which he clearly did. He told them they stayed in Apartment 7 but had left yesterday. Joel asked if he thought they were going to be away for a long time, and the doorman said he presumed so because they had taken a lot of luggage with them, adding he thought they were going back to South Africa. The doorman, Ben, was talkative; he clearly didn't like George Corfield, but he thought Virginia was lovely. A mine of information, Ben knew the Corfields stayed in the flat about three times a year, no one else used it, and he thought they owned it. There was a management company who looked after its upkeep, and the Corfields had employed the same cleaner, Josie, for years. Josie was in the flat now, and he asked if they wanted to go up, which they did.

After walking up the three flights of stairs rather than taking the lift, they knocked on the oak door of the apartment, which was just as imposing as the front door of the building. A small red-haired woman in her sixties opened the door. Joel saw there was a security chain, and Josie peeped through the gap between the door and the frame. Fiona introduced them and showed Josie her warrant card, which Josie examined thoroughly before releasing the chain, opening the door and inviting them in. Fiona said they wanted to speak to the Corfields, but Josie confirmed they left for South Africa the previous day. Mr Corfield had called her and told her to come in yesterday and today as the place was covered in dust and there were hairs everywhere. Josie thought this was nonsense, but Mr Corfield said he was asking the management agents to come round and check tomorrow. Josie didn't like George Corfield either.

Fiona explained to Josie they wanted to search the flat but would need to get a warrant, and she didn't want Josie to do any more cleaning. Josie was relaxed about this; she had been paid in cash by Corfield the previous day and was almost finished. She only needed to do the bedrooms. Josie locked the flat up and Fiona asked her to keep the keys until they could get a search warrant. Josie suggested she left the keys with Ben the doorman as she lived in Putney. Ben was delighted at being involved, particularly when Joel said not to let anyone in and to contact him if anyone tried to gain entry. Fiona and Joel left Josie and Ben trying to work out what Corfield had been up to.

As Fiona and Joel walked back to the police station, Fiona phoned George Corfield's mobile number. It was unobtainable. Joel rang Heathrow police station intelligence office and asked them to see if the

Corfields had been on any of the flights to South Africa the previous day. It was surprising how helpful people could be for a Detective Inspector from the Commissioner's Office. Joel asked them to pass the results of the enquiries on to Billy, which they refused to do, just in case the check was fraudulent, so Joel then asked them to pass the results to Commander Nugent, the Commissioner's Chief of Staff. There was no further challenge, and Joel phoned Eric Nugent to give him the heads up.

While Joel was on the phone he was aware Fiona was organising a search team to be at Belgravia police station at eleven. He thought it was rather premature; they didn't have a warrant yet. At the police station they prepared the application for the warrant. Joel phoned Ali, who fortuitously was already in Oxford about to visit the lab, and asked him to divert and come to Belgravia. Fiona also phoned the Coroner to tell him about the developments in case of any media interest, and then phoned the Met's own press bureau. Things were moving fast again, but it hadn't been any different for the last few weeks, Joel thought.

Fiona went to Westminster Magistrates Court to apply for a search warrant for the Corfields' flat in Hans Place. The application was detailed; it had to be as it was an unusual one. Joel waited in Belgravia to meet the search team and to try and find out who owned the flat. The management company details they had been given by Ben turned out to include an accommodation address in Kensington, and the telephone number went to an answerphone.

Whilst Joel was waiting, Eric rang back to say Heathrow Intelligence had the information for him. Joel phoned them and discovered George and Virginia Corfield had not left for South Africa the previous day, but taken a Swiss Air flight to Geneva. There were no details of an onward flight. The intelligence officer said obtaining information from the Swiss was not as easy as from some other countries, but they would attempt a search of the carrier databases in case the Corfields had travelled on. Joel appreciated it; they were being really helpful.

Ali arrived at the Belgravia police station just as Fiona was returning from court with the search warrant. She said the district judge questioned her closely about the background and nature of the warrant application. They both briefed the search team: what they were looking for was hair, blood or body fluids, not one of their usual searches for stolen property, guns or drugs.

Chapter Forty-One

Fiona initially went with Ali and the search team to Hans Place before leaving the experts to their task and returning to Belgravia police station and Joel. He had been busy. Heathrow Intelligence phoned back and said the Corfields had bought connecting flights in Geneva not to South Africa, but to Tel Aviv. This was very odd.

Joel phoned Matthew to see if he had heard from his parents. He had not, and was so concerned about what was going on he had not gone into Chambers, choosing to remain in his flat to await a call. Fiona said they should go to see him and they made their way back to St John's Wood. En route Ali rang to confirm the search team had found hair from brushes in the flat and a number of other possible sources of DNA. Joel told Ali he needn't go any further for the moment, wondering what Ali meant.

Ali said while they were in the flats a man purporting to be a representative of the management company arrived, but when Ben the doorman told him the police were in the flat, he had turned and left. Ben didn't recognise him and discreetly followed him to a nearby car. He'd taken the car's number and they were checking it.

Returning to St John's Wood, Fiona and Joel explained to Matthew what they had found out, including Matthew's parents going to Tel Aviv. Matthew was really surprised. His parents had been in Israel earlier in the month and had friends there, but they did not mention any plans for a return visit. Matthew understood what was going on in the Hans Place flat, and Joel also explained what Robert and William had been researching after reading Jess's dissertation. Matthew found it fascinating. While he had discussed Jess's work with her, the suspicions regarding uranium smuggling were news to him.

Joel then mentioned Cantact in the context of being an agent in South Africa suspected of being involved in smuggling uranium and the name of the firm which ran the club possibly connected to the fire at Sarah's shop in Budleigh. Matthew again looked shocked.

'Cantact? You said Cantact, Joel?' he repeated.

Joel said, 'Yes, Cantact.'

'Cantact is the company which owns the flat my parents stay in. It's part owned by James Davies who used to work with my father in SIS. You may recall me telling you about him, Joel, years ago. Remember? He was a witness in a case I was involved with, and my father and I fell out about it. Then my father employed Davies. Surely you remember, Joel?'

'It's coming back to me now, but I didn't put two and two together. There is a Cantact director called David Davies, could it be the same man?'

'It is the same man. David James Davies, better known as James Davies,' said Matthew. 'He would do anything my father asked him. My father told me way back, how Davies was a wealthy businessman even before leaving SIS, which I found really odd.'

Fiona said, 'This gets more and more intriguing. I think we need to regroup, Joel. Matthew, have you any idea where your father may be in Israel, or with whom?'

'I'm sorry, I have no idea. I don't know their friends, they're business associate types, but if I do hear anything I will let you know.'

They said their goodbyes and Fiona and Joel returned to Islington. Ali phoned to say the search team had finished at the flat, and while they were there a solicitor turned up, acting on behalf of the management company, to see what was happening. The solicitor was told the flat was being searched and was given Fiona's details if they wanted any more information. Ali said he was going straight to Oxford and the lab with the samples they had collected.

Fiona suggested Joel update Robert, and when Joel spoke to him William Goble was still there. They were intrigued by the further Cantact connection, but also more than a little pleased their research had paid off. After the conversation with Robert ended, Joel and Fiona sat down, Fiona put a proposition to him.

Joel was relaxing in the Business Class Lounge at Heathrow when his evening flight to Cape Town was called. He boarded the 747, settling into the business class seat as if he was a regular, scanning the horizon for the "s the k" and thanking the steward for the glass of champagne.

Just four months ago he had been on the same flight, going to South Africa for the first time. This time he was going on holiday: official holiday.

He had been working in the Commissioner's office full time for the last four weeks and enjoyed this very different work immensely. Fiona and he agreed, following the revelation of Cantact's possible involvement in South Africa, the fire in Sarah's shop and George Corfield's connections with the company, things were a little too close to Joel and he needed to stand aside from the investigation. He hadn't initially taken it very well, but he came round to the fact Fiona was right on many levels. It was all a little too close to him.

In the interim, Fiona continued to move swiftly.

George Corfield was last seen taking a motor launch out of Tel Aviv Marina, having left a note for his wife and Matthew. The letter was not a suicide note; it was an apology for accidentally killing Jessica. It said she had confronted him on the fateful night about his involvement in uranium smuggling after leaving SIS back in the eighties. He said he'd had too much to drink and had grabbed Jess by the throat to shake her and explain it was all very different then. She fell to the floor, dead. He didn't mean to kill her. He panicked but, knowing the Kem was seen leaving the house, the answer was there for him. He said he was sorry to Virginia and Matthew; interestingly there was no apology to Kem or Robert. Joel wasn't surprised. Virginia and Matthew found George's letter very difficult to comprehend and come to terms with, from Jess's death, to the deception for all those years, to his disappearance.

The launch was found, empty and out of fuel, about thirty miles off the Israeli coast two days after leaving Tel Aviv. George was not on board, and some thought, hoped, he was dead. Joel remembered Robert Maxwell's disappearance, which proved to be fatal. Joel was not convinced about George.

One of the things arousing Joel's suspicions was the car used by the man who visited the Hans Place flat. It had been traced to a false address in North London. However, it was given a parking ticket later the same day in Old Court Place, Kensington. The driver had an argument with the warden who was taking a picture of the car. Unfortunately the photo didn't show an image of the driver, but the numerous CCTV cameras, situated at the rear of the Israeli Embassy, produced good images of the incident. Ben, the porter, identified the motorist as the man who had visited Hans Place, and the Diplomatic Protection officers at the Embassy identified him as a diplomat from the Israeli Embassy who returned to Israel days after the incident. They didn't say, but the motorist was clearly Mossad.

It transpired Corfield was intimately involved in organising the smuggling of yellow cake out of South Africa in the eighties. He discovered how to do it while visiting the Vaal River during his time with SIS, and this was the reason he had left. Corfield found out through Kem's father, who had grown up in the area, and Corfield ruthlessly exploited the villagers, using his position and Cantact, which had been set up by Davies as the cover. He gained legitimacy and favour with the South African Government at the time by facilitating the importation of machinery from Israel and Germany, which was used in the nuclear industry. Ever the far-sighted individual, Corfield had seen what a dangerous game he was playing. After making a fortune, he moved to the Western Cape and handed the business over to corrupt, retired government officials who continued the exploitation in human and economic terms. Corfield had taken advantage of Kem's father through the use of his fellow villagers, abused Kem, leaving him to rot in gaol, and crushed Kem's family through years and years of suffering. He was also suspected of organising the attack on Kem but as the main witness Mhkize had died, there was no evidence. George Corfield was truly a really nasty piece of work, concluded Joel; he could think of many other adjectives and nouns which would also apply!

Peter and Matthew's civil ceremony had gone ahead. Virginia attended, which Joel thought was only right, and he enjoyed it too. Surprisingly, the events brought Matthew and Joel closer than ever.

David James Davies, Reginald Arthur Husband and Leonard Alfred Jancer had all been charged with conspiracy to cause grievous bodily harm and arson with intent to endanger life. They were remanded in custody awaiting trial. The actual instigator was Corfield who had contacted Davies. Joel's evidence wouldn't be contested, he'd been told, Jancey confessed all, as did Bunny. Davies was implicated through telephone traffic and a money trail, which seemed surprising for an ex-spy, but perhaps not, bearing in mind Matthew's views on Davies's competence. Joel felt sorry for Wildo, who had been killed in a car crash some weeks ago. Joel heard it was an accident!

The arrest of Katherine Thornley caused the Crown Prosecution Service unusually, to appoint Queens Counsel immediately, resulting in her being charged with misconduct in a public office and conspiracy to pervert the course of justice. Most of the surveillance team were prosecution witnesses, although three had been charged with telecommunication offences and conspiracy to cause a public nuisance, along with Thornley. It transpired Thornley had received a number of emails from Pennard, mentioning Joel and asking for her help in getting him back to the United Kingdom. The emails said Joel was upsetting things in Cape Town and was causing trouble for friends of the party in South Africa. Piers also mentioned it looked as though Pennard and Thornley were having a sexual relationship, which came as a shock for the soon to be ex Mrs Pennard. Pennard himself had left Weisners' to return to the United States of America.

Joel was dragged from his internal review for a brief interlude by dinner: chicken pasta washed down with a little more champagne. He then settled down to sleep, but his mind continued to recap recent events.

He hadn't heard from the Investigatory Powers Tribunal but he met with Arthur Walkden, who was open with him about what had happened. There was now an inquiry into Hydra by the IPCC, and Arthur had assured Joel he would hear about its findings. Interestingly, almost as soon as Joel started work on the eighth floor, AC Bobbin and DAC Dennis were seconded to the College of Policing and the Inspectorate respectively. There was a strong rumour Arthur Walkden was going to be the next Deputy Commissioner of the Met. Joel hoped so; he liked Arthur.

The Belmont Gardens Quintet, too nice a title for Magnus and his traitors, Joel thought, had all been committed for trial at the Crown Court, together with Yellop and a Chief Superintendent. They had all been remanded in custody; Joel could only imagine their treatment in prison, despite being in segregation.

Things in South Africa hadn't stood still. The lab had matched George Corfield's DNA with the samples from Jessica's fingernails which, when coupled with the other evidence, convinced the courts in South Africa Kem Siblisi should be released on bail pending an appeal hearing. Frederick and Marta were delighted, as were the whole Siblisi family who couldn't understand George Corfield's selfish and dreadful behaviour. It transpired some of those who died of uranium poisoning in the Vaal Valley were related to Kem and he had spoken to Jessica about this, but failed to make the connection between Corfield and the tragic events.

Robert was already in South Africa awaiting Joel's triumphant return; well, Robert described it in this way. Joel didn't feel triumphant.

He felt sorry for Kem and his family for what they had endured; for Jess and Matthew for what they had lost; for Virginia Corfield who had also lost so much and had been lied to for so long.

Joel's mind continued to bounce around. The Somerstown street gang had been sentenced to a total of sixty years in prison, not bad, Joel thought. He had been in touch with his victim, even when on the sick, and whilst she was still suffering badly, she was glad the court believed her. And then to Croydon, to Weston's Yard and an event he'd learnt about. Ron Weston and his wife had been out for the morning, and when they returned to the yard they saw a lean, fit besuited man with short hair talking to their sons. Obviously Old Bill. The boys' heads were down and they were clearly having the riot act read to them by the cop.

Ron jumped out of the car and said, 'Everything all right, Officer?'

The policeman turned to him and asked, 'Are you Ron Weston?'

'That's my name. What can I do for you?'

'I'd like a word with you. Somewhere private, please,' said the cop.

It was barely a month since the Belmont Gardens arrests, and Ron suspected this was the new team coming to put the arm on him.

'Come into the office,' said Ron while The Missus went straight over to the boys to find out what had taken place.

The policeman said, 'I understand you've been paying rent to my colleagues over the last few years.' Ron gave no reply. 'My name's DCI Messenger, I'm the new head of CID here.'

Ron thought, so much for the clear out. Here we go again. The fit young man then put his hand in his pocket and pulled out an envelope, which he handed to Ron. It contained a bank cheque, made out to R. Weston MBE, for forty-three thousand pounds, signed by G McKnight and issued by the bank's Hereford branch.

'Is this some kind of wind up?' Ron said, puzzled by the unfolding events.

'It's no wind up. Do you recognise the name on the cheque?' Piers asked.

'I knew someone with that name a long time ago.'

'In the days before the Lottery, when everyone did the football pools?'

'Yeah, about then,' Ron spluttered.

'When people who worked together used to have syndicates for the pools? When in your line of work you paid a year in advance, just in case anything happened?'

'Yeah, but…'

'After you disappeared and never went back to the mess,' Piers interrupted, 'you won £700,000 between you in the 1970s. Of course there was no publicity, so you wouldn't have seen anything in the papers. The army couldn't give an address because you didn't have one, and so the money has been sitting in the bank, collecting interest and being looked after by Gerry McKnight who, by the way, would like to see you down there soon.'

'I don't know what to say. Thanks, son, who are you again?'

'I'm DCI Piers Messenger, head of Belmont Gardens CID and a friend of Joel's.'

'Joel! Joel!' The Missus screeched from the door. 'I told you he was a good lad, and this one too by the sound of things. What have you got there, Ron?' She snatched the cheque out of his hand. 'Bloody hell, Ron, what's this?' Ron explained over a cup of tea with Piers. Before he left, Piers got an assurance Ron would ring Gerry McKnight.

After Piers left the yard, Ron's sons came into the office. 'What do you two want? No work?' Ron barked.

'Dad, what did you do exactly in the army?' asked the elder son.

'You know your dad doesn't like talking about that, son, now come on,' said their mother.

'But Dad, that cop told us you were a hero and you were one of the bravest people he'd heard about. He said he used to serve in the same unit and people were always talking about you,' said 'Boris One'.'Weren't you a driver or something Dad? Are you a hero?' queried 'Boris Two'. The Missus challenged, 'You're going to have to tell them, Ron.'

'OK. Sit down, lads, it was like this…'

Ron hadn't realised at the time, but Piers was from the Regiment as well, which was how he knew the details.

Joel loved a happy ending, he felt tears of happiness weeping from his eyes, few would believe it of this outwardly tough detective.

He was still unable to sleep and picked up a copy of the Evening Standard. The front page headline read, 'Home Secretary resigns to spend more time with family.'

Justice, thought Joel – not being one to bear a grudge, of course!

Acknowledgements

To our friends and family who have supported us throughout, particularly those who have provided editorial comments. Special thanks to Mark Hamlin for his visual creations, Alan Young for his technical assistance and Anita Smith whose contribution, help and assistance has been invaluable.

Find out more about the authors and their work at
www.looktheotherwaythebook.com

Lightning Source UK Ltd.
Milton Keynes UK
UKOW04f2202160115

244611UK00002B/40/P